SIXTH LOVER

ALICE GAINES

ISBN-13: 978-1-940854-00-7

PROLOGUE

Manhattan Island, New York, 1880

The lady was too old for him. Also, too rich, too clever, and stunning in a way that filled Thomas Deering's mind with sweet lethargy. At seventeen, he'd already worshipped her for seven years. Still she had no more idea he existed than she realized that he could hear every word she and her friends uttered in what they thought was a private conversation about lust. And every time the lady's pacing took her past the narrow opening at the threshold to the dining room, he could see her from where he stood in the hallway.

"You should take a lover, my dear," Mrs. Standen said. "Or, better yet, two or three."

Mrs. Rutherford—Carole, as he called her in his daydreams—fingered the petals of a rose in the bouquet on the sideboard. "I couldn't. Mr. Rutherford's no young girl's dream, but he's never mistreated me. I wouldn't hurt him that way."

"He wouldn't need to know." Another of the women. He didn't recognize the voice.

Carole released the flower. "I'd know."

"Very admirable, I'm sure," Mrs. Standen said. "But you're missing out on your youth."

Carole turned toward the doorway, and for a moment, he got a glimpse of her face. Before she could spot him, he flattened himself against the wall. Her image remained in his mind, though. The honey-blonde hair, green eyes, and pursed lips. She wore clothes of the latest fashion—elegant and no doubt wildly expensive. The waist cinched, emphasizing the curve of her breasts and swell of her hips below. He had to smother a groan as his member grew long and stiff in his pants. She might think of him as a boy—if she thought of him at all—but he had a man's reaction to her.

"Does he satisfy you, my dear?" Mrs. Standen again.

Silence stretched out long enough for the clock to strike the half-hour without interruption. Finally, Carole sighed.

Thomas crept forward again and peeked inside. Carole had turned away and held her hands stiffly by her side.

"He doesn't," Mrs. Standen said.

"I don't know how to answer that," Carole said. "He makes me happy enough."

"Does he make you spend?" the other woman said from outside his vision.

The back of Carole's neck turned a bright pink, and she didn't move a muscle.

"He doesn't," the woman said.

Mrs. Standen clucked her tongue. "I came twice last night before Philip even put his cock inside me."

"We shouldn't be talking like this," Carole said, but she made no move to leave. Her skin had grown even redder.

"Don't believe that nonsense about women not enjoying sex," the other woman said. "If anything, we require it even more than men."

Could that be possible? He'd heard stories. He understood the words "spend" and "come." Could women experience those things the same way men did? He'd kissed a few girls. Some enjoyed it more than others. None seemed as deeply moved as he became when he lay in his bed, stroking himself until he exploded with lust. Could a female lover feel the same things—becoming aroused, climbing to the peak, and losing herself in that ultimate moment?

Could Carole do all that? Did she do it with Mr. Rutherford? He held his breath, waiting for any clue.

"You're approaching your peak, my dear," Mrs. Standen said. "At only a few years older than you, I craved sex constantly. When Mr. Standen couldn't keep up, I found someone who could."

"That's disgraceful, Muriel," Carole said. "I won't do it to my husband. I took a vow."

"Don't you think he'd break that vow if the right woman crooked her finger?" Mrs. Standen said. "They all do it."

"I don't believe it."

The other woman huffed. "No sense talking to a fool."

"Or, an innocent," Mrs. Standen corrected. "You were a virgin on your wedding night, weren't you?"

Carole turned again, and Thomas jumped back silently before she could spot him. The rustling of skirts and the scrape of a chair told him Carole had taken a seat at the table. When things had settled, he dared a glance and found her sitting, her shoulders slumped.

"I thought it so gallant of Mr. Rutherford to want to wait until after we'd married," she said. "Instead, it turns out the marital act strains his heart."

Mrs. Standen's jeweled hand covered Carole's. "But he has known you."

"We indulge from time to time," Carole said. "Carefully."

"Dear God in heaven, that's no way to live," the other woman said. "Someone should be drawn and quartered for what society does to girls."

"You're absolutely right, my dear," Mrs. Standen said. "Boys experiment before they settle down. Girls should, too. Otherwise, how will they know when they've found the right man to make them happy for the rest of their lives?"

"They should take at least three lovers," the other woman said. "No, four."

"I say five," Mrs. Standen said. "No woman should bind herself to anyone before her sixth lover."

"What a fanciful idea." Carole sighed. "I have such dreams at night. They follow me around all day. Men so taken by passion, they take me up against a tree. Men so well endowed the sight of their sex frightens me. Sometimes, I imagine myself with more than one man."

"And you should have all those men, my dear."

Thomas's throat had gone dry, and his blood pounded in his ears. Already hard, his cock throbbed, as he imagined himself as one of her lovers, pushing her back against something, lifting her clothes, and shoving himself into her. Imagine, six lovers. Could a woman really want that many? If so, he'd give Carole everything she wanted…even share her with other men, if that made her happy. Anything to see her smile and share the pleasures of her body.

"You should have all that, Carole," Mrs. Standen said. "It's your right as a human being, no matter what public morals tell us."

"I can't. I won't be unfaithful to my husband."

Soft footsteps came up behind Thomas. As quietly and nonchalantly as he could, he pulled the dining room door closed. Then, without looking back, he started up the hallway as if he'd only been passing through toward somewhere else.

The ploy didn't work. A hand came down on his shoulder. A very familiar hand. He stiffened but didn't move.

He didn't need to. His father turned him around, stared at his face and then down to the front of his pants.

"What's got you in that state, boy?" he father demanded.

"Nothing."

"Nothing?" Robert Deering snorted. "It takes something to create a cockstand like that."

"Erections come easily at my age," he said. "You should know that."

"Liar. You're not fooling me." His father jerked his head back toward the dining room. "What was going on in there?"

"Nothing."

"Tell the truth, or I'll take it out of your hide." Before Thomas could brace for the blow, his father cuffed him on the ear. "You were watching something. Two of the servants rutting? Maybe a pair of young girls with their faces buried in each other's muffs."

"It's none of your business."

Murderous rage entered his father's eyes. Thomas had seen that his entire life. It used to frighten him into doing anything the bastard ordered—at least, until he realized that nothing he could do would have any effect on the man's rages.

"You'll keep a civil tongue, or I'll beat you to a bloody mess," Robert snarled. "I can still do it, even though you're grown."

They'd see about that. Thomas stood taller than his father now, and he was younger and more agile. He'd learned to box at school, although he hadn't shared that information. If the bastard tried beating him again, he'd get a rough surprise.

"Let's go see what's going on in there." His father grabbed him by the upper arm and pulled him toward the door. "I might enjoy the sight myself."

When they got there, his father put his hand on the knob, but Thomas covered it with his own. "Don't do this."

"Don't think you can order me around." His father opened the door and half stepped inside.

Carole jumped from her seat, her eyes wide. "Mr. Deering."

His father scanned the room. Aside from Carole's slight alarm, the scene was one of three ladies engaged in simple conversation. Nothing remarkable unless you'd overheard the subject matter.

"Sorry to interrupt you, ladies," his father said after a moment. "We'll be on our way."

He closed the door again. Thomas pulled his arm from his father's fist. "I told you it was nothing."

"Then, you're a fool as well as an ass," Richard said. "The Mrs. Standen and Wilson are little more than whores, despite their finery and their rich husbands. It seems the Rutherford woman isn't any better."

"You take that back!"

This time, his father slapped him, hard, across the face. "Don't use that tone with me."

Thomas stood his ground. "You will not speak of Car...Mrs. Rutherford in that way."

A cunning smile crossed his father's face. "So, she's what's got your cock in that state. Does she read you a bedtime story before she fucks you?"

"Shut up."

"All right. You've been asking for it, and now I'm going to give it to you."

He stood and watched his father come nearer. Had he asked for the beating that had broken his arm when he scarcely came up to the man's knee? Had his mother asked for the kick to her belly that had caused her to miscarry his little brother? The man had bullied them both for too long, and he'd learn now he couldn't do it any longer.

His father's eyes narrowed in suspicion when Thomas didn't back down or beg for mercy, but he kept coming, his fists raised. Thomas waited for the right moment and then swung for the bastard's chin. He missed, damn it all, and his momentum allowed his father to grab him by the scruff of the neck and slam him, face first into the wall.

His vision swam, but he held onto consciousness enough to hear the sound of other footsteps running in their direction. They'd have an audience. Good. The witnesses could either watch him humiliate his father or they could see what a violent bastard the man had always been.

He stayed where he was, both to let his head clear, and to lure his father closer. Sure enough, a hand landed on his shoulder and yanked him around. That gave Thomas an opportunity to pound his fist into his father's belly. When that won him a loud "oof," he followed with several more punches to the ribs. A crunching meant he'd cracked at least one, and his father stumbled backward, open to any assault Thomas cared to inflict.

He glanced up to find an expression of utter astonishment in his father's eyes. And fear. Glory hallelujah, fear.

Now, he took a better stance, fists raised, weight on the balls of his feet. His father looked on—paralyzed, having no idea which way to move. Thomas struck, his right fist connecting with the man's jaw and then his left coming up under his chin.

Robert staggered but remained standing. "Why, you little whelp."

"Not so little anymore," Thomas answered.

"I'll kill you. I swear to God, I will."

Enough. Thomas swung again, this time with his entire weight behind the blow. His fist struck his father's temple, and the man crashed to the floor. For a moment, he seemed unconscious, but then his eyes opened. They didn't focus, though, and they shut again as he went limp against the floor.

Reality returned. Mr. Standen and a few of his servants clustered, kneeling, around his father. Standen looked up at him. "What in hell have you done?"

"No more than what he's done to me," he answered. "Numerous times."

A soft gasp sounded behind him. He turned to find Carole, her fingers covering her mouth. For a moment, they stared at each other as if she remembered that afternoon. Her wedding day when his father had given him a black eye and she'd comforted him with a flower from her bouquet. The exact second he'd fallen in love with her.

Then the recognition in her expression dimmed—if it had ever been there at all. She looked on the whole scene with horror.

"I'm sorry," he said. Two puny words. Completely inadequate. *Come away with me. I can make you happy. I love you.*

He could never say that, though, so he wiped the blood from under his nose and headed toward the back of the house to make his escape. One more visit to his parents' house to convince his mother to leave with him. If he could manage. If not, he'd take what money he had and a certain book that had a rose pressed inside it. He wouldn't see any of these people again for a very, very long time.

CHAPTER ONE

Thirteen years later

Freedom at forty was its own sort of prison, at least, for a woman. Yes, Carole Rutherford had all the money she'd ever need for anything. Yes, she had the social status that won her invitations to parties and balls. Yes, she controlled her own body now. But what man would look at a woman her age, even though her lack of childbearing had spared her body some of the ravages of aging?

Men liked younger women. That's how she'd ended up married to Oscar Rutherford. Even though he'd died, he still held the rights to her, it seemed, and the black of her mourning clothing didn't help matters.

"You have guests, Mrs. Rutherford." Mayne, her butler stood in the doorway of the sitting room. "Mrs. Coats, her niece, and a young man. Shall I show them in?"

"Of course. I'd forgotten they were coming."

Mayne bowed. "Very good, Mrs. Rutherford."

"And would you ask cook to send up tea and something? Apologize that I forgot to warn her."

"I'm sure she'll manage just fine." Mayne left, and Carole braced herself for jollity. Although Edna Coats was a relative by marriage, she didn't resemble her cousin, Carole's husband, in the slightest.

Edna bustled into the room with two younger people behind her—Edna's daughter, Elise, and a man Carole had never seen.

Carole rose from her chair to greet them. Edna reached her first and grasped her shoulders to pull her close enough to kiss the air next to one of her cheeks.

"It's been too long, Carole," Edna said. "I should have come earlier."

"I've been fine," Carole answered.

"You shouldn't be alone so soon after Oscar's death. I've brought Elise and her new husband for a nice visit."

Elise grasped Carole's hand. "Cousin Carole, this is Richard Gould."

As Elise had married late, Mr. Gould appeared only a few years younger than Carole. But where Oscar had already seemed to age in his middle years, Mr. Gould stood tall and hearty. You couldn't really call him handsome as he put his hands behind his back and smiled at her, but he gave off a sense of masculine power beneath the fine cut of his suit. Physically, he could have come from one of her erotic fantasies. None of those men had faces or personalities. Little more than erections and hard bodies, they seldom uttered a word but merely filled her and drove away the nagging aches inside her. For over twenty years, she'd barely enjoyed anything like a normal sex life...or what she understood as normal, but she certainly shouldn't work her frustrations out on her cousin's husband, even in her mind. She shook herself inwardly to stop from staring at him.

"Won't you all sit down?" she said. "We should have tea and coffee soon."

The newly married couple took the love seat, and Mr. Gould took Elise's hand in his, settling it between them, an innocent gesture of affection that filled her with guilt for how she'd been thinking of him.

"…coming up to Saratoga this summer.'

"I'm sorry?" Carole sat, folding her hands together in her lap.

"I said you really must come up to Saratoga this summer," Edna said from her seat near her daughter and son-in-law. "Losing Oscar so tragically has me determined to get the family together more often."

"Yes, I'm sure it would." Oh, dear, the family. Swarms of them ranging from Oscar's oldest aunt who couldn't walk or hear, to adults, children, grandchildren, great-grandchildren. All of them solid and predictable and not the least bit interesting. Somehow, Oscar had escaped all that solidity and had had a fine intellect and artistic sensibility.

"I'll see if I can join you," she said. With any luck, they wouldn't realize she had absolutely no plans for summer or fall or winter.

"I'd love for you to get to know Richard better," Elise said.

"Everyone's told me so much about you," he added, although he scarcely took his eyes off his wife.

"That's very sweet," she answered. "Welcome to the family, Mr. Gould."

"I'm so lucky." He turned in his seat to stare at Elise head on. Oscar had looked at her that way every day of their lives together—as if she were the most beautiful woman in the world. Oscar hadn't had this man's broad shoulders or solid back.

Damn her, what was wrong with her? She'd had the dearest, most affectionate husband in the world. A man who would have given her Buckingham Palace if the Queen of England would have sold it to him. Why did she have to sit here wondering about another man's build?

The refreshment arrived—a tea and coffee service with a plate of little cakes next to it. The maid set the low table before her, and she could put her mind on serving her guests instead of places where it didn't belong.

"So, what do you do, Mr. Gould?" she said finally.

"I have a large press and book bindery outside Newburg," he answered. "It doesn't make me rich, but I do well enough."

"It's a fascinating business, Cousin Carole," Elise said. "The papers they use and the different materials for binding."

"It must be," she answered.

Edna polished off one of the cakes, dropping a few crumbs onto the floor. "Mr. Gould tells us hardly anyone uses leather any longer. Such a shame."

"False economy, if you ask me. Leather lasts forever," he said.

Oh, dear. He made a perfect addition to the family. Wholesome, predictable, dull. And yet, Elise would have a large, firm body to cling to as she...

"Carole, dear, are you all right?" Edna asked.

"Fine," she answered. Her fingers started to tremble, and her cup clattered as she set it on the table in front of her.

"My poor dear." Edna jumped up and put her arm around Carole's shoulder. "We shouldn't have come. It's too much for you so soon after Oscar's death."

"No, I'm glad you did. Truly." and she'd be equally glad when they went away. What in hell was wrong with her?

"We wanted you to know we love you," Edna said. "And you must come visit as soon as you can."

"I'll do that." and she would. Somehow, she'd make herself do it.

"Is there anything you need?" Elise asked. "Anything at all we can get for you?"

"No, really. I'm fine." She gave them her best smile. "It's just a passing mood."

"You go and lie down," Edna said. "We can see ourselves out."

"Don't be silly. I can do that." Carole got to her feet. Edna hugged her, and Elise joined in. They were such dear people. Why couldn't she enjoy them more? When they all separated, Mr. Gould extended his hand. She shook it briefly and then pulled her fingers from his stronger ones. Before she had a chance to linger on that image, she led the rest of them into the hallway and to the front of the house.

Mayne appeared silently, just as he always did, and opened the door. After a few more kisses in the general vicinity of cheeks, the three of them left, and the butler closed the door behind them.

"Can I get you anything, Mrs. Rutherford?" he asked.

"Thank you, no."

"I put the mail on the side table."

She nodded, and he walked away toward the back of the house. The tray he'd indicated held a few envelopes, so she picked them up and took them into Oscar's study.

She pushed back the roll top of his desk and laid the envelopes on the blotter. Once seated, she couldn't help but notice the fanciful bird hidden in one of the nooks meant for envelopes. An antique of alabaster so fine it was nearly translucent, the figurine had cost a great deal of money. One of the dozens of things Oscar had bought for her simply because she'd wanted it. He'd had excellent taste—far better than her own. But as soon as she'd fallen in love with something, he'd declare it the finest example of whatever kind of work it was and buy it for her on the spot.

The figurine watched her as she sorted the mail—two bills, a shareholder's statement, and another envelope. A letter from a law firm she didn't recognize.

After the settlement of Oscar's estate, she ought to know every lawyer in New York, but this one didn't jog her memory. She opened the envelope and pulled out a single sheet of heavy vellum.

"My dear Mrs. Rutherford," it read. "Please allow me to extend condolences on the loss of your husband."

Oh yes, that. She'd had enough sympathy to last several lifetimes.

"I wish I could be with you during these difficult hours. You won't remember me, but we met a few times several years ago. I've kept the memory of those encounters fresh in my mind ever since. You are not easy to forget."

Dear Lord. What on Earth could that mean? She looked at the signature and found only an initial. T. The person had closed with "Fondly, T."

The envelope gave no clue to the identity of the author. Simply the address of a law office on Fifth Avenue. When had lawyers started writing notes like this? She went back to the letter.

"If it's not asking too much, I'd like to hear back from you. I know this seems an odd request, and I'll be happy to explain at length in another letter if you're interested. Simply reply to Mr. Rose at the address on the envelope. If you don't answer, I won't bother you any further. Fondly, T."

Mr. Rose. She searched her memory. With all of Oscar's family's acquaintances and their friends in New York and the opera society and the people who flitted in for Oscar's intellectual salons, she'd met hundreds of people in the last several years. None of them were named Rose that she could recall. Not even a woman with a first name Rose. and why would the person write to her using a law firm as an intermediary?

He must have meant to protect his identity for some reason, although heaven only knew why someone would feel they had to fear her. Or, maybe he'd only tried to intrigue her. He'd accomplished that nicely. Or, possibly...just possibly...he'd wanted to make her feel safe enough to respond. This way of communicating almost promised a barrier between them, a wall she could throw up if he got too close. Another level of intrigue.

She ran her fingers absent-mindedly over the paper. They stopped at the sentence that had made her breath catch. "You are not easy to forget."

She shouldn't reply. No sane woman would. She might find a maniac on the other end of the chain of communication. She should visit Edna, go to Saratoga this summer, attend more to family manners. Any decent woman would. But damn it all, she'd been decent too long. What harm could a letter do? She'd probably never hear from him again, and if she did, she'd keep things strictly to corresponding through a firm of lawyers. You couldn't get much safer than that.

She fished through the cubbyholes until she found some of her own letterhead. The man had to know her address if his attorney did.

She set the piece of stationery in front of her and picked up a pen.

"Mrs. Oscar Rutherford," the printing said. Good Lord, at least she could have one of her own names back now. She crossed out Oscar and substituted Carole. Then, she began to write.

*

Even in the city, the rose arbor at the end of the garden behind Carole's house felt like a sylvan paradise.

She sat alone on a wooden bench, surrounded by the flowers' perfume and the buzzing of insects. A damselfly whizzed by and landed on a leaf near her head. Its body shone in iridescent blues and greens too brilliant to be real. She watched it until it flew off again.

The time had come for her to settle on what to do with the rest of her life. At forty, she might not even have spent half of her time on Earth. She had her health and plenty of money. She only needed some purpose— something to drive her forward so she didn't just dwell in the past.

She ought to do charity work. Other women in her position spent their time that way. Organize teas for benevolent associations. Host fundraising events for the symphony and ballet. She'd attended enough of those. She ought to know how to run one. The mere thought gave her a headache.

Why try to fool herself? Her head wasn't the problem. Her body was, specifically the spot between her legs. For the last years of his life, Oscar hadn't had the strength to perform. He'd slip into her room from time to time and huddle beneath the covers with her. Then he'd kiss her and smile, but a sadness had filled his eyes, although he tried to hide it. He'd known he couldn't give her what she needed.

She'd loved him, damn it. She'd kept her vows. She'd been a good wife. She deserved more. And now, at her age, she could only tempt another older man. She'd never have what her body craved—a big, hard cock and a man with enough youth and vigor to use thrust it inside her over and over until she went limp with satisfaction.

Enough self-pity. Most women would love to have her life. She only needed to find a way to make the most of the many blessings she'd been given.

She started to rise but then spotted Mayne coming down the path toward her. He had a glass of something in one hand and a bronze salver in the other. When he reached her, he held both out.

"Cook thought you might like some lemonade," he said.

"Thank you." She took the glass and sipped the tangy, sweet liquid.

"And the mail." Mayne set the tray on the bench beside her, turned, and went back toward the house.

The mail consisted of only one letter—from the same law firm that had sent the odd correspondence from Mr. Rose earlier. She'd written back weeks ago and had heard nothing. It seemed she'd have a reply, after all.

She set aside the lemonade and picked up the letter.

"Dear Carole," it began. "I hope I may call you that.

"I had so feared you wouldn't answer my note that my heart soared with delight to see your letterhead and the graceful hand that addressed it. You see, although I haven't had the pleasure of being in your company for years, I think of you so often, I felt your presence near me when I sat down to compose that opening salvo in what I hope will become a long and satisfying friendship."

Oh, my. Odd, very odd. One might even find it frightening. Still, it was only a letter, and one sent through a third party. This Mr. Rose hadn't approached her directly, and she'd be perfectly safe inside her own house with a full household staff if he tried.

"Indulge me, please," it went on. "Is your hair still the golden color of ale it was when I last saw you? Are your eyes as clear and deep as emeralds? Do you still hold your chin at that defiant angle when challenged?

"Forgive me if I seem too bold, but that's how I remember you—a woman of great integrity and beauty. If I've said more than I should, by all means, let this letter be our last. But I do hope I haven't offended you and that you'll dignify my requests with a response.

"Until then, I remain fondly yours, T."

Her heart was racing when she finished reading the note. Although he'd described her poetically, he had the details of her appearance correct. He'd even noticed what Oscar had always called her stubborn jaw. They had, indeed, met, and he'd paid close attention to her appearance.

Rose, Rose. Why couldn't she remember anyone named Rose? She must have noticed him at least once as he so clearly knew her.

She picked up the envelope and studied the return address again. Bradley and Morrison, Attorneys at Law. Fine. Tomorrow, someone on their staff would explain these letters and tell her exactly who Mr. T. Rose was.

*

Carole's heels clicked against marble as the assistant led her into the office of Mr. Eustace Bradley himself. The senior partner of this obviously profitable law firm occupied a corner office that looked out onto Fifth Avenue in a fashionable part of the city. A grandfather clock of polished mahogany stood against one wall, the ticking of the pendulum floating up toward the high ceiling.

She took a seat in front of a huge desk, crossed her ankles under her skirts, and rested her hands on her reticule in her lap. Whoever her Mr. Rose was, he had to have a great deal of money to hire a firm like this one and command the attention of the Mr. Bradley himself. It would cost an ungodly amount to use this law office as little more than a messenger service. Had he known she'd come here and chose this venue specifically to impress her? It had worked.

After a while, the office door opened again, and a portly gentleman with bushy, graying eyebrows entered.

"Mrs. Rutherford, I'm sorry to keep you waiting. I hope my staff offered you some refreshment."

"They did. I'm not thirsty."

"Got right down to business, eh?" He pulled out the huge chair behind his desk and sat. "I wish all my clients were as direct."

"Mr. Bradley, I've come to ask about one of the people you represent."

"So I gather. Mr. Rose."

"Yes."

"Well, you see, I don't actually represent him," he said.

She leaned forward, placing her hand on the edge of the desk. "But his letters come from here."

"But they don't. We're only an intermediary."

"I don't understand."

He leaned back and folded his hands over his belly. "We receive the correspondence from a solicitor in London. We simply pass the material on to you."

"London?" she repeated. "So, Mr. Rose is in England?"

"I wouldn't assume that. The solicitor might be getting them from anywhere, even another lawyer somewhere."

"But why would someone go to so much trouble and expense?" she asked.

"For any number of reasons. The most likely is he wishes to remain anonymous."

"But that doesn't make sense. Why would he ask me to write to him if he doesn't want me to know who he is?" she said.

He rested his forearms on the desk and leaned toward her. "If there's one thing I've learned from this business over the years, it's that people don't make sense."

"How can that be true?"

"Think of the scandals you read about in the newspapers," he said. "Wealthy men destroyed because they try to keep a little extra profit for themselves."

"But this can't be about greed. He hasn't asked me for any money."

"And judging from the generosity of the checks we receive to deliver his letters, he doesn't need any," Bradley said. "But I've had clients kill someone for a trifling reason. Others get themselves caught in places where they shouldn't be. Sense and reason have nothing to do with those things."

"So, how can I find out about Mr. Rose?"

"I'm sorry to say I don't know."

"There must be something," she said.

"We know nothing more about him than you do," he said. "Probably less."

"I'll contact the solicitor in London."

Bradley leaned back again. "I'm sorry. I can't tell you who he is."

"Why in heaven's name not?"

"Confidentiality, Mrs. Rutherford. You'd expect no less."

"Oh, dear." She slumped against the chair.

Bradley's brows furrowed. "Is Mr. Rose harassing you?"

"No, it's…"

"Because if he is, we'll refuse his letters and return his money," Bradley said. "We won't accept it if he's doing something wrong."

"It's nothing like that."

"We can let the man in London know that his client is threatening a United States citizen."

"He's not. I just want to know who he is." Damn, why did that sound so desperate? The man must think her a perfect idiot. Maybe she was, becoming so upset over a few letters.

20

"Let us know if you want the letters to stop," he said. "You won't hear another word, on my honor."

"No, I want them to continue." and there it was—the core truth of the matter. She did want more letters. She wanted the long and satisfying friendship they offered, although what he meant by satisfying wasn't at all clear. He admired her, had called her beautiful. But he could hardly get any physical satisfaction with an ocean dividing them.

"I've upset you, Mrs. Rutherford," Bradley said.

"No, I'm just frustrated. I like getting my own way in things."

He laughed heartily enough for the sound to echo off the walls. "Don't we all?"

She rose. "Thank you for your time, Mr. Bradley."

"One moment." He opened a drawer and pulled out an envelope. It had only one word on it. Carole. In Mr. Rose's handwriting. "I've had this for a while. I'm supposed to give it to you if you come seeking information."

She took the paper and stared at it for several seconds before folding it and stuffing it into her reticule. "Thank you."

"I'll have someone see you out."

"Don't bother. I can find my way."

*

Once at home, Carole went directly to the study without stopping to remove her hat or gloves. She set her reticule on the desk and pulled out the folded envelope. Her hands lingered on it as she smoothed it flat.

The alabaster bird caught her eye as it stared back at her, its head cocked in an almost accusatory gesture. Oscar was dead, and his present to her could keep its opinions to itself. She turned the figurine and pushed it toward the back of the cubbyhole. Then, she took a breath and opened the envelope.

"So, my clever girl, you decided to check up on me."
She could almost hear a male voice speak the words.
"Wise decision, and to be honest, it pleases me that
you've taken an interest in my identity."

How could she not? A man who claimed to have met
her and clearly remembered her looks…a man who
offered a long and satisfying friendship…how could he
fail to pique her curiosity? No, not pique, but engage it
fully. Since his second letter, she'd thought of little else.

"An unimaginative soul might assume that I'm
writing from London," he went on. "But I'm sure you
will have realized that I could be next door to you in
Manhattan, sending correspondence across the Atlantic
to be returned via a web of lawyers. Rest assured that I
am abroad, although not in London, and pose no threat
to you. I only wish to engage in a conversation over
some distance about a subject dear to both of our
hearts."

Curse it all, what subject could that be? If she
couldn't remember him, she couldn't remember his
interests and passions.

"Do write back, dear Carole, and remember that you
can always end the conversation by not replying. If I
hear nothing from you, I'll disappear out of your life
entirely.

"Fondly yours, T."

All right. She would engage in his odd conversation.
She was single now and could establish any sort of
relationship she wanted with a man, especially one
thousands of miles away. In fact, she had perfect
freedom, as she'd never encounter him in person. What a
liberating thought…complete honesty about anything
that came into her head.

She removed her gloves, pulled out a piece of
letterhead, and picked up the pen. Again, she crossed out

Mrs. Oscar and added only Carole. Carole Rutherford, with no reference she'd ever been a Missus.

"Dear T," she wrote. "Tell me honestly. Are you married?"

While she wouldn't have an affair with her Mr. Rose, it wouldn't do for his wife to find overly friendly letters from another woman. She did have some standards.

"If we begin a conversation, I hope we'll follow it wherever it leads. I'm a firm believer in the institution of marriage and wouldn't want to come between you and your loved ones in any way. If you're as unencumbered with social obligations as I am, we'll be able to speak freely with each other."

Was she jumping to the wrong conclusions? He might have meant to discuss literature or art. But then, why the emphasis on her appearance? and why all the intermediaries? It seemed he wanted something more, and she needed to take the risk of letting him know that his overtures would receive a welcome.

"And finally, dear Mr. Rose, I need something better to call you. May I please know your first name? You know mine."

She started to end the letter with "sincerely" and changed her mind. In the end, she settled on "Yours in anticipation, Carole."

She found an envelope, addressed it, and folded the letter into it. Before she could change her mind, she licked the flap and sealed the contents then went to the bell pull and gave it a tug.

Mayne appeared. "May I be of service?"

She held out the envelope. "Take this to the post office immediately."

"Yes, ma'am." He approached and took the letter.

"No, wait. It's only going to Fifth Avenue. Take it directly there."

"Of course," he said. "It must be important business."

"Yes. I think it very well may be."

Mayne left, and Carole went to the window that looked out over the front of the house. After a moment, Mayne emerged with the envelope in his hand. When a cab passed by, he hailed it and climbed in. The driver flicked the reins, and the horse lumbered off toward Fifth Avenue. Let the conversation begin.

*

Mr. Rose—Thomas according to his new signature— wrote back as quickly as two ocean crossings allowed. The note was short and cryptic. She stood in front of her destination and re-read it.

"My dearest Carole,

"To discover my intent, please visit a small book store on Forty-Second Street called Pan's Bookshelf. Ask for the proprietor's wife and tell her I sent you. Then buy whatever captures your fancy. The bill will go to Bradley for payment.

"Take everything home and study it. After all that, if you still wish to correspond, write and tell me of your adventure.

"With ever growing affection, I remain yours. Thomas.

"P.S. I'm single and not attached."

Thank heaven for that last.

Still clutching the letter, she glanced up at the sign above the store. Pan's Bookshelf was an odd name, but the merchandise seemed what you'd expect. Copies of popular books and sheet music filled the display window. When she entered, a little bell went off over the door. The place was tidy and free of dust and held shelves and tables of ordinary books. A slender gentleman wearing a tweed coat approached.

"Are you the proprietor?" she asked.

"Roland Card at your service," he answered.

"I'm supposed to speak to Mrs. Card."

One of his eyebrows went up. "You are?"

"Yes. Is she available?"

"She handles our special customers."

"Mr. Rose told me to ask for her," Carole said.

"I'll see if she's free. Wait here, please." Mr. Card went to the back of the store and disappeared behind a curtain into what likely was a work area. A quiet conversation started back there. His voice and a woman's. The name Rose came up several times, although Carole couldn't make much else out.

Finally, a woman pushed the curtain aside and emerged. "You say Mr. Rose sent you?"

"He told me specifically to come here and ask for the proprietor's wife."

"That's me." Mrs. Card pulled a key chain out of her pocket. "Let me show you what he wanted you to see."

Mrs. Card led her to a corner of the store. A small staircase led down to a closed door. The woman inserted a key in the lock and let them both into a nearly dark room. When she turned up the flame on the gas light, revealing the merchandise, Carole gasped in surprise. The very first thing her gaze had landed on was a glass case full of phalluses made out of a variety of materials. Leather, marble, ivory, even blown glass. They came in all sizes from mere figurines to truly mammoth depictions of the male member.

"You can see why we have to be careful who comes in here," Mrs. Card said. "The prudes would close us down if they found out about this collection."

"I never imagined there were such things."

"Mr. Rose must have wanted to expand your horizons," Mrs. Card said.

She turned toward the woman. "Then, you know Mr. Rose?"

"Not at all. He sent references from some of our other customers."

"Could I be introduced to them?"

Mrs. Card's eyes went wide. "Certainly not. I can't reveal their identity any more than I can reveal yours."

"Of course."

"I will say, though, that some of them are the prudes' husbands."

"Indeed." Carole looked around. The room held all sorts of things. Books, as you'd expect, but also vials of what seemed like oils and herbs. Then, there was strange equipment. Studded collars and leather bracelets. Even whips and riding crops. Costumes and scarves hung from a rack in the corner.

"Can you help me select some items?" she asked.

"New to the voluptuous life?" Mrs. Card answered.

"I was married for twenty years, but all this…"

This room might have come out of her heated daydreams. Even though she couldn't determine the purpose of some of the items, she could recognize the intent. Sexual pleasure, free from any censorship or disapproval. Her "friend," Thomas Rose, had sent her here to free her sensual nature in ways she hadn't been able to during her marriage.

"I'd be happy to help." Mrs. Card picked up a few volumes and handed them to her. "Books are usually a good start for your education."

Carole looked at the spine of one. "The Pearl?"

"An underground English journal. Very naughty. You can learn a lot there."

Carole wandered back to the case she'd first noticed—the one containing representations of the male member. "Do women use these to…well…"

"Not the glass one, I hope. But the leather might serve."

"It's enormous," Carole said.

"That's what some women want."

Mrs. Card might have been speaking directly to Carole's lustful fantasies with that last remark. She'd buy one of the statues. Not to insert into her body, but she'd run her fingers over it, just to get the feel of a hard rod against her palm. To play with it the way she'd imagined toying with a lover's cock.

"I'd like the ivory one."

Mrs. Card opened the case and handed it to her. "It's a beautiful piece."

Carole hefted it in her hand. It felt warm and smooth. "It is lovely."

"Now then, would you like to try a collar or cuffs?"

"For what?"

"You are an innocent. For discipline."

"No, I don't think so," Carole answered. "This is enough for now."

"Let me show you something." Mrs. Card went to the rack and pulled out a garment that was made of some gossamer fabric. Nearly transparent, it would show off anything beneath it. Here and there, feathers attached might hide breasts and the pelvic area, but as the gown moved and shifted it would give onlookers peeks at a woman's private parts. Mrs. Card held it up to Carole. "It's your size, and the feathers would favor your coloration."

"It's beautiful, but I don't have anyone to wear it for."

"A shame, but it'll be here if you change your mind." She returned the gown to its place.

"Thank you for your help," Carole said. "These things will do for now."

"Just one more item you really do need." Mrs. Card picked up one of the vials. "It's an extract of mint. Highly concentrated and quite an astringent."

"What would I use that for?"

"It stimulates sensation on moist parts of the body." Mrs. Card removed the top and shook some of the liquid onto her finger. "Let me rub some on your lip."

Carole leaned forward and allowed the woman to place a few drops on her lower lip. The flesh immediately began to tingle. Almost a burning sensation, but pleasant.

"That is strong," she said.

"Imagine it in other places," Mrs. Card said. When Carole didn't respond, she inclined her head toward Carole's ear. "Between your legs."

"Oh, my…yes. I see."

Mrs. Card stoppered the bottle and handed it to her. "You'll want this."

"Thank you."

"Enjoy your things," Mrs. Card said. "and visit again."

"Thank you," she answered. "I definitely will."

*

This time, Carole locked the study door closed behind her before going to the desk to lay out her purchases. She set the ivory phallus next to her hand on the desk and the book on her other side.

She hadn't spent much time studying the male member. Sex was something she and Oscar had done at night and mostly under the covers. Thinking back now, she could hardly remember enough about his sex to know if he measured up to this sculpture. If only she could have him back for a few hours so she could explore the real thing—stroke it and watch it respond. Maybe even watch the stream of sperm as it shot out in his orgasm.

She sighed. Now, the only man on Earth she could ask was on another continent, separated from her by two sets of lawyers.

She took down another piece of letterhead—this time the new batch she'd ordered with her name reinstated—and began to write.

"My dearest Thomas,

"I can only assume that you intentionally directed me to the sexually explicit materials in the back room of Pan's Bookshelf. I imagine you'd like to know what I bought and what I think of my purchases."

She reached over and ran a finger down the length of the phallus and then circled the head. How would a real man respond if she did that?

"I selected a model of the male member carved out of ivory. I presume it's a faithful portrayal of the real organ. It has an odd appeal I can't deny. The shaft captures the eye and leads my gaze toward the head and at the pucker in the tip. Can you tell me, dearest friend, how greatly men's rods vary in size, shape, and beauty?"

What does yours look like? Is it very large? Oh, dear. She couldn't possibly ask that. At least, not yet.

"I also bought copies of a journal called The Pearl and a book of engravings. I'll leave the magazine for later and tell you a bit about the pictures before I close."

She flipped a few pages, and the book opened to a depiction of an Indian couple. The woman had bent over to clutch her ankles, and the man stood behind her with his organ poised to enter her. Another engraving appeared French—a lady reclining on a chaise, her hand between her thighs. She wore an expression of pure rapture. She didn't seem to notice a man hidden behind a curtain with a very large erect member in his fist.

"I didn't know such material existed," she wrote. "So explicit. So sinful. So delicious. Thank you, my dear friend, for opening my eyes. I feel as though I've been sheltered behind a screen obscured from the larger world of sensation.

"I still don't know how we met or why you would remember me, but I thank whichever benevolent fate sent your attentions my way. I want to study these treasures and will write more at length when I have.

"Farewell for now my dearest Thomas. You'll be in my…"

My what? My mind? Very little of what went on between them—even through the distance and the intervention of lawyers—involved her mind. She had a visceral reaction to everything about him and his letters now. Her breath had caught at the mere sight of his firm hand on the letter that had directed her to Pan's Bookshelf. Now, as her fingers caressed the pages of the book, she could imagine that he had touched them before her. If she stroked the phallus now, she'd have to imagine it real flesh—his flesh. All those images created a slow ache in the pit of her belly and below. No, intellect had nothing to do with this.

"…my most private thoughts," she wrote. "I remain, your devoted Carole."

Coward. She should have said he'd be in her heart because he lived there now. Maybe, she'd find the courage to tell him that in her next letter. Because there would be more letters. They'd discovered something too unique and wonderful to end it now.

She addressed an envelope, sealed the letter inside, and pressed her lips to the paper before going in search of Mayne to have him take it to Mr. Bradley's office.

CHAPTER TWO

When she found Mayne, he wasn't alone. Joseph Stoddard, one of Oscar's partners, stood in the front entryway. He paused in the act of handing his hat to her butler, and his eyes widened when he caught sight of her.

"Mrs. Rutherford," he said. "I hope I'm not intruding."

"I was just coming to find you, ma'am," Mayne said.

"Thank you." She handed Mayne the envelope. "You take care of this. I'll see Mr. Stoddard in the sitting room."

"Yes, ma'am," Mayne answered.

She turned and led her visitor that way. Once there, she gestured toward a chair. "Would you care to sit?"

Stoddard remained standing. "I hope I haven't interrupted anything."

"Why would you say that?"

"You seem short of breath, and your skin is flushed."

She put her hand over her chest, almost feeling her heart beating there. Her bosom was, indeed, rising and falling more than normal. Looking at those pictures and writing to Thomas about them had excited her more than she'd thought.

"I just came in from a brisk walk," she said. Oh, my. Now, her secret friendship with Thomas had her telling little lies. As what she did or where she went was no business of his, the whole thing was really rather fun.

"Did you need my help with something at the company?" she asked. "My signature, perhaps?"

He shook himself slightly. For heaven's sake, he'd been staring at her chest the entire time.

"I just came to see how you are," he said. "We're all concerned for you."

"How thoughtful."

"It's too easy to forget a widow after her husband has died."

"Well, thank you for checking on me."

"You look very well." He cleared his throat. "Very well, indeed."

He stood awkwardly, as if he wanted to say something else but couldn't find the words. "In fact, I hope you won't take this the wrong way, Mrs. Rutherford…Carole…you're glowing."

Warmth bloomed inside her. She shouldn't have enjoyed the comment so much. Joseph Stoddard meant nothing to her outside of Oscar's company. But no one had noticed her as a woman for so long.

Except for Thomas. Impossible. He couldn't have noticed her from half a world away. And yet, he had. He'd entered her life in the most intimate way possible. He was changing her from the inside out.

Stoddard walked toward her and took her hand in his. "I've always admired you. Oscar was a lucky man."

She tried to pull her hand away gently, but he held it fast in his. Short of making a scene, she could only stay where she was and allow him to touch her.

"We all have needs," he went on softly. "Especially once we've tasted the pleasures of the flesh."

"What are you talking about, Mr. Stoddard?"

"You're an intelligent woman. I think you know."

She did yank her hand back then. "Did you come here to ask me to be your lover?"

"I didn't. Honestly. I only wanted to see if you're well."

"Then, what on Earth has come over you?"

"You have." He took her elbows in his hands. "I don't know what's different. You were always a lovely woman, but now...you're tempting beyond resistance."

She stepped backward. "I think you'd better go."

"I'm sorry." He took a deep breath. "I don't know what came over me."

"I suggest you go home to your wife."

"Yes, of course. My wife." He gave her one more long look, and a fever seemed to enter his eyes. "Please remember, though. If you ever find yourself, well, lonely in that particular way. I'd be more than happy to keep you company."

"Understood."

"I'll see myself out, then."

She stepped aside so that he wouldn't have to get near her to leave the room. He did without looking back. She stood, nearly holding her breath, as his footsteps echoed down the hallway. The front door opened and closed, and she could finally relax.

*

"My dearest Thomas,

"You won't believe what happened yesterday. Right after I finished my latest letter to you, I had a visit from one of my late husband's partners. I must have been in some state when I greeted him. Had I known, I would have pleaded a headache and hidden in my bedroom

33

with the voluptuous reading you so kindly bought for me.

"Here's the most remarkable thing about his visit—he told me I was glowing. Yes, glowing. He called me tempting beyond resistance, and he asked if he could be my lover. I must admit that the mere thought that I can move a man in that way gives me more than a little feminine pride.

"I know you must think it odd that a woman who'd shared a marriage bed for twenty years could be so naïve, but I hardly anticipated the power of correspondence like ours. It seems you've turned me into an enchantress.

"Of course, I refused him. Once a woman has tasted the sweetness of a friendship like ours—even if from a great distance—a mere dalliance with a married man holds no appeal.

"In the meantime, I thought I'd let you know how my studies are progressing. I've learned a whole new vocabulary. Priapus, cunny, cockstand. I've read of the joys of coupling in groups. Young girls exploring each other's bodies while lusty men look on. And imagine the wonder of Lady Pokington's clitoris.

"As I read the stories, I keep the images of the sensual paintings in the back of my mind. How much more exciting to picture the dimensions of an aroused member while reading of another's exploits?

"I blush as I write the words, but as much with excitement as with embarrassment. And with no shame in me at all. What use is shame? Surely, the Almighty must have wished us to take pleasure in the act when He directed us to be fruitful and multiply. Otherwise, why would He have given us such powerful drives? Even as I sit here with an ocean separating us, I can feel the brush of your lips on my throat, taste the sweetness of your mouth, hear your labored breathing as you move inside me.

"I dare to write of this because of everything you've shown me. You must share my emotions, or you wouldn't have sent me to Pan's Bookshelf. I bless the day you did.

"Dearest Thomas, I've kept your letters. I'll read them in order now to admire how cleverly you've seduced me. Write again soon.

"Your eager student, Carole."

*

"My darling Carole,

"Fate produced both of your letters in my post on the same day. What an embarrassment of riches.

"First, I could hardly contain my jealousy that some other man should try to win your affections, although I'm not surprised that he would. Or course, you're tempting beyond resistance. You tempt me in my waking moments and in my dreams. Of course, you're an enchantress. You've entranced me completely.

"I'm glad you sent the man away. If he persists, let me know, and I'll have Mr. Bradley share a few words with him. 'Cease and desist' come to mind.

"More important, I'm glad you enjoyed Pan's Bookshelf and thrilled that you brought some items home with you. Lady Pokington is a delight, isn't she?

"I picture you with the ivory phallus hidden somewhere and have a good chuckle. I do hope a maid doesn't find it one day while she's dusting.

"I should warn you before you read further that what I have to say is as explicit and detailed as the stories you read in The Pearl. As always, you have the freedom to put this letter aside or even burn it. Should you finish it and find anything distasteful, you need only decline to reply, and I won't bother you again. It's my dearest wish that won't happen and I'll hear from you soon. We're soul mates, I think, sharing more than lust, although that's quite powerful between us. Now, if you dare, read on…

"You asked about the male member, specifically whether it varies for size and beauty. It does. But truly, my darling, weren't you asking about mine? I think we must be forthright and open on this score, so I'll tell you about my cock.

"I'm holding it in my hand right now. Every time I receive a message from you, it hardens at the mere sight of your handwriting on an envelope. When I read the carnal words of your last letter, it swelled against my trousers, demanding to be released. It's thick, hard, and ruddy in color as I sit here, much as I imagine the ones in your book appear. I hate to brag, but honesty requires that I tell you my instrument is a large one. You'll have to tell me whether or not it's beautiful, as I can't judge that for myself.

"There, now. As I stroke it, it grows even bigger and deepens in color. In a moment, the telltale drop of liquid will appear at the tip. Shortly after that, I'll lose control and will have to race to the inevitable orgasm.

"Before that happens, let me ask you for a favor. When you finish this, take it to your bedroom. Lock the door behind you securely. Draw the curtains. Then, strip out of every bit of your clothing. Take your time and imagine my hands undoing all the hooks and buttons. Picture my lips skimming over your flesh as you expose it.

"Once you're naked, lie on your bed and run your hands over your body. Stroke your face and then your neck. Moving lower, cup your breasts and squeeze them. Tease the nipples until they peak and harden.

"Now, lower still. Past your ribs to your belly. Imagine my head resting there as I explore your thighs with my palm and then slip between them to probe the heaven at the place where your legs meet. Your sex, your pussy, your sweet, sweet cunny.

"Now, reach there yourself. Feel the plump lips that guard your entrance. Are you already growing wet? If so, spread the moisture over your inner thighs.

"My darling Carole, I can hardly continue. Picturing you lying on your coverlet with your legs spread as you pleasure yourself is the most erotic thing I've ever done. My hand moves faster on my aching cock. I must finish quickly.

"Once you've made yourself thoroughly wet, part your lips again and find your pearl. It will be hard and throbbing as my sex is as I write. Stroke it firmly. Find the way to get maximum response from hit. Tweak, pluck, roll it between your fingers. Whatever pushes you faster, do that. Continue, never slowing, never hesitating, until you reach the crest and soar past. Feel the tension build and build until it crashes over you. Then, memorize each contraction as you spend.

"Once you've done that, rest for a bit before taking up pen and paper to tell me about everything you did and felt. Please, I desperately need to know every detail.

"Oh! The orgasm approaches. I only have enough strength now to tell you that I remain your most devoted Thomas."

Dear heaven. Carole clutched the papers in her hand so hard she crumpled them in her fist. Nothing she'd seen in any of the pictures or read in any of the stories compared to *that*. Nothing in her real experiences with sex came even close. She'd been inside his mind, occupied his body, as he'd stroked that magnificent instrument.

It had to be large and beautiful. In no just world could he have strung those words together if he hadn't meant them. Days ago, he'd sat somewhere with a pen in one hand and his sex in the other while he stared at the paper she held in her fingers right now. Fingers that had crushed the pages.

She took a breath to steady herself and spread the letter out on the desk to smooth it out. Her hands shook as she did, but their trembling didn't compare to the hammering of her heart that sent her blood pulsing through her, especially to the place between her thighs. Mere words had aroused her to a point past anything she'd experienced before.

He wanted her to do the same for him. And right this moment, her body screamed for relief. Although she'd occasionally wake up in the middle of a climax, she hadn't manipulated her sex since the first explorations as a girl. Would she even remember how to do it? She'd better, because this fever would *not* go away on its own.

Yes, she'd follow Thomas' instructions, make herself spend, and then write to tell him about it. If he found the reading as exciting as she had, he'd become erect again. He might even have to take out his sex and give himself another orgasm. Because of something she'd written.

She took the letter and its envelope and left the study. If a servant found her as she made her way upstairs, the person would have to notice something wasn't right. She'd think of some explanation, preferably one that required several minutes of perfect solitude with no interruptions.

She encountered no one, though, as she went down the hallway and climbed the stairs. She saw and felt everything through new eyes. The smooth wood of the banister, the soft carpet under her feet. Everything seemed brighter—more sensual—than she'd experienced it before.

The upstairs corridor was hushed and deserted, and she easily slipped into her room undetected. After turning the key in the lock, she removed it entirely, went to the window, and set it on the small table there.

When she pulled the drapes closed, near darkness fell over the room. Now, to undress. She undid the buttons at the cuffs of her blouse and then the ones behind her neck. The silk went over her head and down her arms, and she draped it over the back of a chair. Her skirt unfastened easily, although pushing it past the bustle and hoops took some doing. The strings to remove those resisted untying, but she eventually had the whole contraption free and let it fall to the floor around her feet.

After stepping out of that, she sat and removed her shoes and stockings, taking the garters with them. She had to stand again to undo her stays. She paused to imagine Thomas back there, helping to free her from the corset. His breath would graze her neck as he worked. He might even curse softly in frustration at having to fight her clothing.

He'd be tall and strong. Virile. Thinning hair wouldn't bother her—one had to expect that in men her age—but any man youthful enough to become aroused at the glance of a woman's handwriting on an envelope would have enough vigor to fill her until both had spent copiously and neither had anything left to give.

When she finally had the corset off, she pulled her shift over her head. That only left her drawers. She bent to push them off, and her fingers brushed moisture. She'd already damped the crotch, and she hadn't even touched herself yet. What a miracle that her Thomas could arouse her from half a world away. Now naked, she imagined him sitting on the bed behind her, his fingers closed around his stiff member, as she walked to the mirror to study her reflection.

What would he see in the glass? She had graceful limbs, thank heaven, and they hadn't aged much. Her breasts had grown over the years. As her distant lover had instructed, she grasped the flesh with her hands, squeezing. They seemed to swell to fill her palms, and the nipples hardened. When she rolled them, a current of electricity shot through her, and more wetness seeped out from between her legs. She continued, now teasing the peaks with her fingers until they beaded up tight, and oh so sensitive.

If only Thomas could come up behind her and do this for her. His hardness would press against her rump, and she could get a good feel for its size. No matter how large he became, he'd make her ready for the moment when he eased himself inside her and they began the long climb to heaven.

Maybe, someday they'd do all that. Maybe, they'd meet and they could caress each other's bodies. Right now, she'd picture him as she fingered herself. It would have to do.

She went to the bed, climbed on, and spread her legs. Just lying there exposed heightened the tension building in her belly. She stroked her face, as he'd told her to, and then ran her hands lower. She'd already toyed with her breasts, following his instruction, and honestly, her poor sex couldn't wait any longer. So, after finding the mint extract in the drawer of the bedside table and dabbing some onto her finger, she went directly to her sex.

The moment she slipped her hand between her legs and fondled the lips there, her whole world shifted, and a new reality took its place. She'd wanted to explore her carnal nature her entire life, and now it claimed her. She stroked the flesh there, spreading the salve until she tingled with it. Her pussy—might as well use the right word for it—felt swollen and achy, and more moisture seeped out.

She pressed and squeezed, and a soft cry of pleasure escaped from her throat. She would climax, and soon. Already, a haze of need closed around her mind, leaving only one destination, one way forward.

She stroked herself slowly from back to front and then the reverse. When she reached the entrance to her cunny, she slid a finger inside. Her muscles clamped down on it, immediately, searching for something bigger to probe all the way inside her.

Thomas. She needed Thomas and his stiff member. She needed to take it in her hand and guide it between her lips.

He wasn't here. She only had the images in his letter and on the pages of her book. He'd told her to rub her pearl, and so, without him to take her to the ultimate, she could only follow his instructions.

She found the clitoris immediately. It had hardened into a tight nub. When she touched it, the mint set it on fire. Her whole body stiffened, her back arching, and she bit her lip to keep from crying out. Damn, how could her own hand feel so blessed good? She rubbed it rhythmically, feeling the coil winding tighter inside her.

What had he told her? Remember, remember. To find the exact way to get the strongest response. She tugged gently, and her heart lurched. Yes, yes, that must be it. Then, she rolled it between her thumb and forefinger, and that was even better. She kept right on until her thighs grew damp with the moisture from her cunny. But when she used two fingers to circle the pearl, pressing it into the hardness beneath, she lost all conscious control.

The tension burst over her as she came. For long heartbeats, it held her, crushing her with its power. Pleasure so intense, she could hardly breathe. Then her sex convulsed, all her inner muscles contracting rhythmically. She rode out the storm until it finally released her and she rested against the coverlet and pulled air into her lungs.

When it was all over, she rolled onto her side and clutched her ribs, moaning. Deep inside, the muscles of her sex still fluttered with aftershocks.

Oh, dear Lord. She'd never be the same again.

*

"My dearest Thomas,

"I did it. I used my hand to make myself spend, just the way you told me to, and it was glorious. I've never felt so free. Even as I write this, I might be floating an inch off the chair. I'm that happy.

"I followed all of your instructions—removing all my clothes, touching my face and my chest, squeezing my breasts and teasing the nipples. I even made a study of exactly what my pearl liked best. A firm, circling motion finally set it off, but to be honest, anything might have done it. I'd already become so aroused reading your letter that even the simplest pressure would have driven me past the breaking point.

"Well now, what do you think of the wanton I've become? I can write the most scandalous words without a blush. I think of sex from the moment I wake up in the morning until I fall asleep. I dream of sex. and it's all your doing.

"So, tell me, dear Thomas. Have I made your cock hard with my words? Are you holding it in your fist right now? Are you stroking the shaft and lingering at the tip? Do you imagine my hand there as the flesh turns livid with arousal?

"Most of all, can you picture your sex plunging into mine? Can you feel my juices coating it? (I've grown wet just thinking of that.) Do you think of how I'd grip you as I spent all around your rod?

"Tell me all. Please. and when you next write, send some sort of likeness so that I can see your beloved face. I'll place it on the table beside my bed so that I can look into your eyes as I climax.

"Please write again soon, so we can share even more depravity.

"Your besotted Carole."

*

He didn't write back. Two whole months with no word. Carole should have begun to reconcile herself to the fact that she'd lost Thomas—if, in fact, she'd ever really had him—but each day that went by without a word cut into her more deeply.

For heaven's sake, she'd buried her husband. The man she'd lived with every day for twenty years. The man who'd existed to make her smile and had done his best to make her happy, even if he couldn't do it in bed. She ought to mourn him more than a stranger who'd sent her fewer than a half a dozen letters.

She sat with them now spread out in front of her on the desk. In order, from the first one that did no more than hint at what would follow to the last one—so outrageous and delicious she'd crushed it in her fist out of excitement. There must be some clue in here about what had happened. Some indication of what she'd done wrong. But as many times as she'd read them re-read them and then read them yet again, she couldn't find that clue. She'd only done what he'd asked her to do, and still, he didn't write back.

Damn it all to hell, anyway. Her breath caught on a sob, and she pressed her fist against her mouth to stifle any sound that might escape. She bit her lip so hard she might break the skin. Good. Better that than tears. She would not cry over him. Bad enough she'd made herself vulnerable to a stranger and spoken to him about things she'd never mentioned to anyone else, including her husband. She would *not* allow him to reduce her to a sniffling female. No, she'd put him behind her, and eventually, she'd forget him.

Yes. She took a deep breath. That's what she'd do.

She pulled the roll top of the desk down, locked it, and put the key into her pocket. Then she got up and went to the window.

Life bustled out on the street. Men and women going about their business, some pulling children along with them. Cabs, carts, and private carriages jostled each other on the crowded street. Only she sat inside, feeling sorry for herself. Tomorrow, she'd go back out into the world. She'd call on some of the ladies who were supposed to be her friends. She'd find out about their charity projects and then volunteer for the ones that sounded most interesting. She'd pour tea and cut cake. She'd buttonhole wealthy men and ask them for donations. and she'd smile. Most of all she'd smile, smile, smile. It would all be very upstanding and proper. And soul crushing.

The letters tugged her mind back to the desk as if they could whisper and command her. That one line she kept going back to. What he'd written about the beauty of his member. "You'll have to be the judge of that." The implication leaped off the page—that she'd see his cock. How else could she judge its beauty? He'd clearly suggested that they'd meet. Not just that they'd keep writing, but they'd actually face each other in the flesh. They'd make love. That line promised it. It did!

But then if she could believe him, he'd been stimulating himself when he wrote it. He could have been out of his mind with lust, written anything that came into his head. She'd probably never know why he'd used those words.

Give it up. Give it up. Damn it, give it up! She took a shuddering breath and tipped her head back. "I can't forget it if I can't understand it."

"Mrs. Rutherford?" It was Mayne's voice from the doorway.

She swiped at her eyes and turned. "Is it the mail?"

"No, ma'am, you have a visitor."

"Tell whoever it is to go away. Tell them I have a headache."

"I will." He left, and she went to a chair sank into it. The last sick truth washed over her as it always did when she thought of Thomas. All the things she'd written back. About how she'd touched herself. Squeezed her own breasts. The exact motion of her fingers that had made her come. The urgent plea for his picture. How humiliating, all of it. If the whole thing had been a hoax, he could be laughing at her this very moment.

Mayne appeared again. "The gentleman says he has important business with you, ma'am."

"Oh, for heaven's sake, who is it?"

"A Mr. Bradley."

"Bradley?" All the air rushed out of her chest.

"He asked me to tell you the following. That Mr. Rose said you might refuse to see him, but you should hear him out, nevertheless."

Her whole body started to tremble. "Where is he?"

"In the sitting room."

"Tell him I'll be right there," she said. "Whatever you do, don't let him leave."

"Yes, ma'am." Mayne turned to leave again.

"Never mind. I'll see him now." She bolted from her chair and left the room, nearly pushing her butler in her haste to get by. She used every bit of control she could muster not to break into a run, but suddenly the route between the study and the sitting room seemed to expand in front of her. She finally reached there, and when she entered, the lawyer turned and smiled.

"How nice to see you again, Mrs. Rutherford," he said.

She closed the door and entered on shaky legs. "Mr. Rose. There's nothing wrong with him, is there?"

"Not as far as I know," the lawyer answered. "He hasn't mentioned anything in his letters."

"Then, you've heard more from him."

"Of course. All of it about you."

She put her hand over her chest. "About me?"

"Business arrangements."

She gestured toward a chair. "Please, sit down."

He sat, pulled his case into his lap, and opened it. When she took a seat hear him, he produced a small packet. "Mr. Rose asked me to give these to you."

She opened the papers and stared at them until they made sense. "It's a steamship ticket."

"To London for two days from now," he said.

Her mouth dropped open as she stared at him. "Two days?"

"I know it's soon…"

"It's impossible," she said.

"Difficult, I'll admit, but I've arranged things for you."

Her head swam. For two months, she'd had no word from him, and now he expected her to get on a ship to England—in two days. It was insane, but underneath all that, the message finally registered in her brain. He'd sent for her. He wanted her to come to him. He hadn't ended things. She hadn't repulsed him with her erotic revelations. He wasn't laughing at her.

"…this afternoon," Mr. Bradley was saying.

She glanced up at him. "I beg your pardon."

"Someone from the passport office will visit you this afternoon," he said. "It took some doing to arrange that, but I have a bit of pull at the agency."

"I have a passport," she said.

"There won't be much to do about that then, but you'll need a visa."

"Visa?"

"From the British government," he said. "Someone from the embassy will visit tomorrow."

"Forgive me if I seem confused," she said.

He laughed in that hearty way he had. "I imagine this is a surprise."

"It's bewildering."

"Maybe this will explain things." He reached into his case again and pulled out an envelope. The handwriting jumped right out at her. One word—Carole. Thomas had written it.

Mr. Bradley handed her the letter. She took it, running her fingers over the vellum. She'd thought she'd never hear from him again. She'd thought she'd mistaken his intent. Now, this.

Mr. Bradley shut his case and rose. "I think that's everything."

She got up, too. "I'll see you out."

"I can find my way," he said. "I'm sure you have a lot to do in the next two days."

"I haven't even begun to take it all in," she answered.

"*Bon voyage*," he said. Then, he left her alone with this new letter. She sat again and waited until the front door opened and closed.

Her fingers fumbled with the envelope, but she finally had it open, and she unfolded the paper.

"My darling Carole,

"How you must despise me."

Oh, Thomas. She ought to despise him. He ought to hate him with every inch of her body. But just seeing the words "darling Carole" lifted the dark cloud that had hovered over her heart for weeks.

"I had some arranging to do before I could send for you," it went on. "and to be totally truthful, I thought that an element of uncertainty might make you eager enough to see me that you'd agree to all the details of my plan."

Uncertainty? It had been misery. and as to her eagerness, she had enough of that without any manipulation on his part.

"I hope you'll forgive me," he continued, "and that by the time we finally meet you will have put away any

47

anger so that we may come together as lovers, the way Fate has meant us to."

She jumped up, clutching the letter to her breast, and spun around the room out of pure joy. She'd see him, taste his kisses, feel his hands on her breasts, experience the invasion of his sex into hers. Maybe she would punish him first. She could make him beg. She could command him to make her climax with his fingers first. Or—no, better—with his tongue, the way men did in The Pearl. Not even Oscar had done that for her, and she could have it as soon as she got to England.

She stood in the center of the room, dizzy both from the pirouettes and from the swing of emotions. She opened the letter and read on.

"Now to my plan," it said. "It's outrageous. It may even sound impossible, but I truly believe we must proceed in this manner to find lasting happiness together. Before we meet, I want you to take four other lovers."

Good Lord, he couldn't mean that. She read the paragraph again. She hadn't been mistaken. He was telling her to seek out other men.

"I don't want anyone but you," she said. She read some more.

"Please don't think I make this request lightly, my darling. It's one of the most difficult things I've ever done. The mere thought of you with another man makes my blood run hot with jealousy. I want you for my own. I want you to cry no one's name but mine as you spend. I want your precious cunny to be the private home of my cock.

"Yes, my lover, it's hard now, but Priapus will have to remain in my pants until I've finished this and convinced you to take up this amorous adventure. I'll explain everything when we're finally together, and I think you'll agree that what I asked was for the best.

"Now then, as always, if you wish to have no more to do with me, simply tear this letter up. I assume if you've read this far, you've accepted the steamship ticket from Mr. Bradley. You needn't use it. That stateroom can go vacant across the Atlantic if you decide to remain where you are."

Not go? Impossible. If she ever did get over Thomas, she'd never stop wondering what she'd missed. For heaven's sake, she wouldn't even know what he looked like. But she'd think about him constantly, and she'd no doubt curse herself for not taking this opportunity when she had it.

Four other lovers. How would she even do such a thing? She was forty-years-old, not unattractive for her age, but younger men wouldn't notice her. After everything she'd been through, she wouldn't take a married man. She'd been faithful to her husband for twenty years. She wouldn't help another man betray his wife. Somehow, she'd have to find a way to do as he requested, and quickly. She'd waited too long for happiness to put it off any longer.

She went back to the letter.

"Still reading, my darling?" it said. "Good. Here's how we'll proceed. Bradley's already worked out the details in New York. In two days, you'll board the ship to London. My solicitor will greet you when you arrive. He'll act as our go-between. Once you've taken and dispensed with your first lover, you'll contact him for further instructions. When you've had all four, he'll tell you how to find me.

"I'm trusting in your lusty nature that it won't take long."

If only she could feel as sure.

The letter continued, "I've waited a long time and can find enough patience to wait a bit longer. Hurry to me, Carole. I long to see your beautiful face again, this time on the pillow next to mine.

"As always, I remain, your devoted Thomas."

"Another visitor, Mrs. Rutherford," Mayne said. He'd entered without her noticing. "He says he's from the passport office."

"Show him in."

Mayne turned to leave.

"Oh, Mayne," she called after him. "Tell the staff to take care of things, pack for me. I'll be leaving for London day after tomorrow."

So little time to prepare. She'd have to go through all the clothes before she'd had to go into mourning. With any luck, none of those dresses would have gone out of style. She could freshen them with new hats and other accessories. Less than two days to shop and pack. and to visit Pan's Bookshelf one more time. That feathered, nearly invisible gown would be hers, after all, now that she had someone to wear it for.

CHAPTER THREE

How did one attract men all alone in a city you hardly knew and with no social contact except for a solicitor and his wife? At least, Mrs. Carter had expensive tastes in things and had shown her the best shops for clothing and anything else she decided to buy. She even had a great deal of money Mr. Carter had given her on her arrival. Thomas had sent it, of course, although she had plenty of her own.

Now, here she sat in an elegant teashop, sipping from the finest china, and listening to Mrs. Carter prattle on.

"There's Lady Wendly," the woman said. "Such a shame about her son."

The lady went by, arm in arm with another fashionably dressed woman. She took no notice of either of them, so obviously, Mrs. Carter wasn't a friend or even an acquaintance.

Carole waited until the pair was safely out of earshot. "What's wrong with her son?"

Mrs. Carter leaned across the table like a conspirator. "He drinks. Well, all men do, but not like him, and he's to be the next Earl. If he doesn't kill himself first."

"That must be very embarrassing for her."

"No one speaks of it," Mrs. Carter said. "I only found out because I have a friend who knows the family."

"Do you know a lot of people, Mrs. Carter?"

"I try to keep up. Strictly to help Mr. Carter with his practice."

"Of course." The woman was a busybody and a gossip. How on Earth that could help her husband was a mystery. But, it might help Carole track down the sort of man she could make into a lover.

In fact, she'd already found a candidate. He sat across the room with a beautiful woman wearing a dress with rather too low a neckline for the middle of the day. If she understood body positions correctly, he might very well have his hand in her lap or someplace more intimate.

"Ah, you spotted Mr. Harthorn," Mrs. Carter said. "Women usually do."

"Is he notorious?"

Mrs. Carter's brows floated nearly to her hairline. "Worse than that. A perfect libertine."

Carole tsked a few times. "I pity his wife."

"He isn't married," Mrs. Carter said. "At least, no poor woman has to suffer the disgrace of his frequent flirtations."

"Thank heaven for that." and very handy for her plans. She'd agreed to find four lovers so that she could finally be with Thomas, but she wouldn't interfere with anyone's marriage.

"What a waste of a man he is," Mrs. Carter said. "So attractive and well-bred. His family's quite wealthy, too."

"Maybe that explains his success with women."

Mrs. Carter waved her hand in a dismissive gesture. "No woman will ever benefit from the connection if he won't marry her."

True, but she could enjoy his good looks, as Carole did when he slanted a glance in her direction. His dark eyes held a lazy, insolent glint as he studied her. The exchange took only a second or two, but it gave the impression that he'd assessed her from her hairline to her shoes and found her promising. Then, he immediately returned his attention to the woman with him as if he hadn't noticed Carole at all. An utter scoundrel. Exactly who she was looking for.

For the love of heaven, who would have thought she'd be doing this at age forty? At least, he appeared near her age. Otherwise, the whole idea would be completely ridiculous.

"Oh, my dear, you can't be fooled by his charm," Mrs. Carter said.

"He's nice to look at, nothing more."

"You're best to keep it that way. He's broken hearts all over England."

"My heart?" Carole laughed. "Only one man has ever had my heart."

That was a lie. She had loved Oscar, and now, she'd fallen for Thomas. but Mrs. Carter didn't need to know her business in that regard.

"Don't look, but they're leaving," Mrs. Carter whispered. "They'll have to pass this way."

Carole stared into her teacup and couldn't help but grin. How childish to pretend not to notice someone, and yet, this whole thing was a game. Footsteps approached, but she kept her gaze down. As the couple went by their table, long, masculine fingers grazed the edge—just enough to make sure she was aware of him. When she finally glanced up, he'd opened the door of the shop and escorted his partner outside.

"Did you see that?" Mrs. Carter bristled with anger. "He might as well have touched one of us. The man's a disgrace."

Carole did her best not to giggle. "Well, he's gone now, so we don't have to worry."

"He can stay away, as far as I'm concerned."

Wrong. He could try, but Carole would find him somehow.

*

Somehow, Mr. Carter worked a miracle and got her a complete box at Covent Garden for five nights in a row. Thank heaven, she actually enjoyed opera. Even more miraculous, perhaps, the dressmaker had finished several gowns, so she'd have a new one for each performance. She had to fight the temptation to tug at the bodice, though, as the necklines plunged low enough that she'd never dare to wear it in New York. She wasn't in Manhattan, though. She wasn't even Mrs. Oscar Rutherford, but Mrs. Carole Rose, scandalous American widow. She could manage American widow honestly enough. She'd have to work at the scandalous apart to win Mr. Harthorn's attention.

Still, a strange woman dressed provocatively and sitting all alone in her own box would have to arouse curiosity. Who knew how many nights she'd have to sit here before the word got back to the object of her hunt?

Already, several pairs of opera glasses had been trained on her, and heads had bent toward other heads to pass a private remark. She'd simply smiled, lifted her chin, and pointedly looked toward the stage.

Shortly after the beginning of the second act, she had her first visitor—a woman, long-limbed, very elegant and most likely in her fifties. She forged her way right in and took the chair next to Carole's.

She smoothed an errant curl with a bit of gray in it back from her temple. "Well, young lady, you've caused quite a stir. No doubt that was your intent."

"I don't believe we've met."

"Ah, American," the woman said. "No wonder no one recognized you."

"Mrs. Carole Rose from New York."

Instead of doing the obviously courteous thing—returning the introduction—her visitor pretended to look around. "Mr. Rose doesn't seem to be in attendance."

"He died several months ago."

"My condolences. My mouth gets away from me sometimes. I'm Bertina Hammond, Lady Blakely, but my friends call me Bert."

"I'm glad to make your acquaintance, Lady Blakely."

"Well done, Mrs. Rose." The lady's smile broadened.

"Because I addressed you formally?"

"Because you didn't assume I'm your friend."

The music swelled as the tenor finished his aria. Applause rolled through the theater, as people jumped to their feet. Maybe some of them had listened to the singing. Carole also rose, as did her visitor. They clapped politely for a while and then sat back down.

"So, have you satisfied your curiosity, Lady Blakely?" Carole asked.

"Not entirely."

"I'm not very interesting."

The lady laughed. You couldn't call it actual mirth, but it had a musical quality to it. "A woman alone in one of the best boxes? You had to know you'd attract attention."

"I hadn't counted on you to visit."

"I daresay not, but ah, yes…here he is."

Lady Blakely turned toward the back of the box, and Carole followed her gaze. Mr. Harthorn entered, went straight to her visitor, and placed a light kiss on her cheek.

"Hello, Bert," he said.

"Hello, darling," Lady Blakely answered. "I might have known you'd show up."

"I can never stay away from you for long," he answered.

"Liar." Lady Blakely patted his cheek and rose. "Behave yourself with Mrs. Rose here. She's American and doesn't understand our ways."

"No one understands your ways, Bert," the man said.

"You're such a bastard." The lady rested her hand on Carole's shoulder. "Watch out for this one."

"Thank you for stopping by," Carole said.

Lady Blakely left the box with an angry rustle of silk.

Mr. Harthorn sat in the now vacant chair next to Carole. "You mustn't pay any attention to Bert. Her claws are sharp but don't go very deep."

"Do all people in England wander in without an introduction?" Carole asked.

"We've met."

She studied him. His brown eyes sparkled with mischief, and his sable hair curled around his collar in a style too long for proper fashion. With his long legs and broad shoulders, he cut quite a figure. He was an indecently attractive man and obviously knew it.

"This afternoon, although we weren't introduced," he said. "I'm Roger Harthorn, as I'm sure your companion told you. She was quite scandalized."

"You know Mrs. Carter?"

"I've observed her type often enough." He gave her an insolent smile that dazzled, even in the near-darkness of the theater. "The posture gives them away as well as they way they pretend not to be staring. Dudgeon of the highest order."

She couldn't help but smile, too. He'd described the solicitor's wife to a T.

"Do you enjoy the opera, Mr. Harthorn?" she asked.

"I tolerate it well enough," he answered. "You?"

"I like it very much."

56

"Don't tell me I've finally met someone who comes here for the music," he said.

"I'll admit that wasn't my only reason." Her cheeks grew warm. They'd be quite pink now, but with any luck, he wouldn't notice in the dim light. She'd never learned how to flirt, and at her age, she'd probably never catch up.

"You hoped to be seen, or you wouldn't have taken a whole box for yourself," Harthorn said. "I hope the person's worth all the trouble and expense."

"I'm sure he is."

"A man. Of course. Give me his name, and I'll arrange an introduction."

Damn. What did she say to that? She didn't have a name and didn't want to meet anyone else, anyway. but she'd never find the nerve to tell Harthorn she'd come looking for him.

"A secret, eh? Don't worry. I'm sure he's seen you." Harthorn rested his arm on the back of her chair and leaned close enough to put his lips near her ear. "He noticed you this afternoon well enough."

Ah, yes. The brush of his fingers on her table as he'd gone by. "I don't see how you could know that."

"Mrs. Rose, let's not toy with each other." His voice came low and sweet, his breath tickling her ear. "We forged a connection this afternoon."

"You're exaggerating a bit, aren't you?"

"Not at all. I haven't reacted this powerfully to a woman since I was a lad." He took her hand and set it in his lap, pressing her palm against the front of his pants.

Oh, dear Lord. She tried to pull her fingers away, but he held them there. "I got this way from simply watching you sip tea."

Her heart hammered, and she had to remind herself to breathe. After all these months, she had her hand on a man's member. Through his pants, yes, but the outline was unmistakable—long and thick and so very hard. Exactly what she craved. Deep inside, her own sex got the connection he'd spoken of. Despite the impossible situation, her pussy felt empty, begging for what it hadn't had for so long.

No—had never had. Oscar was never like this.

"So, will you slap my face now?" Harthorn asked.

She swallowed around the lump in her throat. "No."

"By God, you're direct. An Englishwoman would have dodged and dallied."

"I'm too old to dally," she said.

"And thank the Almighty for that." He bent toward her again, this time placing a soft kiss on the naked skin of her shoulder. "May I know your first name?"

"It's Carole."

"Carole," he repeated, before gently nibbling his way toward her neck. Her breathing grew labored as he left pinpricks of fire everywhere he touched her.

"You're trembling," he whispered against her throat.

"You'd better stop. Someone might see."

He straightened and turned her head toward his. "You're an innocent."

"I was married for ten years."

"But you're still innocent, aren't you?"

"I knew my husband on our wedding night." She tried again to free her hand from where it rested against his crotch. He still didn't release it.

"But you were a virgin then," he said.

"That's the way it's usually done."

"How sweet." That delicious smile curled his mouth. "And you haven't had a man since he died."

Since some months before, but she couldn't betray her husband by confessing it. Instead, she bit her lip and did her best to calm her trembling.

"That only makes me hotter, Carole. My cock's throbbing now," he said.

"Shall I stroke it?" Good Lord in heaven, where had that come from? "Through the fabric, I mean."

A light of pure mischief entered his eyes. "You'd like to do that?"

"I find it fascinating." She squeezed him, pressing the head with the tips of her fingers. "Could I make you spend that way?"

He sucked in a breath. "I daresay you could."

"Would anyone notice, do you think?"

"They can't see into my lap."

"Will they see this?" She reached lower, between his legs where his sac would be and stroked it softly. That took the mischief from his eyes, but his lips still stayed in that lazy smile. He turned back toward the stage, pretending to follow the opera, but they both knew none of the music penetrated his brain.

What fun. She'd never, in her life, expected to do anything like this, but Thomas had opened her mind to all kinds of delicious possibilities. Thomas. Darling Thomas. Why had she never asked him if he liked opera? She'd have to do that in her next letter. Then, she'd have to ask if he'd like to sit in a public place with her hand on his cock. For now, she'd pretend he was here with her now as she used gentle pressure against the length of his shaft. Up, down, and up again to linger at the tip.

"You do that very well," Harthorn said. "I wouldn't think you inexperienced."

"I'm glad to hear it."

He let out a soft moan. "This won't take long at all."

"You mustn't give anything away with your expression," she said. "Your friend, Bert, may be watching us."

"She won't tell. She likes her husband's money too much."

"And you know secrets he wouldn't want to hear," she said.

"I say…" His eyes drifted halfway shut. "Could we discuss it later?"

"Of course." She moved her fingers faster, gripping him as tightly as she could manage through the wool of his pants. He sat rigidly, and his eyes went out of focus with pleasure.

"Talk to me," he whispered. "Something filthy."

"Would you like to fuck me, Roger?" There. She'd said it. The worst word she knew.

"God, yes."

"I'd like that, too. My cunny's getting damp for you." That was no lie. Who would have thought that she, a virtuous widow with hardly a dirty thought until a few months ago, would find herself with a perfect stranger like this? Sitting in public, stimulating his sex and telling him she wanted him. "But you won't have me, will you? No, you're going to spend in your pants like a schoolboy."

"Oh…ah…don't stop."

"No one can know what I'm doing to you, or I will stop," she said. "Promise me you won't make a noise when you come."

He gritted his jaw. "Bloody hell."

"Do it, or I'll leave you hanging." She paused in her work on his tool. She wouldn't leave him this way. If nothing else, she wanted to see what he'd do when the climax hit him.

"I promise," he said in a strangled whisper. "Have mercy. Finish me."

She squeezed the tip of him and then stroked his length—hard and fast, all the way to the base. He closed his eyes and clenched his jaw as his body stiffened. His hips jerked as he climaxed, but he made no sound above a soft grunt. Such a sight he made—the male animal consumed by lust. She'd never watched a man face at the ultimate moment before. She'd see Thomas in this state eventually, and he'd witness her ecstasy, too. Right now, Roger Harthorn slumped against his chair, breathing heavily. She finally reclaimed her hand setting it in her own lap.

"That was extraordinary," he said softly.

"I'm glad you liked it."

"Like? My dear Carole. The word is inadequate."

Pride glowed inside her. The idea of taking other lovers had seemed silly and even morally bankrupt when she only wanted one man—Thomas. but she could learn so much before she joined him. How much better to go to him fully prepared to fulfill his wildest fantasies than to have to grope blindly for just the right caresses to make him wild with wanting her.

Yes, Thomas had had it right. She'd experiment with other men and give the benefit of her lessons to her ultimate lover.

"You're grown pensive," Roger said. "That didn't repulse you, did it?"

"Not at all."

"You seemed willing. Even eager." His face showed uncertainty, even worry. For heaven's sake, the scandalous fellow who'd bedded any woman he wanted, actually cared about her opinion of him.

"It was a revelation," she said. "I've never done anything like that before."

"Nor have I. I usually entertain the lady." The wicked heat returned to his eyes. "Would you like me to do the same for you?"

She nearly gasped with surprise. "Your hand under my skirts at the opera?"

"Not right now. It'll be intermission soon."

"You'll have to rejoin your friends," she said.

"Eyebrows will rise if I don't."

"Eyebrows have probably already risen."

"No doubt about that." He chuckled. "Still, I want enough time to do the job properly."

"What do you suggest?"

"Will you be here tomorrow night?"

She smiled and nodded.

"I'll see you then." He leaned toward her again. "In the meantime, don't touch your pearl. I want it hungry for my touch."

"I'll wait."

"Good." He rose. "Until tomorrow."

As he left, the last strains of the second act finale crashed through the theatre. She hadn't listened to a thing from the moment Harthorn had placed his lips against her ear. The house lights came on, and people headed toward the lobby or other boxes for a visit. Carole sat where she was, her hands clenched together in her lap.

Tomorrow.

*

Carole awoke with a start, her sex convulsing in orgasm. She clutched her pillow and let it finish until it tapered off and left her floating halfway between her dream and reality. She'd been lying in a field nude when something hard had thrust into her. Then, it had been a faceless man, holding her hips as he slid a mammoth cock in and out of her pussy. She'd climaxed instantly, waking herself up to tangled sheets in a strange bed. Her hotel room in London.

She sat up and rubbed her face. She'd promised Roger Harthorn that she wouldn't touch herself, and she hadn't. Her lust had made her spend, anyway. But the orgasm hadn't satisfied the fire inside her. It had only banked the embers, leaving the smoldering and ready to leap into flame again. How would she get through this night and the whole, long day until they'd meet again?

She searched the bedside table until she'd found a match and a candle. Once lit, the taper gave off enough light for her to make her way to the table that held the hotel stationery. Once she had that and a pen and ink, she began a letter. To Thomas. Who else?

"My dearest,

"I had a dream just now of a man fucking me with his huge member. We were out of doors, of all things, lying under nothing but the sun. I couldn't see his face, but I know he was you. When we do finally meet, let's do that. We'll make love with breezes caressing our skin. We'll both strip to our skin. I'll wrap my legs around your hips, and you'll take possession of my eager sex."

Damn, this wasn't helping. It only intensified the ache between her legs.

"I've met the first man to fill your requirement that I take four lovers. He's a rake and a cad. Devilishly sexy, but not someone to whom I'd ever trust my heart. He'll have my body, but not my love. That belongs to you."

How odd to be writing to one man about another. But then, everything about this trip lay outside normal experience. Her whole life had become one voluptuous experience after another, and who knew what lay ahead?

"We sat at Covent Garden, this man and I. He took my hand and put it on his member. He claimed I'd made it hard simply by sitting next to him. Can you imagine that?"

She still had to smile inwardly at the knowledge that she could wield such control over a man's body—especially such an experienced one. Harthorn could probably have any woman in London he wanted, and he'd wanted her.

"He came in his pants, simply because I stroked him through the cloth. He called the feeling 'extraordinary.' I can't wait to use what I've learned on your beloved cock. I hope you'll find me extraordinary, too."

She should tell Thomas everything. Confess her plans for her next meeting with Harthorn. But then, maybe it wouldn't merit a full report. She could always write again once she had more to say.

"Thank you for sending me on this adventure, Thomas, even if it delays our eventual happiness together. When we finally come together, I'll be able to pleasure you so well, you'll never want another woman.

"Until then, hold me in your dreams. All my love, Carole."

She folded the letter, put it into the envelope, and sealed it tightly. Tomorrow, she'd deliver it to Mr. Carter and then wait for the sun to go down.

*

Harthorn had arrived in her box during the second act that first night. New evening, new opera, but by the beginning of the third act, he hadn't made his appearance. Carole sat, her back so stiff it didn't touch the back of her chair. Perhaps, he wouldn't come at all. Perhaps, he'd planned the whole thing as a joke at her expense. Perhaps, he and his friend, Bert, were laughing at her right now. If he didn't keep their appointment, she'd sit through the entire performance with her head held high and never come back again. There were plenty of other men in London.

Then, suddenly, he was there. Behind her at the entrance to the box. She felt him as much as heard his soft tread as he approached her.

He walked up to her and rested a hand on her shoulder. "Sorry to be so late."

"No matter. I'm enjoying the music."

His fingers tightened on her skin. "You didn't care if I honored our agreement?"

"I didn't mean that," she said. "That is, I did, but..."

He picked up the empty chair next to hers and put it down closer to her. When he sat, their thighs met.

"You're confused," he said.

"And a little frightened." Damn, she shouldn't have admitted that.

"Of me?"

She looked at his face, finally, and saw clear amusement there. Not in an unkind way. More like a shared joke, just between the two of them.

"You're a notorious scoundrel, Mr. Harthorn," she said. "I don't know what to expect."

"You'll enjoy it. I promise."

She nodded and turned back to the performance.

Her skirts moved—no more than a soft rustle and a tug. His fingers crazed the naked skin above her garter. She stiffened and jumped.

"Do try to relax," he whispered. "You're as tight as a coiled spring."

She took a deep breath and then another as his hand moved upward to the inside of her knee.

Her sex hadn't given her any peace since her dream. The dull ache returned. The craving to be filled. She'd have to surrender part of herself to this man to have what she wanted. She'd have to allow him to touch her in the most intimate places. She'd lose control when she climaxed, revealing herself at her most vulnerable moment. It was madness. She'd only just met him. She had to end this, get away now before things went any farther.

And yet, she needed his touch so desperately. She'd been so long without. If she left now, she'd have to find some other man to give her some relief. Her own hand didn't satisfy, and it wouldn't get her any closer to Thomas.

"Better?" he whispered.

"Yes."

"I'll continue."

She took a shuddering breath. "Please."

"You're skin's so soft. And hot." His hand inched higher, closer to her pussy, and stopped. "You're not wearing drawers."

"It seemed for the best."

He groaned softly. "Good Lord, if I'd known, I would have gotten here sooner, no matter if I'd had to leave the others rudely."

The others. Who might that be? She wouldn't ask, not now nor later.

"You're here now," she said.

"I wish I could dive under your petticoats," he said. "I'd spread your legs and devour your pussy."

Such an image. She'd read about that in The Pearl, but still couldn't imagine a man's mouth there. At least, not while she was sitting in a nearly public place.

"That wasn't our agreement," she said softly.

"I can make that very good for you."

"Your hand only."

"All right," he said. "For now."

"We'll meet again after this?"

"If you'll allow me. I haven't seen you naked." His hand stroked her inner thigh, making slow passes over the sensitive skin from her knee upward. He hadn't touched her sex yet, but it responded, anyway, feeling heavy and swollen.

"Shall I tell you what I'll do when I finally have you all to myself?" His hand reached the lips of pussy.

She swallowed a groan of need. "Yes, tell me."

"I'll strip every bit of clothing off you, and then, I'll just stare at you for a while."

"I'm forty years old. You might not like what you see."

"That gown hides very little of your breasts, and this…" He stroked her from the entrance to her sex and upward toward her pearl. "Tilt your pelvis forward so I can touch you better."

She did as he said, moving her buttocks near the edge of her chair. He plunged a finger inside her, and her muscles clamped down on him.

"Poor puss," he said. "It's been empty too long."

"Oh, God…"

"My cock aches to fill it. Should we try, I wonder? I could unbutton my pants, and you could sit on me."

"Someone would see that."

He sighed. "You're right. I'll have to do this, instead."

He pulled his finger from inside her and used it to search for her clitoris. When he found it, she jerked, pushing her sex harder against his hand.

"You're wet already, dear Carole," he said. "Can you feel how you coat my fingers?"

"Please more," she gasped.

"In good time. Now, where was I?" He stroked her again. His touch was maddeningly gentle. Enough to drive her wild, but not to bring her to the brink.

"When I can bear no more, I'll rip off my own clothing," he said. "Then, I'll go right to work on your beautiful cunny."

His finger kept moving and moving. It dipped inside her and pushed until more moisture seeped from her and spread over her thighs. The world went hazy around the edges. Somewhere beneath her and at a distance, an orchestra played and people walked up and down across the stage, singing. but none of that mattered as much as the burning between her legs.

"I'll feast on you," he said. "Licking and sucking until you spend against my face."

"I can spend now, if you'd only…"

He rubbed her harder, using a circular motion over her pearl. "This way?"

She bit back a cry as liquid pleasure pooled inside her, seeking release.

"I'd rather prolong the fun," he said. "You tormented me last night."

Her vision swam, and blood rushed in her ears. The power of speech fled, taking with it rational thought. She had no choice now but to submit to anything he did to her and trust that when the climax finally came, he'd make it good.

"That's my girl." He stroked her steadily now, feather light, along her lips and lingering at the nubbin. "Once I'm through eating you, I'll thrust my cock inside you and fuck you until you beg for mercy."

She might have laughed at that if she'd been able. She'd beg for mercy now if she could make her voice work. He'd pushed her so close, so close, and yet, he still held her back.

"I'll fuck you until I think I'm going to explode," he said. "Then, when I'm right at the edge, I'll pull out and turn you over so that I can enter you from behind."

Damn. Maybe she should have agreed to straddle him and let him thrust into her, after all. She'd certainly spend on the spot. The box must have a secluded corner where no one else could see them. Why hadn't she thought of that? Too late now, but she would have him inside her. He'd promised.

"I'll keep right on plowing you, until you come all around me." His fingers never strayed from her clitoris now, and he would finish her soon. Every nerve felt stretched to the limit and would snap at any moment.

"You're ready now, aren't you?" he said.

She could only whimper in response.

"The tenor and soprano have nearly finished their duet," he said. "Wait until the very last note before you come."

Please, let them finish. Please, please, please.

The singing continued, damn it all. Long passages of the two voices soaring together, while Harthorn tortured her with touches just this side of firm enough to satisfy her. She couldn't hold on for another second, but he wouldn't push her past the brink, damn him.

The music reached a crescendo, and two voices floated above it. Higher and higher. The sounds hung in the air like a living being as her sex clenched tight.

"Now," he whispered, as his finger played over her. Hard. Fast. Insistent.

She came with an impossible force. Wave after wave crashing through her. The music ended, and loud applause deafened her as the spasms kept rocking her. His fingers never stopped until she'd finished and collapsed against the back of her chair.

Finally, he removed his hand and straightened her skirts. "By God, you'll drive me mad."

"I think you've already sent me there."

"Do you have any idea of the state of my cock?"

She opened her eyes and smiled. "Shall I minister to it again?"

"Not tonight. A hand's not good enough."

"What will you do?"

"I can't go back to my friends with my fingers smelling like this." He waved them under her nose so that she could smell her own arousal. "and I'll be damned if I'll wash it off."

"Should we try to find a dark corner so that I can sit on you?"

"That's not good enough, either. Come home with me."

"Now?" she asked.

"In ten minutes." He rose. "If I can walk with this iron rod in my pants, I'll go summon my carriage. Meet me in front."

"Won't someone see us leave together?"

"I don't give a damn, do you?"

She ought to. She ought to care that a man she hardly knew would take her home to fuck her. In truth, she'd only care if he didn't. "I'll be out front in ten minutes."

He bent and kissed her. Just a soft brush of lips—their first, after all they'd done to each other.

"Ten minutes," he repeated. And then, he was gone.

CHAPTER FOUR

Harthorn's butler didn't so much as blink when his employer brought a strange woman home. He simply took their things with a slight bow. "I left the lamps on as you instructed, sir."

"Good man. Turn them off except for the ones in my bedroom, and then go to bed," Harthorn said.

The butler disappeared, and her new lover, took her hands in his. "Do you like the house?"

"I haven't seen much," she answered. "It's quite grand from the outside."

"It's been in my family for generations."

She stepped closer to him. "Do they always leave the gas lights on so late?"

"I suspected I'd have a visitor after the opera," he said. "Tonight's special."

She couldn't help but bask in his smile and a little surge of pride. No doubt he told all his paramours they were special, but as she had no plans for an actual relationship with him, a little deception didn't matter. He could forget all about her tomorrow. She only needed him for tonight.

"What's going on beneath that beautiful, blonde hair?" he asked.

"I was only thinking of what you promised to do to me," she lied.

"Ah, yes. Cunnilingus until you climax and then coitus until you beg for mercy."

"I think I like devouring and fucking better."

"Vixen." He laughed. "Will you use that foul language when I'm deep inside you?"

She rose up on tiptoe to bring her mouth to his ear. "Fuck me, and find out."

"I've never had a nicer invitation." He escorted her to the stairs and led her up. They went in silence, hand in hand until he opened a door and pulled her into his bedroom and against his chest.

His mouth came down on hers, not clumsily, but with enough urgency to steal her balance. She had to cling to him as she answered with her own lips. This was no sweet caress from an older man. Her hands met solid muscle everywhere they went—his chest, arms, and broad shoulders. She hadn't even thought about his age, but clearly, tonight she'd have a man in his prime.

He kept on kissing her as if he'd drown if he didn't take more and more. Somehow, he walked her backward until her rear met something solid. A post at the corner of his massive bed. His fingers worked at the fastenings of her dress, and soon, the tips found the furrow of her spine.

He pulled his mouth from hers, and took her face in his hands. His breath came heavy and hot against her cheeks. "I'm burning up."

"I know."

"I thought I'd die during the ride home," he said. "I felt every jostle of the carriage in my cock."

She shifted so that she could put her hand over his crotch. He'd managed a very impressive bulge.

"Don't." He grasped her wrist and pushed it away. "Leave me some control."

"I don't want you controlled. I want you to devour me."

"Then, we'd better get you naked."

He stripped her like a master, turning her to undo her dress and the corset and petticoat beneath and then bringing her back to face him to finish. When he'd removed her chemise, he paused, his gaze fixed on her breasts. She tried to cover them, but he pushed her hands aside.

"You're even more beautiful than I'd imagined," he whispered. He cupped one mound and ran his thumb over the tip. "So soft, and see how the nipple stiffens."

Her knees grew weak, and she tried to crawl back into his arms. He held her where she was. "No shyness, Carole. Let me worship you."

She was no goddess but a forty-year-old woman who'd only had one man in her entire life. Now, a strong, virile man could see her every imperfection. She'd disappoint him. Why had she come here?

When he bent and took her nipple into his mouth, her body gave her the answer. She swayed into him and closed her eyes, pinpricks of light dancing behind the lids. The tugs of his lips connected somehow in her sex as she moistened all over again. This time in preparation to take him inside her.

He straightened and held her against his chest, slipping a hand between her thighs. "Wet again, my sweet Carole?"

"Your doing," she whispered back.

"Hardly. It's no secret I've known a few women." He parted her nether lips, and...oh!...touched her bud again. "None of them responded like you."

"None?"

He smiled down at her. "I don't tell tales."

Good. Then, he wouldn't tell hers. "Understood."

"Lie down," he said. "Let me give your cunny the treatment it deserves."

He led her to the bed, and she climbed on. Still smiling, he sat beside her to remove his shoes and socks. His cravat flew in one direction and his jacket in another. After removing his cuff buttons and the studs from his shirt, he set them on the side table and rose.

When he removed his shirt, she got a view of his chest. Solid and finely muscled, the expanse invited exploration, from the few curling hairs to the flat nipples and the planes of hard flesh below.

"If you keep looking at me like that, I'll strut like a peacock," he said.

"I'd enjoy watching." Indeed, she'd never seen anything like him—so tall and masculine and with his own sort of grace. Even the pictures in her book paled in comparison to the reality.

She held her breath as he unfastened his pants, pushed them over his hips to the floor, and kicked out of them. Now fully naked, he offered his entire body for her inspection. Especially, his cock.

Oh, dear heaven. Suddenly shy, she stared at his face. "It seems you don't believe in underclothes, either."

"I'll admit that the rubbing of my trousers always keeps me a bit excited," he said. "But then, you knew I'm depraved."

"A perfect beast."

"Look at me."

It was a command and perfectly clear in its meaning. She was to study his cock, not shy away from it. She finally did.

You couldn't really call the thing beautiful, but once she'd focused her gaze on it, she couldn't have made herself pull away if she tried. It rose from coarse, dark hairs at the base—thick and proud—along the shaft to the head. A ridge of flesh circled that, and a pucker dimpled the tip. His flesh had already turned dark with arousal and stiff enough to reveal the vein that ran along the underside.

"Well?" he said.

She licked her lip. "It's very large."

He threw his head back and laughed. "By God, you will make me strut."

She reached her arms out to him. "You're magnificent."

He got onto the bed, pulled her into his arms, and kissed the tip of her nose. "And you, my little vixen, make me feel like the greatest lover on Earth."

"Right this moment, I think you are."

"Oh, Carole," he sighed, right before he kissed her.

No embrace she'd ever shared matched this one. Not only did their lips dance together as if they'd rehearsed each step, but his body pressed against hers everywhere. Nothing to separate them, just skin sliding against skin. The friction created enough heat to melt her, and she softened beneath him, savoring every passage of his palms down her sides and over her ribs.

His cock pressed against her belly, and he moved his hips in gentle imitations of what he'd do once he'd embedded himself in her. She flexed upward to create more pressure.

He groaned and placed his face against hers. "Don't do that."

"It doesn't feel good?"

"Too good. I'll spend against your belly.'

"I definitely want you inside me for that," she whispered.

"I promised you something else first." He moved then, sliding lower along her stomach. He'd said he'd devour her pussy. She'd never had a man's mouth there, and with the way she'd soaked herself, he'd find it unpleasant.

"Are you sure?" she said.

"Sure?" He used his mouth to tug at one nipple and the other. "I must taste you."

His face went lower and lower, and he parted her legs with his hands. "Here's your lovely puss. She smells so sweet."

"Roger…"

"Shhh." He licked her—one long swipe along her lips and then a flick at the top, just over her pearl.

Her hips jerked upward, and a cry floated to the ceiling. Her cry.

"You taste like caramel," he said. "Delicious."

He settled his mouth over her and continued in earnest. Pass after pass of the most intense pleasure she'd ever experienced. Wicked, wicked, wicked. And more erotic than she'd ever dreamed possible.

Already, all the sensations from the opera flooded over her. How he'd used that maddening touch to keep her near heaven while the music climaxed all around her.

She reached down, found his head, and tangled her fingers in his hair. Without words, she had no other way to signal her approval and to beg him for more.

"That's my girl." He slid his arms under her legs and around her hips to pull her hard against his face. Now, sucked on her lips and then sent his tongue flicking directly against her pearl. The storm built, the clouds of arousal gathering in her belly, each electrically charged. Soon, they'd merge, releasing all that power and taking her with them to oblivion. and he kept right on, knowing what he was doing to her. She'd have to find some way to thank him, but for now, she could only live within her own body and its pleasures and demands.

When he took her nub fully into his mouth and sucked, she flew out of control. She managed one last plea. "Don't stop."

He applied more pressure, and she shattered. The climax rushed through her with such intensity, it tore a sob from her chest. As the walls of her pussy contracted, he finished her. For long heartbeats, it gripped her. When she finally rested back, he lapped at her gently and then rose above her again.

"Carole," he whispered.

She groped to touch him—anywhere—met what felt like his shoulder and stroked the skin. "Yes. Anything."

"I need to feel your pussy around me."

"Yes," she murmured. She slipped her hand between them, and he moved just enough to let her find his shaft. Now tilting her hips upward, she brought him to the entrance to her sex. In one fluid motion, he entered her all the way to the base of his cock.

"You're still fluttering," he said. "Can you feel it?"

Sure enough, little aftershocks continued, only this time, her sex had something to cling to. What an amazing feeling to be filled after all the months of emptiness. and he filled her so completely, even stretching him.

"You're so tight." He pulled back and surged forward. "I'm afraid I won't last long."

"Fuck me," she said.

"Oh, God." He set a rhythm for them—a retreat and return, seeming to go deeper into her with each penetration. The fire inside her hadn't had time to extinguish, and now, it flamed again. She wrapped her legs around him so that she could rise up to meet him on each thrust. Soon, they were straining against with each movement, grasping at each other. Anything for more contact.

Her hands went underneath his arms and up so that she could dig her fingers into his shoulders. He trembled with the effort to keep his weight off her, and his labored breath warmed her neck. She let her hands roam over his back, savoring the tension in every muscle. Lower, she discovered the contraction and release of the muscles that let him pound into her.

At some point, the easy slide of his cock into her pussy had grown into more frantic coupling, as both of them climbed higher toward the pinnacle. She shouldn't be enjoying this—shouldn't even be doing it. They didn't love each other. Might never even see each other again. She'd promised her love to another man, so this one shouldn't be able to command her body so completely. but he did, and soon she'd reach orgasm with a solid shaft of his flesh inside her.

"Oh, damn." He stopped moving and shook his head violently. "I almost lost control. I almost came."

"You can come now. I won't be far behind."

"No." He took a few ragged breaths. "As we discussed. Only your knees."

When he pulled out of her, she rolled onto her stomach. Before she'd had a chance to rise, he grabbed her hips and guided them upward. Immediately, he shoved his member back into her and moved again. So violently, she had to reach for the headboard to steady herself.

"Even better," he gritted. "Now, sweet Carole, come with me."

"I will."

"God, I want to feel it." The thrust wildly, shaking the bed with the force of his movements. She'd never felt such abandon, either in a lover of in herself. The fury built inside her. In a moment, it would catch her up in the inevitable.

"That's it," he said. "Spend for me."

Yes. Yes, yes, yes. The words came out in some foreign language. Guttural cries and sobs.

He continued the savage plundering of her pussy. She braced herself as best she could, holding her body so she wouldn't miss a stroke. Then suddenly, her body took over again, and she climaxed so hard she couldn't even cry out.

His roar filled the room, as he gripped her hard, pulling her back against him, as he slammed into her. A few more massive thrusts, and his body stiffened behind her. Impossible, but her sex seemed to feel the release of his seed as her spasms pulled at him. He held her there as he shouted once again. Then, the two of them fell into a heap.

He didn't move for the longest time, didn't even lift his weight from her. The mass of him, pushing her into the mattress, felt like a blanket. Comforting. She managed a deep breath and then a moan of pleasure.

"I'm crushing you," he whispered into her ear.

"Stay where you are."

"A gentleman doesn't squash his lover flat."

"But you're no gentleman," she said.

"No, I'm not." He moved his hips. He was growing soft but not so soft that he couldn't remind her of what they'd just shared. Then, he rolled off her and scooped her against him. "but I won't be responsible for suffocating you."

She ran her fingers into the hairs on his chest. "Roger?"

He took a breath and let it out on a sigh. "I'm here."

"Was that good?"

"Good?" He chuckled, the sound echoing inside his chest. "My dear woman, you rattled my teeth."

She grinned so hard her face felt as if it'd split. "I'm glad."

"So good, I'm afraid I'm going to what men do after fabulous sex." He yawned.

"Go to sleep," she said.

"Can't keep my eyes open." He trailed his fingertips over her back. "Stay the night with me?"

"Yes. Oh, yes."

*

When Carole next woke, she found herself in almost total darkness and with a solid, warm body beside her. Naked, as was she. A vague memory entered her sleep-clouded brain. Roger coaxing her to get under the covers and wrapping himself around her. He must have already turned off the gas lights. Now, he lay with his back toward her, his buttocks jutting against her hip,

She rolled onto her side to get a better look at him in the dim light that penetrated from the street lamps outside. His shoulder loomed in front of her, so she ran her palm over it. He was solid, yes, but soft, too. Smooth and warm to the touch. A body so foreign to any she'd encountered before. and so luxurious.

She pulled her hand back under the covers and traced the furrow at the center of his back. More muscle, topped by velvet skin.

He shifted and made a noise—halfway between a grunt and a word. She ought to stop, let the man sleep, but she needed to learn more about men's bodies before she finally coupled with Thomas's. Thomas would feel like this—sleek and powerful. Thomas's body would warm her and shelter her. She couldn't know that, as her mind constantly reminded her, but she'd listen to her heart where Thomas was concerned.

She let her fingers travel lower, savoring the curve of his hip and then settling on his buttock. The roundest part of him, firm and tight. These muscles had made those amazing thrusting motions as he'd filled her. She cupped him and squeezed gently.

With no warning, he made a soft growl and rolled over onto her. She did the only natural thing—open her legs to give him a place between them. He made the only natural response—finding the entrance to her pussy and driving his rigid cock into it in one glide.

She gasped in surprise and pleasure and wrapped her legs around him so that she could rock with him. Such an unexpected treat—to come together so easily.

She studied his face. With his eyes still closed, he seemed still wrapped in sleep. He'd brought her to full alertness, though. Excitement built to arousal as his chest pressed against her breasts and each forward passage of his cock made her pearl more and more sensitive.

"Oh, Bert," he crooned in her ear. "Bert, I love you."

"Roger."

"Leave Blakely and come away with me. We can have this every night." He moved harder and faster.

"Roger," she said more loudly.

He opened his eyes. They took a moment to focus, and he stopped moving. "Carole. Oh, Carole, I'm so sorry."

"Don't worry." She stroked his face. "It's all right."

"It's not all right. It's unforgivable."

"Shhh." She kissed him briefly. "Close your eyes and pretend I'm Bert."

His brows knit. "Really?"

"Really. Only, please finish what you've started."

"Thank you," he said. "You're a saint."

She had to laugh at that. "Hardly, considering where your member is right now."

He pulled back and thrust into her. "Ah, yes."

She groaned with enjoyment and closed her own eyes. He could have his fantasy, and she'd have hers. Thomas. He'd be her age, or a bit younger, like Roger. He'd be healthy and strong, and his cock would always be hard for her. He'd stroke her inner muscles, just like

Roger did. He'd cover her face with kisses and whisper her name. He'd hold off his own release until she'd climaxed.

Yes, Thomas. He was inside her now, demonstrating his love in the most basic way. She'd open herself to him completely, allowing him inside her body and her heart. He'd make her whole.

The man in her arms moved faster, grunting with the effort and his rising excitement. With each thrust, her bud took a jolt. Soon, it reached the point where any pressure could set it off. She held onto his shoulders and tipped her pelvis for the best contact. and oh heaven, she'd come soon.

"Now," he gasped. "Love, please now."

She gripped his cock with her inner muscles, creating maximum friction. Damn, it felt good. Responding came so easily now. Although they'd just met, their bodies knew each other. The speed of his thrusts reached into her pussy to ready it for the inevitable explosion. His groans in her ear, raced along her nerves the length of her body to the very seat of her desire. They started the climb together in a duet as melodic as the one that had driven her orgasm earlier. She arched her back as the climax hit, gasped as it took full possession, and cried out while she convulsed around him. He joined her, releasing his heat into her with a cry that matched her own. When they finished, he rested his body on hers.

"Thank you," he whispered.

"You're very welcome."

*

"My dearest Thomas,

"I've done as you instructed. I've taken a lover. Now that I know the reality of engaging in the sexual act for no more than the pleasure it can give, I can hardly remember what my wifely duties felt like. Before your letters and our delicious correspondence, I had no idea what true carnality felt like. The books you had me buy only produced a pale shadow of the lust I finally experienced. What utter luxury to act on one's wildest impulses with no thought of anything but the final outcome—climax after climax, his providing almost as much joy as my own.

"I tell you more about my adventurous Englishman. His initials are R.H., and he showed me delights I never dreamed of. Before I describe them, my darling, let me assure you that I plan to repeat them all with you and that they'll be all the sweeter because of the love we share—a love founded on trust and the sure knowledge that we were born to be together despite our separation by distance and time.

"First of all, my Englishman taught me the wickedness of indulgence in a nearly public place. I told you about how I fondled him in my box at Covent Garden. The second night, he brought me to orgasm with the world's most beautiful music to cover the cries my release. I attempted to maintain the outward appearance of calm, but as I neared the ultimate and control slipped from my grasp, my face must have contorted with the sort of mask only created by sexual release. Anyone looking on would only have to follow the motions of his arm to realize what mischief his hand was about. Daring, you may say, even foolhardy, but it inflamed us so we had no choice but to seek greater privacy for even more intimate play.

"My darling, until that night with R. H., I had never copulated with my lover entering me from behind. He had me rise on my knees on his bed so he could position himself between my legs and drive himself into my depths from there. Not only did this new position inspire me to new levels of hunger, but he was able to give me yet another shattering climax. How I long to repeat this performance with you.

"The other pleasure he taught me veered so far from what I once considered decent I blush to write it down, even to someone as dear to me as you. To get through the next confession, I'll force myself to write it as simply as I can. He kissed my pussy. No, to be honest, 'kiss' fails to convey the reality of what he did. He used the word 'devour,' and that's surely what he did. His used his lips and tongue to stimulate my nether lips and clitoris until I thought I'd die from arousal too intense to bear. In truth, I did die a bit when he finally finished me and could do nothing for several minutes until my senses returned. He seemed to take great pleasure from the act and pride that he'd satisfied me so well. I hope you'll do the same when we finally meet.

"Now, it occurs to me as I prepare to move on—and I will, my darling Thomas so I may take another lover and bring myself closer to our eventual meeting—that my next task will be to gain more knowledge about the male member. I saw R.H.'s and felt it deep inside me. But I need to learn about its response, how best to stimulate it, and how to give my lover the utmost pleasure possible. It occurs to me that I may best accomplish that last by use of my own lips and tongue on my partner's sex. I intend to experiment with my next paramour's cock, all the while paying close attention to his reactions, with my ultimate goal of learning how best to love yours.

"I'm off to France in a day or two. I leave my Englishman behind. He turned out to be a decent sort, and I hope to do him a favor before I leave London.

"I'll see you as soon as I possibly can. All my love,
"Carole"

*

Carole could have turned down the invitation, but the opportunity to have tea at an honest-to-goodness English lord's townhouse was far too tempting. She might or might not meet Lord Blakely, but no doubt Lady Blakely intended a full scrutiny of the woman Roger Harthorn had visited in the box at Covent Garden.

She'd dressed demurely in a dress that spoke quietly of expense and fashion. Another last minute creation by the insanely expensive dressmaker. The woman earned every cent. The butler didn't give any indication of approval or disapproval but inspected her invitation—in the lady's own hand no doubt—and led her to a pair of double doors. When he pulled them open, she found Lady Blakely sitting near a small table that held a silver tea service. There wasn't another soul in the room. The doors closed quietly behind her.

Lady Blakely didn't rise, but indicated a settee near her. "How good of you to come."

"Am I the only guest?"

"I thought it would be nice to get acquainted." Lady Blakely pointed to the settee again.

Carole sat. If getting acquainted meant prying into her relationship with Roger Harthorn, Lady Blakely had told the truth. No matter. Carole had something to tell her on the subject. It would shock her, and that would be payment enough.

Lady Blakely poured them both tea and then sat back to sip hers. "So, are you settling in?"

She had no intention to settle in in London, but she'd save that for later. "Very well, thank you."

"Don Giovanni was lovely the other night, wouldn't you say?"

A signal that the lady had been in attendance that second night…the one when Roger had slipped his hand under her skirt and the two of them had left together. Perhaps, Bert had been one of the friends to whom he'd failed to return.

"I enjoyed the opera very much." The woman didn't have to know why.

"I hope Mr. Harthorn has acted as an expert guide for you," Lady Blakely said. "He knows the city intimately."

"We've only seen each other a few times." That was true enough.

A slight lift to the lady's elegant brow showed surprise. Most likely not to the mention of a few times, as she would have seen them at the opera twice. Maybe, she was only surprised that Carole would admit it so easily.

"Really," she said. "He's usually much more attentive than that."

Carole took a sip of her tea and then smiled over the rim. "This isn't really about his acting as tour guide, is it?"

That earned her a haughty lift to Lady Blakely's chin. "You Americans are so direct."

"I hope I haven't offended."

"I'll be direct, too, Mrs. Rose. Roger's a charming boy."

"He's a man, I believe."

Lady Blakely waved that away with a brush of her fingers. "He's a charmer. When you have his full attention, you'd think you were the most fascinating woman in the world."

The lady spoke from personal experience, no doubt. Carole took more of her tea and didn't answer.

"He's made dozens of women deliriously happy in the time I've known him," Lady Blakely continued.

"He's a rake."

"After a bit, he finds someone even more fascinating and moves on," the lady said.

"That's what rakes do, isn't it?" Carole answered.

"I see I'll have to be even more direct." Lady Blakely settled her cup in its saucer with a soft click. "He doesn't love you."

"Of course, he doesn't. I don't love him, either."

Lady Blakely stared at her as if she'd never considered the possibility that any woman wouldn't love Roger Harthorn. Yet another indication that the lady's feelings for him ran deep, despite her cool exterior. As Carole watched, the woman became less and less cool, clearly struggling for her next words.

Carole ought to excuse herself and leave, and yet, it didn't sit right to know that the two of them cared so much about each other but couldn't be together.

"Lady Blakely," she said. "I don't know quite how to put this, so I'll say it straight out."

Lady Blakely's fingers trembled just enough to make her cup uncertain in its saucer.

"Mr. Harthorn…Roger," she continued. "He called out your name while we were making love."

The china rattled violently until Lady Blakely set it on the table next to her with a clatter. The lady herself turned ashen.

"He obviously loves you," Carole continued. "and I suspect you feel the same toward him."

"I don't know what to say." Lady Blakely pulled a handkerchief from her sleeve and twisted it between her fingers.

"I know it's none of my business, but he seems like a good man. Can't you find a way to make him happy?"

The lady pressed the handkerchief to her nose. "He's so much younger than I am."

"I faced that in my own marriage from the other side," Caroline said. "I won't deny it's an issue. but you're healthy, and you're very beautiful."

"Mrs. Rose, you quite confound me."

"I'll admit I confound myself." She reached into her reticule and produced the letter she'd written to Roger. She held it out to the other woman. "I wrote this to tell him I'm leaving. I was going to mail it, but maybe you'd like to read it."

Lady Blakely eyed the envelope but didn't take it. "Are you sure?"

"I'd like for you to feel reassured."

"Thank you." The other woman took the letter and held it between her palms. "I'll see he gets it."

"I know I've said too much already, but let me add one thing." Caroline paused to find exactly the right words. "He won't wait forever. Some smart woman will steal him away from you, and you'll always wonder what you missed."

Lady Blakely bit her lower lip, and she straightened in her chair until her spine might creak if she tried to move.

Carole rose. "I'll see myself out. I wish all the best for both of you."

*

As Caroline stood on the dock waiting to board the ship that would take her across the channel, a rose suddenly appeared before, almost brushing her nose. It was attached to a masculine hand. "A rose by any other name would smell as sweet."

The warmth and scent gave away his identity before she took the flower and turned around. Roger Harthorn.

"You're leaving me, Mrs. Rose."

"I see Lady Blakely delivered my note."

"Deuced good of you to set her mind at ease," he said. "Not many other women would."

"I was feeling philosophical and generous."

"I'm sorry we didn't get to know each other better, but before we get maudlin…" He held up a small basket. "Something for you to eat on your journey."

"Prepared with your own hands?"

"I should hope not. I wouldn't want to poison you."

She laughed and took the gift. "How thoughtful. Thank you."

"I didn't know what you like, so I had cook make my favorites."

"I'm sure it'll be delicious."

He put his hands behind his back and stared at the ship for a moment. "I'm not used to women leaving me."

No, he probably wasn't used to that, the devil.

"I don't think I like it," he added.

She had to chuckle at that. "Think of all the women you've left."

"I have been thinking of that." He huffed. "So, where are you headed?"

"Provence, if you can believe it." She had the delightful letter from Thomas with instructions in her pocket. She was to find an amorous Frenchman as her next adventure.

"Wonderful place," Roger said. "You'll love it there."

"I hardly speak a word of French."

"Ah, but you speak the language of love, *mon amour*."

She swatted at his arm. "Now, you're just being silly."

He touched her elbow. "If you return to London, please let me know. I'd like to see you again. I think Bert would, too."

"I'd like to see the two of you together."

He dropped his hand. "That's complicated."

"But not impossible."

He gave her his wicked grin. "I'm a resourceful fellow."

A member of the ship's crew shouted "board," and the passengers started moving forward.

"That's it, then." Roger turned toward her. "Have a safe trip."

"Have a good life." She reached up and kissed his cheek. Then, the rose in one hand and the basket of food in the other, she headed toward the ship and what or whoever lay ahead for her in France.

CHAPTER FIVE

"My darling Carole,

"Oh, what agony your letter caused me. To think of another man's face between your thighs when I so long to be there. Yes, my darling, I'll eat your sweet puss. I'll spend hours worshipping it with my tongue until you've spent and spent and beg me for mercy because you can't take any more. I wish you were here now so that I could dive beneath your skirts, nip through the fabric of your drawers, and make you come so fiercely you soak the cloth with your juices.

"We have to wait, though. I have my reasons, and I'll explain them to you when we meet. You'll understand, I promise.

"In the meantime, I want you to know how much I admire your bravery in completing the tasks I've set out for you. Although I'm filled with jealousy that R.H. has known you in a way that I can only dream of for now, I'm grateful that he turned out to be a man you could only like, not love. How like your generous heart to do something nice for him as you leave. After all, you've already given the greatest gift in the world—your precious body. Actually, not the greatest gift. That would be your heart. I plan to have both.

"On to France to your third lover. Then I only have to wait through your fourth and fifth before you come to me and I can become the sixth and final man to share your bed.

"Your devoted Thomas.

"P.S. I can't even think now about your promise to learn about a man's member in preparation of taking mine into your mouth. It clouds my mind with such lust I'm incapable of rational thought for hours. I only dare to let my imagination go in that direction at bedtime when I have the privacy to take my swollen flesh in my hand and give myself some semblance of relief."

"I say, ma'am, that looks like an interesting letter."

Carole started so violently she nearly knocked the tiny café table over. Crumbling Thomas's letter in her fist, she glanced up at the man who'd spoken. "I beg your pardon."

"I didn't mean to scare you," he said.

The accent registered. "You're American."

"Texan." He gave her an unselfconscious grin. "That's almost the same thing."

She stuffed the letter into her purse and extended her hand. "Mrs. Carole Rose from New York."

"Pete Norfolk." He shook briefly and then released her.

The man was tall and had light brown hair. Pleasant looking in a boyish sort of way. Crinkles around his eyes spoke of maturity, sun, or both. His smooth palm didn't belong to a man who spent a lot of time riding a horse.

"Does Mr. Rose speak French?" Norfolk asked. "Because you clearly need some help."

"Mr. Rose is dead."

"Condolences, ma'am."

"Thank you," she said. "You're right. I don't speak much French at all."

"My friend, Jean-Paul, and I wondered if we could we could translate for you."

Norfolk gestured toward another table where two cups of coffee sat in front of two chairs, one vacant. Another man sat in the second. Of smallish stature and nearly ink black hair, he nevertheless had startling blue eyes. Eyes that he now used to stare at her openly in a way that wasn't exactly decent. Of course, a Frenchman might look at any woman that way for all she knew about the breed.

"I would appreciate it if you'd help me figure the bill," she said. "People here seem nice, but they could take advantage of someone as ignorant as me."

"We'd be happy to, but we'll treat, of course." Norfolk waved his friend over, and the two of them joined her. Jean-Paul had to pull over a chair from a neighboring table. He turned it around, straddled the seat, and rested his arms on the back, leaning toward her.

"Mrs. Rose, this is Jean-Paul Caville," Norfolk said.

"Monsieur." She offered the Frenchman her hand and he clasped it, rubbing his thumb over the back before he lowered his mouth nearly to her skin.

"*Enchante, madame.*" He followed that with some fast French that escaped her.

"He wants to know how long you've been in Provence and how long you plan to stay."

"Tell him a few days and I don't know. My visit is open-ended."

Norfolk translated, and Caville responded with something else she didn't get.

The tops of Norfolk's ears grew red. "Forgive me, ma'am. I don't think I'll translate that."

"What did he say?"

"He complimented you on your beauty but not in a way an American would approve."

"Really?" She studied Caville. His gaze had taken on an appraising gleam. As he watched her watching him, his lips curved into an indecent smile. Teasing the naïve tourist or an attempt at seduction? Who could tell?

She smiled back at him and turned her attention to the American. "How long have you been here, Mr. Norfolk?"

"Close on to a year now. I did the grand tour after college and kind of got stuck here."

"It's a lovely place to get stuck." For Caville's benefit, but not looking at him, she picked up her cup and pressed her lips to the edge, letting them linger there as if in a kiss. Soft laughter came from his direction, but she pretended to ignore it.

"You're a college man, Mr. Norfolk," she said.

"UT Austin."

"My husband graduated from Yale."

"I hear that's a fine school," Norfolk said.

His companion laughed and rattled off some more French.

"I'm not going to tell her that," Norfolk said.

Aha. So, the man did speak English. He could communicate directly with her if he wanted. He was playing some game. He couldn't get the upper hand unless she let him, so she'd continue to ignore him.

"I do appreciate your help, Mr. Norfolk," she said. "You hear such stories about the French, you never know how much of it is true."

Norfolk cast a sidelong glance at his friend and then smiled at her. "What do they say in New York about Frenchmen?"

"That they're consumed with food, wine, and sex to the point that they think of little else."

"The food and wine here are very good," Norfolk said.

"I've enjoyed them so far," she said. "I can't tell if I've had the best France has to offer."

"We could act as your guides," Norfolk said. "Jean-Paul runs his family's winery. He could tell you about that."

"What a shame my French is so bad. I'd love to discuss it with him."

"You know I speak English, madame," the Frenchman said finally.

"I must have misunderstood," she said. "Why would you have said those other things I couldn't understand?"

"Perhaps I was afraid you'd slap my face in public. I'll be happy to translate once the three of us are alone."

"You're rushing things," the Texan said. "Mrs. Rose hasn't agreed to join us."

"*Au contraire*. Mrs. Rose would have dismissed us if she weren't willing," Caville said. "A woman senses when a man wants her. She probably knows you've grown hard in your pants.

"Jean-Paul!" Norfolk said.

"Well, aren't you?"

Norfolk's cheeks flamed with embarrassment. So, he was erect. Fascinating.

She turned toward Caville. "And you, *monsieur*?"

"I'm a Frenchman. As you said, consumed with food, wine, and sex."

Oh, my. What a wonderful surprise. She'd come here to find a lover, but she may have won herself two. Lovers three and four. If she had these two men at once, she'd only need to seek out one other man before she could go to Thomas.

"What do you suppose we should do to ease Mr. Norfolk's condition?" she asked.

The Frenchman's eyebrow went up. "You'd be willing to do that?"

"I'd be willing to do any number of things that might surprise you." What an insane thing to say. She hardly even knew what that meant as a practical matter. The smell of flowers in the air must have intoxicated her. Either that, or the idea that a man could become erect merely by watching her drink coffee had.

"You're adventurous for an American," Jean-Paul said.

"I didn't come to France to hide quietly in my room."

The Texan took her hand. "My dear Mrs. Rose."

"Maybe we should be less formal. Call me Carole."

"Carole," he repeated. He lifted her fingers to his mouth. "You and Jean-Paul and I. I can hardly believe it."

"You'll be our guest at Maison Caville, Carole," Jean-Paul said. "We'll arrive for you at the inn this evening. We'll share the best food and wine Provence can offer."

And the best sex. He didn't have to say it. She'd take two lovers tonight. Two cocks to begin her study of the male member. By the time she could take Thomas's cock into her mouth, she'd know every trick to give him maximum pleasure.

"You should see the look on your face, Carole," Jean-Paul said. "There's nothing more erotic than a woman's excitement."

"Damn, yes," Pete's voice came out husky.

"We'll do our best to earn it," Jean-Paul said.

"I have no doubt," she said. "Until this evening."

*

It was pure idiocy to go off with two men she'd only met that morning. She'd known Roger Harthorn's background before she'd allowed him to touch her and before she'd gone to his home. Now, she'd disappeared into the French countryside without letting anyone know her plans. She didn't know her destination herself.

Yet here she sat in an open carriage, Pete by her side and Jean-Paul on the opposite seat. Someone here had money, quite possibly both of the men, as Pete looked perfectly comfortable in the lavish surroundings. The carriage climbed along the side of a hill marked off by a wall of gray stone with tiny plants growing in the crevices. Beyond that lay vineyards—hundreds or thousands of grape vines following the contours of the land off into the distance. As they went higher, the cultivated land gave way to a glorious disarray of flowers.

"Such beauty," she said. "You own this all, Jean-Paul?"

"In my family for generations. It's been fun to see it all through Pete's eyes, and now, I'll have yours as well."

"We're so glad you've come," Pete said.

She glanced from one man to the other - from the easy smile and soft brown eyes on Pete's face to the Jean-Paul's hooded blue gaze and the dark curl that fell against his forehead. What a contrast they made—each different from her husband and from Roger. She'd learn something from each of them and take her own enjoyment in the process.

"Shall I tell you how we picked you?" Jean-Paul said.

"First, you'd better tell me why you chose anyone at all," she answered.

Jean-Paul leaned back against the seat and glanced at Pete. "You tell her."

"Well, you see…" Pete took her hand and pulled it against his chest while his fingers stroked the inside of her wrist. "Jean-Paul and I have become so close. We've shared everything friends do, but we wanted more."

"A woman?" she said.

"More. A lover," Pete said.

"Have you ever had two men at once?" Jean-Paul asked.

She could think up a clever answer to that, but why play coy? "No."

"Then you've never taken a man's member into your mouth and another man's into your pussy?"

"I think I'm about to," she answered.

"*Bien*. Tell her what I said to you when we first saw her," the Frenchman ordered.

"That he could tell by the way you walked that you liked to…" Pete's voice trailed off.

"He's too shy," Jean-Paul said. "What I told him, in French, was that I could tell from your walk that you like to fuck. Is that true?"

"I'll tell you honestly that I've just learned how," she said.

That clearly surprised Jean-Paul, as he cocked one of his black brows. "But your husband…"

"We had sex. We never fucked."

"*Tres Americaine*." Jean-Paul made a disgusted sound in his throat. "Such a waste of a woman's body."

"I had a lover in London," she said. "He taught me the true meaning of the word."

"An Englishman." Jean-Paul seemed no more impressed with that information.

"He made me come fast and often." She glared at Jean-Paul. "I assume you can do the same."

Pete let out a hoot. "You were sure right about her. I can't wait to get to the villa."

"We'll have a civilized dinner before *foutre*. The anticipation will increase your appetite, *mon ami*."

"I don't see that it needs increasing." Pete said. "I've hardly softened since this morning."

"I have a favor to ask of the two of you," she said.

"Anything," Pete answered. "Just ask."

"I need to learn about men's cocks. How to best stimulate them, how to create intense arousal for my lover," she said. "I'd like for one or both of you to instruct me."

At that, Pete groaned. Jean-Paul leaned forward, placed his hand on her knee, and stared into her eyes. "We'll do that and much more."

*

Jean-Paul's staff remained invisible. When she arrived at her room, her trunk already stood open in a corner, and most of her clothing had been removed. Something unfamiliar lay across the huge bed. A garment of some sort made of scarlet silk. She removed her hat and gloves, set them on the bedside table, and then picked up the brilliant fabric. It might have been a nightgown of some sort, although who would wear such a thing to bed where no one would see it? She held it up to her body. Although it would likely fit her, it wouldn't cover much. And no undergarments lay near it. If she put it on, it would rest directly against her skin.

A pair of matching shoes lay on the floor. Dancing slippers, not meant for bed time. Had Jean-Paul ordered this put here so that she'd wear it to dinner?

She quickly freed herself from the decent clothing that restricted her body. It made a huge and very silly looking pile next to the simplicity of the silk. When she got down to her corset and drawers, she paused. Though the stays would enhance the size of her bust, nothing unnatural belonged beneath that garment. So, she stripped down to her skin—even removing her stockings. Now completely naked, she picked up the gown and walked to the huge mirror in its oval frame near the dressing table.

Stretching, she raised her arms over her head and allowed the silk to slither down her body. The hem stopped just at her toes as if the gown had been made for her. It clung in all her feminine places, too. At her hips, outlining the lyre-shaped curves, and at her bosom. Still a bit shy, she covered her breasts with her hands and squeezed. That made the nipples pucker against the fabric. She giggled and tweaked them with her fingers until they turned into tight points. What would Pete think of that?

Craning her neck, she turned to get a view of her back. The silk clung to her buttocks, too, even showing the crease between them. Oh, dear Lord, she couldn't wear this to dinner with two men she'd only met hours before. What would they think? What would they do?

On the other hand she'd already heard about one man's erection and asked them both to teach her how to fellate them. Timidity certainly didn't fit with that.

Smiling, she went back to the bed and stepped into the slippers. No point delaying. She'd go downstairs dressed in a gown that showed every detail of her body. She'd offer that body to two men she'd met that morning, and they'd surrender their cocks for her education. The mere thought made her breath catch in her chest. Her nipples rubbed against of silk, still stiff. The overall sensation created a show ache of arousal in her pussy. Not a flame yet but ready to blossom inside her.

She left her room and went to the staircase. Running her hand along the banister, she descended the steps of the grand staircase. Both of her hosts stood at the base. In contrast to her dress, they both wore formal attire. In their perfectly tailored suits, all they needed were satin sashes across their chests to look like royalty. Prince Charmings—one small and dark and the other tall and with light brown hair. Heat flared in Pete's eyes as she approached. Jean-Paul's expression remained guarded, but one side of his mouth slid upward in a smile.

When she reached the bottom step, Pete took her hand and guided her to him. "You're a vision. Isn't she, Jean-Paul?"

The other man walked behind her and his palm went from her waist downward over one buttock. She shivered, both in surprise and at the sheer carnality of the caress. No, not a caress but an appraisal and a declaration of possession.

"Do I pass your inspection?" she said. "Perhaps you'd like to look at my teeth."

Instead of answering, he pulled the pins from her hair, letting each one hit the floor with its own tiny clatter. Once the strands fell loose, he gathered them up and draped them over her shoulder. His lips brushed the base of her neck.

Still no word of acceptance or approval. She'd need every shred of dignity she could muster to keep from showing uncertainty, which he'd surely take as a sigh of weakness. What a strange situation to find herself in. One man so clearly eager for her, and the other who refused even to tell her he liked her appearance.

Finally, he went to her side, wrapped her arm around his, and led her into the huge dining room. Lighted candles stood everywhere, and a huge chandelier hung over the table, shedding even more light. They'd see each other clearly over dinner, even though the chair Jean-Paul pulled out for her stood at one end of the long table and he took the seat at the other end. Pete sat halfway between them on her right.

Everything so formal, from the portraits staring down at them from the walls, to the setting of multiple plates and silverware, to the clothing of the men and their distance from her.

She sat, doing her best to appear composed, as if she came down to dinner half-naked every day. She shook out her napkin and laid it across her lap. "Did you find a seamstress to make this gown for me in one day?"

Jean-Paul glanced briefly at Pete and then back at her. "I had it here already. It belonged to my wife."

"Your wife?"

"Don't worry," Jean-Paul said. "She's not here."

"I hope she's not…" She couldn't bring herself to use the word dead. At Jean-Paul's age, his wife must have been a young woman - not the age to die a natural death.

"We don't discuss her," Jean-Paul said.

Pete remained silent through the exchange, twirling his empty wineglass by the stem.

By the looks of things, a good deal remained unspoken in this household. She wouldn't tolerate that if she were to have a true relationship with these two men. For a casual affair, it didn't matter, and she'd let the subject drop.

Jean-Paul rang a small bell near his hand and a servant entered—a balding man in livery, of all things. He set their soup course in front of them, bowing slightly as he set each bowl onto the china, and then left again.

She picked up her first spoon and sampled the soup, a clear broth with deep, rich flavor. "Delicious."

"Try the wine," Jean-Paul said.

She had to select from several glasses. She chose the white wine and lifted it toward both men.

"To new friends." Pete delivered the toast, and they all drank.

"Jean-Paul's fume blanc," Pete said. "One of my favorites."

"I can see why."

Jean-Paul set his spoon in his soup with hardly a sound. "Tell me about your marriage."

So, hers was up for discussion but not his. She had nothing to hide. "He was much older than me. He died after twenty years."

"Did you have sex with him?"

"Of course, I did," she answered.

"That's what I want to know about, not his age."

"Excuse my friend. He can be blunt," Pete said.

"If she didn't want to talk about sex, she wouldn't have come with us," Jean-Paul said. "If she didn't want to have sex, she wouldn't have put on that dress."

"You could be gentler with your questions," Pete said.

"I suspect our Carole has had enough of gentleness," Jean-Paul said. "Am I correct?"

"I hadn't thought of it that way," she said.

"There, you see?" Jean-Paul rang the bell again, and the servant returned to clear the soup and serve the main course. He served her exactly the same way he had before—as if she was properly dressed for a formal dinner and her nipples didn't show through her gown.

When he'd left again, she picked up her knife and fork and cut through the crisp skin of the butterflied game bird on her plate to the tender meat below. The cook had balanced the gamy flavor with garlic and herbs in the brown sauce that accompanied to create a symphony of flavors. The roasted potatoes on the side of the plate provided yet another texture. She'd never eaten anything so delicious in her life, and she forgot her wine until Pete lifted his glass of the red toward her.

She wiped her lips with the linen napkin, sipped from her own glass. Also wonderful. "You've mastered food and wine, Jean-Paul."

He pointedly didn't mention sex but went on eating his own meal for a moment. After a taste of his own wine, he set his glass aside. "Your marriage. Go on."

"There's not much to tell. I don't know why it interests you."

"I want to know exactly how ignorant you are."

"Jean-Paul, please," Pete chided.

"He's right. I am ignorant. I wonder, though, what your servant might hear."

"He intrudes only when I call him," Jean-Paul said. "He doesn't speak English, in any case."

"So, he won't interrupt us, no matter what we do?" she said.

"My staff is well trained," Jean-Paul said. "Continue."

"My husband and I made love on our wedding night."

"You were a virgin," Jean-Paul said.

She nodded in reply.

"Did you climax?" he asked.

This time, she didn't answer at all, but surely, he'd see the warmth flood her cheeks. She picked up her wine and finished it in one swallow.

"I'm sorry, Carole. A girl's first time should be wonderful," Pete said.

"I doubt most virgin brides enjoy the act. Women only come into their own later. In fact, I had a close friend who insisted that no woman should settle down until she'd found her sixth lover," she said.

Oh, dear God. Her heart sank toward her belly. Sixth lover. What Thomas had demanded. The whole reason she sat here with lovers three and four. Could it be a coincidence—a bit of sexual lore common among the adventurous but something she'd never learned? Or had Thomas overheard one of her conversations with Muriel Standen? How long ago would that have happened? She hadn't spoken to Muriel since Oscar's death. He had to have planned all this in advance.

"Carole?"

She glanced up to discover the servant had returned and was in the process of setting out the salad course. Pete stared at her, and Jean-Paul looked on with a faint tilt of amusement on his face.

"Is something wrong?" Pete asked. "You suddenly went pale."

Very likely, as her blood had drained from her face. Her dress didn't provide much cover, and gooseflesh covered her arms.

"Have you seen a ghost?" Jean-Paul said.

"I think maybe I have." How long ago had she had those conversations with Muriel? So many years ago. Had Thomas overheard? No, impossible. It had to be a coincidence.

"Tell us about your ghost," Jean-Paul said.

"No." The word came out with no thought at all. This had nothing to do with Thomas, and she wouldn't tell anyone else about him even if it did.

"Disobedient thing," the Frenchman said.

"I don't have to obey you," she said. "I came here as a guest. If I've misunderstood that, I'll leave immediately."

Jean-Paul steepled his fingers together as his smile broadened. "There is fire in you, after all."

"If there weren't, I wouldn't be here."

"Behave yourselves," Pete said. "Both of you."

"I apologize," Jean-Paul said. "Please go on."

What an insane situation. She ate some of her salad, no more than greens dressed in oil and vinegar. The simple purity only emphasized the carnality of what had come before and what would follow—the dessert and after.

"Did your marriage get better?" Pete asked.

"The marriage was fine. The sex became tolerable," she said. "I knew there should be more. My friend told stories that made my pussy ache."

"Still, you didn't take a lover?" Jean-Paul asked.

"He was my husband. I'd vowed to be faithful." She looked down at her hands. "Then, he became ill and couldn't manage at all."

"I'm sorry, Carole," Pete said. "I wish I'd known you then."

"I still would have been married." She lifted her chin. "He died and left me a great deal of money."

"You decided to experiment," Jean-Paul said.

"I found an odd bookstore. The material opened my eyes. New York held no promise, so I decided to travel."

Jean-Paul finished his salad, pushed the plate aside, and rested his elbow on the table. "Now the Englishman."

"I won't give you his name."

"Not necessary," Jean-Paul said. "How many times did he make you come?"

"Three times in our one night together." She paused. "Four, if you include at the opera."

Jean-Paul hooted. "At the opera?"

"He fondled me under my skirt until I came. The sounds of Verdi drowned out my cries." Ah, yes. Roger's fingers on her pearl. His voice in her ear warning her not to spend until the last notes of the duet. The rhythm of the music as the orgasm approached and then the ecstatic moment.

"The English have become creative," Jean-Paul said.

"My lover was a rake. Very experienced at satisfying a woman." She took a breath. "He took me home, ate my pussy, and fucked me. We did it again in the middle of the night."

She didn't add that he'd called out another woman's name. She'd dreamed of Thomas as Roger had moved inside her. Love for each other had been no part of it. Only their bodies had mattered, as only these two men's cocks did now.

"He taught you to speak dirty," Pete said. "I love filthy language on a beautiful woman's lips."

Clearly, the man did because his skin had flushed. The color didn't come from embarrassment.

"Dessert," Jean-Paul said as his picked up his bell again.

This time, the servant put something that looked like chocolate pudding in front of them and then dabbed a bit of whipped cream on top. This was nothing like she'd had at home, though. When she spooned some into her mouth, it floated on her tongue and then dissolved, leaving a flavor so rich as to be sinful. "Oh, my."

"*Mousse au chocolat*," Jean-Paul said. "I'm glad you like it."

"I've never had anything like it." She ate some more and allowed herself a little groan of pleasure.

"It's my favorite." Pete took a mouthful of his mousse and then stopped when he caught her watching him. His grin turned into an evil expression that would have done Jean-Paul proud, and he ran the tip of his tongue around the edge of his spoon. Exactly the way he might stroke the lips of her sex and then linger at the bud at the top.

She should have learned by now that Jean-Paul did nothing he hadn't carefully planned. The gown, the stroke of her buttock to assert his dominance here, the sensuous foods and wines. He'd drawn out her entire sexual history, and now he'd fed them something designed to arouse her imagination. Indeed, the brocade of the chair seemed to have roughened enough to scratch against her sex through the silk of her gown. The Frenchman had arranged things so that she'd beg them to lick her pearl or fuck her or both. If only she could turn the tables on both of them.

Ah, yes. "You've nearly finished your mousse, Pete. Would you like some of mine?"

He shared a sidelong glance with his friend. "Would you like to sit in my lap to feed it to me?"

"I had something different in mind." She set aside her napkin and returned his gaze evenly as a few silent seconds ticked by. After a bit, she lifted her dessert glass toward him. "I'd like to spread this on your cock."

His eyes flew wide open, and he dropped his spoon onto the tablecloth.

"Don't worry," she said. "I'll lick it off again."

Jean-Paul clapped a few times. "Brava!"

She grasped her dessert and rose. "Turn around so I can reach you better."

Pete also got up and lifted his chair to follow her instructions.

"The other way," she said. "So Jean-Paul can watch."

He obeyed and sat back down, his back to her. She approached slowly so that he'd have to listen to her soft footsteps as she neared him. The back of his neck glowed pink over his collar. More flush of arousal. She walked around him, set her dessert plate on the table, and knelt.

When he parted his legs, she pushed at his knees, giving herself a wider space between them. The action stretched the fabric of his pants so that, as soon as she'd unbuttoned his jacket, the outline of his member showed clearly through the cloth. She pressed her palm against it. "Impressive."

He took in a quick breath. "You inspire it.."

She stroked his length. "It feels like steel. I didn't know a man could get this hard."

"Go easy," Pete said. "I'm ready to explode."

"I do hope so. I want to watch." Though she'd never done anything so brazen or calculated to inflame a man in her life, she opened one button of his fly, taking her time for full effect. She unfastened them one by one while her palm continued to press against his shaft. His breath came faster as she worked.

Finally, she reached into his pants, curled her fingers around his flesh, and pulled his sex free. He grunted his approval.

Grasping his shaft in her fist, she looked up into his face. His eyelids had drooped, and his lips had parted. When she pumped him, he clenched his teeth and moaned.

"What do you think of Priapus?" Jean-Paul asked.

"He's a splendid fellow," she said. "So thick and holding his head proudly erect."

"Note the color. He's highly excited."

"I'm going to spend any minute," Pete said.

"Not until I've finished eating my dessert off you," she said.

"Do it," he said from between clenched teeth. "Oh, God. Please, do it."

She scooped some of her dessert into her hands and rubbed it between her palms to warm it. It slicked her fingers, much the way her pussy grew moist before her own climax. Now, she noted each feature of Pete's rod as she smoothed the chocolate into his skin. Her thumb and forefinger barely circled the bulbous head as she pushed past the dimple at the tip and down along the shaft. She'd need a great deal more to coat all of him, so she repeated the process again until she'd reached the base of his shaft.

He made strangled sounds in the back of his throat as she worked, and his cock seemed to swell and throb at every stroke along his length.

"Now, lick it clean," Jean-Paul's voice said from behind her.

She turned, just briefly, to find him staring at her with intensity that was almost frightening.

"Can't last," Pete gritted.

"You can, *mon ami*," Jean-Paul said.

She continued sliding her fingers along Pete's rod, but now, she bent her face to the tip. A tentative lick at the head got her a loud gasp from Pete. The taste of chocolate danced on her tongue, but a salty tang lay behind it. Not unpleasant at all, so she sucked him into her mouth and circled the ridge with her tongue.

"Damn!" His hips moved, slow thrusts upward that pressed more of his hardness into her mouth. She let her mouth slide down along his shaft and then up again.

"Oh, that is…" He pulled in a ragged breath. "So good. So…damned…. fucking…good."

"Make it last," Jean-Paul whispered. "I'm sure Carole wants to watch the semen spray all over you."

Pete pushed harder now, and she had to grasp him at the base to hold him back from choking her. With so much more of him to lick clean, she pulled her mouth away and then stroked her tongue along the inches she hadn't yet caressed. She clutched at his shaft, moving it this way and that to get to the rest of the chocolate. When she'd finished, she put her mouth on him again, taking as much as she could swallow.

No more words came from his mouth. Only the primitive language of a man at the very edge. No chocolate now, but just his flesh and more salty evidence of his excitement. His fingers went into her hair, pressing her head downward on every thrust of his hips. She'd pushed him too far, and he'd lost control.

His breath turned to gasps, each rising in pitch, as he continued pushing his cock into her mouth.

"Now!" Jean-Paul shouted. "He's coming."

She managed to guide his cock from between her lips, but she continued stroking him. Hard. All the way from the base to the tip. His body went rigid, and he bellowed as a spray of milky liquid flew from the tip of him. Another followed, and then another.

After a moment, he gave a long groan and relaxed against the back of his chair, his eyes still closed with pleasure. His cock softened in her hand but droplets of his semen remained on her fingers. After rising, she used his napkin to clean her skin then dipped her forefinger into the remnants of her mousse. She used that to paint his lips and bent to kiss it from his mouth.

When she straightened, he gave her a lazy smile. "I thank you, ma'am."

"You're very welcome." She turned to Jean-Paul. "It's been a long day. I think I'll retire."

She straightened her hair and walked from the room with as much dignity as the throbbing of her pearl allowed.

*

Images of Pete's rigid member haunted Carole's dream. He was so huge, and her body craved him. No matter how hard she tried to take him inside her, his cock eluded her—always moving away at the last moment. She woke up in a state of excitement too powerful to ignore. So, as Thomas had instructed in his letter from months ago, she slipped her hand under the covers and pulled the hem of her nightgown up so that she could touch her mound. She gasped at the contact. Not what she'd sought in her dream, but the best she could do until one of the men could relieve the ache— assuming she found the audacity to ask one of them outright to fuck her. She had only met them the day before, after all.

As she let her mind drift back into the dream, a small sound penetrated the fog of arousal. Someone walking on the terrace just below her open window. Someone close enough to be listening to what went on in her room.

She walked to the window and looked out. Sure enough, Jean-Paul was standing on the terrace, staring over the wall at the garden and the vineyards in the distance. The moon shone brightly enough to show the black of his hair and the rigid set of his back. As she watched, he turned slowly and gazed up at her. Somehow, he'd known about her restlessness. Somehow, he'd guessed that she'd look out and find him. He wore the usual half-amused expression on his face—as if he could read inside her and realize the height of her need for a lover.

No, not a lover with him. Something more complex. And yet, he was a man and had a cock. He'd watched her fellate his friend to orgasm. He had to have become aroused himself, no matter how much he'd try to hide it. Unless he'd had some relief since dinner, he'd fell the need for coupling as bad as she did. He did nothing to beckon her, though, but simply turned and gave her his back

Not bothering with a robe or slippers, she let herself out of her room and padded down the stairs. She had to go down a series of unfamiliar hallways, using her best sense of direction to find her way to the spot below her bedroom. A tall door stood ajar at a promising spot, so she let herself out through it. Yes, the terrace. Jean-Paul leaned against the stone wall a few yards away, so she went to him and took a spot beside him.

"You should sleep in the nude while you're here," he said without moving his stare from the distance. "We might want to visit you."

"Isn't this a visit?"

"I couldn't sleep," he answered.

"I couldn't, either." She moved closer to him so that her shoulder nearly met his. "I imagine we're both restless for the same reason."

He shrugged. "Pete's probably sleeping soundly. He always does."

"And the staff?"

112

"Safe in their own quarters." He moved finally, stepping behind her. Still not touching her, he reached around and rested his hands on the wall. Until then, the night air had felt warm enough, but now his body heat seeped into her skin. Denied until now, her poor sex moistened in anticipation. He breathed deeply as if he could smell her musk, the evidence that she wanted him.

"Have you ever watched cats mate?" he asked.

"I never kept pets."

"They don't look as if they're enjoying it," he said. "You'd think they were fighting except for the way the female lifts her ass into the air to tempt him."

Finally, he did touch her, putting his palms on her buttocks. Not unlike the way he'd touched her when she'd come down for dinner, but now he kneaded the flesh. "You've been tempting me with this since you came into the house."

"You're the one who left that dress on the bed."

His hands went lower, still squeezing. His fingers slipped between her thighs. Even from behind like this, they neared her sex enough to squeeze the lips and put pressure on her clitoris. More wetness seeped from her, dampening the cloth of her gown enough that he'd have to feel it.

"Damned clothing," he muttered. He fumbled with the tie of his robe and then gathered up the skirt of her gown in his fists.

Yes. Now, he'd do something. He'd either touch her or fuck her. She'd come either way. Finally, his cock pressed against her bare skin. Not as large as Pete's, but rock hard and hot enough to sear its imprint into her flesh. She whimpered with need. Just like in her dream—the hardness so close but not inside her.

"The male cat holds his female down, covering her with his body. She accepts his roughness. It excites her." He parted her legs, stepped between them, and drove his rod up into her. No tenderness. No caresses. No soft words. Just what she wanted. She didn't even have to look at him. She could just take and take and take.

Without breaking their union, he pressed her hands against the rocks of the wall and covered them with his own. His cock went right on moving inside her. Harder and deeper. Like the cat, she arched her back to offer him maximum penetration. He whispered a string of French as he kept shoving himself inside her. No translation necessary, the meaning came through. Soft, sweet, and nasty, the words told the story of males and females in heat. Coming together in the most primitive way possible.

As his thrusts grew more savage, he pushed on her hands so hard that the stones pressed into the flesh of her palms. She wouldn't complain, though. She wouldn't do anything to slow him. The climax was too close— coiling deep in her belly. She clenched her sex down on him, seeking more friction. In response, he grunted and ground himself against her with each thrust.

"Don't stop," she whispered. "Please, don't stop."

He bit her shoulder, right through her gown. Truly animal now. Both of them.

"Come," he whispered.

"Yes…yes."

He let out a growl and continued thrusting. To steady herself, she kept her palm firm against the stones of the wall. "Fuck me."

"Like this?" he said as he drove himself deeper inside her.

"Yes, damn it. More." *Just a little more. Close, so close.* She tensed as every nerve caught fire. She would come now. "Keep fucking me."

He did. Hard. Her sex exploded in violent orgasm, clamping down on him in waves. She screamed as the power of it stole her consciousness of anything but her pussy and the hard male flesh that plunged into it. He roared as he came with her and thrust so hard he nearly pounded her into the wall. Savage and sublime at the same time.

It left her aching when it ended—physically and mentally. Her palms hurt from scraping against stone. Her shoulder stung from Jean-Paul's bite. Her pussy felt sore even as it continued sending aftershocks around his softening cock. Most of all, her mind screamed that she shouldn't have enjoyed that.

Jean-Paul had shown her no tenderness. He still didn't. He slumped against her, breathing hard. Not a sweet word or a gentle touch. He'd truly fucked her the way animals rutted, and yet, he'd given her the most powerful orgasm of her life. How could she not want more of the same? Sex like that could become an opiate.

After a bit, he sighed and pulled out of her, leaving her sex empty and wet with juices from both of them. He didn't move away but stood with his hands on her shoulders. Now, they both looked out over the land that had been in his family for generations. The dark garden and the rows of grape vines that had heard their cries of release.

"*Ah, bien,*" he whispered. "You did well, *cherie.*"

"I did?"

"Yes." He kissed the spot he'd bitten. "The *mousse au chocolat.* Very creative."

"You mean with Pete." She looked over her shoulder, but his face lay in darkness too deep for her to read his expression.

"I could tell he enjoyed it tremendously."

She turned her face away from him. He might as well have just slapped her with that "compliment." Only a moment ago, he'd climaxed inside her, and he only praised her performance with his friend.

Bastard. He had climaxed, and he'd shouted loudly enough to wake up the dead. Maybe Pete had heard. Maybe the servants had. He could give her the back of his hand with his words, but his animal roar told the truth. He'd come as hard as she had. He only wanted to deny it for some reason.

She smoothed her hair and walked away from him without a word.

Chapter Six

To see the three of them, one would assume nothing out of the ordinary. No more than a group of friends on a stroll through the market, the woman's arms looped through the men's. All dressed respectably, all wearing pleasant expressions.

Pete stopped them at a flower stall to buy a tiny bouquet of lavender. When he turned to present it to Carole, he stared at her chest. "I'd hoped to put this into your bosom, but you've covered your breasts."

"Please, we're in public," she said.

"I'm quiet," he answered. "Besides, they all speak French."

"Someone might understand English," she said.

"This is France. We all understand breasts," Jean-Paul said. "Still, if we walk a bit, no one will overhear us."

Pete handed her the flowers and then wrapped her arm around his again. They passed stands of vegetables and fruit—piles of potatoes and eggplants and baskets of strawberries that perfumed the air. All of Provence smelled of flowers and other sweet produce, it seemed.

With the views, the sun, the flowers it seemed a magical place where one could run naked and cover one's body with all the colors and scents. And then at night...what sensual promise the night offered.

"You're shy today," Pete said as they passed a baker's stall. "You hardly speak, and you've covered yourself nearly to the chin. A lover could get suspicious."

She glanced at Jean-Paul. He stared straight ahead with a half-smile curling his lips.

"It makes me wonder if there's a mark on you somewhere," Pete said.

She stopped in her tracks, pulling the other two to a stop.

"Jean-Paul, you didn't," Pete said. His words scolded, but his face only showed amusement.

Jean-Paul shrugged and said something in French she couldn't catch.

"I should have warned you he's an animal," Pete said. "So, where did he put his mark? Your breast, maybe?"

"Good Lord." She glared at Jean-Paul. "You wouldn't bite that, would you?"

"Not with my lover facing away," he said. "Too difficult."

"You are an animal," she said.

Pete laughed softly.

"And you encourage him," she said.

"Of course, I do. You came to the chateau to play with both of us," Pete said. "From the noises you made, it seemed you enjoyed yourself."

Her skin flushed hot. "You heard."

"Half of Provence probably heard. Half of Provence expects that from Jean-Paul."

"I don't know why I'm talking about this with you." She dropped their arms and walked briskly away, still clutching the lavender in her hand. She had to navigate by old ladies with baskets of vegetables and baguettes under their arms, but she finally arrived at a bench near the corner of the square.

She shouldn't be so upset at their frank language, especially if no one listening could understand. Certainly, none of the other people in the market had smirked or leaned in to hear more clearly. She'd fellated Pete to orgasm while Jean-Paul looked on. Later, she and Jean-Paul had made enough noise to wake the grapevines. Of course, Pete had overheard.

Pete appeared out of the crowd and sat on the bench next to her. "Angry with me, pretty Carole?"

"Where's Jean-Paul?"

"Buying a few things for dinner. You didn't answer my question."

"I'd expect him to come with you so he could add to the ridicule." Damn, that sounded petulant.

"Ridicule?"

"Jean-Paul doesn't like me." Dear Lord, where had that come from? And yet, that lay at the bottom of what had made a knot in her stomach since the night before. His "compliment" on how she'd satisfied Pete and not him had really been a rebuke. He had to have done that deliberately.

"Ah well, that's Jean-Paul," Pete said.

"He was rude last night."

Pete put his hand on her shoulder. "He didn't force himself on you, did he?"

"Nothing like that." She paused. "He made me feel small afterward."

"I'm sure he didn't mean to. He tests everyone when he first meets them."

"Did he do that to you?"

"He called me a child," Pete answered.

"There. Do you see what I mean? Rude."

"I was a child."

"Men," she said. "He'd destroy something, and you'd pay for it."

"Probably." He touched her cheek. "But you can't object to some teasing. The three of us are doing something forbidden. Normal etiquette doesn't apply."

"I suppose you're right."

"After the pure depravity of what you did with your dessert last night, I'd expect you and Jean-Paul to make a lot of noise when you finally fucked." He took her chin and turned her head so that he could press his lips to hers in a gentle kiss. "Your sex was good, wasn't it?"

"It was." Despite the roughness, or maybe partly because of it, the orgasm had hit her with a force almost too strong to be borne. And her pussy still felt a bit sore. She'd been well and truly fucked. If they wanted to tease her about it, she could hardly complain.

"There you are, then," he said. "Are we forgiven?"

"You are. We'll see about Jean-Paul."

"You'll forgive him. In fact, I bet he was rough on you because he's afraid you can best him."

She had to snort at that. "You must be joking."

"You'll see." He rose and took her hand to pull her up with him. "Let's go find the bastard and see what he's up to."

*

That night, Carole found a second silk gown on her bed but wore her own clothes to dinner. Although the silk garment from the night before had looked wonderful and felt sinful and delicious, she'd stand a better chance of asserting some control by setting the boundaries herself. She would have sex with both of them again, but they'd know she wasn't some child, as Pete had told her Jean-Paul had thought of him, but an adult woman who'd married and lost her husband and had her own mind.

She chose a low-cut dress that showed off her bosom, and she dabbed perfume behind her ears and between her breasts.

True to form, Jean-Paul and Pete had planned a surprise for her. Instead of a formal meal in the dining room, she found the two men in a side room, sitting at a small table with a deck of cards and stacks of chips in front of them.

When she entered, Pete looked up with a definite gleam in his eye. "The little lady has found us, pardner."

"Isn't that a little too Texan?" she asked.

"You should have heard him when he first came here," Jean-Paul said.

Pete dealt out some cards. "Poker, Miss Carole?"

"That's the widow Rose, son," she said. "And where's the grub?"

"Please, you two," Jean-Paul said. "I can only endure so much American charm."

"There's a buffet on the sideboard," Pete said.

There was, indeed. Composed salads, rigid in their geometric placement of vegetables. Covered chafing dishes offered various hot dishes, and a tray at the end held delicate pastries and fruit. She served herself from the savory dishes and left dessert for later.

When she joined the men at the gaming table, Jean-Paul poured red wine into a crystal goblet and passed it to her. "You play this silly game, I suppose."

"Not at all. I only know bridge."

Jean-Paul sighed. "If only we had a fourth."

"Ante up, folks," Pete said as he dealt a few cards. "Five card stud, only one hole card. Simplest thing on Earth."

When he tossed a white chip onto the center of the table, Carole did the same. "How do I know the two of you won't cheat?"

"I have better things to do than cheat at cards," Jean-Paul said.

"Besides," Pete said. "We're not really playing for money."

"Then, what's the point?" she asked.

"She's right, you know," Jean-Paul said. "We need something else."

Pete leaned back in his chair as an evil glint entered his eye. "The winner gets to ask for a sexual favor."

"That doesn't work, either," Carole said. "You'll both make demands of me unless you want to have sex with each other."

An awkward pause followed. Not for long but enough to suggest she'd said something forbidden. Pete smiled through the whole of it, but Jean-Paul's face turned into the mask he wore so often.

"I know," he said after a few seconds. "The winner gets to ask the person with the worst hand anything he likes. The loser has to answer truthfully."

"I'm game," Pete said.

Jean-Paul lifted his wineglass toward Carole. "And you, *cherie*?"

She touched his goblet with hers. "Agreed."

"Well, then. Carole has an ace showing. If she has another in the hole, she's way ahead of the game," Pete said.

She carefully checked her down card, keeping her expression bland. A six. Probably not a good sign.

Pete dealt each of them another card up. "Jean-Paul has a pair of deuces showing. I have nothing showing, but you don't know what I'm hiding."

"Why don't you shut up and deal?" Jean-Paul said.

Pete gave each of them another card. "No help to anyone. The question remains does the little lady have another ace?"

She stared him in the eyes. "I'll never tell."

"One last card." He dealt one more round. "Ah, I have a pair of tens showing and Carole got a deuce. That only leaves the fourth deuce."

Jean-Paul turned over his hole card. "Which I happen to have."

"Three of a kind beats my pair." Pete gathered his cards up and tossed them onto the center of the table. "What do you have, Carole?"

"Nothing. Just an ace."

"I win. You lose. What should I ask?" Jean-Paul took a sip of his wine, staring at her over the rim of his glass. "Why didn't you wear the dress I had left on your bed tonight?"

"Easy," she answered. "I'm tired of you dominating me. I'm an adult. I can dress myself."

"What if you were suddenly overcome with the desire to have one of our cocks inside you?" Jean-Paul said. "How could we get past your clothing?"

"You're not that irresistible."

Pete let out a whoop. "You didn't impress her last night."

"She hasn't fucked you at all yet," Jean-Paul said.

"Do you two want to talk or play poker?" Carole said.

"Deal." Pete went back to work, and Carole ate some of the food on her plate. Excellent, as usual, as was the wine. She didn't bother to turn over her hole card. She'd find out at the end what it was, and no amount of knowing ahead of time would change the outcome.

This time, she lost again and Pete won.

"Tell me about the first time you had sex," he said.

"My wedding night. I don't want to talk about that."

"You agreed to the rules," Pete said.

"I feel I'm betraying my husband," she answered.

"He won't know about it," Jean-Paul said.

She let her mind go back to that night at the hotel where they'd stayed before boarding the train to Niagara Falls for their honeymoon. How she'd lain in bed, dressed in all the layers of lace a bride collected in her trousseau. She'd made herself avoid the details of what would happen throughout the engagement and even the wedding day. As she'd waited for him, she rehearsed all the reasons for marrying him. Oscar was a kind man. She'd be rich. She'd never do any better. Most of all, any man would hurt her the first time and she might as well give her virginity to this one.

"It didn't take very long," she said finally. "Oscar told me he loved me. He climbed into bed, raised my gown, and took off my drawers. He had to work a bit to penetrate me, and then we coupled without undressing. He finished quickly, thanked me, and went to sleep."

Jean-Paul muttered something in French that sounded like a curse.

"You asked," she said. "Now you know."

Pete collected the cards into a deck and set them aside. "You must have had more love and passion in your life than that."

"I did love him. I was married to him for twenty years. He took care of me, and I took care of him as he died."

"You're not a dishonest woman, *cherie*." Jean-Paul leaned toward her, giving her his penetrating gaze. "That's not the kind of love Pete means. It isn't any kind of passion at all."

"I'm not looking for love." She did her best to smile evenly. "And you two are more than enough passion."

"Borrowed sex," Jean-Paul said, his stare never leaving her face. "That's all we are. Fun for a while and then over."

True, that's all she'd come here for, and she'd leave again with nothing but pleasant memories of a dalliance on her way to her true love.

Thomas. Why did he suddenly feel like an illusion? What was it about the way this Frenchman looked at her that made her question everything—most of all herself? Thomas was real. Their love was real. He had some reason for sending her into other men's beds. He must, or she'd been pursuing a fool's errand and making a fool of herself in the process.

She pushed back her chair and rose. "Enough for tonight."

"Jean-Paul's upset you." Pete glared at his friend. "Why do you have to act like a damned oracle? Carole's our guest."

"It's just a headache. It'll go away again," she said.

Pete got up, too. "I'll order a bath. Scrub your back."

"No need. I'll see you both tomorrow." She left them both, and Jean-Paul said nothing as she did.

*

Carole awoke as a body slid into bed next to her. When she retreated, she found another one right behind her. Warm, solid, and male.

"Pete?" she whispered.

An arm went around her and cupped her breast. "Here, love."

"And that would make you…" She rubbed her eyes and made them focus on the face near hers on the pillow.

"Jean-Paul," he murmured back.

His breath carried the scent of wine—sweet, as if he'd just sipped it. He kissed her gently, letting her sample his lips and the flavors of fruit and sunshine there. As rough as his caresses had been the night before, now he used tenderness. Something melted inside her, and she took his face between her hands to hold him to her so that she could savor the play of his mouth against hers.

Despite her earlier rebellion, she'd obeyed Jean-Paul and worn nothing to bed. Now, his naked body fitted itself to hers in front as she snuggled her back against Pete. Both men gave evidence of full arousal, Jean-Paul's firm cock pressing against her belly while Pete's larger one fitted itself into the space between her buttocks. Not ending the kiss, she let her hands roam over male flesh everywhere.

Such luxury. Not one man, but two. Jean-Paul became the most devoted lover, now kissing her forehead, her eyelids, even the tip of her nose. She stretched and moaned with pleasure as Pete's hand moved to the other breast. Kneading and rolling the nipple, he created a current of desire that traveled along her nerves outward and downward.

"So good," she crooned. "Oh, yes. So good."

"All for you, *cherie*," Jean-Paul answered. "Because you married a man who didn't know how to love your body."

She twisted and glanced over her shoulder at Pete. "My wedding night?"

"Have you ever had two men before?" he said.

"Never."

"Then, you're a virgin." He nuzzled her ear and nibbled at the lobe. "This is your first time."

"Two tongues." Jean-Paul let his trail along her neck to her shoulder and then flicked it over the spot where he'd bitten her the night before.

"Four hands," Pete said as he lowered his over her ribs to her belly. "Twenty fingers."

"Oh, yes," she sighed.

"Two cocks." Pete pulled her back hard against his. "All for you."

They set to their work as if they'd rehearsed exactly how three people could fit together to give the one in the middle maximum delight. A mouth closed around her breast. Jean-Paul's. He sucked on the nipple, tugging and then flicking it with his tongue until it tightened into a stiff point. Palms and fingers went everywhere, warming her and leaving sensitive skin behind. She let the real world slip away as she slid into an erotic trance. Every soft sound, every puff of breath over her flesh sent her deeper inside herself as she let them pleasure her. *All for me.*

A hand cupped her mound and pressed so that the hard nub there pushed against the bone beneath. A surge of excitement rushed through her, and she cried out at the power of it. Already, she'd become so aroused, she'd shatter soon. That wouldn't end her need, though. She wouldn't be satisfied with one climax, not with two lovers so eager to please her. Two male members, throbbing and ready to plunder her. She'd take them both as hard and deep and long as they could last.

Jean-Paul kissed her again. "Look at me."

She opened her eyes, although the lids had grown heavy and she could hardly focus her gaze.

"Come for me, *cherie*," he said. "It's your first time, and I want to you come against my face."

"Please," she answered.

Jean-Paul moved slowly along her body, leaving a trail of kisses over her ribs to her belly. As if by agreement, Pete lifted her leg over his. Now, she lay back against him, her legs thighs parted and her sex exposed.

The two of them had planned this...all for her. Her spirit soared as her body basked in their touches, their kisses, the soft sounds they made. A love song of a sort, and not one she'd likely hear again.

When Jean-Paul reached her pussy, rational thought ended. His tongue flicked lightly against her pearl. Too lightly. She whimpered and arched toward him, but Pete held her fast.

"Trust us," he whispered as his fingers squeezed her breast and then teased the nipple.

Such delicious agony—long, slow arousal. She could trust them. She had to. Jean-Paul paused for a moment, and she lay in Pete's embrace, her body strung tight with need. She needed to come, and she would. She should wait, let it build, but already she'd neared the edge, and still, he wouldn't push her past.

Her breath came in fast puffs now. A struggle to pull air into her lungs. Floating in a sea of lust—a solid male body behind her, his cock pressed against her buttock and a man's face near her pussy.

He licked her clitoris again, faster and harder. Yes, this would finish her. Now, she fought against the release, drawing the ecstasy out. Each extra second pushed her higher.

Her voice rose in pitch as her breaths turned to gasps. To tell him without words…don't stop, don't stop! He continued, now even faster, and she couldn't delay the inevitable. Her sex clenched and then burst into spasms. Jean-Paul sucked on her bud as the climax continued.

When she couldn't manage any more, she went limp in Pete's embrace. After a bit, Jean-Paul joined them, surrounding her with heat, arms and legs in a tangle. Weak as a newborn, she nuzzled her nose under his chin and to his shoulder.

"Happy, *cherie*?" he said.

"Mmm."

"So, you don't want Pete inside you?"

She pulled back and studied his expression in the sliver of moonlight. Instead of his usual hooded expression, he smiled with pride and more than a little amusement. Teasing, obviously.

"I want Pete inside me very much."

"I'm glad to hear that." Pete pushed his hips forward, shoving his cock against her ass. His very hard, very large cock. "Let's see if I can make you come, too."

She kissed Jean-Paul, inhaling her own scent. "What about you?"

"You wanted to learn about the male member," he said. "Use your hand on me, and the three of us will climax together."

"My mouth instead," she answered.

"*Sacre bleu*. Yes, *cherie*."

Pete shifted, allowing her to rest on her back against the tangled sheets. They worked quickly, she parting her legs and Pete taking his place between them. The tip of his sex eased between the engorged lips of her sex. Even after that powerful climax, her body craved more. As he pushed slowly into her, she had to stretch to take his bulk.

"Damn, you're tight. Slick. Hot." He groaned. "As good as your mouth."

"You've filled me," she answered.

"Now, I'll fuck you." He pulled back and then surged forward again. Lord, she'd never had anything like this before, even from Roger and Jean-Paul. They'd driven her to insanity, but they'd never been so deep inside her. As he moved, his body stroked against hers, rubbing her nipples and stirring her flesh back to life.

She lifted her legs to circle him and give him the best angle for penetration. As Pete set a rhythm for the two of them, Jean-Paul knelt near her. He guided his cock to her face so that she could suck it into her mouth.

She was fucking both of them and being plowed with Pete's thick rod. Thoroughly carnal and forbidden and all the better for its sinfulness.

After a few moments of bliss, Pete set a driving rhythm. In, out, stroke, retreat. While Jean-Paul pumped his hips, she tried her own tricks on him, pumping his shaft while teasing the head of his cock with her tongue.

"Good," he gritted. "Just so."

"Can't hold off," Pete said. "I'm going to come."

"Not yet. All of us at once," Jean-Paul answered.

"Hurry." Pete's thrusts came faster. Harder. Deeper. Each time he plunged into her, her pearl responded with a jolt of sensation. Now, she had a cock inside her and another in her mouth.

Both men were breathing hard as if running at top speed. Pete still held his weight off her as he plunged into her, but his eyes had closed. He'd disappeared into the world of his own lust, and it drove him hard to his destination. She closed her own eyes and pictured Thomas above her as he neared the ultimate. She imagined sucking Thomas' beautiful member, as well.

Yes, oh yes, now. When Jean-Paul grunted, she pulled his cock from her mouth and pumped it. Now, the orgasm caught her up again, tossing her into madness. This time, when her inner walls tightened, they squeezed the steel and satin of Pete's member. He shouted with her while beside her, Jean-Paul stiffened and sent a spray of semen over her fingers. Pete followed with a few savage thrusts while her sex continued gripping him.

In the end, they all lay limp, each alone in satiation and each surrounded by the others' nearness.

CHAPTER SEVEN

The day they visited the Roman aqueduct, they took the lunch Jean-Paul's staff packed in a large, rattan hamper, and the three of them sat on the grass, drinking wine and breathing in the perfume of flowers from the fields nearby. Afterward, Pete stretched out on the blanket and fell asleep, leaving her alone with Jean-Paul. When he'd finished cleaning up, he sat beside her, looking over the sun-washed landscape while he twirled a blade of grass between his thumb and forefinger.

"How do you like Provence, *cherie*?" he said.

"How could I not like it?" she answered. "It's magnificent."

"Have you ever visited Texas?" he asked. "Do you know what it's like?"

"Only the stories we hear in the east…that it's full of gunslingers and Indians."

"Translate, please. How does one sling a gun?"

He might have meant that as an insult of Americans or a subtle way to assert his superiority, but he didn't raise his eyebrow or curl his lip. Instead, he seemed concentrated inward as the blade of grass twirled and twirled between his fingers.

"I don't know," she answered. "We don't sling guns in Manhattan. I guess a gunslinger straps it on in case he wants to shoot someone."

"That sounds dangerous. So do the Indians."

"I suppose it is."

They sat, not speaking, for several minutes. He seemed comfortable with the silence, and by now, it didn't grate on her nerves as it might have when she first arrived. She'd only spent a few days with them, mostly touring his estate and eating more delicious food when they weren't having sex with each other. Still, after that amazing encounter in her bed, she could hardly think of them as mere acquaintances. They'd thought to give her a present, both of them concentrated on her pleasure. They'd succeeded, and she'd always carry their gift with her most precious memories.

Pete snorted in his sleep, and Jean-Paul glanced over at him. "This uncouth American's promised to take me to Texas to see it. He says it's the most beautiful place on Earth."

"I doubt that," she said. "Texans do like to brag."

"He says you can ride for days and never reach the end of it."

"It is big. And very hot."

"Yes." He tossed the mashed stalk of grass aside. "One loves the place of his childhood, no?"

"I love it here." She gestured toward the aqueduct. "We don't have anything like that in either Texas or New York. Nor the wine or food either."

He laughed. "Or the sex?"

"Or the sex." She waved a hand in front of her face.

"Do you think you understand the cock now?"

"Much better than when I arrived," she answered. "I thank you both."

"It's hard to believe you were really such an innocent," he said. "Could an innocent have thought to use the *mousse au chocolat* to caress a man's member?"

"I felt challenged. I did the first thing that came to my mind."

"You honestly never did anything like that with your husband?" Jean-Paul said.

"Please, we've been through that."

"You have a passionate nature," he said. "It's good you can explore it while you're still young."

"Is forty young?"

"Forty?" He stared into her face in much the same way he had the first morning they'd met. It had the same effect—a flutter of fear and yes, excitement in the pit of her stomach.

"*Ah, bien,*" he said finally. "You're young, so forty is young for you."

Until that moment, she hadn't thought to ask about their ages. She hadn't with Roger, either. They'd expressed interest in her, so they must have found her appealing enough for a brief affair. Thomas would mean a great deal more. What of his age?

Still, he'd claimed to have known her and Oscar. He must know how old she was. In fact, he might be Oscar's age if they'd been friends. He had to have better health and more vigor. To write those letters, he simply had to.

They'd make a good match. The universe couldn't be so cruel as to dedicate her heart to another man who could only write about the gratification she required.

"Carole, you're wandering," Jean-Paul said.

"Who could help it in a setting like this?"

"I hope we know each other well enough now that I can give you some advice," Jean-Paul said.

"I'd say we know each other very intimately."

"Bah. Sex is body parts. You pay attention, you learn how to manipulate them for mutual pleasure," he said. "I think we can be friends. I think we can trust each other."

"Of course we can. How can you even ask that?"

"I have my reasons. You may know them some day." His gaze softened, showing real affection. Not something she'd expected from him. She sat quietly, waiting for what he'd say next.

He stared out over the fields of flowers again. "You must not settle for what's easy. Love is too important. I know that women have limited choices in these things, but there are even bigger hurdles."

"I don't know what you're talking about." It was a lie, but she used it anyway.

"Your husband was the easy way, I think. He brought you status and security and love of a sort," he said. "You settled for him."

"It wasn't that bad."

"Listen, *cherie*. A woman who eats her dessert off one man's sex and then lets his friend have her up against a wall could not be happy without good sex."

She lifted her chin. "Well, now I've had it."

"You're not going to be with us forever, though, are you?"

"This is only a visit," she answered. In fact, she'd fulfilled this part of her travels a few days before. She'd move on soon to find her fifth lover.

"I hope we've shown you not to take the easy road," he said, "but to insist on the one person who can truly make you happy."

"Don't worry. I know who he is. I'll find him and make him mine."

He held up his hands. "You don't have to convince me. Convince yourself."

"I have," she said. "I know exactly what I'm doing."

"Good then. Let's wake up this oaf of a Texan," Jean-Paul said. "We haven't properly shown you the aqueduct."

*

That afternoon, Carole found the silk gown and matching slippers *du jour* laid out on her bed. Emerald green this time and every bit as stunning as all the ones before it. Jean-Paul's wife had certainly had a lot of them.

Now, this one in the afternoon instead of the evening. Jean-Paul had become creative. What if he'd planned some play for the three of them before they went down for dinner? What had her scandalous Frenchman thought up for her today?

She quickly got out of her own clothes, leaving all the trappings on the bed where a servant would find them and put them away as someone always did. After letting the silk slide over her body, she stepped into the slippers and left her room to explore.

No sound came from the floor below except for very distant suggestions that servants might be moving around discreetly. Good. Upstairs, then. Less chance for someone to overhear.

She walked quietly down the hallway toward the other bedrooms. Odd she hadn't thought to find out where the two men slept. They'd come to her, instead.

The chateau was, indeed, a large place with long hallways in both directions, each ending with a staircase to the first floor. A muffled voice came from one wing. Not exactly words, at least not that she could make out.

As she went in that direction they grew louder and easier to interpret. She'd had enough experience by now to recognize the noises a man made while embedded and thrusting in a woman's sex. She found the source, finally, and stood outside the doorway, listening. Jean-Paul in full rut.

He'd brought another woman into the house? That shouldn't cut her, but it did. Wounded her pride if nothing else. He'd have other women, of course, but did he need one now?

Pete's voice joined his—the same kind of incoherent pleasure sounds. A threesome. Perhaps they expected her to make a fourth.

Yes, she should. Another experience to collect. A small orgy of sorts. Still, why did they want another woman when they had her? Damn, she really did need to be less provincial.

She silently turned the knob and stepped inside to a sight that shoved her back against the door in pure shock.

Pete knelt on top of the bed, his legs spread. Jean-Paul had mounted him from behind and moved his hips as if penetrating Pete's body. But he couldn't. Pete didn't have a pussy. The only orifice he had there…

Oh, no…impossible…they couldn't. Her knees almost buckled, but she couldn't look away.

Jean-Paul spoke in French as he pumped. He'd bent over and reached around Pete's body to his cock, stroking it with the silk gown she'd worn on their first night together. Eyes closed, both men were lost in their passion. Both grunting and straining against each other while Jean-Paul kept up a furious rhythm along Pete's shaft.

She ought to leave—quietly open the door, go back to her room, and pretend she'd never seen this. But witness it she had, and she couldn't lie to herself on that score. She couldn't play the innocent with these men, either. They'd read the truth on her face. So she stood and watched the ballet. Male and rough. Not at all the way they'd made love to her.

No, that wasn't true, either. Jean-Paul had fucked her exactly this way the first time. Total dominance and possession.

Now Jean-Paul straightened, dropping the cloth he'd held around Pete's member. He said a few words in French, almost sobbing them, as he took Pete's hips in his fists and kept thrusting.

"I haven't come yet," Pete said. "Don't do it, Jean-Paul."

The Frenchman ignored him as he kept moving, his face a grimace of lust.

"Damn it!" Pete shouted.

Jean-Paul's head tipped back as he let loose a bellow of completion. No mistaking that sound. He'd climaxed, leaving Pete behind. Groaning, he flopped onto the bed. Pete rolled over next to him, clutching his cock at the base. It had turned a deep crimson, the same way it had just before he'd climaxed that first night at the dinner table. Poor man. Aroused to the point of no return and abandoned.

Jean-Paul's eyes opened, but he showed no sign of surprise to find her standing by the doorway. "Hello, *cherie*."

Pete's eyes nearly filled his face. "Carole! Damn it all to hell. How much did you see?"

"I'm sorry," she stuttered. "I was just...I didn't mean..."

"I think she saw enough," Jean-Paul said. "Welcome to our reality."

"You fucking bastard. You planned this," Pete said, as he clutched his rod as if he'd strangle it.

"So, tell us, darling Carole. Do we disgust you?" Jean-Paul said.

"I can't...I don't know what to say..."

His expression turned hard. "Do we?"

137

Holy hell. She had to answer him. Now. And it had to be the truth. She couldn't lie to them, but how could she tell them how she felt when she didn't know herself? Both of them kept staring at her, and she had to say something.

"No," she answered finally. "No, you don't disgust me."

"Prove it." Jean-Paul's voice had cold steel behind it.

Dear Lord, how did he expect her to do that? Why did he keep making impossible demands on her? With no other clue how to respond, she lifted the silk gown over her head and dropped it to the floor. She let them both watch her reveal her naked body before she went to the bed and climbed onto it.

Pete didn't give her time to get out of her slippers. He spread her legs and shoved himself inside her. She couldn't even manage to get her arms around his shoulders before he started taking out his fury on her.

He moved as if Satan himself drove him, making an animal noise in his throat with each thrust. Yet another way to fuck, and perhaps the best example of that primitive word she'd experienced yet. She'd come if he kept this up, but likely he wouldn't last that long. He'd gotten so close to orgasm already. Her body reveled in the coupling, anyway—at the pure carnality of it. In the end, he nearly pushed them both off the bed as he came with one last punishing thrust. Pushing himself upward, he impaled her as deeply as he could go as he came for long seconds.

She tried to stroke his face, but he fell beside her on the bed, gasping for breath.

None of them spoke for long moments. Jean-Paul sat on the side of the bed, looking away. Pete rested his forearm over his eyes as if blotting out the reality of what had just happened.

"For heaven's sake. This isn't the end of the world." She got up, found her silk gown, and slipped into it. She never had removed her slippers. "We'll talk. After we put on some clothes."

*

They ended up in a drawing room—all dressed by society's strictest standards for decency. Except for Pete's sullen expression as he stood staring into the empty hearth, an observer would have thought they were having afternoon tea. Instead of tea, they drank brandy, though. Carole took a good swallow and studied the men who'd been her third and fourth lovers.

Yes, past tense. Time had come to leave.

A few feet away, Jean-Paul crossed his legs and studied her, his mask firmly in place. "So, what do you think of us now, sweet Carole?"

Pete shot him a look filled with venom.

"I'll be honest," she answered. "I don't know what to think. I only wonder why you involved me."

"Pete can tell you that," Jean-Paul answered.

"Damn it, Jean-Paul. Why did you have to make such a fucking mess of this?" Pete swallowed his brandy in one gulp and put his snifter on the mantle. "You orchestrated this little part of our encounter. You explain."

"Well, you see..." With his free hand Jean-Paul straightened the crease in his pants. "Pete developed a craving for a woman. Usually, he wanders off and comes back sick from having drunk too much and stinking of cheap perfume."

"And you throw a jealous fit even though you gave me permission to wander before I did it," Pete said.

"Your typical married couple, eh?" Jean-Paul's brow went up in that artificial way he had. Whatever charm it might have had had worn off long ago.

"Not typical at all," she said.

"Because we're both men?" he demanded.

"Because most married people don't cheat," she answered.

Jean-Paul turned his insincere smile on Pete. "There, you see?"

"All I see is that you dragged our relationship into the open without my permission," Pete answered. "I didn't want her to know."

"Didn't want her to know what? That you love me?" Jean-Paul glared at Pete. "You do love me, don't you?"

"You know I do." Pete ran his fingers through his hair in a gesture of supreme frustration. "Don't insult me by asking again."

"Would it hurt you to tell me without my begging?" Jean-Paul's voice rose above its usual carefully controlled level. "What we do isn't a sin, no matter what your provincial 'morality' has to say."

"Stop it," she said. "Both of you."

That earned her honest anger from Jean-Paul. "I beg your pardon."

"If Pete loves you, he needs to take care not to hurt you." Dear Lord, how was she even talking about this? Men loving men? Still, with everything she'd done with the two of them, the unusual had become normal. Besides, Jean-Paul's hostility toward her made sense now. Simple jealousy, no more.

"I never meant to hurt you," Pete said softly.

"I know that," Jean-Paul said. "Damn it all."

"But you shouldn't trick Pete into revealing himself against his will," she said. "That was a nasty surprise for both of us."

"What should I have done?" Jean-Paul demanded. "How would you have reacted if I'd invited you to join me and my male lover in a ménage?"

"I don't know. Refused you, I'm sure. But honestly, you should settle this yourselves and not involve a stranger."

"You're not a stranger." Pete left the mantle to take a seat next to her. "You're much more than that."

"He's right," Jean-Paul added softly.

"Then, why don't you explain to me *exactly* how we all arrived here?" she said. "Every detail."

Jean-Paul sighed. "As we told you, I was married, more or less happily, and then this man came along."

"And so you like both men and women?" "Like" was an odd word but the only one that came to her as things became more and more confusing.

"We both do," Pete answered.

"Universal love. Isn't that what they teach in churches?" Jean-Paul added.

"Never mind churches. Go on."

"He moved me like no one else ever has," Jean-Paul said. "Isolde understood. It broke her heart, but she understood. She left."

"And then, I turned out to be a disappointment," Pete said.

"No." Jean-Paul slammed his hand on the table beside him. "Not that. Never."

"Then, what would you call me?" Pete asked.

Jean-Paul turned to her. "He gets restless. I let him cheat, and it kills me. How Isolde would laugh if she knew."

"He must stop," she said.

Pete put his elbow on the table between them and rested his face in his hand. "I know."

"Do you really?" Jean-Paul asked.

Pete straightened in his chair. "I will stop because I have to. I love him more than I love my own life."

"That's settled, then," Carole said.

"Forgive me for dragging you into our problem," Pete said. "I thought you'd be our solution."

"I can take responsibility for that. What a thunderbolt of surprise you were, *cherie*," Jean-Paul said.

"How so?" she asked.

The two men glanced at each other, sharing a secret, it appeared.

"You gave me an erection," Jean-Paul said. "Sitting across the café, reading a letter with your lips pursed and your skin flushed. I haven't had that reaction to a woman since Isolde."

"I almost dropped my coffee in my lap when he told me," Pete added.

Yes, reading Thomas' letter had excited her. They'd commented on her appearance at the time.

"What did he say that you wouldn't translate?" she asked Pete.

"He said that you'd made his cock hard and asked if you'd like to sit on his face," Pete answered.

She laughed. What else could she do? "I'm glad you didn't tell me. It would have frightened me away."

"Why did you come with us, Carole?" Pete asked.

What to tell them? The passion she had with Thomas would remain their secret, but she'd shared enough with these two to give them some explanation.

"I'm on a quest of sorts," she said. "I had so little physical expression…oh, hell, sex. I couldn't satisfy myself surrounded by my husband's friends. I settled on voluptuous travel through Europe."

"With no goal at all?" Jean-Paul said. "Only to blindly chose lovers wherever you land?"

"Not exactly that," she answered.

"I think our Carole is keeping a secret," Pete said.

This time, she picked at her clothing for no good reason and let her silence speak for her.

"*Ah bien,* a man," Jean-Paul declared. "I hope he's worthy of you."

"He is."

Pete took her hand. "If he isn't, I'll get a gunslinger to kill him for you."

"I don't think he'll be in Texas."

"You don't know where he is?" Jean-Paul asked.

"I don't." She drank the rest of her brandy and put the glass on the table at her elbow. "That's why it's a quest."

Jean-Paul tsked. "And you find us odd."

"Not odd," she said. "Perhaps...oh, hell...I'm not going to say anything else on the subject."

Pete stroked her fingers. "You're leaving us."

"Tomorrow," she answered.

"But not because we disgust you," Pete said.

"No. I told the truth before. I hope we can be good friends."

That finally got a smile from Pete. "When we go to Texas, you can visit us."

Jean-Paul sighed in a particularly put-upon way. "We'll all become cow pokes."

"Too hot for me," she answered. "You come to New York, instead."

"That's that, then." Jean-Paul rose. "Let's eat our dinner before it cools."

CHAPTER EIGHT

The luxury train rattled past Strasbourg toward the border with Germany. Even with the best rail transportation, the pen jerked on the page as she wrote,

"Darling Thomas,

"When you read this, I will have arrived in Vienna. I've been very clever or very bad, depending on how you look at it. I've dispatched lovers three and four with one adventure. A Frenchman and a Texan, enjoying my favors at the same time. It was quite an experience, and I learned things that, even now, I can't make real enough in my mind to put to paper. I'll tell you all about that when we finally meet.

"I did learn one thing, though. Love is love in all its forms. It gave me faith that our love will bridge any differences between us."

She set aside the book she'd been using as a desk and stared out the window. Countryside not unlike what she'd seen in upstate New York went by, but every village the train encountered proved yet again she'd come far from the United States. Medieval architecture and gingerbread details drew her eye away from her task at hand—a declaration of love to a man she'd never met.

She sighed and rested her head against the glass. Had she gone on a wild goose chase? Any sane person would think so. She'd had sex with three strangers now and had headed off in search of a fourth. Worse, she'd enjoyed every encounter—the orgasm in the semi-public opera box, the first time she'd gone to a man for no reason except that her body wanted him, the night two men had crawled into her bed for no purpose but her pleasure. Could she forgive herself for that?

Of course, she could Thomas had given her permission. No matter how things worked out in the end, she'd owe him gratitude for that. She'd thank him when she finally joined him. For now, she'd find her fifth lover and enjoy him.

She picked up her letter again.

"I've become quite the voluptuary, my darling. My husband's family would never recognize me. I believe this a good thing. As sweet as they all are and as attentive to me as a widow could hope, I must admit I look on them with some alarm. They're so predictable and set in their ways, hardly stepping outside their own homes and circle of friends. Imagine—I had to go to France to meet a Texan.

"If you hadn't come into my life, my dearest Thomas, I would have become just like them, but even sadder with no children or grandchildren of my own.

"No, I'll satisfy myself with the treasures of the flesh. Already, my poor sex feels empty. It pines for your magnificent cock."

She had to pause and smile at that. Pete and Jean-Paul had taught her well. She knew the feel of the male organ now. How it swelled already in a man's pants just from looking at a woman he desired. How it grew harder as she slid her lips along the shaft and sucked the head.

How it turned a deep crimson just before he came. She'd deal well with Thomas's now. Perhaps his cook made chocolate mousse.

"I know I can't have you just yet, but as I find the final lover you've required of me, I'll know that each orgasm—mine and his—brings us closer together."

The conductor approached. "There's a spot for you in the dining car if you'll share a table with a married couple. Very good people, *Fräulein*."

"*Frau*," she corrected. "I'd be happy to share a table. Do they speak English?"

"*Natürlich*." He gestured toward the forward car.

She folded the letter and placed in inside the book then rose. "I'll come."

He led her between the seats until they reached the connection between cars and he turned her over to a waiter. Stepping carefully, she entered the diner. With the table linen, crystal, and heavy silver, the space resembled a fine restaurant. Most of the seats were full, but the motioned her to place across from a middle-aged man and woman. He rose as she approached and pulled out her chair. "I'm Albert Hauf and this is my wife, Greta."

Carole nodded toward his wife. "Frau Hauf."

The pair were both substantial, round and ruddy-checked. Frau Hauf straightened the silver as her husband studied the menu. Carole looked around the car.

The tables had nearly filled, perhaps with strangers sharing as she had. One stood empty as the waiters guided passengers by it.

Frau Hauf leaned over the table toward her. "Do you suppose the rumor's true?"

"I didn't hear the rumor," she answered.

"An extra car was added in Paris," Frau Hauf. "A private car."

"Now, *liebling*, it's not our business who may travel with us," her husband said.

"One has to be curious," Frau Hauf said.

Carole picked up her own menu. "Would you order for me, Herr Hauf?"

"Of course." He gave her a bow, small but smart. When the waiter arrived, Herr Hauf rattled off some German, and the man went away again.

Frau Hauf stared openly at the car ahead of them. "There was some talk among the Parisians at the station."

"About our mystery passenger?" Carole asked.

"You know how the French are. I could hardly get the story for all of their exaggerations." Frau Hauf glanced toward the door and then toward Carole. "But it seems our guest is Klaus Waldberg, the artist."

"Greta, *bitte*." Herr Hauf followed that with rapid German she'd never decipher. Frau Hauf stood up for herself, firing back as quickly as her husband. While they debated, the door to the private car opened, and a waiter entered followed by a tall man dressed just as formally as Herr Hauf but more expensive in cut and materials. The whole room hushed as he went by, his golden head held high as if he didn't care to acknowledge the rest of humanity around him.

When he sat, she had a better view of his face framed by the shocking gold-silver of his hair. That, itself, belied any Teutonic ideal of austerity. Long and wild, it curled around his collar. Beneath his tall forehead, his eyes flashed in an almost unnatural blue.

"It is Waldberg," Frau Hauf whispered.

"Who is he?" Carole asked.

"An artist. Very scandalous," the other woman said. Her husband cleared his throat in obvious disapproval.

"Even the French were shocked," Frau Hauf added.

As the waiter delivered their food, Carole took the diversion to study Herr Waldberg a bit more. Although compelling, his face would never meet a definition of pretty or even handsome. His nose was curved like a beak, and his eyes had a hard glint to them with no sign of laugh lines at the corners. He caught her staring, and his lips curled into a smile that held a bit of cruelty at the corners.

When Carole turned back, the Haufs had taken up their silverware in preparation to eat. She did the same and sliced off a bit of the cutlet on her plate.

"He was in Paris for an exhibition and shocked everyone who saw it," Frau Hauf said as she cut through her own veal.

Beside her, Herr Hauf chewed his meal and then brought his napkin to the corner of his mouth. He very pointedly didn't join in on the conversation.

"Most people are used to nudes in art," Carole said. "What could be so shocking?"

"Not the bodies themselves…" Frau Hauf blushed, her round cheeks turning a violent pink.

Herr Hauf set his fork aside. "Since my wife has brought the subject up, I'll only say the poses and subject matter were highly indecent."

"Erotic," Frau Hauf added softly.

"So we're told. We didn't see them." Herr Hauf gave his wife a stare that forbad further comment.

"Oh, dear." Frau Hauf put her fingers over her mouth and giggled.

"What is it?" Carole asked.

"Don't look, my dear!" the other woman said.

"Don't look at what?" Why had she bothered to ask? Klaus Waldberg would be the answer. What else?

"I do believe he's sketching you."

"Really?" Despite Frau Hauf's warning, Carole glanced over her shoulder at the scandalous artists. He held a pencil in his hand and made quick strokes over the back of his menu. He met her gaze and gave her the same unsettling smile before going back to his work.

She turned back to her companions. "I don't know why he'd want me as a subject."

"You don't know him?" Herr Hauf asked.

"I'd never heard of him until a moment ago." She didn't have to explain herself to this stranger, but in this particular case, she was innocent.

Herr Hauf cleared his throat again, and the three of them ate without speaking. The back of her neck prickled the whole time, as if her skin sensed the attention of Waldberg several tables away. An artist, creator of erotic works. The most logical choice for her fifth lover, if indeed, he had any interest in her.

After a while, the dining car fell silent again, and the prickles at the back of her neck zipped over her skin. Frau Hauf looked down at her plate as footsteps approached and then stopped at their table.

Klaus Waldberg stood there in his golden bird-of-prey glory. He bowed, clicking his heels together softly, as he placed something on the table beside her. The menu he'd used for a sketching pad. As she picked it up, he went on toward his own car and disappeared inside it.

The drawing was nothing out of the ordinary, just a pencil sketch of a woman, neither erotic nor romantic. An honest appraisal of her own face but with her hair floating around it as if in a breeze. Without thinking, she reached up to the French knot she'd fixed with pins and found them all in place. He'd added that part out of whimsy.

"I'd say he thinks he knows you," Frau Hauf said.

"I don't know why." She turned the menu over. At the bottom, he'd written in a sparse hand. "Join me in my car."

"Well." She slipped the menu into her book, taking care not to smudge the pencil marks. "It's been a pleasure to meet you."

Before they could ask any questions, Carole stood, picked her book from the table, and headed toward Waldberg's car. The Haufs would know where she was going. The whole car would. Let them.

When she got to the door, a conductor opened it for her, and she stepped over the threshold. Waldberg stood at a silver coffee service on a sideboard at one side of the lavish space. He'd shed his jacket and tie, and his shirt hung loosely from his shoulders to the waistband of his pants. Now, she could appraise his body, and it was magnificent. Tall and long-limbed, he'd make an impression anywhere. His trousers fit more snugly than most men's, showing off narrow hips and finely muscled thighs.

He turned, a small cup in his hand. "*Kafee*?"

"*Bitte*."

"*Mit Schlag*?

She had to search her memory for the meaning. Ah yes, whipped cream. "Yes, thank you."

He scooped some *Schlag* from a silver bowl into her coffee and handed it to her. After setting her book on the sideboard, she took the cup from him. Waldberg watched as she took a sip and licked some cream from her upper lip.

"*Gut*," he declared. "You will sit, please."

After retrieving her book, she went to an upholstered arm chair and settled onto it. He picked up his own cup, sans *Schlag*, and took a matching seat close enough to her that, when he crossed his legs, his foot grazed her skirt.

"I saw you board the train," he said in precise but clipped English.

"I didn't see you," she answered. "I would have remembered."

"Save your breath. I'm used to flattery."

Was that meant to be direct or simply rude? She nearly choked on her coffee. "I beg your pardon."

"In fact, I dislike flattery intensely."

"I only meant that you cut an unusual figure," she said. "You're tall and very blond."

He quirked an eyebrow. "You honestly weren't trying to win my favor?"

"I didn't sit in a crowded dining car sketching you," she said. "I didn't invite you to my private car."

"Why did you come? Surely, the people you were with told you how I am."

"Perhaps I should have stayed with them." She got up, clutching her book, and set her cup on the sideboard. "Thank you for the sketch. I'm sure it'll be very valuable some day."

"Stop acting like a prig and sit down," he answered.

"I beg your pardon," she repeated.

He gestured toward her chair. "Please."

She still hesitated. Given his domineering nature, she ought to go back to her own car and ignore him the rest of the trip. Still, he not only enjoyed eroticism in art but created it, if the Haufs were to be believed. Despite his hooked nose, or perhaps because of it, he did have a commanding appearance. His body, certainly, offered firm expanses for a lover's hands to explore. If he had any decent cock at all, he'd provide quite an adventure in bed.

His eyes widened briefly as though he'd read her thoughts. Perhaps he had noticed her gaze wandering over his long limbs.

"Forgive me," he said softly. "A person in my position grows used to people fawning over him. It twists one's perceptions."

"I wasn't fawning," she said. "But I might have been admiring."

He laughed. "Honesty. How refreshing. Please sit down again."

She did, still holding her book. He could see the sketch, of course, because he'd done it. But she wouldn't let him read her letter to Thomas. "You must have admired me a bit to do my portrait, even in pencil."

He set his coffee on a table nearby and lounged back enough for the toe of his shoe to tap her leg through her skirt. "You intrigued me. For one thing, two men saw you off."

"They're friends."

"You looked…um, wistful…as if it hurt you to leave them."

"Parting's hard when you don't know when you'll meet again," she said.

"You kissed them both on the cheek."

"Friends do that," she said. "At least Americans do."

"Then why are you blushing?"

Her skin had warmed, starting at her cheeks and going downward. Still, she didn't owe this man an explanation, so she simply gazed back at him as evenly as she could manage. "The two men—Pete and Jean-Paul—are friends."

He put his hands on the arms of his hair, his fists gripping the ends. "Fine. We needn't tell each other everything. I have secrets of my own."

"I don't know why you'd expect me to tell you anything at all. I only met you ten minutes ago."

He sat almost totally still, as if he'd turned into a Germanic demigod. Wotan contemplating Valhalla and the strange liaisons that had gotten him there. His silence, the austerity of his face, set her heart to racing badly enough that her hands might tremble if she reached out to touch him. But why would she do that? Just to feel the firmness and strength of his body?

"You'll sit for me," he said finally.

"For a painting?"

"You object?"

"I…" How strange. She'd surrendered her body to three men now. She'd gone away with Pete and Jean-Paul the same day she'd met them. The mere idea of posing for this man sent a thrill of fear through her. And a thrill of excitement that reached all the way to her pussy. And her pearl, which now hardened, becoming sensitive to even the rhythm of her breathing.

"Those people told you about my art," he said.

"They called it scandalous, enough to shock Paris."

He barked a laugh. "That took some effort, but I managed."

"You can see why that would make me hesitant to sit for you."

Now, he brought his hands up, steepling his fingers in front of his chest.

"More drew me to you than your 'friendship' with those two men." He put an ironic emphasis on friendship. "There's an air of contradiction about you that could make you my Mona Lisa."

"Mona Lisa?" She couldn't help but laugh at that idea.

"You're an unusual combination of innocence and depravity," he said.

"Depravity?"

He made a tiny bow in the chair. "I used the wrong word, I think."

"Depravity," she repeated.

"You were dressed respectably, with your hair tied up in that impenetrable knot, but your mouth lingered on both men's cheeks, and your fingers dug into the tall one's jacket."

153

Oh, dear. Had they really?

"You followed the two of them with a hungry look just before you boarded the train," he said. "I want that expression in my art."

"That's very flattering, Herr Waldberg."

His expression turned stony again. "You're about to give me a weak excuse for refusing."

"I don't want my face in art scandalous enough to shock Paris."

"I see." He rubbed his chin. "What if I used your face in paintings like the sketch I gave you and reserved your body for more…evocative…works?"

"Do you think my body's good enough?"

His gaze roamed over her from top to bottom, lingering on the more intimate places. Even through her clothing, she could feel him, and her sex responded by clenching.

"You're good enough," he said.

"I've never posed nude."

"Fine." He threw his hands into the air. "I can't make you do it."

But he could make her want to, and he had. Imagine, sitting unclothed while he looked from her to the canvas and back. Hours at a time. He might become aroused. Erect. They might couple, and she'd feel his strength and steel against her body and inside it. He'd become her fifth lover. He could even paint an erotic portrait of her that she could take to Thomas. She'd pay him for it, so the rest of the world would never see it.

Even if she didn't have an affair with him, such a painting would make a wonderful gift for her ultimate lover.

"Under those conditions, I'd be happy to sit for you," she said. "And honored."

"*Gut.* Return to your own compartment," he said. "My people will collect you when we arrive in Vienna."

*

The main entryway to Schloss Reinhof stood back from the crowded street. A wall shut off the small courtyard that led to the ornate wooden door. The splashing water of a fountain played an accompaniment to the echoing of her footsteps as she crossed the space and climbed the steps to the main entrance.

Before she could knock, the door opened and a servant in satin knee breaches and powdered wig bent in a bow. She might have returned to a previous century when Mozart roamed the streets.

The servant ushered her inside a grand foyer of gleaning marble and tile. All very magical and charming—and lavish—unless you noticed the statuary. Small pieces all, but with prominent erections, except for the ones that were no more than phallus in their entirety. Oh well, she'd known what to expect.

She followed the servant up a curving staircase to the floor above and then down a corridor lined with thick oriental carpeting. Here and there, small tables held vases of flowers and more sculpture similar to what she'd seen below. Finally, the man opened a door and gestured for her to go inside.

Truly, a princess could occupy such a room. Hardwood floors with more carpets here and there. A large bed with four posts holding up a canopy of lace. A small fireplace had logs already laid out inside. Over the mantle hung a painting of...oh dear lord...not something she'd stare at while a male servant was still in the room.

"A full water closet," the man said from behind her.

"Thank you." She turned her back on the painting.

The man seemed not to notice but stood very formally beside a door he'd opened. "With a bath."

"That sounds wonderful."

"I'll leave you, then. Ring if you require anything." He exited, pulling the door to the corridor closed behind him.

Heaving a sigh of relief, she turned to study the picture. Asian, by the look of it, although she lacked the knowledge to tell if the ideographs along the side were Chinese or Japanese. It depicted a couple in the process of having sexual intercourse. The woman lay in her back, her legs parted, and her lover's member was posed to enter her. but oh, what a cock. As thick as a woman's forearm and nearly as long. Far too big to fit inside a woman's body, and yet this woman seemed happy—no impatient—to take it.

To think…she'd have to look at that when she blew out her candle every night and again in the morning when she opened her eyes. The thing didn't frighten her, if she was truly honest with herself. The possibility fascinated her. If she could take the image into her dreams, she might experience a sexual delight impossible in the real world.

After removing her hat and gloves, she went to the mantle and stared up at the picture. The huge tool seemed alive and poised to enter his lover's waiting sex. Very carefully and lightly, she traced the outline of the cock with a fingertip. Doing her best to memorize the dimensions for a dream.

It would seem she'd found a refuge to experiment. A sensual world hidden from the city's bustle by the wall outside. The inside might well serve as a temple to the phallus. Or perhaps even better…a retreat for worshipers to pay homage to that organ. She'd study here for a while before heading to her ultimate destination. Tomorrow, she'd write to Thomas to tell him she'd found her fifth lover and she awaited instructions on how to come to her sixth, and most desired, lover. In the meantime, she'd sample the pleasures of her bath.

Removing her clothing took some time with all the hooks and buttons. Finally, she'd laid her dress and small clothes on the bed and left her shoes and stockings at the side. Now naked, she studied herself again, running her hands over her breasts, past her ribs, to her belly. So, Waldberg wanted to paint her nude, did he? He might not have realized he was talking about a forty year old woman with the firm skin and blush of youth behind her. If he changed his mind, she'd leave without knowing him and find her fifth liaison somewhere else, even though it would be a shame to miss the opportunities to learn what this man could teach her.

The bath beckoned. Even a luxurious a way to travel offered few opportunities to clean thoroughly. She went to the water closet, as the servant had called it, and found fixtures that fit the small room, including a tub with hot and cold water spigots and soaps and a sponge on a shelf within reach.

The water came out hot enough to create a cloud of mist in the cool air of the room. She climbed in and let it wash over her legs and hips. The soap lathered on the sponge, and soon she'd washed herself clean and leaned back to enjoy the soak.

Closing her eyes, she let her mind wander back to Provence—to the smell of flowers and the warm night air as Jean-Paul had nipped at her shoulder and then slid his cock up into her. Then she pictured the Asian painting, only now, she took the place of the woman lying on her back with her legs parted. Without thinking, she closed a hand over her breast and squeezed, savoring the hardening of her nipple against her palm. She'd become so responsive now, just a touch starting the slow ache in her pussy.

"So, how do you like the *shunga*, Frau Rose?"

She opened her eyes and sat straight up in the tub. Waldberg lounged against the doorjamb, his arms crossed over his near-naked chest.

"How did you get in here without me hearing you?" she asked.

He shrugged. "I live here."

"but so silently…"

"Think of me as a cat," he answered.

Except for the gleam of cunning in his eyes, he bore no resemblance to a cat, and certainly not a domesticated one. A blinding white shirt of some soft material fell from his shoulders and hung low around him, the hem brushing against his thighs. Though buttoned from the waist down, it hung open over his chest, giving her a view of skin unmarred by a single hair.

When he shifted position, the shirt flowed around him, hiding his lower body. Clever man. He'd managed to appear casual while covering his crotch so she couldn't see if he'd had any reaction to her nakedness.

"The *shunga*," he said.

"I'm sorry. I don't know what that means."

"The artwork." He gestured with his head toward the bedroom. "Over the hearth."

"The Asian painting."

"Exactly." His gaze wandered over her body, daring her to cover herself.

To hell with that. She wouldn't show him any fear. She settled her arms next to her, pointedly allowing him to look any place he wanted.

"The *shunga's* rather unusual," she said. "Do you suppose Asian men are really built like that?"

"All men think of themselves that way. When the male member is hard and eager, nothing else in the world matches it in importance."

She stared right back at him, assessing him with her gaze, pausing at the cloth covering his crotch.

"You try to see if I'm excited," he said.

"It's a natural thing to wonder about."

"You're the subject here, not I."

"You only plan to paint me?" she asked. "Nothing else?"

"This is tiresome," he declared. "Put your hand between your legs and touch yourself."

She coughed and then sputtered. "I beg your pardon."

He straightened. "That's the third time you've said that. Twice on the train and now again."

"You counted?"

"I don't like it." His eyes widened in what looked like outrage. "Don't say it again."

Her mouth fell open, so she shut it and sat, gaping at him. He seemed honestly and truly angry. Worse, the tension of his body suggested he might act on that anger. She should have felt fear, and she did to a certain extent. But the fear came laced with something else—excitement, even desire. What power might his passion release?

He obviously had gauged her response to him and approved, because he smiled and rested his shoulder against the doorjamb again. "You understand."

Understand what? Something had just happened between them, but if she asked what, he'd show her that anger again.

"Now, then," he said. "Put your hands between your legs and touch yourself."

She did it, almost automatically obeying his command. When she brushed her pearl, a shock of arousal made her gasp and shudder with its power.

"You see?" he said. "You wanted to. You can't really defy me, you know."

She wouldn't dispute him. At least, not now. Right this moment, her mind went blank of everything except the pressure of her finger on her bud.

She shouldn't get such pleasure from this. A barked order shouldn't have possessed her to the point where she'd perform so intimately for a stranger. She ought to feel humiliated, not aroused. So, why couldn't she move her hand nor slow her finger? Why did she press harder and make circles over her pearl? Why did she tremble and gasp for breath?

"Make yourself come," he said. "I want to see your expression."

She would come, and soon. She wouldn't give him any warning, though. That much power she could keep for herself.

Though she tried to swallow her cries or rising excitement, they came out as soft grunts. Her hand moved on its own now, and a good thing, as her brain had stopped working. The world disappeared as the looming cloud of near-orgasm closed around her. She kept pushing herself higher. Pushing, pushing until she broke free. She shouted as the spasms rocked her. Water sloshed around her while she finished herself. A few more strokes and it passed. At last, she fell limp against the porcelain and sighed with satisfaction.

So forbidden to act this way while a stranger watched. And yet, his command had freed her of responsibility and made the forbidden sweet. She'd thank him when she found her voice.

She lay with warm water lapping at her skin for several moments and then opened her eyes.

He was gone. The threshold was empty, as if he'd never stood there at all.

CHAPTER NINE

Waldberg's studio occupied a large space on the top level of the *Schloss*. He would have had the skylights installed as no buildings had them at the time of the original construction. She stood just inside the room where the liveried servant had left her and watched as he mixed paints and dabbed them on his artist's palette.

He moved with all the certainty of a master—even more commanding than he'd been in her bathroom the evening before. She wouldn't disturb him. He'd had her summoned and must have heard her and his servant enter. Odd, she'd never shown so much deference to anyone. Not even her husband.

"You will take that chair, please," he said without even turning to look at her.

"Take it?"

"Sit in it." He pointed to an armchair a few feet in front of his easel.

"Of course." She walked to the chair and lowered herself onto the velvet seat cushion.

He picked up a pencil and began to sketch on the canvas with confidence strokes. "You enjoyed your dinner, I hope."

"It was delicious." The tray he'd sent up had held a wonderful dish of stewed meat over noodles. Fragrant with paprika and enriched with sour cream, it had surprised her taste buds.

"We'll become more acquainted as we go on." He glanced at her briefly and then went back to sketching. "Or not."

"May I ask you something?"

"Hold still," he snapped. "I can't capture your likeness with you flailing about like that."

"I wasn't failing."

"Then, hold still." He turned his attention back to the canvas.

Of course, now that he'd told her not to move, her every muscle wanted to do exactly that. She had to breathe deeply and consciously make herself relax, one part of her body at a time. Eventually, she settled into her pose. Now, his movements—glancing at her and then sketching on the canvas—took on a soothing rhythm, further easing her.

"What did you want?" he asked.

"I'm sorry…"

"You wanted to ask something."

She had. But what? "I don't remember."

"*Gut*. I'll ask the questions." He set aside his pencil and stood for a moment, studying her. "What made you as you are?"

"I'm afraid you'll more specific than that."

"You sit there very primly, and yet, you defiled yourself last night at my request," he said.

That brought her head up, whether he liked it or not. "That isn't defiling myself, and you commanded me to do it."

His eyebrow quirked. "I can command you?"

"Well, you did." That was a lie. She wouldn't have done it if she hadn't wanted to.

"Interesting," he said.

He stood there like a sphinx. Unreadable. Odd how he could make her feel more uncomfortable fully clothed than he had when she was naked.

"Were you disgusted by what I did?" *Do we disgust you?* What Jean-Paul had asked her when she'd interrupted him and Pete. Imagine. Having to live with the fear of judgment all the time. Thank heaven she'd given him the right answer.

"The look on your face was like a glimpse of paradise," he said. "I'll paint it for you."

"I can't maintain that expression for hours."

He tapped his forehead. "I have it all here."

He went back to painting, and she sat, more or less relaxed as a few minutes went by. Sun streaming in from the skylight warmed her shoulders, and a clock chimed in the distance. Cooking smells wafted up from the floors below, reminding her she hadn't eaten anything except a pastry since the night before. It had appeared on a tray with coffee much the way her dinner had arrived. Quietly, efficiently, and with the minimum of human interaction.

"So, you're an innocent," Waldberg said after a while.

"I was married. My husband died."

"Did the two of you ever experiment with...how shall I say?...exotic practices?"

"Certainly not."

"But you have since," he said. "On your own."

"I wouldn't call anything I've done exotic." An orgasm at Covent Garden, licking chocolate mousse from a man's member, a threesome in her bed. Maybe she should revise that answer.

He gave her a penetrating stare as if he'd read her mind. "Your two friends."

"I didn't do anything unnatural with them."

"They did with each other, didn't they?" he said.

Damn it. Pete and Jean-Paul's love was natural for them. "That's their business."

He smiled. "I see."

"How dare you judge? You don't even know them."

"Watch your tone." The flash of anger returned to his features. He turned so easily from conversation to fury. Or perhaps not fury. More like command or possession. Issuing orders the way you might to a child or a dog. As illogical as it might seem, his display worked on her as it had the evening before. She instantly fell silent. Not even her husband could have commanded her so easily.

He smiled again, clearly realizing his victory. "I don't judge. You said unnatural. My word was exotic."

"You're right."

He continued with his work, dabbing his brush in paint and then applying it to the canvas with confident strokes. "So, you're innocent of anything unnatural, and yet you have the smile and the walk of a woman who's been well...what is that word you Americans use?"

"Fucked."

"Ah, yes. Fucked."

"You can tell that from a woman's walk?" she said. By now, she shouldn't have been surprised. Jean-Paul had said the same thing.

"Virgins and prudes mince. They hold their legs together as if any man they meet might fall on them consumed with lust," he answered.

"I gather I don't do that."

"You walk as though you wore nothing under your skirts and your sex was already wet."

"Really?" She didn't walk like that at all. He had to be saying it to get a reaction from her. He succeeded, as her skin burned hot with embarrassment from her cheeks all the way down her neck.

"And you smile as though your lips have just lingered on a thick cock," he said. "You have taken a man's sex into your mouth, haven't you?"

She waited before she answered. He was trying to shock her, obviously, as if that might win him something. He couldn't unless she let him.

"I licked his dessert off his erection," she answered.

His brow rose again. "What else have you done?"

"I brought a man to orgasm in my box at the opera, and I allowed him to do the same to me."

He chuckled. "Mozart?"

"Verdi," she answered. "I took two men to my bed at once. I spent days letting them both pleasure me."

"Were all these men strangers?" His eyes widened as he stared at her. "Like me."

"They were."

"So, you've sucked and fucked your way across Europe," he said.

"I wouldn't put it that coarsely."

"There, you see?" he said. "That's the contradiction of you. Madonna and profligate."

"And what you wanted to paint."

"Exactly." He set his palette and brush aside. "Let me show you something."

She rose and rolled her head to get a kink out of her neck. After leading her to the other end of the studio, he opened a small door and made room for her to look into the next room.

"I encourage my people to use this space to give me ideas," he whispered.

And indeed, it was in use. A young woman was bent over a table, her legs spread. A servant she hadn't seen before stood behind her, his pants unbuttoned and his erect member sliding in and out of her pussy. The woman had closed her eyes in bliss, and the man stared unseeing at the opposite wall as his buttocks worked to thrust rhythmically. They both would have heard Waldberg speak, even so softly. The obviously knew they were being watched and didn't care.

This room had its own skylight, making every detail of their coupling visible. The rosy flush of excitement on the woman's face, how her knuckles had gone white with the effort to hold onto the table's edge, the slickness of her juices as they coated the man's shaft.

"Not very imaginative today," Waldberg whispered. "But satisfying."

So, fucking looked like this. The man shifted slightly, giving them a better view of how the woman's pussy gripped at him as he continued plowing into her.

She couldn't have looked away, even in Waldberg had ordered it in his most commanding tone. Each passage of the man's rod into his lover's chamber felt like a stab into her own. The woman's rising cries resonated in her own chest, making her nipples harden against her corset cover. She'd had Pete's cock inside her only a few days before, but now, her pussy demanded more. It demanded exactly what this woman was enjoying. Bending over, spreading her legs wide, and submitting to the demands of an erect cock.

Both of them breathed in ragged gasps as his hips moved faster. They were approaching the peak, and the woman pressed backward in a silent plea for more.

As his thrusts got faster and deeper, the woman responded with a loud cry and an arch of her back that pressed her even more firmly against him.

"*Gott, Gott,*" she shouted as she came, her body shaking with the force of her orgasm.

He kept thrusting as she finished and then pulled his sex from inside her. Gripping it tightly, he pumped until the flesh turned crimson and semen shot from the head to land on her naked buttocks. He grunted with each spurt and then took a shuddering breath when he finished. Sighing happily, the woman reached to her ass and smoothed his pearly liquid into her skin.

Waldberg silently closed the door. "Did you enjoy that?"

She ought to deny it, but he'd no doubt detect a blush on her cheeks. "I did."

"*Gut.*"

"I remember my question now."

"Speak."

"Did you invite me here to pose and nothing else?"

Hi lifted his smock to show her the front of his pants. "See my staff."

Sure enough, he was hard, and the outline of his erection showed plainly against the fabric of his pants. Not particularly long, but thick.

"You'll feel it eventually," he said. "If you find the right way to tempt me."

*

The very servant she'd watched copulating earlier in the morning appeared to serve the midday meal as if he found nothing unusual at all about setting plates of food before the people who'd watched his cock erupt in orgasm only hours before. Carole's cheeks flamed every time he approached her place at the table. Partly out of embarrassment and to be honest, partly out of fascination with the image of his swollen flesh penetrating the woman's folds.

At the end of the meal, he poured coffee into tiny cups and then set an elaborate confection of chocolate and cream in front of her. When he'd left, she stared at the dessert and then pushed it away. "I'm sorry. It looks delicious, but I couldn't eat another bite."

"The Viennese diet is rather rich," Waldberg answered.

"I thought that supper last night was the big meal of the day."

"You managed the rabbit and the dumplings," he said. "So, you may be excused."

"I don't want to insult your cook."

"Don't worry. She bought them somewhere, I'm sure." He set his napkin aside and rose. "Would you like to see my work?"

"Oh, yes." Before she could she could push her chair back, he'd moved behind her to pull it out. All very courteous and proper. He didn't even let his fingers make contact with her shoulder.

"The paintings from the Paris exhibition came back in my private car," he said. "They've been rehung in my gallery."

"I'd love to see what shocked the jaded Parisians."

He gestured. "This way."

He led her into a very real gallery, indeed. It must have been the Schloss's original dining hall. Long in comparison to its width, the room featured soaring walls and a huge hearth on one side. Clean of all ash, it hadn't seen a fire in years. And no wonder. Any smoke would have damaged the dozens of paintings that lined the walls.

Between the lack of heat and the tall ceiling and stone walls, the space held a chill. She hugged herself for warmth, but Waldberg walked along as though noticing nothing but the artwork.

"Not all of this is my work," he said. "But I own everything here."

She stopped in front of a large canvas depicting several red-haired nymphs seducing a man into their river. Their expressions seemed innocent enough, but their bare breasts and the obvious invitation on their faces had clearly destroyed their captive's will to resist.

He would follow them into the river and wouldn't emerge again.

"Women always go right to that one," Waldberg said from so close behind her his breath warmed her shoulders.

"The colors, I imagine," she answered softly. "The use of light."

"Nonsense. Women enjoy witnessing their sexual power over men."

"It seems to me the men hold all the power in this world."

"In most things, we do, but not in this." He bent so that the side of his head rested against her cheek. "See how she saps his will with her pleas. 'My lips need yours. I'm empty without you. Come to me, or I perish.'"

"You think she's telling him that?"

"Or worse. They could demand his soul, and he'd give it to them." He said it in a deep, soft voice that had ice beneath. Despite the heat of his body behind her, she trembled.

"His life, maybe," she said. "Surely, not his soul."

"Women know they have treasure between their legs and that men will surrender anything to have it."

"What nonsense." She forced herself to turn, even though the movement brought her flush against his chest. His eyes widened in surprise, and he took a step back.

"It's my experience that men take what they want," she said. "If they can't get it from one woman, they'll find another."

"Perhaps you're right." He linked her arm with his and guided her past several smaller paintings. More *shunga*. He owned quite a bit of it. After a few of those, they came up to a European version. A plump woman reclining on a couch, readying herself to take her lover's huge phallus into her sex. Slender and tall, with unruly blond hair, the figure might have been a portrait of Waldberg. No, a self-portrait, according to the signature.

"It's you," she said.

"An impression of me."

She'd seen the outline of his member. It wasn't anything like that size. "Do all men think they're that large?"

"It represents the greatness of his need, not a literal size."

Unlike in the Asian version of shunga, the female subject showed mixed emotions. Awe at the size of her lover's tool but also no little bit of fear. And when she studied the man again, she found the cruel tilt to his smile. The whole effect was rather chilling.

He didn't say anything about her hesitation at that picture but guided her farther along the line of paintings.

At the next canvas, she couldn't hold back a gasp. This one showed a man and woman in the act of coupling. The man's face disappeared at the top. Only his torso showed, his hips firmly between the woman's legs. Leather ties bound her so tightly her flesh bulged around it, especially at her breasts. Her face featured prominently, and it made a perfect picture of bliss. She'd been trussed tightly enough to cause real pain, and it had added to her rapture.

"Now you see the dark side of my art," he said.

"It's very powerful."

"Admit it. You disapprove."

"It's only a painting." She stared up at him. "Isn't it?"

He didn't answer. He didn't have to. She'd asked a stupid question. Only a painting. He had to have painted it from life to get so much realism into it. Even if he hadn't drawn the couple in the act of coitus, he'd had a female model tied up like that.

Maybe he'd "discovered" this exact event in progress in the small room off his studio.

"The French pretended enough sophistication to enjoy this canvas," he said. "It was another that offended their sensibilities."

Of course, he'd show that one to her. He'd contrived the whole exercise—ever since she'd arrived, each detail right down to the *shunga* in her bedroom—to see how much she'd tolerate before she cried "enough." Somehow, she'd sensed that from the first, and she'd responded without thinking. She'd accepted his challenge. Now she challenged herself. She could leave and find a safer man, or she could stay and discover a darker side of sexual expression.

"This way," he said, as if he'd read her mind.

The canvas was huge and the figures larger than life. A demon of some sort, plunging himself into a human female from behind. The view from their tower room showed a cityscape in the distance.

Disturbing as the subject was, it caught the eye and held it. The creature's mask of fury, his claws that covered his paramour's breasts, the bright red where he'd drawn blood. The woman, though, showed no sign of fear or disgust. Instead, her expression told of complete rapture. Maybe Waldberg had ordered another woman to bring herself to climax while he watched and used her as a subject. This one clearly had reached her peak, her eyes tightly shut, her head thrown back, her mouth open in a shout of completion. The memory of her own climax washed through her, leaving her breathless and aching.

"What do you think?" Waldberg asked.

"It's compelling. Real. Almost overpowering."

"It wasn't the sex that aroused their ire but the title," he said.

"The title?"

"It's called it Notre Dame at Midnight."

The significance didn't register at first. The great cathedral. The male was a gargoyle, not a demon. The cityscape showed the streets of Paris. And…oh, dear Lord…the pile of clothing beside the woman—all black with a scrap of white—a habit. The woman was a nun.

"You showed a nun copulating with a gargoyle," she said.

"At the very top of their beloved church," he said. "I don't think I'll be invited back."

She turned to him. "But why?"

He shrugged. "Because I could."

"No, there's more than that."

"How perceptive of you Frau Rose," he said. "Perhaps you'll understand before you leave."

*

"My dearest Thomas,

"I write now to tell you of my last destination on the strange journey that brings me to you. I'm in Vienna, staying a *Schloss*. The moment you receive this, immediately send word back on how I can find you. By that time, I will have met your last requirement—to know my fifth lover. This latest man is a bit of an odd fellow with some interesting tastes in the physical—not all of them anything I would have considered at all. I feel, or perhaps even fear that he'll broadened my horizons as a voluptuary before I leave here. I think he can teach me things the others didn't, and if I can learn how to please you in some way I hadn't imagined before, the lesson will have served me well.

"Now that I'm so close to the most desired moment of my life—the instant when I can first rest my gaze on your beloved face—my body sings with anticipation. These other men have only whetted my considerable appetite for you. How I long to cast aside the pale imitations of passion I've experienced since embarking on this insane adventure and find true fulfillment in your embrace. I think when this last man brings me to climax, I'll imagine that you've done it. I'll picture his shout at climax as coming from your throat, the last few powerful thrusts to be your glorious cock plunging deeply into me. When I release my own lust, I'll imagine that it's your sex filling me.

"Send for me soon, my own dearest heart, I can't wait much longer."

*

Carole hadn't thought at all before accompanying Waldberg to his home. She hadn't exercised any more care with her other lovers, either. Thank heaven, this man would be the last lover before she could finally join Thomas.

Now, she found herself naked with her latest dalliance, and he hadn't touched her. She'd lived in his home for days, and aside from that one exposure of his hardened cock in his pants, he hadn't shown any sign of desire at all. He seemed only interested in making her vulnerable to his gaze and giving nothing of himself.

"You will sell me this painting when it's done, I hope," she said.

He stopped in the process of dabbing paint onto the canvas in front of him. "Afraid of who might see it?"

"I don't want anyone to see it." Except for Thomas. She'd present it as a gift once Waldberg had finished and shipped it. Heaven forbid she'd have to stay here until he'd completed work. She'd have to convince him to make love to her before then so she could leave. He'd said he wanted to, hadn't he?

No, he'd only promised she'd feel his staff.

He put his palette on the table hard enough that the pots of oils rattled. "What is it now?"

"Nothing."

"Then, why did you move?"

"I'm sorry. I can't lie perfectly still for hours."

"My usual models can," he said.

"Then, maybe you should get one of them." She shook out her arms and rolled her shoulders. If he wanted to play the put-upon, she would, too. Besides, the cramp in her neck did hurt.

He cursed a bit in German. At least, it sounded like cursing. His scowl fitted profanity. After a moment, he pinched the bridge of his nose. "Frau Rose..."

"Why do you call me by my last name?"

"We're more formal here than in your country," he said.

"For the love of God, I'm naked," she said. "You've watched me masturbate."

"All for art."

"What utter nonsense." She got up, found her robe, and slipped into it. The floorboards chilled her feet as she crossed the huge room and stared out the window. Outside, a storybook setting held real life of carriages and people going here and there. Here, behind the castle walls, she'd isolated herself with a man she couldn't read. He didn't seem the least bit interested in her as a sexual creature aside from how he could portray her in his art.

"If you're through with your tantrum, would you care to return to your position?" he said from behind her.

She hugged herself for warmth. "I'm not in the mood."

He sighed loudly. "What would put you in the mood, madam?"

She turned and studied him for a moment. So cool, self-contained. So sure of himself. No wonder he made her furious. "You want me to play some combination of madonna and whore, no?"

"I wouldn't say it exactly that way."

"But you want me to somehow look sexual and innocent at the same time," she said.

"That's what attracted me to you," he said. "I was quite overtaken by your contradictions."

She went back to the couch and sat down. If she'd been wearing petticoats, an onlooker might have said she'd flounced. "I don't feel sexual."

"As you pointed out, you're naked," he said. "Or nearly so."

"Have you ever done this?"

"I'll admit I haven't."

"Trust me. It isn't sexy at all."

He crossed his arms over his chest and glowered at her. "What, pray tell, would make you feel sexy?"

"A story." Yes, that was it. Turn the whole thing back on him. "A story out of your own sexual history."

His eyes widened in what looked like pure disapproval. For a moment, he resembled a teacher...or a minister...who'd caught a child doing something very naughty. She could have laughed.

"Now, who's the prude?" she said.

"I don't see why I should have to reveal anything to you."

"You don't?" she said. "You expect so much from me."

"I expect you to pose."

"I'm not a professional. Find someone else."

"Very well. I'll do as you ask." His eyes fairly shot sparks of anger, and his fair cheeks turned a livid pink. He made an impressive figure standing there so tall and blond and obviously displeased. "Remove your robe and take your position."

She obeyed, draping herself over the cushions in the pose he'd arranged earlier—lying back with her hand covering her mound. After a loud huff, he picked up his palette and brush. "I'll tell you how I lost my virginity."

"I'm sure it's more interesting than how I lost mine."

"No doubt." He gave her another glare and then resumed his painting. "I was little more than a child in my mind, but my body had matured. Some older girls trapped me in the hayloft over my father's barn."

"How old were you?"

"Fourteen," he answered.

"That is a child."

"I was quite tall for my age. They no doubt thought me older."

"And you say they trapped you?"

"Please, hold still," he said.

"I'm sorry."

He painted a bit more—angry strokes that could hardly appear sensual on the canvass. Still, he was the artist.

"There were four of them. One said she'd seen her father's stallion cover a mare and asked her mother if men were built that way. The mother had refused to answer, so they decided to find out with me."

He hesitated for a moment. No doubt no one asked the great Klaus Waldberg embarrassing questions and he'd never had to face telling such a story. Still, she hadn't asked about his virginity, and he could have chosen some other incident.

"I'd been getting erections for some time, as all boys do, but when they held me down and pulled off my pants, my penis failed to impress them."

"They held you down?"

"Don't move!" he shouted.

Damn. She'd asked for this, and now, she'd have to do her best to hold her pose while he told her of his sexual humiliation. How was she supposed to look seductive when she only felt pity for his fourteen-year-old self.

"Two of them held my arms while a third sat on my legs. I struggled but couldn't free myself. Then, the fourth took my cock in her hand and stroked it." He closed his eyes tightly for a moment. "I became erect."

"Of course, you did."

"It felt good," he said. "I hated that. I hated her. I hated my cock"

"Did you climax?"

"Not at first. The other girls took their turn. Petting my little man, they called it."

She held as still as she could

"They continued that way, and eventually I stopped my outward struggle," he said. "Inside, I fought for control because I knew what would happen."

"They'd see you spend."

"I'd had dreams…so many. At night, I'd awakened after one and found I'd soiled myself."

"It's not soiling yourself!"

He pinned her with a stare full of venom. "Lie still."

She did her best to relax back into her position. "Well, it isn't."

"I didn't know that. I didn't understand what was happening to my body." He paused for a moment, and his expression went flat. "I knew what those girls would see if they won, though."

"Klaus, I'm sorry."

His features turned to stone.

"Never mind," she whispered.

"Then, one of them wondered what it would feel like to put her mouth on me. They dared each other, and finally, the oldest said she'd try. I think she was of an age that she'd developed appetites of her own."

Carole lay as still as she could, but in truth, he seemed to have lost any interest in painting at all. She might have not been there at all for all the attention he paid. Imagine what that must have felt like—a child, all elbows and knees, confused about his own body and abused to satisfy the curiosity of other children.

He closed his eyes. "*Gott, hilf mir*. I'd never known such heaven as the feel of her lips on my cock. I resisted with every bit of strength I had, but I knew I couldn't win. But at least, when the lust spurted out of me, it would go into her mouth."

"And did it?"

"Actually, no. After a few moments of delicious torture, she declared that she'd take me inside her the way the mare had taken the stallion." He focused on her finally, and corner of his lips turned up in that cruel way he had. "Later, I realized she was no innocent and knew very well how men were built. She used me as an excuse to fuck."

"Didn't the others tell her not to do it?"

"They held me down while she climbed on top of me. I met no barrier at all, and in a heartbeat, I was thrusting up into her. I couldn't help it."

She didn't say anything. Nothing came to her, and she'd only make him angry if she tried.

"I came almost immediately," he said. "But at least, they didn't see it."

"How absolutely dreadful for you."

"Why would you say that?" A cunning gleam entered his eye. "It was one of the best orgasms of my life."

"They used you. They forced you."

"One can find freedom in being forced."

Her mouth fell open, so she shut it again. "I don't understand you."

"You don't need to," he said. "You only need to pose."

"Yes. Right." She lay on the couch. Completely naked and full of emotion. Confusion, certainly. Pity for the boy and more than a little fear of the man. Maybe that one experience had twisted him. Maybe more.

Maybe he'd been born to create a twisted world around himself. No matter how, she'd entered that world now, and she'd take part of it away inside her when she left.

"Thank you, Frau Rose," he said.

She couldn't help but turn her head to look up at him. "For what?"

"Your expression," he said. "It was exactly what I wanted."

CHAPTER TEN

"My darling Carole,

"You've made fast work of the tasks I set before you. I hope I'm not too vain to hope that your eagerness has urged you to find four lovers quickly so that you could hurry to my side.

"Now that our time approaches, my poor brain can manage nothing more than to paint mental pictures of the moment when we'll finally come together. My first glimpse of your face. The first taste of your lips on mine. Our first true embrace.

"Priapus devils me constantly. Always swollen and pressing against the inside of my pants. He doesn't understand why he can't have your precious cunny. He seems to think I only need to turn one more corner to find you. Surely, *this* time when I blow out the candle and roll over in my bed, I'll find you waiting there, tucked under the covers and ready to accept my aching rod into your heat.

"I'm no longer able to perform the simplest tasks and snap at the staff out of impatience. Hurry to me, my darling, before they all leave me in disgust.

"Take pity on this poor soul who loves you so. I can't stand another moment apart from you, and so I won't.

"Enclosed is a ticket to Lucca in Tuscany. I've arranged for this letter to be delivered at this precise moment so that I'll know exactly when it arrives in your hands. If you take the train that leaves Vienna tomorrow at nine in the morning, you'll arrive in Lucca at five the next day. I'll have a carriage waiting there.

"In this way, I'll know exactly where you are on your journey. I'll trace your progress on the map. I'll know the instant the train arrives and you climb off. In my heart, I'll sense the moment you step into my carriage and begin the last leg of your journey into my life.

"The day after tomorrow, my darling. I'll see you then. After all this time apart, we'll find each other as the Almighty has intended for so very long.

"Good night, my sweet Carole. I won't sleep a wink until you're with me.

"As ever, your own Thomas."

Damn it all to hell. Carole could have crushed the letter out of frustration, but she folded it neatly and put it with the others in her case. The train ticket mocked her briefly before she shut the lid and stuck the whole in a drawer of her dressing table.

She'd written to Thomas too soon. She'd felt so sure of Waldberg, but now, after days of posing for his cursed painting, he'd hadn't touched her. Now, she had one night to accomplish her purpose—seduce him—and she didn't even know how to excite his passions. He'd spent days staring at her naked body with no sign of arousal. She might have been a still life of fruit and flowers for all the lust she provoked in him.

If he didn't want her, after all, she'd need another man, and quickly. She couldn't very well walk the streets of a strange city like a prostitute. And she wouldn't offer herself to the servant who'd performed in that small room off the studio.

Wait, that room. She could use that room, if only she could puzzle out how. Walking often helped her to think, so now she paced toward her bed, turned, and went back to the dressing table. That room. Waldberg had become excited that day. Carole had asked him then if she was more than a model, and he'd said she'd feel his staff. That word had more than one meaning, of course, but he'd showed her his erection when he'd said it. In that moment, he'd wanted her.

She'd have to get in there and get word to him that she was waiting for him. She'd hold him down and sit on him, if she had to. The same way those girls had done. She'd recreate the whole scene for him, if that's what he wanted. He could pretend to struggle against her. Being forced had freed him that day, or so he'd said. He'd had one of the best orgasms of his life. Yes. She'd offer to do that for him.

Searching through her wardrobe yielded nothing like the right costume. She needed clothing that would come off easily but resembled something a young girl would wear. Or maybe she wouldn't have to strip completely but only lift her skirts. That had its own appeal, actually, as it had that night at Covent Garden when she'd waited for Roger while her sex grew eager and moist with no drawers to cover it. This could be fun.

She removed her dress and tossed it onto the bed. Her petticoats followed. Bending, she took off her shoes and stockings and then reached beneath her shift to remove her drawers. As she began to unlace her stays, she caught her reflection in the mirror over the dressing table. The corset pushed her breasts up and cinched her wait. She'd look younger with it, her figure plusher, so she left it on. A housecoat hung on a hook on the inside of the wardrobe, so she slipped into that and headed out.

No one interrupted her as she made her way to the studio. The huge space stood empty except for Waldberg's easel and canvas and the couch she'd posed on. For a moment, she paused in front of the painting. She could easily lift the sheet that covered it and see what he'd done with her own image, but that might anger him. So, she left it and went to the side door.

Locked. The knob didn't turn when she tried it. She checked again, using more force. Damn it, he hadn't used a key before. Clearly, she'd have to find one now.

She went back out into the hallway only to find that same servant emerging from a nearby door. A little mental geography told her he'd been inside that room and had come out a different entrance. He bent to lock it behind him, gave her a tiny bow, and proceeded to walk away.

She ran and caught up to him, grasped his arm, and turned him around. "I want you to let me into that room."

He smiled and shrugged, clearly not understanding. Fine, she could pantomime.

Still holding his arm, she led him back to the door and pointed to the lock. "Open that."

Understanding entered his eyes, and he shook his head.

"Don't tell me no." She pointed toward the door again. "I'm ordering you to let me into that room."

He grew agitated, shaking his head even harder. "*Nein. Ach, bitte, nein.*"

He could take his neins straight to hell. Before he could stop her, she reached into his vest pocket and snatched the key. Then, she stuffed it into her own bodice where he wouldn't dare try to get it back. His eyes grew wide, and he scurried off. No doubt he'd tell Waldberg what had happened. All the better, but she'd have to work fast.

When he'd gone, she pulled out the key let herself into the room. She'd remembered it empty except for the table, but in reality several objects stood here and there. Half a dozen or so whips hung on hooks in a neat row along one wall beside a collection of leather straps and trusses that looked like the sort of tack you'd find in a stable—except for the fact that some had jewels and feathers attached. A glass case nearby held a series of ornate knives arranged from the smallest to long, curved blades. Even the little ones looked lethal if used properly. The largest item stood in a corner she wouldn't have noticed without entering the room. It resembled a loom—a big one, over six feet tall and wide. Cuffs dangled from all four corners.

She shrugged out of her dressing robe and walked around to study the odd collection more closely. She'd just approached the empty frame when the door opened and Waldberg stepped inside.

In a floor-length robe of golden silk, he might have been an ancient priest, if not a pagan god himself. He gave her a predatory smile. "I wondered how long it would take for you to let yourself in here."

"I couldn't let myself in," she said. "It was locked."

"And yet, here you are. You must have wanted to sample what I have here a great deal."

"I was curious."

His eyes gleamed. "Is that what you wear when you go exploring?"

"Not usually."

"*Gut*, then let me show you my toys." He went to one of the whips and gathered up the ends in his hands. "I believe you call this one the cat."

"Cat o'nine tails."

"There's an extra knot of leather on each tip. Very effective." He dropped that and fondled the handle of the next whip. "Nothing exotic here, but it stings well enough."

"Do you like that feeling?"

"I don't suffer in this room," he said. "I deliver the pain."

Curse it, she'd miscalculated. She couldn't understand these things with her limited experience, so she hadn't imagined that she might play the victim. Her little drama with Waldberg suffering humiliation at her hands had turned into something far more sinister at her expense.

"Don't be frightened," he said. "I won't hurt you, unless you want me to."

"I hadn't thought," she stammered. "That is...I only knew...this room..."

"...is where normal rules don't apply, where one is free to explore the darker side of lust."

He walked around her, so close she could make out the scent of his cologne. Pausing, he brushed her hair off her shoulder, bent, and pressed his lips to her ear. "Do you want to stay?"

"Yes." The word came out of her before she'd had a chance to think about what she'd agreed to. She hadn't lied, though. Aside from needing him to become her fifth lover, she wanted him to push her past her limits. Already, her breath had become rapid enough to rub her nipples against the cotton that held them.

"Not the lash for you. I'd hate to raise welts on skin like yours," he said as her circled to stand in front of her. He studied her up and down, rubbing his chin in thought. "I'd dearly love to see your body stretched out on my rack. Yes, with your breasts pointed upward and your legs spread so that I can smell your heat."

She glanced at the frame again. If he fastened her wrists and ankles to the corners, she would be helpless, unable to move a limb. She'd have to trust him not to hurt her. She'd even have to trust him not to arouse her and leave her wanting.

Before she'd had a chance to consent, he grabbed her wrist and pulled her none too gently to the frame.

"Wait," she said. "I didn't say I wanted this."

"Your silence did." He yanked one hand upward and fixed it in the cuff and then caught her other wrist in a firm grip.

"I haven't decided," she said.

"I have." The bound her other wrist. "If you try to kick me, you'll feel the cat. Do you understand?"

"Why are you doing this?"

"Because you asked for it."

"I didn't."

"Don't lie." He knelt and pulled first one leg to the side to fasten the cuff around her ankle and then repeated the process on the other side. Now, she fairly hung from her wrists, stretched out on her toes, the lips of her sex wide open. One hand went up her leg and grasped her mound, rubbing back and forth. When his finger grazed her pearl, her body jerked so hard pain shot into her shoulder. He straightened and held his fingers under her nose. "Smell yourself. You're already wet."

The aroma told her nothing new. Liquid had pooled inside her and now seeped hot into the hairs that covered her mound. Her nubbin had come to life, becoming hard and begging for friction she couldn't give it.

He went behind her to where the rest of his instruments waited. She looked over her shoulder but could only see him from the corner of her eye as he lifted the lid of the glass case. He came back and worked a blade under the laces of her corset. Cutting upward with sharp jerks, he severed them and let the stays fall to the floor in front of her. Then, he held the knife over her shoulder so she could see it.

"Here's the one rule," he said. "You choose a word. When you say it, I'll stop whatever I'm doing."

"A word?"

"No amount of begging will make me stop. In fact, if you beg, I'll push you harder," he said. "So, choose your word, and don't forget it."

A word. She could use Thomas because she'd always imagine him in the place of all of her lovers. But Thomas didn't really belong here in this strange and dangerous situation. And she certainly wouldn't explain to Waldberg who Thomas was. Still, what word could she use to signify the man she'd finally make love to in only a few more days?

"Tuscany," she said finally.

"*Ja, gut*. Tuscany." He slid the flat side of the knife along her chin and then eased the tip behind her ear. She yelped with surprise and jerked her head to the side.

"Take care," he said. "Any movement and the blade could cut you."

"It's cold," she said, even though the chill of the metal hadn't caused the tremor that had rushed through her.

What had he said? Force brings freedom. She could do anything now and blame it on her confinement. She could let her pussy pass its wetness freely. She could come and come, shrieking loudly. She could beg him to fuck her or, better yet, beg him not to do it so that he'd shove himself inside her with a violence she wouldn't have allowed herself otherwise.

So, when the knife slipped under her shift and cut through the fabric that held it on her shoulder, she trembled at the sensation of steel traveling over her skin and the sound of cotton tearing.

Half of the garment fell away, exposing her breast and the aching peak. He cut away the other side of the shift, baring her other side. Only her hips held the cloth up and kept her from total nudity.

After dropping the knife, he fumbled a bit behind her and the silk of his robe whispered downward. When his naked arms went around her, his cock pressed against her buttock. Even through the cotton, it pressed into her skin, impressing its length and thickness there.

Oh, yes. He'd fuck her now. Fully aroused like that, he wouldn't be able to resist but would bury himself inside her wetness. She'd let him do it because she had no choice, and when she spent, she could blame her abandon on him.

Everything was his fault. The way her blood rushed in her ears. The way her sex wouldn't stop releasing rivulets of need. The way her pear responded to every jostle with another flare of lust. All of it.

He palmed her breasts, squeezing them roughly, and then tugged at the nipples until she cried out.

"Did that hurt?" he murmured.

"No. Yes. Do it again."

He didn't, though. He simply held her breasts, relaxing his grip.

Damn it. "Don't do that. It hurts. Don't."

Chuckling, he ran his thumbs around the nipples and then added his forefingers to twist. Pain, yes, but oh, the pleasure. He knew exactly how much pressure to use to make her want to jump out of her skin. She arched her neck backward, the motion pulling at her limbs and jostling the sensitive bud between her legs. How she ached for something there—a hand a finger, even a rough cloth to rub against. And she could do nothing to give herself relief.

Now, he knelt behind her and retrieved the knife. It went beneath her shift between her hips and then along the crack between her buttock. Blade upward, it cut away the rest of the cotton easily. Now, he gathered up the tattered garment and cast it aside, leaving her naked.

For a moment, he stayed where he was. Could he mean to stroke her pussy? Might he slide his fingers along the lips and linger at her pearl? The poor thing waited for it, becoming even more sensitive so that it detected even a current of air over its head.

"Don't touch my sex, please," she gasped. "Anything but that."

"You don't fool me, witch," he answered. "That's exactly what you want."

"No, please. Truly."

"You think I'm stupid. You want me to press my hand against your wet pussy and rub it until you come."

"No." Damn, damn, damn. There had to be some way to make him do exactly that.

"I know how to punish you for trying to fool me." He reached between her legs, covered her sex with his big hand and squeezed. She swallowed a shout, but it came out as a grunt.

"Ah, yes." He removed his hand and rose. "That will work."

"What are you going to do?"

His cock slapped against her buttock a few times. He had to have grasped it by the base to hit her with it. "I'm going to put this into you, but I won't allow you to climax."

She could have laughed at that if her body hadn't become one raw nerve. How would he stop her from climaxing? He might as well stop the planet in its orbit.

"You want this, don't you?" He crouched behind her and positioned himself between her legs so that the tip of his cock eased between the folds of her sex.

Close. So close. If she could only move a few inches, she could have him inside her, but the bonds at her hands wouldn't let her lower herself onto him. She could have wept with frustration. "Don't put that inside me. I couldn't bear it."

"You're lying." He thrust into her slowly. Just the tip at first and then a bit farther. "You've drenched me with your lust."

More. Please, more. She wouldn't say it out loud. If she admitted how much she needed him, he'd think of some other torture. He'd take her now. He had to. No one could have enough self control to resist.

Sure enough, he thrust upward, embedding himself inside her. Her ankles strained against the cuffs, the leather cutting into her skin, but the pain receded to the back of her mind as the currents of pure sexual need eddied and swirled inside her.

Hanging helpless, trussed and spread wide for his invasion, she should have objected. She should have used that word to get him to free her. No rational woman could enjoy this treatment. But rational thought had no place in this reality as he filled her, withdrew, and filled her again. All the movement—the up and down and slamming into her—jostled her pearl, irritating it just enough to send her close to the edge but not push her over.

He groaned as he kept moving. "You're enjoying this."

"No," she whispered back.

"Don't lie. I can feel how you grip me."

"I can't help it."

"You're going to climax."

"No, really. I can't. You're hurting me."

"I can show you pain." He made a savage move inside her and then another and another. Her limbs stretched as though they'd tear, and she screamed, but not from agony. The perfect savagery of the moment, the blinding pleasure. Surely, she couldn't endure any more without shattering.

The bastard left her, then. He pulled his rod from inside her and stepped back.

She couldn't suppress a sob. "You stopped."

"You were going to spend. I told you not to."

She couldn't manage words but simply pulled against her restraints in protest.

"I know how to deal with your sort." He stepped away, and the glass case opened and shut again. She didn't even try to see what he'd done but hung, helpless and miserable with unspent need.

He approached finally, now facing her, and held up a large dagger with a jeweled handle and an evil looking curved blade in front of her. "Do you see this?"

"Please, let me go."

"It's sharp." He touched the tip of the knife against her skin, just between her breasts. A drop of blood appeared, even though she'd hardly felt the nick. Smiling, he bent to lick it from her skin, trailing his tongue from the spot to her nipple. The slight rasp set her nerves on edge. Damn, but the man knew how to torment her.

He straightened and moved behind her again. Now, when his cock pushed back into her, he held the knife at her throat. "If you come when I forbid it, I'll cut you again."

But she had to come. Soon, he'd push her past the breaking point. Each thrust brought her closer and closer.

"Witch," he gritted. "You're making me do this."

"No. Please." *Oh, God.*

"I'll teach you to tempt me." His other hand went to her sex and immediately settled on her pearl. Rubbing, circling, teasing.

She pulled against the restraints, gritted her teeth, and shouted from between them. She couldn't endure this. Not...one...second...more.

"Tuscany!" she screamed. The word let loose the storm inside her, and she came with a force that convulsed her whole body. She barely heard the knife clatter to the floor as her sex continued its contractions.

Waldberg's shouts drowned out her own as he joined her in orgasm. He stiffened, shoving her upward one last time before going limp behind her.

When he pulled out, she hung, too exhausted to fight against her restraints. Deep inside her, the aftermath of her orgasm still fluttered, numbing her mind into a trance-like state.

When hands reached up to release first one wrist and then the other, she didn't immediately realize that Waldberg's servant had done it. Only when she stood on her own power and looked down to see him freeing her ankles did she realize that Waldberg had left.

The man made quick work of unfastening the cuffs, and without looking at her, he found her dressing robe and held it out to her. He left the room finally, and for a moment, she stood clutching the lace against her, unable to take a step.

*

Carole never laid eyes on Waldberg again. No one saw her off at a dock with a basket of food for her journey. She had no innocent kisses before she boarded the train. This part of her journey hadn't given her a lover as the others had. No clever conversations, no declarations of friendship, no affectionate touches. She hadn't even seen any more of the city than the views from the castle.

No, this experience had been about one thing only. How far her body would take her when it demanded satisfaction. She now knew its power. And from that, she knew she could exercise the same power over a lover. It was a terrible knowledge, and she'd use it again only within the bounds of complete trust. What would have happened if she'd forgotten to say Tuscany?

As she stood on the steps in the courtyard of Schloss Reinhof, she clenched her eyes shut to blot out the memory of the feel of that knife cutting into her skin. Was the man mad enough to have killed her? She couldn't imagine it. Wouldn't let herself imagine it, and yet…

She took a deep breath and opened her eyes again. A soft drizzle had started, making the stones of the courtyard and the wall that separated it from the street a dismal gray. The rain couldn't penetrate her clothes, but occasionally, a drop would accumulate on the brim of her hat and plop from there onto her jacket.

The coachman finished loading her things and held the rig's door open for her. She turned to the servant beside her, the same one who'd released her naked body from the frame the night before, and held out the note she'd written by candlelight in the early morning. Though she couldn't instruct him, the words "Herr Waldberg" on the envelope would get it to the right person.

If he'd wanted her to stay, he would have appeared at breakfast or now. More likely he felt just as done with her as she did with him. No good-byes necessary.

Without looking back, she lifted her skirts, raised her head, and stepped into the carriage. Finally, she could go to the man she loved but had never met, but she carried a small, dark secret with her.

CHAPTER ELEVEN

Thomas Deering stood at an upstairs window of the palazzo and watched the carriage roll up the long drive from the road. His legs would hardly support him, his knees had gone that weak. He'd waited for this moment for ten years. No, more like twenty of the thirty he'd been alive. Carole Rutherford, nee Whitmore, would soon step out of that carriage and into this house and back into his life.

He rested his forehead against the glass and closed his eyes. Could this really be happening? Would he see her now? Not from a distance as he'd had to before. He'd touch her, hold her against his breast, taste the honey of her lips. His whole life would come down to this moment.

The rumble of wheels and the creak of springs brought him back to reality. The carriage had pulled up outside. The footmen had dropped down to deal with her luggage. His butler had opened the front door. The coachman had gone to help her descend.

Her foot appeared first and a bit of skirt. Then more. Stylish clothing and a plush figure. Her hat blocked a view of her face until she looked upward. He saw her for an instant before she turned away, and all the breath went out of him.

Oh, God, she was beautiful. The same ale-colored hair. The same green eyes—large and slightly curving downward at the corners. They gave her a sad look, or lost. Any man seeing them would have to offer himself as protector. He'd could get lost in those eyes and never find his way out. Soon, he'd see them on the pillow in the morning as he kissed her awake. Right now, he needed to gather himself enough to greet her.

His feet managed to take him into the hallway and down the steps to the second floor. By the time he got to the top of the grand staircase, his butler had let her inside. He let her look around for a bit so he could drink in the pleasure of being in the same room with her before he found the strength to clear his throat.

She looked up, and her fingers fluttered to her mouth. Her normally pale skin drained of all color until she resembled a marble statue. "Thomas?"

His own name floated up to him like a breeze, and she began to tremble.

"Don't come up. I'll come down." He gripped the banister for support as he descended the stairs. At the bottom, he went to her, closing the distance between them. The distance, the time, the difference. All barriers gone.

Finally, he stood before her and took her hand. "Carole."

"Is it you?" she asked. "Is it really you?"

He pulled her hat off and tossed it aside so that he could cup her face with his hand. "Let me look at you."

"I saved all your letters. I have them with me."

"I have yours. We'll read them to each other."

She bit her full lower lip in a way that made his gut clench. "Not in front of the servants."

"What servants?"

She glanced over her shoulder at the entryway where they now stood alone. "They're all gone."

"They had strict orders to disappear the moment we met."

"Clever man."

"Beautiful woman." Close up, she beguiled the eye even more than the view from the upstairs windows had. She'd filled out from the slender figure when he'd last seen her. All the better for his tastes. He'd drape her in silks and ribbons and take great delight at taking them off. When the time was right. Her lips were as full and pink as they'd ever been. A few lines at the corners of her eyes only made her more intriguing. Yes, every bit his Carole and more.

"Now that we're alone, I can do this." He grasped her chin and pulled it up toward his so that he could kiss her. Her sharp inward breath and the way she leaned into him, her hand pressed against his chest, told him she welcomed this meeting as much as he did. When her eyes drifted closed, he hesitated. He'd pictured this moment so many times. How her lips would part—there, they did just now—how she'd yield softly against him. His fantasies paled in comparison to the reality of her.

When he touched his mouth to hers, all the world's sweetness answered back. Gently at first, he tasted her the way a parched throat could take only sips of water at first. If he gave in to the hunger years of wanting her had created inside him, he'd put her up against a wall and take her fast and hard. His Carole deserved perfection, and he'd give it to her if it killed him.

She had less patience, though, and her mouth urged his on with pass after pass over his lips. Holding her closer, he tilted his head and answered, nibbling at her lush lower lip and then stroking it with his tongue. She made a small noise at the back of her throat. Exactly the note he'd hoped to hear as they coupled. It threatened to snap his tie to reality, sending him into the heated dreams he'd had of her.

Soon, they were clutching at each other, desperate for more and more contact. And just as soon, his cock came to life, thickening until it threatened to burst from his pants.

He straightened and tucked her head against his chest so he could fight for sanity. They both were breathing hard, and she'd be able to hear his heart racing. No matter. He had everything he'd ever wanted in his arms, and he'd never have to live without her again.

After long moments, she stepped back and took his hands. "Let me look at you."

"Take your time. I'm not going anywhere."

She did for a moment and then pursed her lips. "You're younger than me, aren't you, Thomas?"

"I am."

"How much?" The soft tone of her voice hinted at some fear below. Why? Did she think he'd reject her?

"It's not important."

"You knew my husband?"

"Somewhat." A lie, and she'd learn how much, but not before he could feel secure in her love. He'd only seen her husband a few times and knew nothing about him except the lucky bastard couldn't possibly deserve her.

"I should remember you," she said.

"You honestly don't recognize me?"

"I'm sorry," she said. "You look familiar. That's all."

The fact that she hadn't noticed him stung, of course, but it served them well now. She might have different feelings when she realized his true identity. With any luck, he'd have her so seduced and so in love with him she wouldn't care how much younger he was by then.

He lifted her hands to bring them to his mouth. When her sleeves fell back, marks around her wrists became obvious. Some blisters, but mostly a rash, like a rope burn.

"How did this happen?" he asked.

"The last…" She blushed. "The fifth…"

"Lover."

"Do you want to know about them?"

He turned her hands over and kissed both palms. "In time. Right now, let's get you settled."

"I would like a bath."

"I'll show you to your room."

She cocked her head. "My room, not our room?"

"You've trusted me so far. Can you do it a bit longer?"

Her brow furrowed. She didn't understand and she wouldn't likely understand for some time. She'd have to forgive him for more than one thing before they'd finished. For now, he took her arm in his and led her up the stairs. He'd deposit her in her room for now and prepare for a battle later.

*

No matter how many times Carole pinched herself, no matter how many times she closed her eyes and opened them again, the reality of Thomas Rose never changed. So tall and straight and strong, broad shouldered and long limbed—he was every girl's fantasy of the perfect male form. His dark hair, just long enough to defy respectability, and sparkling blue eyes made him truly beautiful. and oh, his mouth. His wicked, delicious mouth. She could kiss him for the rest of her life and never get enough.

As they strolled through his garden in the twilight, he wrapped an arm around her, and she fitted herself against his side. So natural. Even their steps adjusted to match each other's.

And the biggest miracle of all. As much as she admired him, he returned the sentiment in full or more. When he gazed on her, such a light entered his eyes, such softness of expression. No one had ever done that, not even her husband, and it humbled her as it stole her breath.

Now, he stroked her arm and pressed a kiss to her forehead. "I hope the task I set for you was a pleasant one."

"To take four lovers?" She wouldn't use coarse language with him. In fact, she wouldn't even discuss the others as if they mattered at all. They'd served as means to bring her here, no more.

"It must have seemed odd for a man who loves you to send you to another man's bed." He stopped and turned her toward him. "You do know I love you, don't you?"

"I have to. I see it in your eyes."

"And your eyes..." He took an uncertain breath. "What they do to me."

In the next instant they were kissing again. It took no conscious thought, and she couldn't have said who started it. His arms went around her, and hers reached upward for his shoulders as their lips met, retreated, and fitted together again. So solid and warm, his body offered shelter and temptation. Her breasts crushed against his chest as a fog of arousal settled in around her mind. Far more narcotic than any of the others, he so easily sent her into a place where she could shed her clothing and beg him to take her on the ground, on bare dirt if need be.

When he moved his mouth from hers and laid a path of kisses along her jaw and up to her ear, her legs could hardly hold her upright.

"Make love to me, Thomas," she whispered.

"I want to." His breath slid into her ear, sending a current of need through her.

She managed to move away and took his hands in hers. "Let's go inside."

He squeezed her fingers. "Let's talk a bit more first."

He had quite a fondness for conversation, it seemed. They'd done nothing else since she'd dressed after her bath. They'd sat together at the end of a long table at dinner, talking. For heaven's sake, she'd fellated Pete at her first meal in Jean-Paul's villa. She hadn't done anything more than kiss the man she really wanted, and he didn't seem interested in going further.

"Please, sit down." He pointed toward a marble bench.

She sat and stared around the darkening garden. Surely, they should be in a bedroom by now, removing each other's clothes and caressing the newly exposed skin. The fact that they sat here now spoke of a problem. But what?

"I've asked a great deal from you," he said. "I need to ask more."

"You're frightening me, Thomas."

"Don't look so serious. There's nothing wrong." He took her hand again and stared down at her fingers, not meeting her gaze. "I'd just like a delay."

"A delay?" she repeated. "What the he… What kind of delay?"

"I may as well say it straight out." But he didn't. He seemed to struggle with himself for several seconds. "I'd like to wait until after your monthly."

She pulled her hand away. "What are you saying?"

"Please understand. Any child of yours is precious to me. I'd love it as my own."

"But it wouldn't really be yours." Her insides turned to ice. He wanted to know if she'd conceived with one of the other men.

"I'd make the child mine. The world would never know different," he said. "But I need to know."

"I don't believe it. You'd actually deny us both on the tiny chance that I might have conceived a child with another man."

"Is that so unreasonable?" he said.

"It's insane. After everything I've done for you, after everything I've endured, you're worried about paternity." She put her head in her hands as cold reality closed around her. "I've come halfway around the world, and now you're going to hold me at arm's length."

"We've already waited so long. We can wait a bit more." The man had the nerve to sound angry. "I only want to know the truth."

She lifted her head and glared at him. "Well, here's the truth. I'm forty years old—too old to be having children. I never conceived during my twenty year marriage, so I don't think I'll be producing any bastards."

He glared right back. "Don't you dare talk about yourself that way."

"I have no reason to feel superior," she said. "I just fucked four strangers. On your orders."

His face flushed with fury. "Don't talk that way, either."

Unbelievable. She got up from the bench and pace in front of him. "Let's see. I last had my monthly somewhere between London and Provence, so Roger wouldn't be the father."

He sat and watched her, a muscle twitching at his jaw.

"Jean-Paul and Pete were both brunets, but Pete was much taller, and Jean-Paul more swarthy," she went on. "So, a small dark one would be the Frenchman's, and a big, fair one would belong to the Texan."

"You're enjoying this, aren't you?"

She didn't stop pacing. "Now, Waldberg was quite slender, tall, and shockingly blond. You couldn't mistake his spawn."

Thomas's head jerked up. "Waldberg the artist?"

She stopped in her tracks. "You know him?"

"All of Europe does. He's..." Finally, he had the decency to look ashamed. "I had no reason to think you'd encounter him."

"Oh, but I did," she said. "He has some interesting tastes in sex."

"The marks on your wrists."

"I have matching ones on my ankles," she said.

A pained expression settled onto his face, and for a moment, he closed his eyes. When he opened them again, they were filled with sadness. "I'm sorry. I couldn't have known."

"So, you see, I've been well tutored in the amatory arts. I've..." Her voice broke as the accumulation of all the things she'd done crashed in on her. Stretching on a rack and allowing the touch of Waldberg's knife. How Jean-Paul had bitten her like an animal in heat. Licking that mousse. Even with Roger...letting him couple with her when she knew he loved another woman. All the things she'd done for this man, and now he was rejecting her.

"Don't cry, Carole," he said. "Please."

She raised her fingers to her cheek and encountered wetness. Tears. No. She couldn't give in. If she'd fooled herself—if she'd come all this way and committed all those acts for a man who didn't want her, after all— every bit of joy she'd taken from him, every dream would turn to sand and blow away. She had to find some way to hold herself together so she could think.

Yes, think. She clenched her hands into fists by her sides and breathed as regularly as she could. She'd go back to her room—alone. She'd sit and work this all through from the very first letter she'd received from him all the way up to this minute. She'd puzzle it all out somehow. She wouldn't eat or sleep until she had.

Her vision blurred as more tears filled her eyes, but she brushed them away with angry swipes of her hands.

"Carole, please." He rose and tried to put his arms around her, but she pushed him away.

"Don't touch me."

"Sit down again. Let me explain."

"You've explained it very well, I think." She willed her back to stiffen and her chin to rise. "I'm going to bed now. I'm tired."

*

The candle barely cast enough light on Carole's face for Thomas to make out the lines at the corners of her eyes. More light and more noise might awaken. He'd come to watch her sleep and to make up for his earlier clumsiness in explaining why they should postpone the ultimate expression of their love for now.

Lord help him, make her monthly come soon. She'd known about him for months, but he'd wanted her for years. This near to her—so close he could make out the soft sounds of her breathing—his body demanded satisfaction with more urgency than it ever had before. Even more powerfully than it had when he'd hovered between childhood and manhood and had had no control over himself at all.

Now, stretched out beside her, between sheets perfumed with her scent, he could so easily lose himself in her beauty. Wake her softly and then urge her to full readiness. Then, he'd have to satisfy her. He could tell himself the next morning that he'd had no choice. But then, he'd have to wait to see if she'd conceived, and if she had...

Damn him for an idiot. It shouldn't matter. If he'd cared so much about her carrying another man's child, he shouldn't have put her in other men's paths. But again…he had to know. She needed to have enough experience to choose him, not just settle for him as she had with her husband. The sixth lover, her friend had said. She wouldn't know who she really wanted until she'd tried six men. Now that she'd known five, he'd be the sixth and final one.

She whimpered in her sleep as her body twisted away from him. Going up on one elbow, he kept her within his embrace as he watched her face ease back into a half smile. Beautiful, even with the evidence that she'd left the first blush of her youth behind. He pushed some hair back from her cheek and out of her eyes. Still, she slept on, so he trailed his fingers along her temple to her jaw and downward over her neck. Her skin was soft and warm. As pale as alabaster in the dim light. He went lower to the base of her throat and across as much shoulder as her nightgown would yield.

She sighed and stretched a bit, arching her body upward. The action rolled her onto her back, and now, her breast lay only inches from his hand.

Touching it would wake her up, but he did it, anyway. It filled his palm—not overly large but firm and round. The nipple hardened as he kneaded it through the cloth. So entrancing, he almost didn't notice when her eyes opened.

"Thomas," she whispered. "I dreamed you were with me."

"I am."

Her eyes came into better focus, and she glanced around. "What are you doing here?"

"I came to see you."

"See me? Your hand is on my breast."

"All right. I came to touch you."

She stiffened. "I thought you weren't interested in having sex yet."

"That's not what I said at all."

"That's what it amounts to."

"Are you going to stay angry with me forever?" he said.

"Are you going to set all the rules for us?"

"We've waited a long time," he said. "Is it asking so much to wait a little longer?"

"Fine. Good night, then." She turned, giving him her back. They'd see about that.

He reached over toward her hand. "I want to see what Waldberg did to you."

She let him guide her arm across her body so that he could lift the wrist to his mouth for a kiss. "Did it hurt very much?"

"It must have. Look at the welts."

"What do you mean 'It must have'?"

"I was distracted at the time," she answered. "If you must know the truth, I enjoyed what he did to me. Most of it."

"What did he do?" Thomas whispered.

"I don't want to tell you." A little tremor went through her. "I'm not proud that I enjoyed it."

"I'm sorry. I couldn't know you'd run across anyone like him."

She rolled onto her back again. "What did you think would happen?"

"An affair in London. A fling in Paris. Pleasant dalliances. I don't know." He stroked the side of her face. "Was it horrible?"

"No, and that's the problem. I should have felt disgraced. Filthy. I should have done with them as quickly as possible and come straight to you."

"My Carole's a voluptuary." He couldn't help but smile, although it only made her scowl at him.

"You're incorrigible."

Her other arm lay across her chest now, where he could reach it easily. He took it and kissed that wrist, too. "You told me about your ankles. Did Waldberg hurt you anywhere else?"

"There's a small cut on the side of my breast."

"Really?" He started in on the tiny buttons of her gown. Thank heaven they went far enough down her torso to reach her breast.

She grabbed the material. "I don't know that I want you to do that."

"Do what?"

"Undress me."

Still working at the tiny pearls, he pressed his lips to her ear. "Why not?"

She took a sharp inward breath. "You're not going to make love to me."

"I'm not going to couple with you." One more button, and he could push aside the cotton of her gown and feel the skin of her breast under his palm. "There are a lot of other things I can do."

"I shouldn't let you," she said, but she did nothing to stop his fingers from finding the nipple and circling it with his thumb until it stiffened.

"You shouldn't stop me, either." He spread himself over her, propping himself up on his arms so she wouldn't have to take his whole weight. Of course, his cock pressed against her lower belly. She'd have to feel it and realize how much he wanted her.

This would cost him, because he would make her climax without satisfying himself. He deserved no less for disappointing her.

He took a moment to hold her face in his hands and stare down into her eyes. In the dim light, the color had turned to emerald. She gazed back up at him, trusting, which made his heart swell with pride. But there was a note of wariness, too, as if she feared he'd hurt her, not with his touch but with his words. The fear stabbed him deeper than her anger ever could.

He moved his pelvis against her, so she couldn't deny, even to herself, how fully lying beside her has aroused him.

"You know how much I want you," he said.

"Then, make love to me."

"Soon, I promise."

She started to speak, so he covered her mouth with his own before she could form a word. Kissing her like this amounted to pure torture. So close. Only a few layers of cotton separated them as their lips met. He sampled every inch, from the corners to the fullness of the center. He could do this for hours. He could do it for decades and never learn the whole of her response. Her hands went around his ribs and clutched at his back while he ravished her mouth. More addictive than an opiate, her kiss sent his mind into a haze of lust at the same time, all his senses came alive to every nuance of the feel of her. Her sounds. The way she tasted.

Before he lost control entirely, he broke off the kiss and moved lower along her body. Pushing aside the material of her gown, he found the tiny wound at her breast. A clean cut, already on its way to healing. The bastard must have used a sharp blade, indeed.

He'd kill the man if he ever met him. For now, Thomas kissed the cut and then stroked it gently with his tongue. Carole trembled, gasping softly. Lust or fear and maybe shame? When he found the nipple and took it into his mouth, she made a crooning sound. Definitely satisfaction.

The peak hardened under his tongue as he sucked, and her fingers slid into her hair. She held him against her while he went to the other breast. Of course, this one proved as powder soft as the other and as responsive.

She stroked his face as he worked his tongue around the peak and then pressed it against the roof of his mouth.

Her breath came shallow and fast now, and when he finally released her breast and laid his head over her heart, it thumped loudly beneath his ear.

Exactly how his chest and heart labored, as if he'd run a great distance at top speed. She'd parted her legs to make a place for him between them. His sex lay only inches from his now. All he'd need to do was push aside some cotton to position himself to drive his cock home.

Not tonight. Soon, but not tonight.

Besides, he had so much more of her to explore. He somehow found the strength to push himself off her.

"Thomas," she cried.

"Still here," he answered. "I'm not going anywhere."

"Why must you be this way?"

"I haven't kissed your ankles yet."

She propped herself up on her elbows. "My ankles?"

"That's it. Slide up and let me see them."

She sat up, the action moving her toward the head of the bed. Wait until she discovered why he'd wanted her to do that.

After tossing the covers off the foot of the bed, he discovered that her gown had ridden most of the way up her legs. Dear God, he could have slipped inside her so easily. He nearly groaned aloud.

Instead, he stroked her foot, running his fingers along the arch. With the candle so far away, he couldn't make out the marks on her ankles. Well enough. They'd only make him angry.

He lifted one foot and kissed the delicate bone of her ankle then pressed his lips against her instep. "Better now?"

"Some." Her voice still held a note of anger.

When he'd set that foot down and lifted the other, she tsked. "You're a very silly man."

"I'm in love."

She stared at him for a long moment. "Are you really?"

"Of course. How could you doubt it?"

"You're not acting like it."

He looked up toward her. "I'm not?"

"If you loved me, you'd want to make love to me."

"I want that more than I can tell you."

"I'm here. I'm willing," she said. "You're behaving very stupidly."

"I'm a very stupid man," he said.

She crossed her arms over her chest as if to say she agreed.

"But you know I love you," he said. "A man doesn't write letters like that to a woman he doesn't love."

"Still, I'm older than when we first met," she said. "You might have changed your mind when you finally saw me."

He lifted his nightshirt to show her the state of his member. "Does he look disappointed?"

Her mouth fell open slightly, but she quickly closed it again. "Oh, my."

He dropped the hem again, covering himself. A few of his lovers had had a similar reaction to seeing him for the first time. Most men would take pride at such a reaction. It had always embarrassed him, but if he pleased Carole, so much the better.

"I'm sorry," she said. "You surprised me."

"I didn't frighten you?"

She bit her lip and slowly shook her head.

"Then, be a good girl and part your thighs for me," he said.

She might have expected him to give up and join with her, or she might have expected what he would, in fact, do. In any case, her legs fell open. Going quickly, he ran his hands upward from her knees, opening them even wider. Now he could lie between them and bury his nose in the hairs that covered her mound. Already she gave off the sweet perfume of an aroused woman. The scent went right through him to his gut, making his cock throb almost painfully. He wouldn't make it through this night without coming. When he'd satisfied Carole, he'd slink back to his own room and use his hand. Again. Right now, he needed to take care of his woman.

Feeling with his tongue, he found the bud at the apex of her thighs.

"Oh," she cried, as her body jerked. "Oh, Thomas."

He kissed each lip there and then ran his tongue along her slit from the base to her pearl.

Her hands went into his hair, and her breath became so labored it reached his ears even tucked, as they were, between her thighs. He kissed her again, this time lingering at that most sensitive place. Her answering moan told of pure carnal pleasure.

She was perfect. Hot, sweet woman, surrendering to the pleasures of her flesh. He took her more hungrily now, sucking on her lips and flicking his tongue over her pearl.

Her gasps turned to whimpers and then cries as she neared orgasm. His own sex threatened to explode and spill his lust against the sheets. Already, his hips moved in a sow rhythm, pushing his sex against the bed.

"Good," she whispered between harsh breaths. "So good."

He could take pride at that. His efforts gave her pleasure, not the size of his rod. To give her even more, he slipped two fingers inside her and probed. Still, he kept up the friction against her pearl, rubbing and pressing it.

She shuddered so violently he had to hold onto her with his free hand to keep her sex against his mouth. Damn it, he couldn't make his hips stop. He was going to come. The orgasm already coiled in his balls. No way to pull back from it.

"Don't stop!" she cried. "Please, please."

Damn, damn, damn. Desperate, he urged her pearl into his mouth and sucked. In answer, she screamed, and her inner muscles tightened around his fingers. When the contractions started, he kept moving his hand as she shouted in her release.

In the end, he lost his fight. The climax rushed through him, shoving his cock down into the mattress with one last thrust as semen shot from him. He stifled a roar against her thigh as it kept coming. In all his life, he'd never come so hard. It left him weak, all the strength drained from him into the wetness beneath him.

He couldn't even pull himself up to see to her. Couldn't ask if he'd managed to finish her properly. Heaven help him if he hadn't because he couldn't do anything about it now.

Her fingers found his head again and stroked his hair. "Oh, Thomas…That was…oh…"

"Did you…" Even speaking was difficult. "Did it satisfy you?"

"I've never felt anything like it."

That, finally, solidified his bones enough for him to pull himself up beside her and take her in his arms. "Could I have done that if I didn't love you?"

She planted her face against his chest and shook her head.

"I think there's something you need to say to me," he said.

"I love you, too." She looked up at him almost shyly. "Can I ask…"

"Anything."

"Did you spend, too?"

"I did."

She pulled herself against him, sighing. "I'm so glad."

He held her as she drifted off again. Maybe now that he'd found some relief, he could stay with her. So he scooped up the covers and tucked them around their bodies.

Yes, he could stay with her, but he likely wouldn't sleep.

CHAPTER TWELVE

No one glancing or even staring at the two of them could possibly guess at the images racing through Carole's mind as Thomas gave her a guided tour of the local church. Both of them dressed quite properly—she in a modest dress that buttoned to a high collar just below her chin, Thomas in an elegant but understated suit of charcoal grey wool. They didn't even touch as they walked, Thomas keeping his hands behind his back and his eyes only meeting hers for a quick glance from time to time. No, a very respectable American couple, which would make them rather more prudish than many Europeans. So, no one would guess that she could think of nothing else but the sight of his erect cock.

"This is a small church but a lovely one," he said as they passed along beneath stained glass windows.

They stopped in front of a particularly ornate, although small, portrait of the Madonna and child. So many pieces of colored glass set between narrow bars of lead. A brass plate beneath it held the name Alessandro Del Moro.

"The artist went on to do several important pieces at the Vatican," Thomas said.

"Fascinating." She turned her back on the holy scene to face him. "I don't feel very consecrated after last night."

He lifted her hand in both of his and kissed her gloved fingers. "God invented sex, Carole."

"For procreation only," she answered. "Or so the priests say."

The corner of his mouth turned up in a smile. "And what do you think?"

"I think that if God only wanted for us to have children, He would have made us like the animals."

"How so?" He stared down on her with a devilish light in his eyes.

"Animals are only interested in sex when they're ready to conceive," she said. "Humans think about it all the time."

He leaned closer. "I know I do."

And so did she, ever since she'd started receiving his letters. Now she'd met him and had lain in his body warmth. She'd awakened to detect his scent on the pillow next to hers. All that was wonderful, of course, but mostly, her mind kept going back to that moment when he'd lifted his nightshirt to show her the evidence of how much he wanted her.

She'd only seen five other aroused men before, and they'd ranged from small to Pete's impressive member. Thomas dwarfed them all. Long and thick and perfectly rigid. Just taking the knob would make her stretch. What a feeling it must be to have something so magnificent to join them.

"Thinking about last night?" he prompted.

"There you see? That proves my point," she said. "Humans want sex all the time."

"Perhaps we should explain your theory to the priest."

She pulled her hand from his. "I'll do no such thing."

"What a joy you are." He twined her arm around his and resumed walking. Large windows set higher in the walls beamed sunlight of various colors over them as they went.

"You said you knew my husband in New York," she said.

"Briefly."

That hardly made sense when you did the arithmetic of their ages. Although he wouldn't tell her exactly how much younger than her he was, she'd noticed the difference easily. Given that she'd married a much older man, Oscar would have to have been old enough to have fathered Thomas. What kind of business could they have done together?

"Did you and I meet?" she asked.

He stopped walking and stared toward the front of the church. His eyes didn't seem to focus on anything, though. "I saw you several times. We only really met once."

"Why don't I remember you?"

"It was a long time ago."

"How long ago could it be? You're a young man."

His jaw clenched tightly for a heartbeat or two. "Trust me."

"That's all you've asked me to do is trust you." Her whisper came out harsh enough that the sibilant words hissed.

"Not much longer. I promise."

"I don't remember seeing you at any parties," she said.

"Ah, but I saw you."

"Which one?"

"A mansion on Central Park. The Standens', I think."

"Gerald and Muriel. One of my husband's associates and his wife. We went there all the time."

"You were wearing something modest, in contrast with the hostess," he said.

"Muriel likes to dress provocatively." The woman had had half-a-dozen or more affairs behind her husband's back. She'd claimed he did it, too, and insisted what was good for the goose was good for the gander. She declared women were every bit as sexual as men and maybe even more. Carole hadn't believed it until now.

So, he'd met Muriel Standen. Why couldn't she remember him? If she'd seen such a handsome man, she would have noticed, even if he'd been young. If he'd admired her from a distance, she would have kept the knowledge close to her heart. Why couldn't she remember?

"So, you know the Standens," she said.

"Somewhat."

"How?"

"Friends of my family."

"I swear, you're speaking, but you're not saying anything."

"My father ran an import business. Mostly tea and some other spices. He was a major customer at Standen's bank," he said. "There's the entire story. Does that tell you anything helpful?"

"You needn't get angry."

"The Standens knew hundreds of people. Most of them attended their parties. I saw you at one. That's all."

"That was enough for you to remember me after all this time?"

"One look at you is enough."

How could she remain upset with a man who said something like that? How could she do anything but thank heaven for a lover who used his tongue with such precision on her pearl? How could she interrogate a man with so wonderful a cock? Why did she have to question everything? She ought to take what he offered and realize what a lucky woman she was.

Still, more was involved here than her body. She'd loved him since before she'd set eyes on him, and now that she had, he was all the more perfect. A handsome man and well endowed. Thoughtful and clearly besotted with her. She couldn't lose him now. But how could she keep him if she didn't understand him?

"And so, you met my husband through Gerald Standen."

"Yes."

"You didn't come to our house," she said. "I would have remembered."

"No."

Wonderful. Now, even the single words he gave her had only one syllable.

"Were you a business associate of Oscar's as well as Standen? Did you go to our church? An acquaintance?"

"That's it," he said. "An acquaintance."

"You're impossible."

"Carole, please don't rush things," he said.

"It's been weeks since I left New York," she answered. "Months since we started writing to each other."

"I promise you'll know everything," he said. "Can't we get to know each other first?"

"Do I have any choice?"

He stood in silence. Lost in thought, or so it seemed. A bluish light played on his face, cast by a pane of glass high up over the altar and slanting as the day moved toward late afternoon.

"You wouldn't leave, would you?" he said softly.

"Thomas!" she said. "Of course not."

"Then, do it my way. Please."

"You bewilder me."

"Good," he said. "You'll never get tired of me."

"I might get tired of waiting for you."

"Really?" He turned and took both her hands in his. "Will it be so long before we know?"

"Soon. A few days at the most."

"I can wait."

"And then until it's all done," she said. "I want our first time to be perfect."

"I can wait for that, too." He bent to put his mouth next to her ear. "Even though my cock firmly disagrees."

"How firmly?"

"See for yourself." He glanced quickly over his shoulder to see if anyone was watching. Satisfied with their relative privacy, he pulled her against him. A long ridge of hard flesh pressed into her belly. Her memory hadn't exaggerated the dimensions, not one little bit. She moved her hips, rubbing herself against him.

He sucked in a breath and put her away from him. "Naughty girl. Would you unman me in a church?"

"There are a lot of things I'd like to do to you," she answered. "Even in a church."

"Then, I'd better take you home so you can do them properly."

*

The estate had a statuary garden surrounded by walls of hedge. It would never have occurred to Carole to take a picnic lunch there with plans on making sex the dessert. Or at least, some form of sexual play, as Thomas had shown no indication that he'd given up on putting off their first full knowledge of each other for the time being.

Before she'd started on this strange journey of carnal exploration, she would never have imagined sneaking off in the middle of the day for a dalliance. Indeed, she never would have imagined doing anything erotic for the mere pleasure. Now as she walked with him between marble depictions of Roman gods and goddesses—all of them nude—she had to thank the other men for preparing her to make this a delicious encounter, indeed. She might feel strange about undressing in the outdoors, but the pleasure of seeing Thomas's body under the light of the Tuscan sun would more than make up for any shyness on her part.

He stopped in front of a life-sized statue of a female—nude, of course—and set the picnic basket on the grass. "Venus will enjoy watching, I think."

"Good choice." Naturally, the goddess's body was perfect. Not the hourglass figure of modern fashion but still rounded where it mattered—at the bust and hips. Thomas would have to compare her with all that marble perfection. She could outdo the goddess of love in the thighs and buttocks, but at her age, she couldn't match the smooth skin or firmness of muscle. Did the man have any idea what a forty-year-old body looked like?

"Help me with the blanket," he said.

He'd actually brought a quilted coverlet from the house. It wouldn't scratch like wool and it would give them plenty of room to stretch out. She took one end and helped him to spread it in front of the statue with the picnic basket right beside.

Then, he walked to her and turned her around. "I don't imagine Venus will mind holding your clothes."

"Put something over her head, why don't you, so that she doesn't have to see me."

His fingers had started unfastening the hooks at the back of her dress, but they stopped now. "You're not frightened, are you?"

"Clothing can cover a lot of flaws."

"We were nearly naked last night."

"In the dark," she answered.

"I could feel you. You were exactly how I've dreamed of you." He kissed the skin behind her ear. "Haven't you ever had a man in love with you before?"

"My husband."

"Lucky man. I'll bet he thought you were perfect."

"He said so, but it didn't have to do with sex. That was just something we did. Occasionally."

"Then he was stupid," he said. "I plan to make love to you constantly, even if only with my hands and tongue for now."

"I can do the same for you," she said. "Now that I know how."

He let out a little grunt of approval. "That sounds delicious."

"Then, you'd better undress me, don't you think?"

He continued with the hooks, and she stood, letting him do it. He'd have to see her naked, and she might as well let him do it now. Maybe he was right, and he'd find her beautiful. Maybe he'd forgive and then forget her imperfections. She'd been willing to do the same when she'd imagine him older and less vigorous than he'd turned out to be. As more and more of the cloth of her dress fell open, exposing her shoulders to the sun that warmed her through her shift, her mind drifted off to the memory of his face between her legs the night before. Today she could return the favor and watch his huge instrument release his lust.

He kept on with the fastenings until he had them all done and the dress fell into a pile of fabric at her feet. When he took her hand she stepped out of it, and he scooped it up and draped it over one of Venus's outstretched arms.

Her petticoat tied in the front, so he undid that and pushed it over her hips before going behind her again to unlace her corset. "I don't know why you'd wear one of these. You don't need it."

"Why do men wear ties?"

"A tie doesn't squeeze a man's neck the way this does your waist."

"It also pushes my breasts upward."

"Your breasts are perfectly fine without it." He finished with the laces, removed the corset, and tossed it aside. Reaching around her ribs, he cupped her breasts. "There you see? Perfect as they are."

She gave a sigh of pleasure. "Are you going to finish or keep talking?"

"Demanding wench."

"And all your fault."

"I'll take the credit, not fault." He tugged her shift up her body. When she lifted her arms to help him, he pulled it over her head. Now the sun beat down on her exposed shoulders and torso. Her nipples had already hardened under his touch, and here skin had flushed from excitement and maybe embarrassment. Scooting downward, he pushed her drawers toward her ankles. Now she wore nothing but her stockings held up by garters and her shoes. When he helped her out of those, she was as naked as the day she'd been born.

He didn't move or make a sound for a moment. But before she could glance back to see what he was doing, his palms covered her buttocks. "You have the most perfect ass."

"Don't be silly."

His lips followed his hands, kissing first one buttock and then the other. "Glorious. I want to use it for my pillow forever."

"Wonderful. I'll lie sideways on the bed with my head hanging off one side and my feet dangling from the other."

He slapped her softly. "Don't disturb my fantasy."

"You're a very silly man."

"Just wait and see how silly you've made me."

She looked over her shoulder to find him grinning up at her. He resembled an impish boy who'd just done something naughty but knew his cuteness would prevent any punishment. The expression melted something around her heart. "Are you going to kneel there all day worshiping my backside?"

"I could."

"That isn't what you promised."

He heaved a fake sigh. "I guess I'll have to worship the rest of you, then."

He rose and helped her to step out of the mounds of clothing all around her. She stood at the middle of their blanket, fully exposed to his view.

His expression softened and his gaze went up and down her. She'd never seen a light like that in a man's eyes. It was frightening, actually. He gave her so much power over him. The power to hurt him more deeply than she'd ever thought of before.

At least, he seemed sincere in his adoration, and she could stop fearing she'd disappoint him. Finally, he held his arms out. "You're beautiful, Carole. Even more than I dreamed."

She went to him and put her arms around his neck. Instead of pulling her close, he kept his hands at her ribs to hold her away while he kissed her.

Though his mouth moved gently on hers, the caress did little to hide his hunger for her. Each pass of his lips over hers urged an equal response, demanding that she want him as badly as he did her. He needn't have worried. She'd gone way past wanting with this man. He owned her heart as surely as he'd own her body when the time came.

After a few moments, he eased her away from him. "Stop before I lose my head completely."

"I wish you would."

He kissed the tip of her nose. "Be good, or I'll have to swat your bottom."

"Isn't it about time you undressed?"

"Why don't you undress me?"

"All right." She undid his tie, or tried. The knot worked oddly in and out and back on itself. How odd to discover that, at age forty, she had no idea how men's clothing worked. Men put on and took off their clothes themselves, and neither her husband nor her lovers had ever asked for her help.

He grinned and removed the tie himself.

At least, his collar buttoned, and buttons were buttons. That opened easily enough, and she started on his shirt.

He cleared his throat. "You won't get very far with the shirt if you don't take off my jacket first."

"I know that." She hadn't thought of it, though.

"You've never undressed a man before, have you?"

She lifted an eyebrow at him.

His grin grew even wider. "I think I'm flattered."

"I'll do a lot more than flatter you," she said. "I'll have you begging."

"I don't doubt that a bit." He didn't wait for her to take off his jacket but shrugged out of it and tossed it to the side. "Here, let me help."

Now, she could open his shirt, and what a delight she exposed as she unfastened each button. An expanse of chest and abdomen. Only a few dark hairs clustered here and there on skin that felt smooth under her palms. Solid muscle. The body of a man in his prime.

She pulled the tails of the shirt from his pants and burrowed her arms under the cotton, running her palms over him everywhere.

Damn, he was glorious. Sleek and warm. Male and beautiful. She pressed her face against him and breathed in his scent. For long moments, she simply leaned into him, her breasts against his solid body.

"Carole?" he said.

"Shut up. I'm worshiping you."

He put his arms around her. "Darling, I'm holding your naked body. I don't feel like a god right now."

"You feel like a god to me. Like the ones in this garden."

"I'm as hard as they are."

She smiled up at him. "I want to see."

"Then, finish undressing me."

She pushed his shirt off his shoulders, and he shook out of it. Instead of making another awkward mistake, she knelt to remove his shoes and socks. Now, she looked up at him, right at the huge bulge at the front of his pants. Oh my goodness. And he thought he wasn't a god.

She took her time unfastening his belt and then moving to the buttons of his fly. His eyes closed as she twisted each one slowly. She'd said she'd make him beg, and maybe she would. She'd learned something by experimenting with Pete, and she could use that knowledge to make him regret not coupling with her now. She'd satisfy him, but not until she'd made him mad first.

With the last obstacle gone, she pulled the trousers downward. He wore no underclothes, so his cock came free, standing stiffly away from his body.

The thing was every bit as imposing as she remembered. So thick at the base she could hardly circle it with the fingers of one hand. She stroked it from the bulbous tip to the sac at the base and then licked the underside of the head.

"Ah, Carole," he gasped. "You own me."

"I wish that were true." Still grasping him in her fist, she glanced up at his magnificent body.

"Do you doubt it?"

"If I owned you, I could order you to do what I want."

"I will. Trust me."

"I trust this fine man." She ran both hands over him petting his shaft. "I have such plans for him."

"He's up for anything."

"He certainly is." She sucked the head into her mouth, savoring the feel of his velvet against her tongue.

Groaning loudly, he grasped her face and pushed gently forward. "It's too good. You have to stop."

She didn't release him, though. Let him want her as much as she did him. After another slow thrust, he pushed her head away from him with enough force to say he meant business.

Resting back on her heels, she stared up at him. He'd closed his eyes, but now he swallowed hard and opened them again. "You're like a drug, I swear."

Pride warmed her heart. She'd studied well in her travels. If she'd come to him directly from New York, she'd never have known how to arouse a man and then satisfy him. She wouldn't have realized the power she could hold over a man's body. She certainly wouldn't have developed her own sexual appetites. Now, she'd become the lover Thomas deserved.

He reached down to help her up. "I want my wits about me so I can admire you."

"Do I really please you?"

"You're my dreams come true." He took her chin in his hand and lifted her face to his. "I wouldn't lie about something like that."

"Then, we're perfect for each other, I would think."

"Come. Lie down with me."

He took her hand and led her to the blanket. When she sat, he guided her onto her back and rested, propped up on his elbow, beside her. "Your face was the first thing I noticed about you, of course. Especially your eyes."

Ah, yes. They'd always been her best feature along with her hair. They hadn't changed much—only a few white hairs no one ever noticed and the beginning of crow's feet.

He stroked her cheek with the backs of his fingers. "And your skin…how it glowed that day. I couldn't take my eyes off it until I noticed your mouth."

She couldn't help but blush. No man had ever talked about her like this before. No man had ever looked at her with the same heat in his gaze as Thomas used now.

"I couldn't look at that mouth without imagine kissing it," he went on. "As soon as I did that, my body betrayed me in the most embarrassing way."

She nearly choked. "I never heard of anything like that happening around me."

"There are ways to hide the reaction with clothing."

To think, she had not only missed this handsome man's presence in the same room. She hadn't realized she could make him hard with a glance. All the years wasted.

Of course, she wouldn't have cheated on Oscar. Or would she? Muriel might have talked her into it. None of that mattered now. They'd come together as free people and could enjoy each other without guilt.

"I had no idea what your body would look like beneath your clothing. Female trappings disguise so much. Once, I saw the curve of your breasts above your bodice, though." He cupped one now, and it seemed to swell at his touch. The nipple still stood erect, and the contact sent a shock through her system.

"So soft," he murmured. "I love the way it yields for me."

"Any part of me will yield for you."

His eyes closed again, and an expression that almost resembled pain crossed his features. When he looked at her again, his gaze followed the progress of his fingers over her ribs to her belly. Her sex realized his destination and reacted with a dull ache that wouldn't take much to turn into a wildfire of arousal. He knew how to do that, as she'd discovered the night before.

"You're plush and feminine," he said. "Such luxury."

"Some men might like a more slender woman."

"Only a fool. I want a soft reception when I sink into you," he said. "Not bones sticking me."

She had to laugh. "No danger of that."

He stroked her hips. "The lyre shape. The most perfect female form."

"I've plenty of that, too."

Now his fingers went to her inner thigh and stroked from her knee upward. So gentle, so tantalizing. She stretched like a cat having its ear scratched. He'd soon touch something much more intimate than her ear.

"Your thighs," he said. "When I learned about…"

His voice trailed off. She might have found that odd if she could think of anything besides how close his fingers came to the lips of her sex on every upstroke.

"When I thought of wearing them around my ears, I knew I'd never find any greater heaven."

She glanced up at him. "You didn't think of that when in a crowd, I hope."

"I wouldn't have dared," he answered. "I saved that for more private moments."

"And now, you've done it, and very well, too."

"I have. What a precious cunny you have." He touched the lips, grasping first one and then the other lightly between his fingers. They swelled and parted for him, opening to accept his cock. That wouldn't happen now, but she could wait. She had to. After the night before, she couldn't doubt he'd satisfy her. No not

227

satisfy. Nothing but taking him inside her would do that. But he'd make her spend, and he'd make it good.

"You like that, I think" he said.

"I wish I could purr."

He chuckled. "I'd love to hear that."

"Just don't stop."

"I know what wants my touch." He rubbed her pearl, and her hips jerked upward. "Here it is."

He knew what he could do to her, the devil of a man. No matter how angry she'd been the night before, he'd used her body to bend her to his will. He could do it again with a touch.

And what a touch. His finger moved with maddening precision. Firm and fast enough to make her strain upward for more. He toyed with the tip, pressing and releasing. Her nerves caught fire there, and her sex clamped down, grasping at nothingness inside her. The most beautiful cock imaginable was only feet away from her.

As his hand drove her closer to climax, she rested back and pictured the day they'd finally join. He'd hold his member by the base, trying to maintain some control after days of depriving them both. She'd make him wait, stroking him and kissing him until his whole body shook with need. Finally, when she'd tormented him long enough, she'd let him take his place between her legs and drive himself into her.

He kept caressing that sensitive nub. "You should see the look on your face."

She ought to open her eyes and insist that he take her. Surely, she could manage that somehow. Just now, she could only lie nearly paralyzed with the pleasure his strokes created against her pearl. That and the mental image of feeling him ease into her one inch at a time.

"I can watch you spend," he said. "It's daylight, and I don't have my face between your legs."

She ought to recoil in shyness from that. Her carnal nature wouldn't let her, though. Nothing could penetrate the cloud of desire he'd created around her brain.

"Your chest is the loveliest shade of pink, darling Carole," he said. "You've coated my fingers with your moisture."

"Don't make me try to talk."

"Not at all. Just enjoy." He smoothed the wetness over her lips and then rubbed it into her pearl. Deliberate now, he knew he was pushing her to the brink. No more hesitation, she let him finish her. Her sex convulsed, and her throat opened to release a harsh cry. The orgasm lasted for long seconds, gripping her tightly, and then dropped her into near unconsciousness. She drifted for a bit, almost feeling the ground rock beneath her like the ocean.

When rational thought returned, she sighed and opened her eyes. He was still there beside her, gazing down with the side of his head in his hand. That soft look of love still shone in his eyes. Miracle of miracles, he'd seen her every imperfection and still wanted her.

"My turn," she said. "You and your letters and those books taught me how to worship Priapus. Care to see what I've learned?"

He groaned. "You'll probably kill me."

"Only the small death," she said. "You'll recover to die again."

Enough conversation. She sat up and placed her hand on his shoulder to urge him flat against the blanket. His whole body stretched out for her view. Sleek and finely muscled, he could have posed for one of the statues around them. Even his feet were beautiful. From there she let her gaze wander up his strong legs to the sac between them and the huge shaft that lay erect against his belly.

She took that first, curving her hand around the base. She'd estimated the girth well. Her fingers couldn't quite encircle him. She pumped him and watched as his eyes closed in bliss.

She'd done this before, of course, but this was Thomas surrendering to her. This was the member she'd craved for months without even knowing how impressive it would be when she finally could touch it. Still holding the shaft, she placed a finger of her other hand against the dimple on the head and then circled the rim. Smooth and hard, it tempted her to all kinds of mischief. She bent and flicked her tongue over his tip.

His chest rose on a ragged breath and then relaxed again with a sigh. Sigh? She'd have him doing more than that before she finished with him.

Smiling inwardly, she ran her lips over him, taking him into her mouth to suck. When he trembled, she increased the pressure and slid her lips downward, although she could only manage the first few inches.

His hand pushed hair back from her face, and she glanced up at him. He'd opened his eyes halfway and watched her with a fevered gaze as she swallowed as much of him as she could manage.

So, he wanted to see what she was doing, did he? She'd give him a show. Smiling, she released his cock but held the shaft against her cheek. "See how big you are and how dark in color?"

His only answer was a parting of his lips to take in shallow breaths.

"I'm going to lick you all over until you spend." She started at the base, sticking her tongue out so that he could follow as she tip glided along his length to the head. She repeated the action several times all around until she'd tasted every solid inch of him. Still, his eyes remained half open, even though the rapid rise and fall of his chest showed that he was struggling to hold back his orgasm and losing in the effort.

"This is what you really want, isn't it?" She took him into her mouth again, sliding her lips along his shaft. This time, she pulled him out again, gripped him in her fist and pumped. "Want more?"

"God, yes."

She sucked him again, deep and hard. This time, he surrendered, resting his head back and closing his eyes. She'd finish him now, but not inside her mouth. She'd have to judge carefully—taking him right to the point of orgasm and then using her hand. Such a marvelous instrument. She'd feel it come inside her later. For now, how sweet to watch it release its treasure onto her hand.

He groaned with every breath now, and she kept working him. Up, down. Deeper. Sucking, licking. When his hips moved, she used her hand to keep him from thrusting too hard into her mouth.

His breath came in gasps and grunts as he kept pushing up into her mouth. "Oh, God...I'm going to come."

She had him now. Close. A few more seconds. She kept on pumping him and loving him with her mouth.

"Now," he shouted. "Damn. Carole!"

She moved her face just in time to watch him go rigid as he climaxed with a shout. A spray of pearly liquid shot from the head of his cock. Another followed, hot and strong. She kept up the pressure until he'd finished. He'd coated her hand and droplets had fallen onto his belly. She smoothed it all into his skin and then stretched out next to him so she could enjoy the expression of satisfaction and peace on his face.

After a moment, he took a deep breath and pulled here against him. "Amazing."

"You liked that."

"You took the top of my head off."

"I'm glad." She snuggled close to him burying her face into the crook of his neck.

"You went close to the edge," he said. "Another second or two, and I would have filled your mouth."

"I couldn't let that happen. I wanted to watch."

He chuckled softly. "I'm sure you got a show."

"Quite a sight."

He kissed her forehead and stared into her face. "Where did you learn how to manipulate a cock like that?"

"From the books you had me buy." Her cheeks grew warm. She'd done more than just read. "I…um…also experimented."

"With one of the others?"

She bit her lip and nodded.

"Don't be ashamed. I sent you to them."

"Do you want to know about them?" she asked.

"I do." He hesitated for a moment. "Perhaps this is a good time. I could use some fortification first."

He sat up, reached to the picnic basket, and pulled it next to him. He acted as if having a meal outdoors while in the nude were something perfectly ordinary.

He uncorked the wine and poured tumblers for both of them. It tasted of fruit—rustic, rather than refined. It fit perfectly with the hunk of bread he tore from the rounded loaf and passed to her as did the salami.

The cheese was a revelation, though. Somewhat softer than cheddar and full of grassy, nutty notes. She inhaled deeply and let the flavors dance on her tongue.

"Sheep's milk," he said. "Do you like it?"

"Wonderful. It makes everything else taste even better."

He cut off a few more slices of sausage, handed one to her, and then rested on one elbow. "Tell me about the others."

She took a deep breath. "I met Roger in England. He was what the English called a rake."

"A lady's man," he said. "How was he in bed?"

"Good," she answered. "Even better than he was in the box at the opera."

He paused in the act of bringing his piece of sausage to his mouth. "The opera?"

"Covent Garden no less. That's where we shared our first orgasms."

"You had sex at the opera?" he said.

"With our hands," she answered. "I made him come in his pants."

"By God, Carole, you were little more than an innocent."

"A respectable widow. I surprised myself. But I'd been writing to you and reading those books."

"So, he pleased you."

"He taught me how to enjoy my body for its own sake," she answered.

"You didn't fall the least bit in love with him?"

"He was in love with another woman. We parted as friends."

"So, you went on to France."

"Jean-Paul and Pete." She found her glass of wine where she'd rested it in the grass and took a swallow. "The Frenchman and the Texan. Pete's was the first cock I ever put my mouth on."

"Did he make you do it?"

"I volunteered. I wanted to learn how to do it."

He took his glass and clinked it against hers in a toast. "You learned very well."

"The fact that I'd smeared it with chocolate mousse helped."

He roared with laughter. "You're amazing."

"Jean-Paul didn't like me much, but he had me, anyway. Up against a wall the first time. He bit my shoulder in the process."

"Was he an idiot? Why didn't he like you?"

"Jealousy. He and Pete were lovers. Practically an old married couple."

"Ah, that sort."

"I'll say. I caught them in the act one day," she said. "Jean-Paul had staged it so I'd find them."

"With one's cock inside…" He left the rest unsaid.

"Jean-Paul was on top."

He touched her thigh. "What did you do?"

"I made love to Pete to show them both I accepted what…who…they were."

"Was it terrible?"

"No." She set her wine down and rolled onto her stomach, holding herself up on her forearms. "It was flattering that Jean-Paul wanted me at all. Pete did whatever made his cock happy."

"And then Waldberg," he said. "How did you meet him?"

"He saw me kissing the two men good-bye when I boarded the train in Paris. We met in the dining car. He sketched me."

"Do you have the sketch?"

"In one of my books," she answered.

"I'd like to see it."

"Of course," she said. "He wanted to paint me. He claimed I had the look of a Madonna and a harlot combined. I quite intrigued him."

"So, you posed for him."

"Painting me seemed all he was interested in until I forced the issue."

He didn't say anything but stared up at her with concern that bordered on fear in his eyes.

"He had a small, locked room off his studio. It had various instruments. I got inside, and he found me."

"What did he do?"

"He had a frame…a sort of rack device. He cuffed me into it, spread-eagled, and threatened to cut me."

"The wound on your breast."

"It was lethally sharp. When he had me scared to his satisfaction, he shoved himself into me and put the knife at my throat."

"Carole, I'm so sorry," he said. "I couldn't imagine that would happen."

"We'd agreed on a word. If I said it, he'd stop. I used it just before I climaxed."

His face flushed. Anger? Shame? Who knew? "I wish I could take that memory back for you."

"Don't. It was incredibly exciting. Although, I don't think I'll do that again."

He put his hand on her shoulder and urged her to roll onto her back. "I never imagined that I'd ask so much of you."

"Why did you?"

He ran his fingertip along her jaw to her chin. "I've heard it said that a woman shouldn't settle down until she's met her sixth lover."

Oh yes, that again. He seemed fixed on it.

"Women don't experiment before marriage the way men do," he said. "I wanted you to choose me once you knew what the world offered."

"Thomas, you knew I loved and wanted you."

He stretched out next to her. "I think I've made some mistakes. Forgive me."

"We're together now."

CHAPTER THIRTEEN

He caught Carole closing the center drawer of his desk when he entered the library. She did her best not to look guilty, but the pink of her cheeks gave her away. She'd seen the calendar.

"Looking for anything in particular?" he asked.

"Paper," she said. "I thought I'd write a letter."

"In the pigeon hole above. And who would you be writing to?"

Her lips curled up at the corners. Just a hint of a smile but enough to send a warning. She planned on toying with him somehow.

"My distant lover," she said.

He took the chair nearest her. "Roger? Pete? Waldberg, perhaps."

"Not them." She waved a hand. "They were only experiments."

"Then, who?" She couldn't have anyone in New York, or she wouldn't have written him the way she had. She wouldn't have taken off for London and leave the man behind. She couldn't have anyone else here because she hadn't been out of his sight except to sleep. She was definitely playing some game.

"Thomas Rose," she said. "Maybe you've met him. He's American but lives abroad."

"Never heard of the fellow," he answered evenly. She meant him, of course, although she couldn't know that his name wasn't Rose. He'd reveal his identity at some point, but not until he could feel more certain of her love.

"What a shame," she said. "I think you two would like each other."

"Not if he's my rival for your affections. I'd kill him with my bare hands."

"Threats of violence. You're an animal under all those fine clothes."

"You know exactly what I am under my clothing."

"Do I really?" Her smile became absolutely evil. "I haven't really known you."

"That's just a matter of time."

"Time you appear to be following with some help." She opened the drawer, pulled out the calendar, and dropped it open on the desk. "You're trying to calculate my menses, aren't you?"

He snatched the calendar, closed it, and put it in his lap. "Do you blame me?"

"Blame you? I have to laugh at you. You have no idea of my cycle."

"How could I?"

"You've tried to calculate when I left for France because I had my monthly about them," she said. "You're not far off. Your problem is you don't know whether I'm regular or not or how long my cycle is."

"Perhaps you'll tell me and put me out of my misery."

"Your misery?" She sounded positively offended. "This is all your doing. You could have had me in the front entryway the moment I arrived if you'd wanted."

"Damn it. I've explained my reasons."

"And ignored my wishes in the process."

"Carole, please."

"So, I'm going to do what I always do when I'm feeling unfulfilled," she said. "I'm going to write to Thomas."

He reached to the desk, pulled out a sheet of paper, and set it on the desktop. "Here you are. Pen and ink are over there."

"No." She pushed back the chair and rose. "I'll dictate. You write."

He moved to her seat, still warm from her luscious bottom and put the calendar back into its drawer. Then, he inked a pen and held it over the paper. "I'm ready."

"Start the way I always do. 'My dearest Thomas.'" She paced to the window, tapping her lips. "'I ache for you, especially in that secret spot between my legs.'"

He scribbled as quickly as he could, but images of her secret spot—the musky perfume of her arousal, how her pearl hardened in his mouth as her cries signaled her onrushing orgasm—clouded his brain and made his hand shake.

"'This latest lover torments me,'" she went on. "'He has the cock a lustful woman dreams of. Long and thick with a head…oh, the head! A work of art.'"

The cock in question felt more like an instrument of torture at the moment. It never totally softened when he was around her, and now it swelled in his pants. Soon, it would be fully engorged and throbbing.

"'He let me put my mouth on it and then watch as it erupted in orgasm,'" she said. "'An amazing sight. It went on for the longest time, spraying his seed everywhere.'"

He stopped all pretense of writing down her words and set the pen aside.

"'But he won't put it inside me, the cruel man.'" She turned away from the window to face him. "Do you think that might make him jealous?"

"I think it'll make him hard."

"Good. That's what I want," she said. "I always become aroused writing to him. I like to think of him touching himself as he reads."

He swallowed. The answer would probably kill him, but he had to ask, anyway. "Do you touch yourself when you read his letters?"

"Not usually during. I get wet, though."

He squeezed his eyes shut, but that only made the mental pictures clearer. Her thighs, moistened in her excitement in anticipation of accepting his swollen member inside her.

"Afterwards, I often retreat to my bedroom and undress. Then I lie on the bed, naked, and finger my pearl. Always, I imagine his thick rod sinking into me to the hilt."

"Do you come?" His voice came out in a croak.

"Always. Sometimes violently."

"Would you like to right now?"

"I haven't finished my letter to Thomas," she said.

She started pacing. He didn't watch her. He couldn't. He'd become almost unbearably hard, and if he even looked at her, he'd be sorely tempted to lift her skirts and take her up against a wall. So, he stared at his desk, his hands in fists on the top.

"Now, where was I?" Her footsteps approached him and then retreated to the window. "Ah, yes. 'He won't use that huge instrument where I most need it, and I have to endure unsatisfied desire for it every waking moment. Sometimes, I dream about fucking him.'"

More pacing. The only other sound came from the clock on the mantle. A tick-tock that somehow went in rhythm with the throbbing of his member.

"'I know you wouldn't treat me this way, my darling Thomas,'" she said after a moment. "'After I'd stroked you enough to make you stiff...'"

"You wouldn't have to do that," he interrupted.

"I wouldn't?"

"You'd only have to tell him about the ache between your legs to make him more than ready."

"Interesting," she said. "Men are such amazing creatures."

He didn't feel amazing just then. He felt like a beast in full rut as his cock threatened to burst from his pants, the head bumping up against the waistband.

"'No, my dearest love. You'd gently undress me, lay me across your bed, and give me every inch of you until I screamed out in my release.'"

Damn it all to hell. He'd do exactly that as soon as she'd had her monthly. He could wait for that scream. It would have to come soon, even if he couldn't know the exact date. If it didn't, they'd assume she'd already conceived, and they'd prepare for the birth of the child. He could still make love with her for several months if they did it carefully.

He'd been so concentrated on the building lust in his cock and the sac below, he didn't notice she'd come up behind him until her hands rested on his shoulders.

She bent to him, placing her face next to his. "Why, you naughty boy. You haven't written any of this down."

"I..." He tried to take a deep breath and failed. "I can't write that fast."

"Oh, dear." She clucked her tongue. "I'll have to repeat it all."

"No need. Every word is burned into my memory."

240

"Why, Thomas, one would think my words have excited you."

"You have no idea."

"I think I do." Her tongue licked around his ear and then dipped inside.

He almost came out of his chair. "God!"

"Poor thing." Her hot breath was almost as rough on his nerves as her tongue. He had to bite his lip to keep from shouting again.

"I have a surprise for you." She straightened and pushed on his shoulder to turn him in the chair.

"I'm not sure I can take any more surprises."

"You'll like this one." She perched on his knee and put her arms around his neck. "I started my monthly this morning."

"Carole!" She was tall enough in his lap that he had to turn his face up for a kiss. She obliged immediately, parting his lips with her own for a deep connection that had his head spinning within seconds.

Not even caring if he was too rough or not, he dug his fingers into her hair to angle her face so that he could devour her mouth. No matter how much he took, she gave and gave, and still it wasn't enough. Lips, tongues, even teeth. No way of knowing where he ended and she began.

While their mouths tangled, her hands went roaming—under his jacket, over his chest and ribs, and downward. When she touched his cock, it fairly jumped in his pants. Even through the cloth, she'd set him off in another moment.

He shoved her hand aside and began tearing at her clothing. The buttons on her bodice flew as he yanked the halves aside. Now, he could plunder her corset cover for treasure. He got one breast free and covered it with his mouth, sucking at the nipple until it stiffened to a hard point.

She let out a whimper and freed the other breast for him so he could lavish his tongue on that while he massaged the first with his hand. Her chest rose and fell, and the skin turned a rosy color. Bless her. She'd become aroused, too.

Still toying with her nipple, he pressed his face to the perfumed crook of her neck. "We can make love. I can finally thrust my cock into your cunny."

"Not now. I'm bleeding."

"It doesn't matter. I don't care."

"I do. I want to be perfect for our first time." Her hand went back to the front of his pants. "I'll make you come this way."

"Not good enough." He pushed her hand away again and pulled her skirts upward.

"What are you doing?" she demanded.

"I can make you want me."

"Don't," she said, as she gathered dress around her. "It's messy."

"I love you, Carole. Everything about you is beautiful."

"It isn't to me." Her traitorous hand found its way back to his instrument and pushed against it through the wool of his pants. "Here. This will last you for now."

He went to remove her fingers but only ended up pressing them against himself even harder. Damned impetuous flesh. It would have what it would have and wouldn't give him any peace until it did. "Spread your legs for me. I need to be inside you when I next come."

"Then, you'll have to hold off for several days." She climbed off his knee and straightened her bodice. "Because, now it's your turn to wait."

With that, she turned on her heel and left the room.

Damn it all to hell. He smashed his fist onto the top of the desk so hard the ink well clattered. Wait several days, she'd said. He couldn't walk around like this that long—if he could manage to walk at all. She'd driven him mad with her talk and her kisses. Worst of all, she'd learned exactly how to tease his cock to such readiness that the slightest jostle would set it off.

Already, his sac felt tight and heavy. Already, a droplet had appeared at the head of his cock to warn of the orgasm to follow. He couldn't stop the inevitable now, but he wouldn't give her the satisfaction of calling her back to finish what she'd started.

No, he'd have to take care of this himself, no matter how he'd promised himself he wouldn't have to do that once he had his ultimate lover. He'd find some way to make her pay for reducing him to this. A pleasant way, of course, but something that convinced her not to toy with him.

He opened the top button of his pants. *Holy hell!* Too late for even that. He fumbled madly with the second, but before he could undo it, he came so hard he nearly buckled over. Only the desk kept him from toppling to the floor as semen shot from him in wave after wave.

Though she'd left him, somewhere in the house she'd have to hear his shouts.

*

Thomas towered over the local girl who'd acted as maid to Carole since she'd arrived. A tiny thing, she'd hardly seem capable of blocking a bedroom door on her own, and yet, with all the fire and independence of the local people, she'd managed quite nicely.

"What in hell is she doing in there?" he demanded.

"*La signora* she's tell me you no come in."

"This is my house, and I'll go in there if I want to." He lunged for the knob, but the girl managed to block him with her body.

She let loose with a string of Tuscan Italian he couldn't hope to understand but it all boiled down to one word. No. By God, the next time he hired any of the townspeople, he'd make damned sure he could scare them.

"Carole!" he thundered. "I've had enough of this nonsense. I haven't seen you all day."

Not a sound came from inside, and the maid stood there, her arms crossed and her nose stuck up at him. Oh, hell. He shouldn't be in such a foul mood simply because she hadn't shown herself since the night before. It was only a bit after noon. She might not feel well and hadn't wanted to face the day yet. But if she was sick, she'd surely come to him, wouldn't she? He'd want to take care of her, make sure she had everything she needed. Why would she shut him out?

"Damn it, woman, what's wrong?" he called.

Still nothing. He shouldn't lie to himself. The fury had built for the last five days. Mostly unreleased lust, but she'd made matters worse with her constant touches and grazing of her lips against his ear. No matter how he'd reasoned and even begged, she wouldn't tell him how long he had to suffer through her monthly. Perhaps she'd had a point that he'd acted just as mercilessly by making her wait before they made love. But that didn't help now after five days of constant, nagging arousal.

"Carole, I'm sorry I shouted," he said. "Please, let me in. I'm worried about you."

More silence greeted that. He looked down at the maid. "She is in there, isn't she?"

"She said you no go in."

Of all the damned, idiotic…he raised a fist to smack it against the door. The maid cringed and darted away. Of course, she'd thought he meant to hit her. The woman inside was making him crazy.

He lifted his hands, palm outward, to ease the girl's fear. "Not you. I wouldn't hit you. Please don't be frightened."

The girl's eyes had widened to fill half her face, and she quickly crossed herself.

"Damn it, Carole. I'm losing my mind." He paced in front of the doorway. "All right. You win. I'll do whatever you want."

"Come in," she called finally.

The maid turned the knob and stepped aside. Finally, Thomas crossed the threshold and all the breath rushed out of his chest.

Across the room, Carole stood by a window, the sun lighting her from behind. She wore something nearly transparent. Feathers adorned it over the private parts of her body—her breasts and mound—but they didn't hide anything, really. In fact, they drew the eye right there.

He immediately turned to face the wall. Too late to keep her imagine from being burned into his brain.

"Don't you like this gown?" she said. "I bought it at Pan's Bookshelf. Rather, you bought it for me."

"Money well spent," he managed to squeeze out through a throat that had gone tight.

Fabric rustled behind him, and he could have sworn he heard her footsteps coming his way, although her bare feet on the carpet wouldn't make a sound.

"I know you're angry with me, but have some pity," he said. "If I touch you, I'll have to make love with you."

"Poor Thomas." Her fingers landed on his shoulder.

He gritted his teeth and did the best to hold still.

"I bathed this morning," she said. "I'm clean."

"Don't toy with me."

"I'm not. Not anymore." Her grip tightened on his shoulder, and she turned him around to face her. "I'm sorry I put you through that, but you deserved it."

"Agreed." It was the only word that came to him as he stared down at her half-naked body.

"You're not listening, my love." She put her hands behind his neck and stepped closer. "I'm done bleeding, and I've bathed to make myself ready for you."

"We can make love," he whispered.

"Please."

"Oh, God." He dragged her hard against him and bent to take possession of her mouth in a kiss. They twined their arms around each other, fitting together along the length of their bodies. When he couldn't get her close enough, he pushed a leg between hers. With his hands on her buttocks, he pulled her upward to ride his thigh. Now thrusting, he shoved his cock—still contained in his pants—against her sex. He must have hit her pearl because she let out a cry and trembled in his arms.

"The bed," she whispered into his ear.

"In a moment." He tore the pins from her hair, letting it fall down her back. Now that he could have her, he'd take his time—at least as much as his rock-hard member would allow him. Her gown resisted removal, but finally gave way as he yanked it upward and tossed it aside.

Now, every part of her body was exposed, and as he kissed her, her skin blossomed with the scent of soap and clean woman. From the heavenly spot behind her ear to the curve of her jaw and the hollow beneath. She stroked his face as he went and arched her neck so that his lips could skim over every velvet inch.

By the time he reached her breasts, her breathing had become erratic. His hand covered one while his mouth explored the other. He found moisture beneath from her earlier bath and licked it away. And all the while she encouraged him with sighs and gasps—her song of rising excitement.

When he dropped to his knees, he could bring her ultimate offering to his mouth—her sweet pussy. His hands went behind her to grasp her buttocks and pull her legs apart. That way, his fingers could reach the lips of her sex from behind while he could find her pearl with his tongue.

It had already elongated and offered itself for his explorations. Her hips moved, but he continued kneading her buttocks and pulling her sex to him. Her lips swelled and parted like a flower as he stroked them, and her moisture collected on his fingers. Lapping at it made his senses reel. Somehow, his member would have to find some control, because she'd offered herself to him completely, and he meant to know every inch of her by the time he'd finished.

Her cries came more often now and higher in pitch. Her knees wobbled, but he held on. Swirling his tongue, he pressed and teased the seat of her lust.

"Thomas," she gasped. "Oh…oh, God…I…oh…oh!"

Yes, my love. He licked all along the slit between her legs and then took her pearl firmly into his mouth.

Screaming, she climaxed and released her honey onto his face. He didn't let her go until her whole body shook. Then as she let out a groan of satisfaction, he rose and scooped her up and into his arms.

She felt as limp as a sack of rags against him, and if it weren't for her breathing and an occasional flutter of her eyelids, one might have thought she had no life in her. Then, again, the rosy hue of her skin suggested health and satisfaction. He couldn't take his eyes of her face as he carried her to the bed, finding his way through memory alone.

When he set her onto the coverlet, she stretched and smiled, opening her eyes in a lazy grin. "Undress for me."

"Try to stop me." He had to sit on the bed to remove his shoes and socks, but he stood for the rest—both so she could watch and so he could toss his clothing aside as soon as he could get out of it. He could make undressing a lingering affair at some other time. Right now, he had little patience for anything more than making sure she was ready for him before he thrust inside her.

Her gaze followed him as he threw his jacket in one direction and his tie in another. His vest followed...why in hell did people wear so much clothing?...and then his shirt. Finally, he could undo the buttons on his pants with a bit more control than he'd had that other day in the library. Her eyes widened as he pushed his pants over his hips, freeing his member.

As he pushed his pants to his ankles and kicked out of them, she slid her fingers between her legs. "May I have all of you now? Finally?"

"As much as you can take and more." He lay beside her and moved her hand from her sex. "Let me do that."

She parted her thighs for him, and he immediately found her pearl. Distended again, or perhaps still. When he tugged at it—oh, so gently—she made a noise half between a grunt and a gasp.

Her hand moved to his cook and squeezed the head. "I want this."

Damn, he should make her stop. She'd make him so wild he'd take her roughly. He'd wanted too many years and it felt too good to stop now. She squeezed and rubbed until he might lose his mind. She saved him, though, or her sex did. She grew wetter and wetter, and when he slipped a finger inside her, her muscles clutched at it. All the while, her breath came faster.

So when she arched her back and spread her legs to make room for him between them, he didn't hesitate but took his place and moved toward her.

She guided him by reaching between their bodies to grip his cock and press the head against the entrance to her body. The entrance to heaven.

He made himself go slowly at first so that he could feel the passage of his flesh into hers. She gripped him.

So hot and wet and tight. In the end, he had no choice but to surge forward, filling her.

She sucked in a breath and let it out on a hiss as her fingertips dug into his shoulder.

"Did I hurt you?" he whispered.

"So good. So good. I've never felt anything like it."

"I love you, Carole. My whole life. I've never loved anyone but you."

"Yes, Thomas. Yes."

He paused to savor the moment he'd worked for ten years and longer. Her face a mask of ecstasy, his cock fully embedded in her all the way to the base. When he'd stored every detail in his memory, he began to move. Slow thrusts first, stroking her inner walls. He watched her as he slid in and out. Watched her lips part as she struggled for breath. Watched as her eyes clenched shut in a grimace of pure arousal. Watched as she tipped her head back and arched up into his body. He'd done all this. He'd given her this pleasure. And he'd be the one to make her climax for the second time. He was her sixth lover and her last. She'd never want anyone else to touch her again.

The thought made the miracle of their joining all the more powerful, sending his need to a new level. He had to close his eyes and concentrate on the sounds of her cries in his ears and the grasp of her muscles caressing him. She wrapped her legs around him so that she could rise to meet his thrusts, taking him inside her more deeply, although that couldn't be possible. Her hands clutched at his shoulders and back as though she couldn't get close enough and needed more and more.

He gave it to her. Hard and fast. Plowing into her until he couldn't stop. He was going to come, damn it. Too soon, he'd have to give in, and this bliss would end. Worse, he'd leave her unsatisfied. He couldn't help it. He couldn't hold an orgasm this powerful off for long.

Moaning, he lowered his head to her shoulders and let his hips take control. Savage, violent thrusts. Brutal. He might hurt her, but he couldn't stop.

Sorry...make it up to you...have to come...now...now!

Before his last thread of sanity snapped, she tensed all around him. Clamping down on him. Hard. Her climax. The ultimate. Her shout rang out in his brain as her spasms started. Sucking at him along the entire length of his cock. He bellowed like a beast as his orgasm slammed into him, crashing him past a barrier into a world of blazing light. He exploded inside her, releasing his seed in one bust after another. It went on and on, draining strength from every part of his body. Unbelievable. Impossible but real.

Finally, he collapsed onto her, his face resting alongside hers. He had to get his weight off her, but his bones had melted, and he couldn't have moved if his life depended on it. She didn't seem to mind but sighed happily and stroked his back. Good for her. She had more strength than he did. Oddly, though, her cheek was moist where it met his. Had she been crying, or had he?

Her shuddering breath gave him the answer. That put some strength back into his arms, and he pushed himself above her just as a tear escaped her eye.

He kissed it away. "Hush, my darling. Don't cry."

"I never dreamed…"

He kissed one eyelid and then the other. "Don't be sad."

"I'm not sad," she answered. "I'm in awe. I never thought sex could be like that."

"Lovemaking, not sex. I love you."

Another uncertain breath, and another tear, which he also removed with his lips.

"Tell me you love me," he said.

"You know I do."

"Say it."

"I love you, Thomas."

He nearly cried himself. Although he'd softened, his cock was still inside her, the most perfect expression of their love. Hearing her say it now filled the moment with even more joy.

He continued kissing her face, punctuating each caress with another "I love you."

When his heart felt as if it would burst with too much happiness, he rolled onto his side. The movement pulled his sex from hers, but he gathered her into his arms to keep her close.

She sighed and buried her nose in his chest while he stroked her spine, up and down, up and down.

"I love you, Carole," he whispered.

"I love you, Thomas." She followed that with a deep yawn.

"Marry me."

She stretched and then relaxed again and sighed.

"Carole?"

"Thomas."

"Marry me," he repeated.

She didn't answer, but her soft breathing told the story. She'd fallen asleep.

*

When Carole next opened her eyes, enough of the afternoon had passed that the sun spilled through the curtains at a slant and some corners of the room held shadows. She'd ended up under the covers somehow, and Thomas lay at her back. One of his hands covered her breast, squeezing it gently. Just enough to restart the fire banked in her belly. She nearly cooed in approval.

"Awake finally, sleepyhead?" He nibbled at her neck and then down to her shoulder.

"You worked some magic on me."

251

"I'm ready to work some more." He moved his hips, pressing his member against her ass. His very thick, very hard member.

"Randy fellow, aren't you?" she said.

"That's the magic you've worked on me."

"You'd better feed me first," she said. "I'm hungry."

"Your own fault for staying in here and missing meals."

"I thought I'd toy with you a little more before I gave you what you wanted," she said. "You deserved it after the way you deprived me."

"It was torture. Hell. I was like this most of the time." He thrust again to make his point. "I only had to look at you to swell almost painfully."

"Poor thing. I didn't mean to hurt you."

"Then, make it better. Marry me."

"This is no time to discuss something as serious as marriage."

His hand went to the other breast where he plucked at the nipple gently. She would never have thought that pleasant, but the way he did it sent sparks along her nerves to her heart and lower.

"This is the perfect time," he said. "When I have you at my mercy."

"Unfair."

His hand moved beneath her breasts to her ribs and stroked her. "Marry me."

"Thomas, please."

"Thomas please what? Thomas please put your hand between my legs? Thomas please stroke my pearl? Thomas, please put your cock into me?"

"All those sound wonderful," she said.

"Agree to marry me."

"That's blackmail," she said as his hand went to her belly. Lord, but he could make her do anything with those skillful fingers. He'd do it in a minute, and she'd agree to jump off a cliff if he asked it.

The very fingers stroked the hair of her pussy. Close to where she'd started to throb for him but not close enough.

"Say you'll marry me," he whispered into her ear and then followed with a flick of his tongue. She'd done that to him and gotten quite a reaction. He'd probably learned it from her and now used it to shock her whole body into nearing full arousal.

"You've had your way with me," he said. "Now, restore my honor by making me your husband."

"Don't make me laugh."

"I won't make you laugh. I'll make you come." He touched her, stroking her pussy and moved slowly to her nub and back. "Already moist."

"Don't sound so smug."

"Not smug, only sure of myself." His hand brushed her most sensitive spot. "And of you."

"Fine, then. Make love to me."

"Marry me." He followed that with another stroke. Firmer this time and lingering on her nub.

Her mind went off to that semi-real world of sexual excitement where everything slowed down and came in filtered through physical need. The sound of his breathing behind her, the feel of the sheets against her hip, the smell of wood polish—all of it existed somewhere, but only as it complimented the coiling need in her pussy. She'd climaxed once with him inside her. How much more powerful would it feel with his hand on her pearl, too?

"I want you," she said.

"Do you mean this?" Again, he pushed his tool against her back. "Say you'll marry me, and I'll give it to you."

"We'll talk," she said. "Afterwards."

"See reason. We belong together."

"We are together. We'll talk."

He plunged a finger into her as his thumb kept up the pressure on her pearl. The cad knew what he was doing to her, and still, he wouldn't show her any mercy.

She arched back against him, but that only reminded her of what she could have if he'd stop tormenting her. His amazing cock would probably imprint its image against her ass. As with Waldberg, she needed a safe word.

"Thomas!" she cried.

"Promise me you'll think about it."

"I promise," she gasped. "Now, please."

He lifted her leg up and over him. He had to shift downward to bring the tip of his member to the entrance to her pussy. In this position, her body had to stretch to accept a cock as large as his, but as wet as she'd become, he soon passed easily until he'd embedded himself firmly inside her.

And oh, what a whirlwind of sensation. To be filled so completely while he toyed with the exquisitely sensitive bud between her thighs. She could have shattered on the spot, but she'd hang on as long as she could to prolong both of their pleasure.

He pulled out and surged forward again. "Damn, but you're tight."

"You're just big."

"I wish you could feel the way you grip me," he said as he kept moving.

"Believe me, I can." Her sex had a will of its own, and while her mind tried to fend off the orgasm, her body closed hard around him, creating maximum friction. Now, her pearl responded to every touch with a threat to spill over into climax. He'd set a fire between her legs that would soon ignite and take her past reality into oblivion.

He went faster, surging in and out of her. "Woman, you make me wild."

"I like you wild." Lord, what a feeling. Impossible, but he seemed to have swelled even more. "You're so good when you're wild."

"I want to feel you climax again." He rubbed her pearl constantly, gentle and fast and then more firmly. Impossible to predict and even more impossible to resist.

"Don't stop," she gasped.

"I love the noises you make when you climax."

He'd hear them soon. She'd fought as long as she could. Not even one more moment...not even a second. The orgasm started where his fingers played her bud, where his cock continued to plunder her. It spread like a tidal wave, looming over her and then crashing to smother her. She screamed as her sex went wild, clenching at him rhythmically.

He stayed with her until she'd finished and then grasped her hips and held on as he made his own last thrusts. So deep, so hard. He shouted too and emptied himself inside her. Such a perfect moment, and she could have this any time, just by reaching for him.

CHAPTER FOURTEEN

Thomas obviously wouldn't give up. He had an idiotic idea that they should get married, and he wouldn't give her a moment's peace until she agreed. He didn't even seem to plan on asking her but assumed she'd already said yes.

It started over the antipasto. He put down his fork and wiped his mouth with his napkin. "I assume you'll have family you'll want to invite to the wedding."

"I have no one but my husband's family," she answered.

"Hmm. They may not take well to your remarrying."

"Thomas, I haven't agreed to this."

"Of course, you did."

"I agreed to discuss it," she said. "That's all."

"I don't see what we have to discuss. We love each other. We should be married." With that pronouncement, he picked up his wine glass and drank as if he'd closed the subject.

"For heaven's sake," she said. "I don't even know you."

"I think we know each other very well."

"I wasn't talking about sex."

"Lovemaking." He put his wine glass down with a bit more force than necessary. "Call it what it is."

"All right, lovemaking. But that's only one way of knowing someone."

"What more do I need to tell you?"

"Where you come from? Who's your family?" She gestured around at all the opulence. "How you can afford this?"

"Worried that I can't support you properly?"

"Don't be silly. My husband left me more money than I'll ever need."

He leaned back in his chair and crossed his arms over his chest. "You need to check into my background, then."

"I need to know who you are."

"Aside from the man who had his cock inside you an hour or so ago?" he said.

She leaned across the table toward him. "Please, the servants."

"No one's here. Besides, they're discrete."

"Why won't you tell me about yourself?" she asked. "What are you hiding?"

"All right." He let out an angry huff. "I was born and raised in New York. My family moved in your husband's circles."

Which, of course, would mean he'd moved in the same circles as she had. He'd tried to obscure that fact for some reason.

"Maybe you should get in touch with them to tell them of your plan to get married," she said.

"No." The word came out hard and flat. "Nor will they attend the wedding. I have nothing to do with them."

"Who are they? What are their names?"

"They're no one, and their names aren't important." Real anger flashed in his eyes. "As to my wealth...I learned the sea as a common sailor. I saved my money and used that and a small inheritance to buy a cargo ship. I built that into a successful business."

"You don't work at it."

"I retired to pursue other interests."

"What interests?" she asked.

He hesitated for long moments. For a while it seemed he wouldn't answer at all. Finally, he gazed out the window toward the terrace and then back at her. "You."

"Me." What could that possibly mean? "But we'd never met before you sent your first letter."

"Not formally."

"What does that mean?" Damn it, in a minute she'd do more than lower her wine glass with a thud. "How did we meet if not formally?"

"It doesn't matter. You don't remember me, in any case."

"Why are you being so secretive?" she asked. "What do you have to hide?"

"After what we've shared, I would think you could trust me." He tossed his napkin on the table, rose, and went to the fireplace, resting his arm on the mantle and staring into the empty hearth.

Fine. He could be angry. She had enough anger of her own. "I've given you my body. That shows some trust, I think."

"Then, why won't you marry me?"

"Marriage is for a lifetime. For a woman, a bad one is a trap. As my husband you'd own everything that's mine."

His head snapped around. "I don't want anything of yours but you. Your heart is mine already, isn't it?"

"I love you. I've told you that."

"Then, prove it."

"Damn it." She slammed her fist on the table hard enough to rattle the china and silver. "I slept with four strangers for you. I don't think I have to prove myself."

He looked ashamed of himself finally. "I'm sorry. This means so much to me."

"I have to ask again. What are you hiding?"

He stared back into the fireplace again. As angry as she'd been, her heart still ached for him. He looked so confused, even lost. For a moment, a fragment of a memory teased her. Someone who resembled him but not exactly. The same expression, though—the tension in the jaw and eyes wide with disappointment. No matter how hard she tried to retrieve more details, nothing came to her, except that her memory was of a much younger man. Then, the image faded.

She got up from her chair and went to him so that she could put a hand on his shoulder. He avoided her gaze but covered her hand with his own.

"Thomas, how old are you?" she asked.

His shoulder tensed. "We established that. I'm younger than you."

"How much?"

"It's not important."

His posture said the exact opposite, as did the fact that he wouldn't look at her. He was keeping information from her. Information she needed to make a wise decision about marrying him.

"Is Rose even your real name?" she asked quietly.

"No. It isn't."

"For the love of God. You've lied to me about your name?"

"You're right." He straightened and turned to her. "This isn't the time to talk about this."

She didn't say anything. Absolutely nothing entered her mind. What could you think when you discovered that the man you'd fallen in love with—the man who'd just insisted you marry him –had lied to you about something as basic as his name?

"Let's sit down and eat our dinner." He gestured toward the table.

She resumed her seat and picked up her napkin. At least, eating made sense.

*

Damn, he hadn't thought things through fully. Thomas sat on the terrace of the palazzo he'd bought and furnished in hopes of someday sharing it with Carole Rutherford. Although he'd come so close to fulfilling that dream, he now found himself with nothing but a stiff drink for company and the light of a waning moon to illuminate the grand estate that should have impressed her. He'd made such a mess of things tonight.

He hadn't looked at things from Carole's point of view. He'd loved her for so long, he'd assumed that if he could make her love him back, marriage would naturally follow. She had loved him, too, even before she'd left New York. Perhaps, he should have left things at that…identified himself and hoped that she'd accept him. Instead, he'd sent her on an outlandish quest ending with a confrontation with a complete stranger she knew only through letters. Of course, she'd have reservations, and his high-handed manner hadn't helped matters.

Love had blinded him. When he'd set about to make himself rich so that he could deserve her, he'd had no way of knowing if she'd ever become available to him. Despite her husband's age, the man might have outlived her. The chance look at an American newspaper's notice of Rutherford's death had hit him like a thunderbolt. Fate had sent him word that he could complete his plan and have the woman he'd wanted his whole life. Since then, he'd planned every move of bringing her along carefully, using caution with his first letters and only answering her fervor with equal desire of his own. He'd even waited out those three months between letters to make her want him desperately. The lapse had made him perfectly miserable, too, but he'd done it to win her complete devotion. It must have worked because she'd come halfway around the world to find him.

He took a swallow of his brandy, but it only made the roiling in his gut worse. He'd sent her to four other men, even though reading her letters about them had nearly killed him. Over-caution, perhaps, but he'd get her to sow her wild oats so that she'd never regret settling down with him. Besides, she had an investment in him now. If she tossed him over in the end, she would have done all that for nothing.

Holy hell, when had he become such a calculating bastard? What he'd put her through. He'd make it up to her. He already had in large part. They loved each other. They created magic in bed. He'd make her a good husband and spend the rest of his life giving her everything she wanted.

He set his drink aside and went to the edge of the terrazzo where a staircase led down to the gardens. He'd created all this for her. Yes, he'd enjoyed the place before he'd learned of her husband's death, but he'd put every detail in place with her in mind. He'd seen her with violets pinned to her blouse once, so he'd made sure to have them planted in abundance. He'd chosen Italy based on a remark he'd overheard that she'd like to visit here. He'd put every item in place imagining how she'd react to it.

He descended the stairs and followed the gravel path to the spot below her window. Two bedrooms down from his own. No light shone from inside. She'd be asleep by now. Alone in the bed he'd shared with her earlier in the day. Coward that he was, he hadn't followed her there for fear she'd send him away. Perhaps she'd expected him and was now angry or worse.

Perhaps she thought he'd rejected her. One stupid error after another. First trying to force her to agree to marry him when she didn't know him well enough. Then, not making things up with her immediately.

Now, he had to think of a way to undo the damage. He hadn't lost her yet. She hadn't run away in horror. She hadn't even upbraided him for lying to her all this time. She'd seemed perfectly astonished and had even eaten her dinner before excusing herself and going to her room. If she felt uncertain what to do, he could act before she made up her mind. More calculation. More manipulation. But all for a good cause. And maybe he'd take a page out of her own book to do it.

*

Carole stretched against the sheets and found herself just as alone in bed as she had been when she'd retired the night before. She and Thomas hadn't discussed the matter, but it seemed only natural that they'd sleep in each other's arms. He hadn't come to her nor asked her to go to him. Maybe it was just as well he'd stayed away. She had to figure out how she felt about the latest revelations, and more of his unbelievable sex— lovemaking—would only fill her brain with feathers.

She'd fallen in love with a man who wouldn't tell her who he was. Or how old. Could he want her for her inheritance? He appeared wealthy enough on his own, but she couldn't know that for certain. but if money motivated him, he could as easily have courted her in New York.

No, he loved her. No matter how good an actor, he couldn't feign that. He had some mystery he didn't feel he could share with her. At least, not yet. He'd *have* to reveal his identity before he married her. The laws couldn't be so different in Italy that he could keep his name from his own wife. With patience, he'd tell her.

She'd wait. What choice did she have? Leave him and go back to New York?

She sat up and swung her legs over the edge of the bed. A flash of white caught at the edge of her vision. An envelope that had been slipped under the door. She went to it but already knew what it was. Her name in that familiar and dear hand told the story. Thomas had written it.

Holding it against her heart, she went back to the bed and tore it open. Inside lay a letter like the ones she had tied together in a ribbon in the top drawer of her dresser.

"My darling Carole,

"I've decided to take my cue from you and unburden my heart in a note."

Unburden his heart. Would a sad message follow? He couldn't be saying good-bye.

She read on. "This won't be about sex, although poor Priapus misses you already. It won't even be about lovemaking but about love.

"How easily we use that word with each other without examining its real meaning. 'I love you' comes naturally to the lips of passionate people as we join together and ascend toward heaven. But remember, my darling, that I cherish you every moment. When I'm shaving, when I stand staring into the sunset, and most especially during those first moments of waking when I become aware of the world and realize to my joy that I share it with you.

"I have to confess to you finally that I've loved you for a very long time. For years, in fact. Long before you were ever aware of me."

She could have howled in frustration. Instead, she set the letter in her lap. Damn it, why couldn't she remember him? Such a strong and handsome man couldn't disappear into a crowd. She would have seen him, and even though she'd never have committed adultery, surely, her mind would have wandered in the direction of "what if?"

She'd had that one flash of recognition the evening before—a brief moment when he'd seemed familiar enough for her to place him. To give him a name. Then, the moment had ended like a door closing and shutting out light. Only one thing remained. Whoever he reminded her of had been terribly sad when she'd met him.

She picked up the note again. "When I learned of your husband's death, a tiny bud of hope blossomed inside me. If I could catch your interest, I might be able to lure you to me. How can I express my surprise and delight at your honesty and willingness to share your amorous nature with me? We were truly made to fit our lives together as perfectly as our bodies do."

Dear God, the man owned her. She could credit his way with words for her utter inability to refuse him anything. But that would ignore the larger issue—he was only telling the truth. He was the man she'd dreamed of for her entire life.

Throughout her marriage, she'd ached for something more. As much as she'd hated herself for the feelings, she'd wondered about what she'd missed. The great romance, the breathless kisses and whispered endearments. As time went on and Oscar grew sicker and older, she'd harbored fantasies she had hardly admitted to herself—a man constantly hard for her. Tearing at her small clothes in his eagerness to plunder her. Need so great it demanded fulfillment now! no matter the circumstances or the setting. A man with the endowments and stamina to exhaust her. Now, she'd found him.

"I do love you, Carole, and although that means my body craves you every waking moment—and also in my dreams—it also means that your smile fills my heart with sunshine, your laughter is my favorite music, and my thoughts never wander from how blessed I am to have your love in return.

"Forgive me for sending you on a difficult quest to surrender your precious body to strangers. Forgive me for pressing the question of marriage so quickly. Especially, forgive me for keeping secrets from you. I only hope to forge a bond between us so strong even the Almighty couldn't break it. If that's blasphemy, then I'm damned, because I won't surrender our love even to our Creator.

"Please allow me to win you over. I will explain everything at the right time. You trusted me enough to take up my challenge and come to me. Trust me a little longer in the interest of forming a perfect union that will last for the rest of our lives and beyond.

"As always, your adoring Thomas."

She sighed deeply and sat for a bit, holding the letter in her hand. She had no choice but to trust him. The alternative was too bleak. Go back to New York, limit herself to Oscar's friends and relatives, perhaps develop eccentricities to entertain herself. She could collect stray cats and talk to imaginary companions.

Or, she could stay here and continue to love and make love with a stranger. Share his life and his bed and more happiness than she'd believed possible.

Without even finding a dressing gown, she went in search of him. She didn't get more than a few steps, because as soon as she opened the door, she found him waiting in the hallway outside. He wore that lost soul look that tore at her heart.

"How long have you been standing there?" she asked.

"It feels like hours. If you hadn't awakened in a few more minutes, I would have found a chair."

She shifted her weight from one foot to the other. "I shouldn't have gone to bed alone. It was stupid of me."

"Even more stupid that I let you."

"I didn't mean to reject you," she said. "I've never done anything like this. I don't know the etiquette."

"New territory for both of us." He gave her a small, nervous smile. "You read my note?"

"It took my breath away."

"I don't want you to stop breathing."

A burble of happiness escaped her lips, and she held out her arms toward him. He caught her up in his embrace, spun her around, and set her back on her feet. Not releasing her, though. Oh, no. He held her hard against his chest and tucked her head under his chin.

"What a long and miserable night," he said. "I hardly slept."

"I kept dreaming about you and waking up."

Stroking the side of her face, he gazed down into her eyes. "You're so precious to me."

"I love you, Thomas."

"Promise you'll never leave me."

"I still don't know who you are," she answered.

"I'll tell you everything when the time is right," he said. "Only, first promise you'll stay with me."

"I don't plan to leave."

"Not good enough," he said.

"Why are you always demanding things from me? Isn't it enough that I love you?"

Still holding her against his chest as if he'd never let go, he sighed. "I suppose it has to be for now."

"Don't make things sound so bleak," she said. "I don't plan to go anywhere. Come into my bedroom so we can recreate one of my dreams."

"That sounds delicious, but we don't have time."

"No time for a fast tumble?" She bit her lip in her best imitation of a pout. "Are you getting tired of me already?"

"Tired of you?" He huffed in feigned outrage. "My dear woman, you'd only have to put your hand on my pelvis to see the lie of that."

She moved to do exactly that, but he caught her fingers and brought them to his mouth for a kiss. "Don't tempt me. Today is for romance only."

"Romance," she repeated. "We've gone far past that."

"Not at all. We skipped it completely. Another of my mistakes."

She stepped back and crossed her arms over her chest. "How, exactly, do you plan to romance me?"

"I'm going to take you out and show you off. Let the world bless our match."

"Who are you going to show me off to?" she asked.

"The local people. It's the church's saint's day. The celebration will go way into the night." His eyes twinkled with mischief. "It's time you met Father Reynaldo."

Her jaw dropped. "A priest?"

"That's why they call him Father."

She took a step backward. "I'm not going to meet a priest. I'm not even Catholic."

"You have priests in your church," he said.

"Episcopalian ones, and I don't want to talk to one of them about our relationship, either," she said. "Besides, how do know what church I go to?"

"I knew your husband remember?"

"Then, I'm sure you know even my church wouldn't approve of what you and I do," she said.

"Fine. You don't have to tell Father Reynaldo anything unless you want to make your confession." He bent toward her. "I'm sure that would be the high point of his year."

"You're laughing about this," she said. "You're a disgrace."

267

"And yet, you love me." He pulled her against him again and kissed her. Her body fit itself against his as though she'd always rested there while she took his sweetness. The first of a new day.

Too soon, he pulled back. "I had your maid find some local clothes for you. I'll escort my *signorina…*"

"*Signora*," she corrected.

"Either way, I'll escort my special lady to the best festival the town has to offer." He grinned again. "We'll all get silly drunk on local wine—including Father Reynaldo—and have a wonderful time."

"You're insane."

"Now, go back inside and get ready. The maid will be up in a moment." He turned her around and swatted her on her bottom. By the time she turned back to kick him or something, he'd already made it halfway down the hallway toward the stairs. With nothing within reach for throwing, she went back into her room to wait for her maid.

*

The whole day turned out to be great fun, even if Carole had no idea what was going on around her. They'd joined the procession after mass, helping to guide the statue of Saint Filipa down the winding street to the town square. There, they'd witnessed a children's pageant of Filipa's good works, sprinkled here and there with a miracle or two. Tables set up with food, constantly changing. Simple and delicious beyond belief. The cheeses. Oh, the cheeses.

Now, after all the speeches and singing, lanterns provided only enough light to show the handful of musicians and the dancers while she and Thomas sat on a bench with glasses of red wine in their hands.

An older woman approached them. She was bent from age, but her eyes held a gleam of wisdom and laughter. She took Carole's hand in her two rough ones and uttered a string of Italian that completely escaped Carole's American ears.

She glanced at Thomas. "Do you know what she's saying?"

Thomas shook his head. "Sorry."

The woman kept on, now more emphatically. Carole smiled at her. "*Scusarii. Non capisco.*"

The woman never stopped her chatter, but now, she touched Thomas's chest with one forefinger—right over his heart—and did the same to Carole with her other hand. She then brought her fingers together and kissed the tips.

Thomas laughed. "That seems clear."

Her cheeks warmed. Shyness, suddenly, laced with more than a little pride that someone would link her in public with such a handsome man. She'd been a wife for so long and then a widow, not standing out in either guise. Tonight, she felt young and admired. When Thomas put an arm around her and kissed her forehead, the lady clapped her hands together and spoke even more rapidly.

The priest found his way toward them, not entirely steady in his gait. When the old woman spotted him, she crossed herself, took his hand and kissed it. They spoke briefly, while the woman pointed to them and to the father a few times.

Father Reynaldo finally sat beside Carole. "So, you are the English ones."

"American," Thomas corrected.

"From the palazzo, si, si," the priest said. "You come to mass some day, eh?"

"That would be delightful," Thomas answered. Carole nudged him in the ribs, but he ignored her. "This is my intended, Signora Rutherford."

Reynaldo's brow went up. "*Signora.*"

"I'm widowed." She'd leave aside the question of Thomas's intentions for her. For heaven's sake, she didn't even know the Catholic Church's position on widows remarrying, and she wasn't about to attend a Latin mass, anyway.

"Can you tell us what the lady's saying?" she said.

"Mama Fernelli, yes," the priest said.

The mention of her name sent the lady into new streams of words, her eyes dancing in the lantern light.

"Mama is part gypsy. She's what you call a seer," Reynaldo said.

"A fortune teller," Thomas said.

Reynaldo lifted a warning finger. "Not approved by Holy Mother Church, mind you. I look the other say, you understand."

"Of course, but what is she saying?" Carole asked.

"She sees the light around you two. Very strong, very pure," the priest answered.

Pure might not be the right word to use for her relationship with Thomas, but strong certainly fit. Now, he squeezed her against his side, running his hand over her arm in a declaration of ownership. It shouldn't have felt so good to display their status as lovers in public. In front of a priest especially. But the wine and food and music had worked their magic, and even Father Reynaldo smiled with the same approval Mama Fernelli showed on her face.

"She says the light is your blessing and you would sin to lose it," Reynaldo went on. "Everyone has a little light, but she's never seen it as bright as yours."

"She's absolutely right," Thomas said. "Thank her for us."

Reynaldo spoke to the lady briefly, and she nodded and clapped her hands together again.

"*Grazie, mille*," Thomas said to her.

Mama Fernelli patted him on the cheek, and then took Carole's face between her calloused hands. When the lady pressed her lips to Carole's forehead, the caress felt like a benediction. Carole's throat tightened as though she might cry. Such a simple act and yet full of love. From someone she'd never met before. Nothing like this would ever have happened in Manhattan, at least, not among the people she knew. Profound and uncomplicated at once and very, very welcome.

"*Che bella figlia*," someone shouted, and glasses raised in a toast. Thomas found hers and pressed it into her hand. Somehow, it was full again. She lifted it in reply and then drank deeply. Maybe too deeply, but the occasion called for it.

The musicians started up another song—something lilting and energetic—and the crowd began to dance. Somewhere in the crush, Mama Fernelli disappeared, leaving her alone between the man who wanted to marry her and a priest. Thomas had probably planned it that way.

"So, you two come to the church," Father Reynaldo said. "I hear your confession. We make plans."

"I won't speak for the lady, but my confession will take some time," Thomas said.

She elbowed him again, harder this time. She leaned close so she could whisper in his ear. "Don't say that sort of thing to a priest."

"He understands," Thomas said. "Don't you, father?"

"If men were all perfect, they wouldn't need the church," the priest said. "Or me."

"I'm not going to confess to anyone," she whispered directly into Thomas's ear.

"You must excuse my intended," Thomas said. Talking right past her again. "She's a bit shy about these things."

"Understood." Father Reynaldo pressed his finger against the side of his nose. "You must be sure, my dear that all confession is kept secret between us."

"I'm sorry, father. You see, I'm Episcopalian." The priest seemed puzzled by that, so she added. "Anglican."

"Ah," he said. "We can fix that, too."

"Father…"

Before she could try, once again, to explain politely that she would neither make her confession nor come to him for the sacrament of marriage, a girl of about ten approached the priest and grabbed his hand. Father Reynaldo only hesitated to put his glass in Carole's free hand before he let the child lead him to the center of the piazza, where they "danced."

"There, you see?" Thomas said. "We've been approved by a gypsy *and* a priest.

"Well, I'm neither, and I'm not making a confession or turning Catholic."

"We'll find an Anglican church," he said. "There must be one in Italy somewhere."

She shoved the priest's glass into his hand. "I didn't agree to marry you."

"No, but we're negotiating, so that's progress." He set the priest's glass onto the bench, drained his own, and rose. "Come on. Let's dance."

"I don't know how."

"Finish your wine. It'll help."

"That makes no sense," she said.

"Try it. Humor me."

She took a swallow and then another. A very pleasant brew, it went down easily. When she'd finished it, he grabbed the glass and dropped hers and his to the pavement, where they broke. "Come on."

Oh, heaven's, why not? If the local priest could make himself look silly by flapping his arms and hopping around one of his smallest parishioners, she could join in the fun, too. Besides, the music had her feet moving, despite her better sense. So, she watched the steps, let Thomas link arms with her, and did her best to keep up.

Soon, she was out of breath, but the exertion felt good. When the crowd formed a circle, she joined it. The steps were simpler now, and she did a decent job with them, so she could throw back her head and laugh. When had she last felt so alive? Probably not since her childhood, and even then, nothing came to her.

The circle broke off into couples, and she found herself with a different partner. A slender man, not quite her height, held her loosely. Though their bodies didn't touch, he guided her in the dance so skillfully she soon had the right rhythm. Now, she seemed light enough on her feet that she could float. When partners changed again, she continued with another and another and even Father Reynaldo, before she'd completed the circle and paired with Thomas again.

He pulled her away from the others, took her in his embrace, and spun them both around. His own laughter came rich and dark as they spun and spun. The distant lights blurred and as her head swam and her heart thundered in her chest.

"Stop," she finally cried. Not enough breath remained in her lungs to speak, but her heart was filled with laughter. "Oh, stop. The world's spinning."

"Dizzy?"

"I'm out of breath, and I can hardly stand, but it was so much fun."

"I have another idea for enjoying ourselves. Come on." He grabbed her hand and led her away from the piazza at a half-run. They didn't go far enough to lose the sound of the music but to the side of a nearby building. Once theme, Thomas pushed her up against the wall and kissed her with all the energy he'd spent on the dance.

He might have been a hot-blooded, Mediterranean lover—Casanova with his passions inflamed. His lips moved over hers with a combination of hunger and skill that had her mind reeling. As dizzy as the dance had made her, this caress made the world tilt crazily.

She did her best to keep up with him, taking his mouth, his breath, his heat. His body nearly overwhelmed hers with his size and solidity. Though she knew every inch of him by now, he'd never come to her with such ferocity before. His hands went roaming down her sides, stroking and massaging, as he pushed her even harder against the boards behind her.

When he released her mouth and slid his lips along her throat, she gasped for air. "Thomas, what are we doing?"

"You know that word you like to use?"

"Fuck?"

"I'm going to fuck you." He fairly growled the words.

"Here?" she whispered. "They'll hear us."

"Not over the music." He pressed his forehead to hers. "Unless you scream. Maybe I'll make you scream."

"You're insane."

"You make me that way. I can do the same for you." Her peasant blouse offered no protection for her breasts, and soon, he had one free. The chill of the evening air made the nipple stiffen. He lapped at it with his tongue, creating a swirl of sensation inside her that went deep to her belly and below.

She gasped as the hunger built inside. "This is crazy."

"It's the wine."

"I thought that dulled the senses," she said.

"Must be drugged." He moved his hips, pushing his sex against her. Long and thick, straining against his pants. "Tell me it worked on you, too."

Maybe not the wine, but something certainly had because here she was, hiding behind a building with her lover's fingers on her naked breast, and she only wanted more. Judging from his behavior and the state of his member, he had no plans to take her home before he fucked her. and unbelievable as it seemed, she'd let him do it. Right here and right now.

"You looked like a wild woman dancing," he said. "Your mouth was open, panting for breath, and your hair flew everywhere."

He pushed the sleeves of her blouse down, pinning her arms to her sides. Now, he uncovered both breasts and kneaded them with his palms. If she'd wanted to get away from him, she couldn't because his weight still held her fast against the wall. but she'd never escape the fire he'd started in her core. Only he could move her so powerfully, and only he could satisfy her.

"I suddenly had a vision of my cock buried inside you as you twisted and turned to the music." He slid lower along her body, his mouth tracing the furrow between her breasts. He stopped briefly to swirl his tongue over each peak. The flames leapt higher inside her, burning away all but a trace of a connection to the outer world. The dampness collected between her legs. The sign that she'd become aroused enough to make sex inevitable.

"Suddenly, I *had* to be inside you," he said. "I'd die if I couldn't feel your muscles around me."

"Hurry, Thomas."

"You want this?"

"Touch me and see," she answered.

Now on his knees, he reached under her skirts and pulled her drawers down so that she could step out of them. Now, his hand went back to her pussy and stroked the swollen lips. She nearly drenched his fingers with her need and groaned with pleasure as he brushed them back and forth across her slit.

He rose and brought his hand to her nose so she could smell her own aroused scent. "Do I have your permission to fuck you?"

"Do it hard."

He yanked her sleeves farther down so that she could free her arms. Now, she wore nothing at all from the waist up, and he cupped her breasts and rolled the nipples. Instead of hurting, the rough treatment only caused her to release more wetness. She throbbed and burned, aching for him to fill her. Despite how firmly he had her pressed against the wall, he made room for her hands as they went searching for the fastening of his pants. He shuddered as she opened each button, but soon, she had them, and his huge tool filled her palms.

As long as she lived, she'd never get used to its beauty. When he moved to lift her skirts, she wouldn't let him take his shaft out of her hands. She petted his length for a moment and then squeezed the tip.

He growled and yanked her skirt upward, taking control. Again, his body forced hers against the wall, while his hand went to her wet pussy. With no grace whatsoever, he separated the lips and plunged two fingers inside her. His thumb found her pearl and rubbed. Hard.

With anyone else, this might feel like crude groping, but Thomas knew her body perhaps better than she did. The roughness only added a new level of excitement, and soon, she'd approached a level of arousal that matched the frantic beating of her heart.

"Thomas," she gasped. "Inside me. Now."

"You're wet. I want you wetter." His thumb kept on with its maddening movements over her nub. Back and forth. Pressing, flicking.

"You'll make me spend." She swallowed a cry. "Damn it, Thomas."

"Hotter," he whispered. "Wetter."

The man was impossible. She couldn't fight him. He'd do things in his own time. He wouldn't leave her wanting. He'd put that hard, huge tool inside her.

Clinging to his shoulders, she gave in to whatever he had planned for her. His chest rubbed against her breasts and the already highly sensitive nipples. His fingers kept plunging into her until her moisture ran freely. Surely, he'd take her soon. Surely, he needed the connection as badly as she did.

She lifted her leg and wrapped it around him. "Give me yourself now, or I swear, I'll scream."

"You want an audience, do you?"

"I want you."

"Then, you shall have me." Keeping her back against the wall for support, he grasped both of her legs and guided them around his waist. The tip of his cock pressed between the lips of her sex as he sought entrance to her body. No wonder he'd wanted her wet, because in this position he felt so damned huge—as if she'd never manage to take his bulk. He eased in slowly, filling her by inches while her heart raced and her breath nearly failed her.

He groaned. "I need to feel you come."

"Fuck me."

His hands held her buttocks as he began thrusting. "I'm going to make you come, but you have to be quiet."

"Yes, yes, anything."

"Carole, if you scream, they'll all hear it, and we'll be discovered."

Honestly, how could he expect her to worry about the outside world when he'd drawn her into another reality with the glide and stroke of his flesh in her pussy? Every movement rubbed at her pearl as well, causing friction so delicious she'd lose all control at any moment.

"Anything," she whispered. "Just don't stop."

He did stop, though. He held her buttocks and pressed her against the boards while his breaths rasped in her ear. "Remember, quiet. I don't want Father Reynaldo to find me with my cock buried in your cunny."

"All right. I promise. Now, please, more."

He moved again. Hard thrusts, penetrating to her deepest, hidden places with each move. He'd split her in two, and she'd only love him more for doing it. She'd been created for this—pure, unadulterated lust.

Somehow, he picked up the rhythm of the music in the distance. This dance was more frantic, the steps driven by the thrusts of his hips as he plunged into her again.

"What you do to me," he whispered. "I feel as if I'll burst."

"Come with me."

"I won't have any choice," he said.

Oh, God, yes. That and that and that. He'd pushed her past endurance. Each forward surge brought the inevitable closer. The climax would take every part of her body.

"Now," she gasped.

"Don't scream."

Curse him, he was right. She bit down on the collar of his shirt as her body took over, throwing her into orgasm. The spasms started as he thrust into her. Impossible to separate his reaction from hers. Muffling her cries, she clung to him while the madness continued.

Then, he was coming with her. He grunted several times and smashed her up against the wall as he moved a few more times and spilled his seed inside her.

After long seconds of heaven, they floated back to Earth. He slumped, resting his head against the wall, and pulled his softening cock from her body.

She had to cling to his shoulders for balance as she lowered her feet to the ground. Every bone in her body felt liquid, and she'd no doubt bruise in several places, but she wouldn't have changed anything about the last few minutes for a bucketful of jewels. In her entire life, she'd never imagined she'd have a lover like Thomas.

"I meant to romance you," he whispered.

"I'd say you did a rather good job of it."

He chuckled. "Shoving you up against a wall and fucking you? I don't even use that word."

"You can fuck me any time you want."

"Minx," he said.

"Libertine," she answered. "Rake."

He lifted his head and stared into her eyes. "God, I love you."

Words failed her. She could only gaze into the light of adoration in his eyes and wonder at the miracle that had given her this man. She stroked his face and kissed him briefly. "I love you, too."

"I probably hurt you."

"Take me home and make it up to me."

He stepped back and helped her to get her hands into the sleeves of her peasant blouse. When he found her drawers on the ground, he brought them to his nose and smiled. "I think I'll keep these."

CHAPTER FIFTEEN

The light from the fire reflected off the copper tub, giving his bedroom a warm glow. The scene might have been quite romantic, even idyllic, if it weren't for the marks on Carole's back. Kneeling behind her, he dipped the cloth into the bath and then squeezed water over the scrapes without actually touching them. Even that made her flinch before she could hide her reaction and relax.

"I can't believe I did this to you," he whispered. "You should have said something."

"And stop all that delicious fucking?" she answered. "Never."

"Perhaps that's why I'd rather make love than fuck. It's gentler."

"Some occasions call for roughness," she said. "Don't try to tell me you didn't enjoy it."

"Enjoy doesn't come close to the way I felt." It had been astonishing—something he would have thought fantasy if he hadn't lived it. One moment, he'd been pleasantly tipsy, dancing until he grew dizzy. He shouldn't even have managed an erection at all, let alone suddenly find himself as hard as steel and aroused to the point of no return. Either that old lady had cast a spell on him or Carole had. Even an aphrodisiac couldn't have had an effect like that on him.

"You seemed unusually large, even for you," she said.

He pressed a kiss to her shoulder. "Don't flatter me. You were tight."

"It isn't flattery if it's true." She gave him a contented sigh. Clearly, she didn't resent or regret anything he'd done, despite the fact that he'd hurt her.

"I know how I am. That's why I tried to stretch you," he said. "You wouldn't cooperate."

She turned her head so that she could smile at him. "My dearest Thomas, most women would kill to have a lover so well-endowed."

"We'll discuss my endowments later. Now, face forward so I can finish with your back."

She stretched her arms out by her sides and sighed again. "It was glorious."

"It wouldn't have been if we'd drawn a crowd."

"I loved unfastening your pants and letting your stiff cock fall into my hands. It was like opening a Christmas present."

"Now, you're being silly."

"Not at all. Should I tell you what you look like?"

"I know what I look like." During his youth, he'd spent a good deal of time manipulating himself—always with pictures of this woman in his mind as he did. At first, only vague images of her loving him. As he'd become more experienced in sex, he'd filled in details. Reality with her exceeded them all.

"You look like a classical statue," she said. "But sculpted out of muscle and flesh."

He dampened the cloth and washed more water over her back. "You'll make me blush."

"The vein on the underside of your shaft pulses as you become more and more aroused."

He put his mouth to her ear. "Now, you'll definitely make me blush."

"Then, before you come, your cock turns a reddish color. It's really quite striking," she said.

Was she tempting him on purpose? Already Priapus stirred beneath his silk robe. Less than an hour ago, he'd spent inside her so copiously he'd thought he'd have no more to give for at least tonight. Surely, she'd be sore, and not just her back. He'd shoved so rudely inside her.

"You should see your own chest as you climax," he said. "You glow pink from your breasts all the way up your neck."

"I wish I could see that."

"You're far too distracted when it happens," he said.

"Thomas, do you think it's love that makes the sex so good?" she said quietly.

The way she said it—softly with great care on each word—hinted this was no simple question. Still, the answer came easily.

"I'm sure it is," he answered. "Why do you ask?"

"Because, with the others…" Her shoulders stiffened. Only a loving eye would notice, but he'd loved her long enough to catch it.

"Yes, I think our love makes the lovemaking what it is," he said.

"The sex with the others was good, too." That came out even softer.

"I'm glad. I wouldn't have wanted you to be hurt."

The fire hissed as a log split. For a moment, that was the only sound in the room until she scooped some water into her hands and let it sluice over her breasts.

"Aren't you jealous?" she asked.

"At the time, I was nearly insane with fearing you'd like one of them well enough not to come to me."

She glanced over her shoulder at him. "Why did you send me to them?"

"I wanted to be your sixth and final lover."

"Why six? Why not three or seven?"

"Call it superstition." He gathered her hair, draped it over one of her shoulders, and bent to nibble the base of her neck.

"That's crazy."

"True." He'd tell her everything soon. About the day they'd first met and how he'd loved her ever since. How he'd hatched his plan to win her during endless monotonous tasks at sea. How a chance remark by one of her friends had settled him on the number six.

"Besides," he said between nips and kisses along her throat, "you've used all you learned with them on me. To my very great pleasure."

She let her head fall to the side to give his lips easier access to her throat. "Not everything."

"Does that mean you have more in store for me?"

"Maybe. As soon as you've had some rest."

"What makes you think I need rest?" Lord knew he ought to. He'd climaxed only a short while ago. He shouldn't even want to think of sex, let alone swell under the silk of his robe, but stiffen he did.

"A man can't get hard again so quickly."

He reached around her and covered her breasts with his hands. "Maybe other men can't."

She took a sharp inward breath. "Oh, that feels good."

"I think you need to recover, though." He massaged her until her nipples became tight, little points against his palms.

"I don't need my back for what I had in mind."

"Really? How about here?" Bending forward, he placed a hand over her mound. The sleeve of his robe got wet, but touching her was worth any damage to the silk. "Are you sore here? I was quite rough."

"Touch me, and I'll tell you."

He parted her lips and found her bud. He stroked her gently until she sighed and seemed to melt back against the tub and against his chest, where she dampened his robe.

By God, she was an amazing woman. If her adventures on the way here had made her into this lustful creature, they'd been well worth it. Her passion fed his, and now, he needed her as much as he had back in the piazza when she'd looked so wild with her eyes flashing and her hair whipping out behind her.

"Are you really erect again?" she whispered.

"I have been since you told me you had plans for me," he answered. "Are you going to tell me what they are?"

"Move your hand so I can think."

"Oh, no. It feels too good right where it is."

He tugged gently at her pearl, and she shuddered, making the bathwater slap against the side of the tub.

She gasped. "I'll make you pay for that."

"And this?" Now, he used circular motions. They always seemed to excite her past resistance. In response, she stiffened and let out a cry.

Before he could finish her, she pushed his hand away. "You're terrible."

"I want to watch you spend."

"You will, but I'm not ready for that yet."

She rose, and he sat back on his heels to watch her. What an ass she had. Rounded and firm. He'd held it in his palms as he'd shoved inside her, and now he could worship it in the firelight.

She climbed out of the tub and turned, standing before him and dripping onto the rug. She didn't even dry off but went to the pile of her clothes and retrieved her stockings.

After that, she fiddled with the robe he'd given her to match his own. With a wicked gleam in her eye, she turned toward him, her hand held out. "Give me your belt."

He rose and obeyed, finally placing the strip of silk in her hand. His erection would have made itself known with no help, but now the robe fell open, revealing his arousal.

She stared at it for some time, tapping the silk strands in one hand against the palm of the other. "What a lusty fellow you are."

"You've made me so."

"Not I." Her eyes widened in mock offense. "I was a virtuous widow until you seduced me with your words."

"The seduction went both ways, and you know it."

She swatted at him, using the cloth in her hand like a whip. It hit his upper arm softly and fluttered downward.

"Don't lie," she said. "That'll only add to your punishment."

"Punishment? What for?"

"For taking me up against a wall while a priest was nearby," she answered. "You might have corrupted him, too."

"Hardly. Father Reynaldo's nice enough, but he doesn't appeal to me that way."

She "whipped" him again. "Do you think this is funny?"

Damn, what made her say that? It hadn't occurred to him, but the image of a naked woman lashing him with stockings all the while pretending she could hurt him did make him want to laugh. It also made him excited as all hell. She had some power over him—a sexual muse, who could command his rod with a look or a gesture.

"I know what you're thinking," she said.

"That wouldn't surprise me at all."

"You want to put that thing into me and take your pleasure," she said.

"You do know what I'm thinking."

"You're a naughty boy, and if you don't do as I say, I'll go away and leave your unsatisfied."

He cast his gaze downward in the best subservient manner he could manage. Laughter still lurked dangerously close.

"Now then, it's my pleasure we'll worry about tonight," she said. "You're forbidden to spend until I say you may."

"I always work to give you pleasure." That was true enough.

"Good, now to go the bed and stretch out on your back."

He obeyed, shrugging out of his robe and lying back, and then waited to see what she'd do. He had a guess, and he'd never done anything like that, but if she thought she could torment him with silk ties, he'd let her try. Sure enough, she tied one end of her stocking around his wrist and the other end to a post at the head of the bed. He pulled on it and found the material surprisingly strong. Another tug only made the silk dig into his skin.

"If you tie my hands, I won't be able to touch you," he said. "How can I caress your breasts and stroke your pearl?"

"Don't you worry about that," she said as she worked to secure his other arm. "I don't want you touching me, anyway."

"Why not?"

"You're sinful. Besides, I can touch myself."

"I'd like to watch that," he said.

"Be quiet." She paused in the process of tying one of his feet to the post at the end of the bed. Tugging on his own robe belt, she yanked his limb almost painfully. "This isn't about what you'd like."

"I can see that."

She finished with his other foot and walked to him, finally taking his chin between her thumb and forefinger to turn his head toward hers. "There's only one thing you can do for me that I don't have."

"My cock."

"Tonight, I own it. It will do what I want." She released his face and straightened. "Now then, here are the rules."

Rules. What sort of rules did she need when she'd tied him so securely he could hardly move? Still, the game had excited her. Her face had flushed beyond what the warmth of the fire could explain.

"You'll submit to everything I do to you," she said. "If you complain about something, I'll only do more of it."

"Should I be frightened?"

"And no back talk. You'll keep a civil tongue in your head."

"My tongue can do a great deal more than talk. Untie me, and I'll show you."

"I know your tricks well enough." She climbed onto the bed and straddled his chest, moistening his skin with her pussy.

"By God, you're already wet," he said.

"I didn't give you permission to speak." She grabbed his hair and pulled his head back, exposing his throat. He had no choice but to allow her to kiss along his stubbled jaw and then down his neck. She acted as if she'd devour him, nipping and sucking and leaving a wet trail of caresses.

When she reached his chest, she circled her tongue around his nipple. He'd done the same for her without understanding how it would feel. The contact sent a rush of desire to his gut. He groaned and arched his back, which pulled his feet against their restraints. The tip of his cock butted against her rear. If she'd stretch out and move a bit lower, he might be able to slip the head between her folds into the wetness that had already accumulated there.

She didn't move, though, except to shift to his other nipple and lap at it until it grew sensitive as if his every nerve ended there.

Suddenly, the room seemed empty of air, and he had to struggle to draw breath. Each inhalation became a moan of pleasure until she finally took pity and sat upright again. "You liked that."

"Dear God, I never imagined."

"You do it to me all the time."

"I hope it has the same effect on you," he said.

"Let's see, shall we?"

Now, she scooted upward and bent over him, taking her breast in her hand. She guided the nipple toward his mouth, and he circled it with his tongue before drawing it between his lips.

"Ah, yes," she sighed, as her sex released a tiny waterfall against his chest. "Do more."

He happily obliged, sucking harder and pressing the nipple against the roof of his mouth.

She moved, pressing her pelvis against him in imitation of the way he'd thrust into her. "So good. So good."

"Give me the other one," he said. "Please."

She did and continued rocking until he'd sucked that nipple into a tight point. Her scent—the perfume of her arousal—filled his nostrils. If he were free, he'd prepare her now—rub her pearl until she neared the boundary to climax. Then, when they joined, her sex would suck at his eagerly until they spent together.

He released her breast and gazed up into her face. Her eyes had gone unfocussed with sexual excitement, and she worked for breath the same way he had.

"Release my hand" he said. "Just one. I can make you come."

She shook her head and took a few deep breaths. "You'd like that, wouldn't you?"

"I should think you'd like it."

"You're not as clever as you think you are. You won't get into my cunny with sweet words and promises. I'll take you when I'm ready," she said.

"Carole, you're ready now."

"We'll see who's ready. She climbed off him and lay down, her head pointing in the direction of his feet. After propping herself up on one elbow, she took his cock in her hand and stroked it. "Now, what do we have here?"

"Be careful, or you'll make me spend."

"But you wouldn't dare do that without my permission."

"I won't have any choice."

"Well, then. Why don't we just see how long you can last?"

"Oh…damn…"

"I do so love to pet this." She used her fingers, now, tracing the ridge around the head of his cock and then down his shaft. At the base, she feathered them over his sac. Not enough to cause pain. Just enough to threaten to send his excitement to a new level. He clenched his teeth, but a growl got through them, anyway. "Do you know what you're doing to me?"

"That doesn't feel good?"

"That feels…oh, God…I can't describe it."

"I gather that means yes."

His heart hammered so fast it might beat out of his chest. The pressure built inside him. "I can't take much more."

"But surely, you can."

"You'll kill me, I swear."

She laughed, actually laughed. "I won't. It'll only feel as if I have."

"Now then, back to this fine fellow." She took his shaft in her fist again and pumped. After one pass, a drop of pearly liquid appeared at the tip. She had to know what that meant—that he'd neared the end of his tether and would snap in another moment.

Instead of climbing onto him, she licked the droplet off. "Salty. Nice."

"You can't mean to…not now…I'm too close."

"This?" She licked him from his sac to the head and then swirled her tongue around that.

"Carole, I mean it. Do not put your mouth on me."

"You're not giving orders here. I am." With that, she bent and slid her lips down onto him. The warmth and wetness of her mouth closed around him the same way her pussy would when he finally got inside her. Or, if he got inside her. He might not last long enough. Instead, she'd get a very good taste of him, indeed. He'd warned her. He ought to simply let her pleasure him and suffer the consequences. It felt so damned good.

And yet, this wasn't some voluptuous adventure with a woman who'd taken temporary a fancy to him and would leave his life the next day. This was Carole, the woman he adored. He couldn't enjoy this if she didn't, too.

She kept sucking on him, taking him deeper and pushing him closer to the edge. He clenched his fists and pulled on his restraints—anything to cause some pain and distract him from the tension coiling in his sac. *For the love of God, Carole, stop!*

She did. Maybe he'd said that aloud, and she'd agreed. Maybe she'd realized on her own the state of his cock. In any case, she held it in her fist as if showing it to him.

"You see?" she said. "This is the color I told you about."

"Yes, yes. Whatever you say."

She rubbed her thumb around the head of his member. "I suppose I ought to let you spend."

"Lord help you if I ever decide to take revenge for this."

"Oooh, a threat. but you see, my darling…" She released his rod and gave him a sweet smile. "…I'm sure any revenge you'd take would be delightful."

"I wouldn't count on that, if I were you."

"Enough talk. My poor cunny feels empty without your cock inside it. I'm afraid your torture is near the end."

"Thank God for that."

Grasping his shaft again, she swung a leg over him. After parting the lips of her sex with her other hand she guided him to her entrance and lowered herself slowly.

Could there be any more erotic sight than to watch his cock disappearing into the body of the woman he loved? Though nearly blind with lust, he kept his eyes open to watch Carole—his Carole—accept him. Every inch, all the way to the base.

She sucked in a breath and then let it out with a hiss. "Oh, Thomas…you feel so…ohmygod I can't describe it."

"Enjoy me, love."

"Oh, yes." She put her hands on his ribs for leverage as she pushed herself upward and then sank against him. "You're so deep inside me."

Though he could barely move, he did have enough room to thrust up into her, and honestly, he couldn't have stopped himself from doing it in any case. She cried out when he did it and then continued moving with him. She met every upward surge with a downward glide, repeating the miracle of their joining a dozen or more times. She bathed him in her moisture as she neared her peak. Though her spiraling need had cost her the will to torment him, he had to hold off his climax for the sake of hers. Not only did he need to satisfy her, the orgasm would be all the more shattering if he could feel her quiver around him when he came.

He grunted and bit his lip as he continued thrusting, reaching with his mind for anything that would distract him from how wonderful she felt, how much he wanted her, how much he loved her.

"Don't stop!" she cried as she straightened, giving him a clearer view of their joining. She cupped her own breasts, and squeezed them as she let her head fall backwards.

Such a carnal creature. His Venus. In that instant, she owned his soul as completely as she owned his body. She was everything sinful and sublime. And she was his.

One of her hands left her breast and traveled over her ribs and past her belly to her nether lips. The tip of her finger pressed between her folds to her pearl, and instantly, her sex clamped down on his in the first stage of her orgasm.

She screamed as the convulsions started, but her finger didn't stop moving. His body took over as the world went mad with lust. Finally, he could let loose all the pent-up need, and he exploded in orgasm. Stream after stream of hot semen shot from him as his shouts joined hers.

It seemed to go on forever, both of them lost in this perfect moment. His response merged with hers until there was no I and thou but only us. United in one being.

Even when it ended, it wasn't over. When she rested on his chest, her sex still fluttered around him. The peace that followed became all the deeper for the madness that had created it.

"If you'd told me that was possible, I wouldn't have believed you," she said.

"You're amazing."

"Does that mean you won't be taking revenge against me?"

"Definitely not tonight," he answered. "You've exhausted me."

She sighed and hugged his ribs. "I love you so much."

"Do you think you can untie me? I'd like to put my arms around you."

"Oh, my goodness. I'm sorry." She freed one hand easily enough, but she had to struggle with the knot at the other one. Once she had that free, they both worked on releasing his feet and then fell back together, their limbs tangled.

Oh so carefully, Thomas stroked her back from her shoulders to her buttocks and even threw a leg over hers. No matter how hard he tried, he couldn't get her close enough. The fire still cast warmth and light around them, and her hair was still damp from her bath. Even in his most fantastic dreams of having her all to himself, he'd never imagined anything quite as precious as this moment. He had to find some way to make her his own for the rest of their lives. She had to become his wife.

"You'd never leave me, would you?" he whispered.

"What a thing to ask."

"I don't know what I'd do if I lost you now."

She pulled her head from under his chin and gazed into his face. "Why would you ever lose me?"

"You won't marry me."

"We've been through all that." She pressed her face against his neck again.

Yes, they had, and she had good reason to refuse. How could you marry someone when you didn't know the person's name? He hadn't trusted her with the truth, and until he did, he couldn't form the ultimate bond with her. He'd have to tell her everything.

Not now, though. They'd never been closer than right at this moment. They might never manage to get closer, although he'd happily spend the rest of his days trying. Still, he couldn't risk her refusal now. If she did refuse him once he'd revealed his identity, he'd need these memories to cling to.

So, when she fell asleep in his arms, he gathered the coverlet around them and just held her as the fire burned low in the grate.

CHAPTER SIXTEEN

"Come, I want to show you something." Thomas held out a hand to her, and of course, she took it.

His mood seemed rather grim this morning, which was odd after their incredible lovemaking of the night before. Or, not grim, but guarded. As if he needed to take great care in how he handled her. She probably ought to be angry that he felt he had to handle her at all, given the level of intimacy they'd achieved. No doubt she would once she'd discovered what this something he wanted to show her was. For now, a sense of worry nibbled at the back of her mind.

He didn't lead her any place unusual or secret but only into his study, stopping in front of a bookcase she'd seen dozens of times. After pulling a large volume from a shelf, he opened it and produced a flower—a rose that had been pressed between the pages. "Does this look familiar?"

"It's a yellow rose. It looks very old."

"Twenty years."

She searched his face for a clue. "Should it mean something to me?"

He put it in her hand. "Study it more carefully."

She did, but honestly, it was just a flower. "I'm sorry. I don't understand."

"It doesn't look at all familiar?"

"I had some like it in my bridal bouquet." She hesitated. "Twenty years ago."

"It is from your bouquet."

"How is that possible?" She stared up at him. "How could you have gotten it?"

A muscle jumped at the corner of his jaw. "Think, Carole."

"My maid of honor gave the bouquet to me right before the ceremony. I had it the whole time until I tossed it. Ruth Davenport caught it. Did she give the rose to you?"

He took the flower back, returned it to the book, and put that on the shelf. "I don't know Ruth Davenport."

"This isn't making any sense," she said. "but somehow, you're frightening me."

"You wanted to know who I am. I'm trying to tell you."

"Why do you look so serious?"

"Listen, Carole." He took her hands in his. "You gave me the rose."

"That's impossible. I didn't even know you."

"We met that day. Try to remember."

"Wait. I did give a rose to someone." A vague recollection started to take form in her mind. She'd been outdoors. She'd met someone else there.

"I stepped outside for a moment to get away from the crush," she went on. "There was someone else. A little boy, sitting on the steps, crying."

"Go on."

"Someone had hit him bad enough that his eye was already blackening. I remember I sat down beside him, despite my gown."

More and more of the details came back. That insane day. All the people. All the expectations. Dread of what the wedding night would bring.

"I sat down beside him and pulled a rose from my bouquet," she said. "I told him not to give up on his dreams and everything would be fine."

"Yes, you did."

"He was the son of one of my husband's friends, only a little boy of eight or nine."

"Ten" he said.

"And his name was…" Cold reality clenched in her belly. "Thomas Deering."

"That's how I met you, and I've loved you ever since."

"Oh, dear God." She covered her mouth with trembling fingers. "You were just a child."

"That was twenty years ago. I'm a man now."

She searched blindly for a chair and settled onto a love seat before her knees gave out. "He was so innocent. You were so innocent."

"Sexually, yes, but I'd lost my faith in goodness years before."

She searched her memory for more details. She'd known nothing of children and especially not about little boys. He'd seemed so small, his shoulders bony under his jacket when she'd put an arm around them. So fragile and so brave as he'd tried to hide his tears from her. Dear Lord, she'd been fucking that little boy.

Thomas sat next to her and tried to pull her into an embrace, but she held him off. "Don't touch me right now. I have to think."

"My father had beaten me that day. As usual, my mother knew about it and did nothing."

"Your mother. Agnes. I still see her at church." She sat in the pew across from his parents every Sunday. What would they think? What did she think of her own behavior? Little Thomas Deering. She'd tied him to the bed the night before, and then, she'd…she'd… The world swam around her, and she closed her eyes against the vertigo.

"You won't see my mother in church again, Carole," he said. "I won't, either. I'll never set eyes on my parents again."

"They're your mother and father."

"My father's a vicious brute who bloodied me at a whim. I left him and his money behind and made my own fortune." He took her hand in both of his. "I did everything for you. All of it."

"Don't say that." Though she took even breaths, her heart hammered. She'd taken this whole insane journey—having sex with men she'd only just met—because a little boy had seen her in her wedding gown and developed a crush on her. He'd plotted for twenty years and then concocted this plan to make her love him. Lord, how she loved him. But he wasn't some mysterious stranger, a man of the world. He was Agnes Deering's child. She'd fucked Agnes Deering's child.

"I feel so filthy," she whispered.

"Carole, no. Please." He reached for her again, and this time she didn't have the strength to pull away.

She stared over his shoulder at a spot on the wall. "All those men."

"I'm sorry about Waldberg," he said.

"Not just him. I interrupted two men having sex. I fondled a man at the opera and let him do the same to me."

"You only did those things so we could be together."

"Why?" She pushed away from him. "Why did you order me to take other lovers?"

"Something your friend, Mrs. Standen said."

"Muriel?"

"I listened to you talking," he answered. "She said no woman should take a mate until she'd had five men. I swore right then I'd be your sixth and final lover."

"What idiocy," she said. "You didn't hear me agreed with her, did you?"

"You kept saying you had to be faithful to your husband. That only made me love you more."

"I can't believe it." She bent and put her head in her hands. "That silly conversation lead to all this."

He dropped to his knees in front of her, moved her hands away from her face and looked into her eyes. "Do you remember that day?"

"Barely. There was a commotion in the hallway. You'd beaten your father."

"No worse than he'd done to me. The good thing was, I felt for the first time since you'd given me the rose that you saw me. You really saw me as a man."

"How old were you?"

"It doesn't matter."

"Oh, no. If there's one thing I know about you now it's that when you won't answer a question, it matters very much."

"It was thirteen years ago," he said. "I was seventeen."

"Oh Lord, Thomas." She stood and pushed past him. "I'm forty years old."

He rose quickly. "And I'm thirty. I'm a man, not a child."

"How would you feel in my position? What if you found out your lover was much younger than you'd thought and she'd had lustful thoughts of you since she was a girl?" she said. "Or maybe you didn't think about me that way when you were seventeen."

He didn't answer with words, but the blush that covered his cheeks told the story.

"What if you knew her parents, even went to church with them?" she said.

"It's not important. It can't be important."

"For heaven's sake, Thomas, think!" She started to tremble, at first no more than a shaking of her knees, but soon her whole body shook. "It's all wrong."

He rose and put his arms around her, holding her when she might have fallen. Resting against his body felt so normal now. He was her haven and shelter, and yet, he was also that little boy and the seventeen-year-old who'd lusted after her.

"I love you, and you love me," he whispered into her ear. "How can that be wrong?"

"You don't understand. How could you? You're living in a child's fantasy."

He stiffened. "You won't leave me, will you?"

"I'm afraid I have to." She stepped back, her trembling over as a heavy calm settled over her. He wore a lost expression, his eyes wide. The same way he'd looked twenty years ago when she'd given him the rose. Dear Lord, what had she done?

"I'm sorry, Thomas," she said. "I'm so terribly sorry."

*

She'd made restless noises all afternoon. Every time Thomas had gone to her bedroom door, he'd heard her pacing inside. He'd lifted his hand to knock more than once and then backed away out of fear of what he'd find. She'd look so frightened when she'd realized his identity. No, not frightened but horrified. She'd trembled so badly in his arms, his heart had ached.

So, he shouldn't have been surprised when she didn't come down to dinner. All the china and silver lay on the table waiting for their meal as if this evening would play out like all the others—good food, laughter, finally the short trip to his bed. Everything for another wonderful evening and night together except Carole.

All these nights together. All the years he'd planned for them to be together. All the dreams of a life together. It all horrified her now. His bones ached at the thought.

He turned away from the dining table and went to the French doors that overlooked the terrazzo. Placing his hands behind his back, he did his best to hold off a cloud of misery. He'd fix things somehow. He'd make her see reason. He'd beg if he had to. He couldn't lose her love after wanting her for so long and finally having her.

"*Signor?*" a voice said behind him.

He looked over to find his major domo looking at him with some concern.

"*La signora,*" the man said. "She's asked for a carriage for the morning."

"Damn." What he'd feared so much he hadn't dared to contemplate it. She'd leave him.

"I thought you'd like to know."

"Thank you." He brushed past the servant on his way to the front of the house and the stairs to the floor above. He'd stop her, by God. She hadn't given him a chance to explain. She owed him that, at least.

He went upward two stairs at a time and then dashed down the hall to her bedroom. Without bothering to knock, he threw the door open. She turned toward him, a lace nightgown in her hand. He'd seen it before—on her otherwise naked body. Today, she had no come-hither look in her eyes. In fact, she went back to her work, folding the gown carefully before putting it into a bag on her bed.

"You'd leave me so soon as tomorrow?" he asked.

"I can't stay." The words came out measured, as if she'd weighed each individually for their exact meaning.

"Why not?" His voice rose until he was shouting. "Why in God's name not?"

"You needn't sound like that." She slowly picked up a shift from a pile of things on the bed. Slowly, but not calmly, as her fingers trembled as she did it.

He went to her and snatched the thing from her hand. "I'll use any tone I want when the woman I love is leaving me for no good reason."

"Oh, really?" Her emerald eyes flashed fury at him. "You can't think of any at all?"

"An age difference isn't good enough."

"Maybe you're right." She grabbed the shift back and glared at him. "It was a shock but probably something I could learn to forget."

"Then, what in hell is all this about?" He threw up his hands in frustration.

"You don't have any monopoly on anger, you know," she said. "As soon as the surprise of who you were lessened, I started getting angry, and the more I thought, the more furious I became."

"What do you have to be furious about?"

"Good Lord." She stared at him for a long moment. "Think, Thomas. You've done nothing but lie and manipulate me from the first."

"I only did what I thought best."

"You invented Thomas Rose and made me fall in love with him."

"Everything I wrote was honest," he said. "I only made up the name Rose."

"And how I fell in love with him." She bit her lip, clearly trying to keep control of herself. "How do you think I felt when you stopped writing? After the most intimate things I'd written to you, I didn't hear from you for months."

"I needed time to arrange things." Liar. He hadn't needed that much time, and he could have written. In fact, he'd picked up his pen more than once out of desperation to see her handwriting on a return letter.

He'd made her wait so she'd be eager to agree to his next proposal. A risky maneuver, but it had worked.

"For months," she repeated. "I thought I'd disgusted you."

"You couldn't have thought that."

"I'd touched myself, brought myself to climax. And then, I'd written to you about the experience. What else could I think?"

"I don't know," he stammered. "I never considered that."

"You'd rejected me. I felt humiliated."

"Carole, no." He reached for her, but she held out a hand to ward him off.

"Don't touch me," she said as she backed out of his reach. "And then you demanded that I take other lovers. What's wrong with you?"

A look of utter terror crossed her face, and she wrapped her arms around herself, clutching her ribs. "More important, what's wrong with me?"

"There's nothing wrong with you, Carole, stop it."

"Oh God, I enjoyed them," she said. "Even Waldberg. What does that make me?"

"It makes you a passionate, brave woman," he said. "You didn't do anything wrong."

"Then when you finally allowed me to come crawling to you…"

"It wasn't like that," he bellowed. Curse him, he had treated her like his marionette. He'd done it for the best of reasons, or so he'd thought. But had he really considered her feelings or only his own?

She took an unsteady breath. "When I finally got here, you held me at arm's length. You wouldn't lie with me until you'd learned if one of the others had gotten me pregnant."

"I only wanted to know if any child would be mine." He groaned inwardly. How petty that sounded, and for good reason. If he wanted to accept her offspring, what difference did it make who'd fathered it?

"I put up with all of that. All if it," she shouted. "And you wouldn't even tell me who you were."

He didn't answer. What could he have said? Every item was true, every accusation right on the mark. He'd behaved like a perfect bastard. His father could hardly have done worse with his fists.

"I asked you to marry me." The only decent thing he'd done throughout this whole affair. "I'll beg you, if you want."

"Yes, you asked, but you still hadn't told me who you were. Dishonest to the last."

"You're right." Something wrapped around his heart and squeezed until he could scarcely get a breath. "I only meant well. Please, know that."

She didn't say anything, but stood, clenching the shift in her fists. She'd nearly twisted it into a knot.

Thomas turned and left the room, although his feet didn't seem to remember the way, and he had to consciously put one in front of the other.

His servant met him in the hallway. The man had probably overheard the whole argument. Another sin to add to his long list of mistakes. He pulled the door closed behind him.

"Have the carriage sent round for Mrs. Rutherford in the morning."

"Yes, sir." After a tiny bow, the man went off to follow the order.

*

When Carole descended the stairs in the morning, her gloves on and bag in her hand, all her luggage stood in the entryway, packed and ready for loading into the carriage. Sun shone through windows high in the walls, warming the tiles of the floor. Another glorious day. Years from now, she'd remember the details, whether she wanted to or not. She'd probably retain more images from today than she did of her wedding, although not happy ones.

Thomas's manservant approached. "Signor Deering asked me to make sure you have everything you require."

Everything except the man I love. "Where is he?"

"In the library."

"I'll speak to him myself."

The man bowed and disappeared the way all good servants do. She took a breath to steel herself. This wouldn't be easy, but she owed him a face-to-face goodbye.

The door to the library was open, but she knocked, anyway, before going in. He glanced over his shoulder as she did and then went back to staring out the window, his hands folded at his back.

"Come to list my shortcomings one more time before you leave?" he said.

"Of course not."

"Good. I thought I might have committed another sin after we argued last evening."

"Please don't act this way."

"What way would you like me to act?" He turned to face her. "I've never had the woman I love run off before. Perhaps there's some protocol I should know about."

His eyes held a wild, forlorn look. It took her back to the first day they'd met. He was a child again, not understanding why the world was so cruel. And yet, the child had become the man who'd made her love him. If only she could walk into his embrace, feel his arms close around her as she found the sanctuary of his body. If only they could make love with such ferocity it would cancel every objection to a happily-ever-after.

For a long moment, neither of them spoke. Finally, he sighed. "Write to tell me you arrived safely in New York."

"Thomas…"

"It's not a trick. I only want to know you're all right."

"Very well," she said.

"I do love you, you know," he said. "I have for this long, so I doubt I'll ever stop."

"That isn't healthy," she said. "You should find a younger woman who can give you children."

His face flushed with anger. "I don't want another woman. I want you."

"The world doesn't revolve around what you want." Damn it, why was she arguing with him again? She came here to say goodbye, so she ought to go ahead and do it and leave. But she couldn't get past the knowledge that she'd never set eyes on him again, and she'd have the image of him standing here, looking like that lost little boy, in her memory forever.

"*Signor?*" It was the servant on the threshold. Two workmen stood behind him, a narrow wooden crate between them.

Thomas rubbed the bridge of his nose between his thumb and forefinger. "What is it?"

"The delivery," the servant said. "From Vienna."

Thomas seemed puzzled for a moment, and then his features fell. "Good Lord. Not today of all days."

"What's in the crate?" she asked.

"You may as well see it."

When he gestured, the men carried the crate into the room. One of them pulled a small crowbar from his belt and pried open the slats. Finally, a frame of some kind appeared, covered by a rough canvas. Thomas took the whole, set it on a chair, and turned to the men. "Leave us."

The three left the room. Thomas stood for a long moment before reaching to the covering over the painting and sweeping it off.

Carole's breath caught in her throat. "It's a painting of me...naked."

"Waldberg. It's the nude of you he started," Thomas said. "It was going to be my wedding present to you."

"You're in it, too." And he was, as if he'd posed for it. She reclined on the couch as she had those days in Vienna—on her back with her hand barely concealing the hairs on her mound. Thomas lay behind her, propped up on his elbow. Also naked except for one thing. He wore a wedding band.

"How did he paint you into the picture?" she asked.

"I sent him a photograph and instructed him in what I wanted," Thomas said.

She walked toward the painting and then to the side, taking it in from different perspectives. Like the work of art it was, it became more complex and intriguing the more she studied it. "It's beautiful."

"And damned expensive. It'll grow in value over time," Thomas said. "I'll send it to you in New York."

"I couldn't take it from you."

He shrugged. "I don't want to look at it. If I keep it here, I'll only store it somewhere."

"What a waste that would be." The more she looked at their images, the more Waldberg's tendencies toward magic emerged. Her skin seemed to glow, and her eyes were a deep, dark green. The man behind her wore a proud smile, as if he'd claimed the most wonderful creature alive as his own.

"Waldberg always had a fantastical side," she said. "Who knew the bastard was a romantic?"

"What do you mean by that?" Thomas demanded.

"Well, look at it. There's a glow all around us that I never noticed in Waldberg's studio. It's almost mystical," she said. A realization hit her heart. Mama Fernelli had said there was a light around them—stronger than she'd ever seen before. Waldberg couldn't have known about that, and yet, the light had appeared in the painting.

She pointed to the woman—herself—in the portrait. "It's so erotic, so flawless."

"Pure realism," he said.

"That doesn't resemble me," she said. "Well, it does superficially, but honestly…"

"It's you exactly."

"Really, Thomas. My skin has aged, and so has my body. My eyes never were that deep color." The woman's breasts were so full in the painting, the thighs smooth and firm. Not like her forty-year-old reality at all.

He walked to her, took her chin in his hand and forced her to gaze up at him. "You look exactly like that. You did the first day I met you, and you do now."

"That was twenty years ago."

"You haven't changed. You never will." He set his jaw in cold determination, but his eyes continued talking. He was the vulnerable boy who'd fallen in love with her all those years ago, and he was the man she loved with equal ferocity.

If she left him, she'd have to go back to the life where she'd settled for what she could get rather than reaching for what she needed. Somehow, against all odds, Pete and Jean-Paul managed to express their love for each other. Why couldn't she be as brave? Yes, she and Thomas had an age difference to deal with, but hadn't she urged Lady Blakely to find a way to overcome a similar obstacle?

She'd learned a lot on her voyage here, it seemed, and little of it had to do with sex. She'd discovered a great deal about life and love, and she couldn't go back to her former life if she tried. So, she wouldn't. Her heart softened and warmed as a tiny beam of light penetrated. Hope. Did she dare to let herself hope? Did she have any choice?

She took an unsteady breath. "We could never go back to New York, you know."

"What are you saying?"

"I don't suppose I give a fig for your father's opinion, but there is your mother."

"Carole?" he whispered.

"We should probably stay away from Oscar's family, too," she said. "I imagine they'd think me foolish to have taken up with such a young man."

"I don't care if we ever go back there at all. I'm perfectly happy here," he said.

No use fighting reality as hope and love finally won over her, filling her heart to bursting. She had to face the fact that she could never have left him, even if the painting hadn't shown up. She would have stopped the coach before it got halfway down the drive.

"Why does the impossible suddenly seem so inevitable?" she said.

"Because it is."

He put his arms around her, and this time, she let him pull her against his chest. His heart raced under hers, and his fingers trembled as he stroked her back.

"I'm sorry for everything I've done wrong," he murmured. "I'll make it all right if you give me the chance."

"I imagine I've been stubborn, too."

"Not you. You're perfect."

"Now, you see, it's that kind of silliness that gets us into trouble." She pulled back enough that she could scowl at him, although she probably wasn't very convincing. The time for scowling had passed. "We'll deal honestly with each other from now on. In everything."

"Agreed," he said. "And I won't even bother you about marrying me, although I hope you'll change your mind on your own."

"Really, Thomas." She groaned. "What would I do with a husband ten years younger than I am?"

"Love him, I hope."

She rested her head on his shoulder and hugged him. "Yes, I think I can manage that."

*

Their letters—all of them—lay scattered around their naked bodies on the rumpled bed clothes. Carole picked up one of her own and blushed. Even though Thomas had just treated her to a thorough fucking, she could still feel some embarrassment at what she'd written to a man she'd only known through his words.

The man in question propped himself up on one envelope. "Read it aloud."

"You know what it says."

She set the paper down, but he grasped it put it back in her hand. "Read it."

"'I selected a model of the male member carved out of ivory. I suppose it's a faithful portrayal of the real organ. It has an odd appeal I can't deny. The shaft captures the eye and leads my gaze toward the head and the pucker at the tip. Can you tell me, dearest friend, how greatly men's rods vary in size, shape, and beauty?'" She set the letter aside rolled onto her stomach. "There. Satisfied?"

"Minx." He swatted at her fanny. "I knew you were asking about me."

"And you answered, didn't you?" she said.

"Courtesy demanded a reply."

She snorted, and he slapped her bum again.

"Find your letter and read your answer. I dare you."

He sifted through some papers and found a page of his own handwriting. "'I hate to brag, but honesty requires that I tell you my instrument is a large one. You'll have to tell me whether or not it's beautiful, as I can't judge that for myself."

He gave her his best wicked grin, complete with the twinkle in his eye. "So, what do you say, Mrs. Deering? Is my organ beautiful?"

"Of course it is." She moved onto her side so that she could reach down and stroke his member. "It's my pet."

"You know how to make it sit up and beg."

A glow of pride warmed her because of his words but also because "her pet" stirred as she trailed her fingers over it. Could he possibly respond again so soon?

"Read the later part," she said.

He arched a brow. "Trying to arouse me again?"

"Maybe." She bit her lip. "Am I succeeding?"

"For months, I dreamed of doing this. Reading our letters while making them reality."

"Then, read," she said.

He cleared his throat. "'My darling Carole, I can hardly continue. Picturing you lying on your coverlet with your legs spread as you pleasure yourself is the most erotic thing I've ever done. My hand moves faster on my aching cock. I must finish quickly.'"

"Were you really stoking yourself when you wrote that?" she said.

"I wouldn't lie about something like that."

"What about how you finished the letter?"

"'Oh! The orgasm approaches. I only have enough strength now to tell you that I remain your most devoted Thomas.'" He blushed. "I used a little poetic license there. If I'd been that close to spending, I couldn't have written anything at all."

"But you did come after you finished writing, didn't you?"

"Right there at my desk, fully dressed with only my trousers undone."

"Oh, good." She kept her hand moving over his thickening shaft and thumbed the underside of the head.

"I'll come again if you keep doing that," he said.

"I do hope so."

"More fun if we do it together." He pushed her hand away from his cock and then buried his fingertips in the hairs that covered her mound. Within seconds, he'd found her pearl and brought it back to life.

"Wet," he murmured into her ear.

"You keep me in a near constant state of excitement."

"How convenient." He rolled her clitoris in the slow circles that always drove her mad. Surely, the man had made some pact with the devil to buy the power he had over her body.

Her breath came harsh and fast, and she stretched her arms to him to invite him to enter her. They needed no more words as he took his position between her legs and eased into her.

Thrusting slowly, he smiled down at her. "Is it as good as you pictured that day in your bedroom in New York?"

"Better. I could never have imagined this."

"Nor I. I love you so much."

"Thomas, I love you, too."

"So, you'll keep your second husband and your sixth lover forever?" he said, as he picked up the pace of his movements.

"Forever," she whispered back.

Then speech escaped them and passion took over— the only sounds their sighs and the crinkling of papers beneath them.

And now for something completely different…
The Danislova series. Three contemporary romance
novels to be released in late fall of 2014. The first
book,

KISS THE FROG

CHAPTER ONE

The lot of them were up to no good, and if Felice
Larson could read her friends right, they were about to
drop the trouble into her lap. What the zoology
department laughingly called the graduate student
lounge couldn't hold more than five or six people in
addition to the ratty couch and the Steelcase table with
the ancient microwave on top. With Ben's height and
broad shoulders, which he at present was using to block
the doorway, her buds from Professor Marc Fanley's lab
created quite a crush as they circled in on her. As they
came forward, she backed up. And backed and backed
until her legs hit the couch and she plopped down.
"Okay, what's up?"

Crystal took the opportunity to sit next to Felice,
almost on top of her, actually. "We've come to a
decision."

"Why do I get the feeling it involves me?" Felice
said. "And why are the butterflies in my stomach telling
me I won't like it?"

"Oh, you'll like it." Sandra sat on Felice's other side, bookending her. Both women appeared ready to pounce if Felice so much as tried to stand up.

Alex nodded toward Ben. "Better close that door."

Ben did and rested against it. For heaven's sake, this was starting to look like a parody of a gangster movie. Next thing, they'd be threatening her with cement overshoes and speaking out of the sides of their mouths, even the women.

"Are you going to tell me what all this is about, or do I have to figure out what you've decided on my own?" she said.

Crystal dug her index finger into her hair and twisted a blonde curl tightly around it -- a nervous habit of hers that manifested itself every time she didn't have an answer to a question and had to stall for time. Felice glanced to Alex but got no more than a view of his faded jeans and university sweatshirt. His brown eyes gave nothing away. Ben wasn't any more help. He simply crossed his arms over his chest and stared at the opposite wall.

Finally, Sandra took charge. She grabbed Felice's hands and leaned forward. "You owe us. You said so yourself, remember?"

"Owe?" Felice searched her memory. She'd used that expression lately. Though she couldn't recall what debt she'd incurred, she had a pretty solid feeling she'd paid it off.

"The research trip," Sandra said. Though she was the smallest of all of them, her red hair made her stand out. She joked that no one should cross her because of her temper, but after getting to know her, you didn't dare laugh.

"I can see I'm not getting through to you," Sandra said. "Kangaroo rats."

A shudder went through Felice at the mention of the word "rats." Ever since reading the novel *1984*, she'd had a terror of the miserable creatures.

"The trip we were all supposed to make to the desert," Crystal tossed in. "The one we let you skip out on. The one when it rained for three solid days and we all came home covered in mud."

"It's not my fault you got stuck with the one week the desert got rain," Felice said.

"We all ended up with colds," Alex said.

"And I sat on a cactus," Ben added.

Of course. Her mind hadn't quite managed to block out the fact that she'd bailed on the rest of them and had stayed in her warm, dry apartment while they'd chased over half of the Sonoran desert counting the population of kangaroo rats. Awful, nasty creatures.

"She's got it now," Alex said.

"We're connecting," Ben said from his station at the door. A man of few words, but every one was important.

"I'm writing half the paper," Felice protested.

"And you're first author," Alex said. "Not enough."

"All right, all right. What do you want from me?"

"Well-ll." Crystal let the blond curl loose for a moment, and then went back to twirling it. "You know Dev."

"Of course I know Dev." The new grad student was kind of an odd bird. A few years older than the rest of them, Dev came from a tiny European country, Latstonia or Bardstokia or something like that. He always mumbled the name when people asked. But then, he swallowed most of his words, making it difficult to know for sure if he was speaking English some of the time.

"He's really nice," Crystal said.

"How can you tell?" Maybe Crystal knew him better than Felice did. He glanced away whenever she looked at him. Poor guy. It had to suck to be that shy.

"I've talked to him," Crystal said.

"We all have," Alex added. "We spent six days in the rain with him, remember? If you'd come along on that trip, you'd know him, too."

"I shared a tent with him. He's a good guy," Alex said.

"Well, I don't know him," Felice said. "He hasn't said more than ten words to me, and he's swallowed six of those."

"He only clams up around you," Sandra said. "Which makes you perfect."

"None of you are making any sense," Felice said. "Perfect for what?"

Crystal's finger gave her hair a work-out, twisting and twisting. "You tell her, Alex."

"Not me." Alex glanced at Ben, whose face turned a bright pink.

"Oh, for crissake," Sandra said. "You're perfect to sleep with Dev, that's what."

"Sleep? Dev?" If Felice thought for a minute, she could probably put those two words into a sentence that would make sense – as long as they didn't have "with" between them. Sleep with Dev. "As in have sex with him?"

"Why not?" Sandra said. "He's a good looking guy."

Maybe he was behind the glasses with the huge rims. If he combed his hair out of his face. And burned the corduroy pants. Lord, did he shop at Dorks R Us?

"Look, Dev's been here for months, and he hasn't interacted with a woman except for the ones in Marc's lab," Alex said.

"Heck, he might never have been with a woman," Ben said. "In fact, I'm pretty sure he's a virgin."

"How in heaven's name could you know a thing like that about him?" Felice demanded. This whole conversation had gone from weird to bizarre to insane within less than five minutes. What man Dev's age would be a virgin?

"We didn't have much to do but talk at night in that tent," Ben said. "I asked about women, and he shut right up."

"I've tried to draw him out on the subject, too," Ben said. "He won't talk."

"Think about it. You could be his first." Ben nodded as if that settled the matter.

If Ben thought that made the whole thing better, he'd missed by a mile. "You want me to take a guy's virginity?"

"Believe me, that's one thing a man never misses." Ben stood there, an immovable tower of certainty, and no one else in the room seemed eager to contradict him. True, the first time meant different things for men than women, but still...Dev ought to share that special moment with someone he cared about.

"It just doesn't seem right," Felice said finally.

"We're his friends," Alex said. "We should do this for him."

"Fine. If you all think that's such a great idea, Crystal or Sandra can sleep with him," Felice said.

"I'm taken," Sandra said.

"So's Crystal," Ben added. The two of them had obviously paired off. They'd been giving off signs for weeks. That only left Felice, or the sane and logical choice, which was to let Dev find a woman on his own.

"Besides, he doesn't look at us the way he does at you," Sandra said.

Felice glared at Sandra. "And how is that?"

Sandra opened her eyes wide and imitated a kind of puppy-dog face. "Like he wants to follow you home."

Good God Almighty. Felice rose and paced to the other side of the room. Her hip bumped the table, rattling the microwave. "You all must be out of your minds."

"He's thousands of miles from home. He only knows us," Crystal said.

"He really needs to get laid," Alex said. Always helpful, Alex.

Crystal's expression brightened. "You could make him feel welcome."

"It's your patriotic duty," Sandra concluded.

"Now, I know you're kidding."

Sandra gave Felice her best menacing stare. "Try me."

"You mean this. You really mean this." Felice glanced at each of her friends in turn, from Ben's stern features, to Alex's open expression, Crystal's smile, and the look on Sandra's face that said she knew she had Felice trapped.

"A little action might do you some good, too," Sandra said.

Felice couldn't stop the gasp from escaping, and she charged across the room to Sandra. "I told you that in confidence."

"Everyone knows you've been…" Alex cleared his throat. "…lonely since whatsizname left on his post-doc.

James. It had been three months, two weeks, and a day, not that she was counting. Even the e-mails were getting short and seldom as James slipped off into the ether of her past.

"Give Dev a shot," Crystal chirped. "He might be good."

"A virgin? Good? The first time?"

"Well…you could teach him," Crystal said. "Show him all the things that turn you on."

"I am not giving Dev VonRamsberg a crash course in the Kama Sutra."

Sandra rolled her eyes. "Do it any way you want. Just do it."

"Right." Felice planted her hands on her hips. "What am I supposed to do? Walk up to him and ask, 'If you don't have anything scheduled between seminars, want a pity fuck?'"

"Of course not. You'd scare him to death," Alex said.

"Well, then?"

Alex reached into his pocket and produced a key tied to a loop of string. "He gave me this when I took care of his pet iguana when he was out of town. Sneak in in the middle of the night and ambush him."

"That's just great." Felice threw her hands into the air. "You want me to assault him."

"It's not assault if he likes it," Alex said.

"How do you know what he likes?" Damn, they had her shouting now.

"He's a guy." Ben counted off the points on his fingers. "He's horny. He wants you."

She turned to the two women for some logic. "You couldn't ask me to do something so stupid."

"We not only ask it, we expect it," Sandra answered.

"You owe us," Crystal said.

Well, shit, they meant it. She paced the room again, what little of it there was. She did owe them. She'd meant it as an expression, but they had her. Technically, she didn't have to have collected the data to write the paper and be first author. But what would Marc think if he found out she hadn't gone on that trip? He prided himself on putting out PhDs who'd had hands-on training. How could she explain to him that what he thought of as cute, little rodents were to her disease-ridden, blood-thirsty vermin just dying for the opportunity to put their fangs into her face? She stopped pacing for a moment. "If I do this, I don't owe you anything more, right?"

"That's it," Sandra said. "Paid in full."

"I only have to do it once?"

"Unless, of course, you want more." Crystal smirked at her. Actually smirked. She could smirk easily enough. She didn't have to skulk her way into a near-stranger's apartment, get naked, and do the nasty with him.

But then, she'd only have to do it once, and Dev was a sweet person, except for his fascination with sidewinding rattlesnakes. If he'd never made love before, he might finish quickly, and she could go home to her own bed. Women had put up with worse in their sex lives. In fact, she herself had. She could face a few minutes in the sack with Dev a hell of a lot easier than she could face Marc's disappointment in her.

"Okay," she said. "Give me the damned key."

*

What did you wear to a sexual ambush? Maybe the same sort of thing you wore to a seduction, which meant that Felice didn't have anything right except for the negligees she'd worn for James. She wasn't putting one of those on for another man. She normally slept in sweatpants and t-shirts. Very appealing for a tackling dummy but not so great for a *femme fatale*.

In the end, she threw an oversized sweater over her jeans and blouse and drove to the apartment complex where the guys all lived. The key Alex had given her worked on the outside gate as well as the building's front door, so she let herself in and searched for number one-seventeen. That lock also turned easily, and she found herself inside Dev's living room.

As the door closed softly behind her, she glanced around. Aside from the large glass tank on the opposite side of the room -- the iguana's enclosure? -- it was a fairly standard space for a graduate student. Light that slipped inside between the blinds showed a couch several years newer and nicer than the one in the grad student lounge and a flat screen television. An arm chair and coffee table sat on top of a throw rug. That amounted to the total of the furnishings.

An archway led off to a small kitchen at one end of the room. The doorway at the other end promised to lead to the bedroom. She tiptoed in that direction. If he didn't detect her presence, she could always change her mind and tiptoe right back out again. Since the afternoon, she'd had plenty of time to conjure up images of what she'd be getting herself into here. And plenty of time to buy some condoms.

She might embarrass Dev. He might jump up and demand that she leave him alone. That would be awkward as all hell. She'd have to apologize and spend the rest of the semester trying to make things right between them. The others would have to apologize, too. She wouldn't take the fall for them when they'd thought up this ridiculous scheme to begin with.

On the other hand, he might take what she offered, more or less fall on her and shove his way inside. She could handle that. It wouldn't give her a lot of pleasure, but it'd get things over quickly. That would only leave the problem of him wanting a repeat performance.

She'd rehearsed that whole scenario in her mind. *Dev, I really like you. You're a good person and a great guy, but it was just a one night stand. You'll find a woman who truly cares about you.. A woman who deserves you. I love you, but I'm not in love with you.*

Lame, lame, lame, but it was all she had. The others might well end up owing her something by the time this all ended. She approached the bedroom and stood on the threshold for a moment. No point putting this off any longer. Operation Seduce Dev T minus zero.

The bedroom proved as unremarkable as the living room. Illumination also snuck in through the blinds here. The room held no more than a dresser, an end table, and a huge bed. For a guy's place, it was all pretty tidy, as was the bathroom, at least from what she could see from a night light in there. The display of an alarm clock showed Dev himself lying face down against the sheet, the covers exposing a broad expanse of naked back. He slept in the nude? Interesting.

With no rational excuse to delay, she quickly kicked out of her shoes and removed her clothing. The air cooled her skin, setting up goose bumps along her arms. She shivered, although the air wasn't really all *that* cold. Across the room, Dev's soft breathing brought home the message. She'd soon cuddle up to his body. No matter how shy, he was still a man with a man's anatomy and a man's needs.

After pulling the strip of condoms from the pocket of her jeans, she approached the bed.

How had she never noticed Dev's size before? Sure, he slumped, but she couldn't have missed the fact that he was easily as tall as Ben. Though not as beefy as Ben, Dev nevertheless had shoulders as broad. The back she'd studied from across the room now appeared like an expanse of flesh, solid muscle with a furrow down the middle.

One of his hands lay splayed near his head, the long fingers spread against the sheet. From this close, he didn't resemble any kind of nerdling. dork, or geek she'd ever seen before. His hair had fallen back from his face, exposing a strong jaw, high cheekbones, and a pair of lips sculpted for sin. Only his long eyelashes suggested innocence.

She shivered again, although this time she didn't try blaming it on the temperature in the room. He suddenly seemed so male and big and, well, desirable. A physical knowledge blossomed inside her body...the sort of communication that didn't require words. Her pussy clenched, grasping for something that it hadn't had for months.

Wicked thoughts formed in her mind. What would those fingers feel like against her breasts, her nipples? Would he have a large cock? Would it stay hard for a good, long time before he came? Would she have the courage to show him how to make her climax?

Still clutching the strip of condoms, she lifted the covers and climbed into bed with him.

ABOUT THE AUTHOR

Alice Gaines lives in the San Francisco Bay Area in a fixer-upper house she never fixed up. Aside from writing and reading hot, hot romance, she loves cooking, gardening, and her church. She has a pet corn snake named Casper and a strange, stray cat. She's insanely passionate about the funky soul band, Tower of Power.

You can write to Alice at authoralicegaines@yahoo.com.

Her website is http://www.alicegaines.blogspot.com.

She's AliceGaines at Twitter, Facebook, and Pinterest.

www.ingramcontent.com/pod-product-compliance
Lightning Source LLC
Chambersburg PA
CBHW031246170626
46807CB00001B/12